By JOHN GOODE

Last Dance with Mary Jane

TALES FROM FOSTER HIGH
Tales From Foster High
End of the Innocence
151 Days
Taking Chances
What About Everything?
By Robert Halliwell: A Way Back to Then
Save Yourself
When I Grow Up
Fadeaway

Published by Harmony Ink Press

Jordan vs. All the Boys

LORDS OF ARCADIA
Distant Rumblings
Eye of the Storm
With J.G. Morgan: The Unseen Tempest
With J.G. Morgan: Stormfront

Published by DREAMSPINNER PRESS
www.dreamspinnerpress.com

JOHN GOODE

151
DAYS

Published by

DREAMSPINNER PRESS

5032 Capital Circle SW, Suite 2, PMB# 279, Tallahassee, FL 32305-7886 USA
www.dreamspinnerpress.com

151 Days
© 2021 John Goode

Cover Art
© 2021 Paul Richmond
http://www.paulrichmondstudio.com
Cover content is for illustrative purposes only and any person depicted on the cover is a model.

Trade Paperback ISBN: 978-1-64405-853-4
Digital ISBN: 978-1-64405-852-7
Library of Congress Control Number: 978-1-64405-852-7
Trade Paperback published May 2021
Second Edition
v. 2.0
Previously published by Harmony Ink Press, March 2014

Printed in the United States of America
(∞)
This paper meets the requirements of
ANSI/NISO Z39.48-1992 (Permanence of Paper).

Kyle

FOR EVERY action, there is an equal and opposite reaction.

This is Newton's Third Law of Motion, and it is a pretty standard concept that is universally accepted in science. It's a cornerstone of physics since forever. Well, not actual forever, but before color television, so close enough for what I'm talking about. It states that whenever object A interacts with object B, they exert forces on each other that forever changes the trajectory of both objects. Everything in the universe can change anything it comes into contact with. No one escapes unscathed.

I'm pretty sure you know I am not talking about physics.

There is no way to exist in this world without affecting it. Trust me, I tried. Most of my life, I tried to place myself outside the world. A boy in an emotional bubble, never touching anything, never letting anything touch me, just my own little island of nothing, trying my level best to just move forward.

I didn't want friends.

I so desperately wanted friends. I mean, in the same way that boy bands wanted to stay relevant past their third album desperate. But I had no idea how to make friends. Hell, I didn't even like myself. What were the odds someone else would like me? No, better not to engage and ignore all that socializing.

I didn't want love.

Now, this is complete bullshit and we all know it. I mean, who doesn't want love? I wanted love the same way people who believe in UFOs want to be abducted. Both of us would be completely shocked by it and then find ourselves utterly unprepared for the actual occurrence. I wanted to be loved, but I had no idea what it would feel like if someone did.

I didn't want to be seen.

This one is true. I hated everything about me, which seemed like it wasn't really a big deal because I hated almost everything else, but it was. See, I hated myself for all the things I wasn't, and I hated everyone else for being everything I could never be. Things like normal, cool, and chill were beyond my grasp, and I grew up loathing all the reasons why I couldn't be like that and hated the people who were.

I wanted not to exist, I wanted a pain-free life, I wanted to get out of high school in one piece.

Turns out I was better off wishing to be abducted. At least then all of my failure would have been contained to a spaceship.

1

Let me show you the chain of events that led to this clusterfuck of a life I live.

Brad Graymark's dad was a douchebag and didn't use protection in high school when he had sex.

That created Brad. He's object A.

Brad desperately wanted to be loved and accepted by his father, but couldn't get it because, and again I refer back to, his father was a colossal douchebag. For Brad that meant playing baseball the very best he could. Because Brad was so good at baseball, he became one of the most popular guys in school. Because he was so popular, he didn't think he needed to do anything except play baseball.

Turns out he needed to maintain a GPA above a negative number.

So to keep playing baseball, which would keep him popular, which would magically change his father to show emotion and say he loved his son, Brad had to find a tutor.

That's me, object B.

We met, he kissed me, I had a stroke and kissed him back, and then all sorts of shit started to happen.

The school decided to say very loudly that they didn't like gay people, which then caused our parents to rise up and threaten to sue them if they kept it up.

See? Action to reaction.

Since the school couldn't openly be hostile toward us, it allowed everyone else to be hostile, which meant it was open season on gay people at Foster High.

Action to reaction.

Being openly attacked forced Brad and me to make new friends—well, new ones for him, my first ones. Those people had been treated shitty for just being different, so we all kind of came together.

Can you see how every single thing has caused a completely different thing to occur?

That led to us crashing a popular-people party, which led Kelly, a friend of Brad's, to admit he had feelings for Brad, which led to Jeremy, don't ask, to film it and put it up on YouTube, which led to Kelly shooting himself in the head.

You know, that makes it sound like Brad being born is at fault; let me start over again.

If I had never been born then Brad would have found someone else to tutor him, Kelly could have gone on crushing on him in silence, and none of this would have happened. So if I was dead, Kelly would be alive.

We all got that?

So now we are here, 151 days left in this school year and we're a man down. I know that sounds flippant, but think about it for a moment. Our senior year had

2

a literal body count; that's how bad it had gotten. But the clusterfuck that was this year wasn't done yet.

Because Kelly killing himself caused people to lose their minds. They wanted someone to blame. Some found that blame in the school, some found it in Kelly, and most of the people at school found it in me.

See, to everyone else, I was object A, the first kid in school to stand up and say, "Yeah, I'm gay. What's your problem?" which led to Kelly being object B and killing himself. Sure, there were a lot of steps in between, but in their head the line from me to him was pretty simple. Gay guy to dead guy. End of story.

But they're wrong. It isn't the end of the story. In fact, it's the start of a whole new one.

Because Kelly killing himself was object A, and trust me in this:

I'm object B, and I am pissed.

This town killed Kelly, this attitude that normal is a religion and anyone who doesn't worship under it is a sinner who deserves to get punished. Maybe you shun them, maybe you hurl derogatory comments at them, and maybe you hold them down and beat the shit out of them in an empty gym. Well, if that's the case, I am not a sinner, I am the fucking devil, and I refuse to stand by and let anyone else end up being sacrificed on the altar of normal.

I have 151 days left in the school year before I blow out of this town like a cartoon roadrunner. That leaves me a little under five months to fix Foster and make sure this never happens again.

So if I were you, I'd buckle up, because I'm not playing around anymore.

JANUARY 15:
WAITING ON THE WORLD TO CHANGE
151 DAYS LEFT

Brad

"So, I have a plan," Kyle said during lunch.

Jennifer and Sammy sat there with us for lunch, but to be honest, no one felt much like eating. A week had passed since Kelly died. School had been closed, and today was our first day back. Foster, which was the center of the world to a lot of us, lurched to a halt as people tried to deal with the fact that one of our own had shot himself. Students who sent him nasty messages on Facebook were all buttsore now that they had been outed to the rest of Foster by Kyle and us printing out their hate. By the end of the week, all the talking and texting quieted down and sadness settled in.

The whole school seemed in equal parts shocked and outraged about the situation. However, by lunch, the four of us knew that the rest of the student body had agreed on one point. Our little quartet of freaks was to blame.

No one was pointing fingers and calling us out, nothing like that. But you know when someone is giving you the stink eye. Even if you never hear the words, you can just tell when someone is talking shit about you behind your back. No one dared to say anything to our faces, but the accusations were there in their expressions.

Kelly's death was our fault.

So to find out he had a plan wasn't shocking to any of us. If you knew Kyle like we did, it wouldn't have shocked you either.

"What now?" Jennifer asked. Her voice sounded tired. The circles under her eyes and her less-than-perfect makeup and hair told me she hadn't slept much more than I had.

I wasn't surprised by her reaction, but I could tell Kyle was. We were all weary, drop-dead exhausted with trying to deal with what had happened and making Kelly's suicide real in our heads. I knew she wasn't blaming Kyle for what happened, but she was having a hard time being excited about another

4

one of his plans; the last one pretty much revealed the school as being full of hating assholes.

Kyle paused for half a second, no doubt trying to process her response. Was it sarcasm aimed at him, or had she been just asking a question? He opted for choice two because he explained, "I want to start a gay-straight alliance here."

Weird. I understood every individual word he said, but strung together, they made no sense at all.

"You want to start a what, now?"

He opened his mouth to answer, but Sammy beat him to it. "It's like an after-school club, but instead of, like, choir or cheerleading, it's a place where kids can talk about their sexuality without judgment." She glanced over at Kyle and flushed a little. "I'm sorry, Kyle. Brad was asking you."

Kyle waved it off. "No, that's exactly right. How did you know what it was?"

Sammy shrugged. "I Googled them before winter break. I didn't think we could ever start one here. But that was before…." She gazed out over the quad.

And just like that, Kelly was there.

I saw him, clear as day, sitting on the steps behind Jennifer, stuffing his face with school pizza and listening along.

God, I was losing it.

"We couldn't have," Kyle agreed. I shook my head and looked away from Kelly. I could tell Kyle was excited by the way his voice sped up. "But I think we can force them to make one."

The emphasis on *force* made me realize what I had thought was mere excitement was really determination lighting his eyes.

"You're talking about the emergency school board meeting this week, right?" I asked. He nodded, and I instantly sighed. "Dude, have you forgotten the last time we tried to go to one of those?"

He smiled back at me and said, "Yeah, but this time we're not going."

That was when I knew the school board was not going to be ready for him, not this time.

His idea was to go to Mrs. Axeworthy and ask her to help.

Now, I don't know about yours, but it seems like every school has one teacher who is just… weird. I was going to say off the beaten path, but *off* doesn't really cover it for Mrs. Axeworthy. She's one of those teachers who never let the class get boring or just went on about the same stuff day after day. She always tried new things, like having class in the quad, or going on field trips to First Street. One time she made us write a song about Foster and its history. Like I said, in her case weird wasn't a bad thing. Mrs. Axeworthy knew she was weird, and I think she liked it that way.

She had talked to Kyle after the last school board thing. From what he said, she had been out on a family emergency or something, so she didn't find out until after the board had ruled if I could play baseball or not, but she wanted to let him know she was on our side. I never knew what *on our side* meant, but at least it wasn't actively against us like most everyone else. I'm going to be honest and say I had almost forgotten she existed until Kyle brought her up again in his plan.

This gay-straight thing had to have a teacher to run it or the school wouldn't recognize it, and since most of the teachers were barely tolerating us, I didn't think asking them to volunteer would be a great idea. But Mrs. Axeworthy had said she was on our side, and Kyle thought that meant something. I silently hoped he was right.

Part of Mrs. Axeworthy's weirdness was her wearing a black cat pin on her blouse every day. However, that afternoon, when we walked into her office, I realized we had not even begun to scratch the weird surface. She collected black cat things. Stuffed animals, pictures, mugs, anything that had a black cat on it seemed to have ended up in her office. I mean, sure, on the weirdness scale, black-cat-thing collecting was way low, but the idea of something like black-cat-thing collecting made me nervous. "Weird" meant "unpredictable" in my mind. Things I couldn't predict always made me nervous, doubly so where Kyle was concerned.

She greeted Kyle like they were old friends and then stood up when she saw me. "You must be Brad," she exclaimed. "I've heard a lot about you!" She looked like she was about to hug me, but then she stopped and held out her hand. It was odd, but I could swear I saw her glance at her door for a second.

I looked and Kyle nodded. He'd seen it too.

"Pleasure to meet you," I said, trying not to sound confused.

"I came to ask you a question." Kyle went straight to the point once she sat back down.

"Well, that sounds serious," she replied, gesturing at the chairs across from her.

I wanted to stand, but then I would have looked like some kind of secret service agent, so I sat down next to Kyle.

"Have you heard of a gay-straight alliance?"

She smiled, but the expression didn't seem very genuine. "Why do you ask?"

I saw Kyle pause. He hadn't been expecting that question at all. "Um, I was thinking that we could use one here at school."

Most adults are pretty good at hiding what they're feeling. Case in point: my dad could be plotting how to kill me and hide the body undetected, and the smile on his face wouldn't waver an inch. Mrs. Axeworthy was not one of those people. Her expression went from fake smile to nervous to almost paranoid as she glanced at the door. She walked over to it and opened it all the way, toeing the doorstop hard so it couldn't close by accident. "That's an interesting idea," she replied, but her voice made the word sound like it was anything but interesting.

"Do you think you can help us?" Kyle asked.

She visibly paused.

"I mean, if you want to," Kyle added. "It was just a thought."

"No, it's okay," she said, sitting down again. "I am glad you asked me, but I'm afraid I can't be of much help."

I saw Kyle's hopes deflate around him.

"Why?" I asked, not really caring if this was a difficult subject for her.

She looked at me, and I could see a sadness in her eyes that hadn't been there before. Seeing a teacher like a real person is weird, but my friendship with Tyler has taught me that grown-ups don't know that much more than kids do. They just hide things better. "It's a long story, and I'm afraid I am not at liberty to share it." She studied her desktop for a moment.

"You don't have to tell us if you don't want to," Kyle assured her.

She gave him a sad smile. "It's not that I don't want to, Kyle." Without knowing it, she'd picked up a pen shaped like a seated cat and started to doodle on a blank piece of paper.

"It's that you can't?" I threw out since she wasn't saying anything.

She looked at me silently.

"Mrs. Axeworthy, you can trust us." Kyle reached across the desktop and put his hand on hers. She sat up a little straighter, eyes widening very slightly.

Then she patted his hand with her free one before gently lifting his hand away and pulling hers clear. At first I couldn't understand, and then it hit me: if someone saw....

"You got in trouble," I blurted out.

"I wish I could help you, but I can't," she stated quietly, not contradicting me. She stood up, ending the meeting.

Kyle got up after her, confused at what was going on.

"I hope you find someone who can help you," she added earnestly.

"It's cool, Mrs. A," I said, standing up. "We'll just keep trying."

"We will?" Kyle asked me, half-stunned.

I smiled and gave him a nod. "Damn right we will."

"Thanks for talking with us," I continued, since Kyle's big brain was too busy thinking to give him the cue that he should say something. She gave me a grateful smile as we walked out. "So what's plan B?" I asked Kyle.

He gave me an odd look. "You tell me. She was my only idea."

"Have to be other teachers out there who will help."

He stopped walking. "You're pretty gung-ho about something you didn't even know word one about an hour ago." He wasn't mad, but he was curious.

I knew what he meant, so I stopped walking. "I know you think this is important, so it is important. I didn't do a thing to help you with Kelly, and that was a mistake, one I am not making again." My voice cracked, as it usually did when I brought up Kelly.

I saw Kelly leaning up against a locker. He wasn't smiling, just staring at me intently.

"This is important, and that means it needs to get done."

He didn't understand my motivation, but I could tell he was happy I was trying to help him.

After school, I went with plan B.

"Me?" Tyler paused and looked at me for a second. I nodded as I pulled another handful of Dallas Cowboys towels out of a box and began to place them on the shelves. "But I'm not a teacher. How can I do it?"

"Well, you're not a teacher yet, but I bet if you asked Coach Gunn, he would sign you up as an assistant coach or something. I mean, you've played college ball—that kind of experience has to be worth something."

"Well, it was barely one year of college ball, and it does count for something. Not enough to get me a degree in education or sports management, which I would need to be an assistant coach." I could tell by the tone in his voice he thought I was only half-serious.

That was his mistake.

"But how many credits are you shy an associate's? I bet if you started at community college, Gunn would hire you on in a second."

He paused what he was doing. "Now you have me going back to school? And who will be taking care of the store between me going to school and coaching?"

Hmmm, I hadn't thought that far ahead.

"What about Matt?" I offered. Tyler and Matt had been dating since New Year's, and though it wasn't serious, I thought it would be enough to ask Matt to hold down the store while Tyler came to school and made everything better somehow.

He laughed and shook his head. "One, he has a job. Two, I don't want to be a coach. And three, you know, even if I did do all of that, there's still a huge chance that they'd say no."

Sighing, I nodded and kept putting the towels away. "I know, but Kyle wants this so bad, and I feel fucking useless."

"You're not useless," Tyler assured me. "It just means it's going to take a little more thinking is all."

"Like I said," I muttered, tossing the last of the towels on the shelf, "useless."

When it came to thinking, I was a bit out of my comfort zone. After all, my claim to fame was being able to hit a little white ball more than 400 feet over the back fence more often than most guys. There wasn't a lot of thinking in that job. But I wasn't going to let Kyle down again.

"You do know just being there for him is enough, right?"

I tried not to look at him like a complete idiot, but I'm pretty sure I screwed that up. "You do know that sooner or later he is going to realize he's been doing all this on his own and find someone who can walk and chew gum at the same time?"

He gave me that sympathetic face that adults give when they are lying their asses off. "You're not dumb, Brad."

"This is coming from a guy who is, like, fortysomething and is just now dating his first serious boyfriend?"

He shot me a look and asked, "What does that have to do with anything?"

I shook my head and slapped a set of golf tees on the shelf. "It means you might not be the best guy to judge if other people are smart or not."

He crumpled up the piece of paper he had been going over and threw it at me, but he didn't disagree with me. Suddenly his expression changed.

"You know, I heard of a club like that back when I was your age."

I tried not to gape at him. "What? Where?"

"There were rumors there was some gay club at Foster. I mean, it could have just been talk. You know how bad the two schools talk about each other behind their backs. For all I knew, Granada had also said there was a dungeon under Foster where we locked up anyone who dared to root for the wrong team or something. I just remember hearing that there was supposed to be a gay club at Foster and that it ended up getting shut down, and someone almost got fired. I wouldn't even remember, but at the time I was scared that my name would somehow get attached to it because I was curious to go see what it was about."

That sounded crazy even for this town, but Tyler wouldn't make something like that up.

THE NEXT day there was no practice, a sure sign the faculty didn't think we were over Kelly's death yet. Kyle was out somewhere with Jennifer, which meant when I was done at Tyler's, I had some time to myself.

Time for plan C.

I sat in my car for about ten minutes, trying to think of a better plan C than the one I had, but nothing came to mind. There were so many reasons I did not want to have to rely on plan C. Then I thought of Kyle busting his ass for the rest of us and told myself to suck it up.

I drove up First Street and turned onto East Avenue like I was going to Kyle's house. Maybe I could just go to Kyle's house… no, I couldn't….

I stopped a couple of blocks up and pulled into the parking lot for Twice Upon a Time.

Robbie was a person I'd barely ever talked to, but for some reason, I didn't like him.

I had "met" him when I was dating Jennifer, since she practically lived at his shop. Robbie was loud, flamboyant, and above all else, stereotypically gay. I admit it was a shitty attitude to have, but guys who didn't act like guys drove me fucking crazy.

He had made a few smartass comments about me when I'd come into the store with Jennifer. I hadn't really heard them because I was too busy biting the inside of my cheek to stop myself from saying something ugly about him and his place.

Sighing, I got out of my car and walked inside. Some show tune garbage being blasted at a speaker-shattering level smashed into my eardrums the minute I opened the door. Robbie's back was to me, and his concentration was focused on the rack of clothes he was sorting. I didn't even think he heard me come in. I called his name, but the music drowned me out. I took a deep breath and roared, "Hey!"

He let out half a shriek and spun around to face me, brandishing the blue plastic hanger he clutched like a sword. "What the fuck!" he yelled at me. "Who just yells at people?"

I pointed upward to the speakers. "It helps if you can hear people trying to talk to you."

He pulled a remote out of his pocket and lowered the music. "Kyle isn't here," he said, stuffing the remote back into his pocket.

I opened my mouth to say something but paused. "I know. Why would you think I was here looking for him?"

He put the hanger up and moved toward the counter. "Well, in the entire time I've owned this place, you've been in three times. Twice with Jennifer, during which you gave me dirty looks, and once to pick up Kyle, during which you barely acknowledged my existence. I don't see your ex-girlfriend dragging you in here, which leaves your boyfriend. Who isn't here," he added.

"I know he isn't here," I snapped at him. "I know where my boyfriend is." I have no idea why I said that, but it seemed like the right thing to say.

"Well, bully for you," he said, sitting down behind the counter. "So now what? You pledging a frat or something? Because I know for a fact there is no way you would ever wear anything that was secondhand."

I began to say something and then stopped. Again he was right, but for some reason the statement pissed me off. "Why do you say that?"

He had pulled a book out from under the counter and was about to open it when he gave me a withering glance. "Well, because every single piece of clothing you have on has an A&F or an eagle logo on it somewhere. Which is impressive, by the way, since the closest store is at least a hundred miles away. You shop online, or Mommy and Daddy make road trips for you?"

I want to point out a few things before I go all ballistic on this guy.

One, it isn't a crime to like nice clothes. Two, I happen to like the clothes they sell at A&F, and I get an allowance every few months to order stuff online. Three, the idea of wearing clothes that other people have already worn gives me the creeps, because all I can imagine is a bunch of other people's bugs wandering all over me. And four, what I liked to wear was none of this guy's business.

"What's your problem?" I asked him, walking toward the counter.

He closed his book and folded his hands on top of it. "Are you serious?" When I didn't answer, he rolled his eyes at me and muttered to himself, "This boy cannot be real."

"Yeah, I'm serious. Why are you being such a dick to me?"

He took a deep breath and let me have it. "Um, maybe because you've given me attitude since day one for no other reason than you're a self-loathing douchebag who is so scared of people not liking you that even now you're pitching a fit because someone is saying they might not like you. Even if that person is someone you can't stand, like me."

I really didn't like that he had a point.

"But putting that aside," he said, moving the book as an example of the metaphor, "the real problem I have with you is that you are so smitten with yourself that you just take for granted people doing good things for you. God forbid you should thank them or even be grateful, not Little Lord Bradley Fauntleroy. Instead you should just go on with whatever issues you have in your own mind because they're more important than anything someone else might say or do."

"You think I should thank you for giving Kyle clothes?" Even as I asked him, that didn't sound right.

"No, you jock dick. I want you to thank me for explaining to the girl you lied to for three years that you weren't a complete asshole because you liked boys the whole time you were using her to hide behind. I would like a small acknowledgment that I took your side even though you have been nothing but shitty to me and that you'd never once consider taking my side if I needed you."

I just stood there, stunned.

"See, I know Kyle told you why Jennifer wasn't holding a grudge against you two, and still you didn't think for one moment about, just maybe, saying thank you. I have no idea why Kyle would waste his time with you… no, wait, I do see it. Let me rephrase. If you couldn't shred cheese on your abs, I'm sure Kyle would have nothing to do with you. Frankly, my dear, you aren't a very nice person. I know, I'm not one either. Now you don't like me for whatever little drama you have in your head, but I don't like you because I went to the mat for you, and you're still acting like a dick when you see me." He gave me a plastic smile and cocked his head. "So you want to go another three rounds there, Sporty Spice?"

The last time I had felt this bad was when the guys in the library thought I was going to beat them up. Every time I think I'm becoming a better person I trip over my own ego and find out I'm still the same asshole I didn't like before.

"You're right. That was shitty of me, and I'm sorry." I would have rather eaten dirt at that moment than apologize, but what choice did I have? Robbie was right. Jennifer had had every right to come after me to carve me up using a dull knife. Instead, she had buried her pain to become friends with me again.

And that was because of Robbie.

"You didn't have to do that, and I didn't deserve it. I apologize, and thank you." I turned to walk out, since there was no way in hell I could ask him to be the alliance's sponsor after what he'd just said.

"So if you weren't here for Kyle, why did you come in?"

I just shook my head and kept walking toward the door. "Doesn't matter. Have a good one."

"Oh, you fucking drama queen! Stop!" he snapped. I paused and looked over my shoulder at him. "I swear to God, one of you butch freaks is worse than any three drag queens." He rounded the end of the counter and came to a halt a few feet away, leaning casually against the glass top. "You came in here for something; then you were read. Now learn humility from that and try again." I gave him a confused look, and he sighed at me. "Why did you come in here?"

I wanted to leave, but I knew I was in it now. "I was wondering… I mean, Kyle is trying to…. Just never mind. It's stupid."

"Oh, for the love of…," he sputtered at me, glaring like he was thinking about taking a swing at my face. "Kyle is trying to…," he prompted me.

"Kyle is trying to get a gay-straight something started at the school, and we need a teacher to run it or they'll say no." I said everything in one breath, certain I had run it together into one garbled phrase.

"A gay-straight something?" he echoed slowly.

"Some kind of club, I think, for gay kids. I don't know. He says it's important." I really wanted to get away from Robbie now.

He seemed to think it over for a few seconds. "You're talking about one of those alliances, right?" I nodded in agreement. "One of those lame-ass groups where no one shows up, and the school thinks it's done something for the poor, misguided 'mos wandering the halls." He went back behind the counter. "It's a waste of time. Tell him not to bother."

I nodded and kept moving toward the door.

"Hold it," he called out. I looked over at him, just dying for him to stop talking. "Why would you come to me for that?"

"I don't know. I was hoping you could get a job at the school or know someone who would step up. I just have no idea where to find someone."

He shook his head. "No, that I gathered. I mean, why are you here pushing for it?" I didn't understand what he meant. "Why do you care so much? Do you even know why Kyle thinks it's so important?"

I had to admit I didn't.

"He thinks it's important, so it has to be" was all I could answer.

"And winner of the worst reason to do something goes to Bradley Graymark and his 'My boyfriend is smarter than I am so I don't need to do any thinking for myself' response. I know why Kyle would think this idea is worth pursuing, but if you have no idea what a gay-straight alliance means, I suggest you get out of the way, because asking people to help you with something that you have no earthly clue about makes you sound dumber than you already are."

I nodded, feeling even more stupid. "Sorry again," I mumbled as I opened the front door.

"Figure out what Kyle is trying to do," he called after me. "If you know why he is doing it, maybe you'll find a reason of your own to ask me to help."

So far it had been the best advice I'd heard all day.

I went to Nancy's Diner because I hadn't heard from Kyle, and I wasn't ready to go home and call it a day yet. A thousand thoughts jostled for my attention, and I barely registered Gayle stopping at my booth, pad in hand, to take my order. "Well, well, well, young Mr. Graymark, as I live and breathe! You ready to order or waiting on Kyle?"

I shrugged and put the menu back next to the sugars. "I guess a Coke and fries." My voice had all the excitement of a guy being woken up in the middle of the night to answer the phone.

She shook her head and then sat down across from me. "I've known you since you had to use a booster seat to eat at this table, and you have never once not been hungry." She gave me one of her "talk to me" smiles. "You and Kyle fighting again?"

"No, it isn't that. I just, I mean, Kyle is trying to do something, and I can't…." I sighed as I realized I was making no sense whatsoever. "I am just tired of being the dumb guy in the relationship."

She gave me a stern look. "How many all-star games did Nolan Ryan play in?"

I didn't even have to think about it. "Eight."

"And how many career strikeouts did he pitch?"

"Um, five thousand, seven hundred and fourteen."

"And how many no-hitters did he pitch?"

"Seven."

"See?" she said, pointing a finger at me. "You are not dumb at all. You just have a very specific skill set."

I rolled my eyes and thunked my forehead against the tabletop. "Awesome. My superpower is remembering baseball stats. I'm sure that will help Kyle immensely."

Something hit the top of my head. I looked up and dodged away from the possibility of another lethal order-pad attack. "I allow a lot of stuff in my place, but pity parties are not on the list. Brad, it takes real brains to remember all of that stuff. It took real brains for you to think past just being reinstated on the team and to demand an antibullying policy for Foster High. Thought I forgot about that, didn't you? Well, I didn't. Brad, the longer you sit there moaning about how dumb you are, the more you're going to believe it. Sorry, son, you have lots of brains, so suck it up, buttercup."

Neither one of us said anything for a few seconds. Finally I blurted out, "Do you think Kyle just likes me for my looks?"

Her eyes went wide, and she bit her lip in an attempt to withhold the laugh that burst out of her anyway. "Do I think Kyle likes the way you look? Of course he does, sweetie. Most of the people in the world would like the way you look." More seriously, she added, "Do I think it is the only reason? No, and let me tell you why. Because Kyle isn't in love with your face or your body or even that smile. He is in love with the guy who set up an elaborate date for him because he wanted to make him happy. He is in love with the guy who stood next to him when the rest of the school was ready to lynch him. Your looks might get you in the door, Brad, but I assure you it is your heart that's the reason you're staying. If Kyle has a problem, you're already helping him. You're there for him, and he knows that."

I began to protest, but she talked over me. "And I know you wish you could do more than that, but I assure you, being there one hundred percent is way more than a lot of other people ever think of doing. Don't sell yourself short there, son." She slid out of the booth, straightened her apron, and snapped her order pad open again. "There are more than enough people in the world who will do that for you. Trust me, they don't need any help."

"But I have no idea what to do." I swear to you, I was seriously trying not to whine.

"You will. Until then, be the guy in love with him." She shook her head. "The two of you are so far ahead of the game, it's silly. Finding the person who makes you want to rush in and save them is almost impossible in this world. Everything else is easy after that. Stop worrying."

It was good advice, but I still felt like crap. I think she knew it, but she knew not to keep talking too.

"I'll get your fries. You sure you don't want a burger?" She watched me think and nodded at the same time I did. Weird. "Yeah, that's one burger too. Coming right up."

She walked away, leaving me to sort out all the crap running around in my head. I really had no one else to ask to help with Kyle's idea; to be honest, asking Tyler and Robbie was me going after the longest long shots I could have found. Gayle brought me my food, and I nibbled on a fry and tried not to feel completely useless.

Then my phone vibrated.

Kyle: *Where r u?*

Just seeing a text from him could get me to smile with insane levels of happiness.

Brad: *At Nancys trying not 2 go home yet.*

It took a few seconds, and he responded.

Kyle: *BRT*

I had to laugh; for someone who never owned a cell phone, he sure had figured out text speak pretty fast. I took my knife and cut the burger in half and divided the fries into two piles as I waited. Five minutes later, Jennifer's car pulled up in front of the diner, and Kyle got out and waved at me.

I felt my face light up as I waved back and then waved at Jennifer before she drove off.

He strode in and tossed his backpack under the table as he sat next to me. "Hey, you," he said, leaning over to kiss me.

I kissed him back, and the feelings of idiocy I had been experiencing all day faded a little. "Hey back."

He looked down at my plate, and his eyes got wide. "Did you wait to eat until I got here?"

I slid my plate closer to him. "I even decided to share."

15

"Oh God, this is the best thing I've seen all day." He grabbed half of the burger and took a huge bite. "We've been running around all day, and we didn't stop to eat." He chewed contently and looked over at me. "I love you so much for this."

I looked at him, confused. "It's a burger."

He shook his head. "No, it was your burger, and now it's ours. That's pretty damn awesome." I felt a warmth in my chest as he leaned closer to me and took another bite. "Not a lot of guys would wait to eat until their flake of a boyfriend could show up. That's why I love you."

I slipped my arm around him and pulled him against me. "How did you get to be so awesome?"

He smiled and shrugged at me. "Genetics?"

We both laughed as we finished the burger.

THE WEEK flew by, and the news got worse and worse.

Kyle had looked up the rules for an after-school club, and not only did it need an adult there but a full-fledged teacher to boot. So my plan of somehow getting Tyler made an assistant coach wouldn't have worked, because he wouldn't have been an actual teacher with a degree and all that. At lunch I brought up asking Mrs. A. again, but Kyle was dead set against it.

"No, she was scared of something. I don't think that's the way to go."

Jennifer sighed and tossed her sandwich into the trash. "This school sucks." She sounded so defeated I was kind of shocked. "Any of you want to cut the rest of the day?"

Sammy raised her hand. She looked like a zombie as well. Most of the school was walking around like that, half asleep, not sure what to do anymore. I'd seen the look everywhere lately, even my own mirror.

I looked at Kyle, and he gave me an "I don't know" look in return. "I better not," I said finally. "They're barely letting me play baseball as it is. If I end up cutting too much, it's just another reason for them to kick me off."

Jennifer stared at me for a long couple of seconds, and for a moment I thought she was mad at me. With as much anger as I had ever heard in her voice she said, "I hate this fucking school." She turned around and stormed off.

"Did I do something wrong?" I asked Sammy and Kyle.

Sammy got up and tossed her Pepsi can in the trash. "No, she's just... we're all just brain-dead, Brad. This school sucks so bad that a guy shot himself to not come here. What does that say about Foster?"

"It says we need to seriously look at why people think Southern people are friendly," ghost Kelly commented.

"That it needs to change," Kyle answered.

She looked at Kyle with a thousand-yard stare and sighed. "Then more power to you." And she walked away.

"What's going on?" Kyle asked me once they were both gone. "Am I pushing too hard? I thought the alliance thing would be a good idea, and the only way we're going to get it is if we bring it up at the meeting Friday. After that they'll never agree.... Should I just shut up?"

I glanced over at Kelly, and he shook his head no and then gestured for me to say something to Kyle.

"No. You're not giving up," I said, looking him straight in the eyes. "They're tired, worn down. They just need some time. So we have two more days. What's your next plan?"

"I don't have a next one," he said sadly.

"You will," I assured him. "We aren't beat yet."

Suddenly I understood what Gayle had said, and keeping Kyle's head in the game wasn't me being a dumb waste of space. After school we went to the library, and he dug through the school rules, trying to find some kind of loophole or some sneaky way to get around it while I sat next to him and looked up what a gay-straight alliance was.

A gay-straight alliance is where kids of all kinds could get together and talk about stuff that was important to them. If you were gay and had questions about being gay, you could ask them. If you were straight and wanted to ask gay people stuff, you could. They generally educated people on the different days, like coming-out day, or no-name-calling week. Both seemed like a long shot, but it was cool that someone was trying to have them. Generally it was a place, once a week, that kids could go to and feel safe no matter what. They weren't freaks, they weren't fags, they were just kids. And though I doubt I would have ever stepped into one before meeting Kyle, I could see how having one was important.

"I got nothing," he said, sighing in frustration. "There is no way to get around not having a teacher."

I grabbed his hand and gave him a smile. "We'll figure something out."

When I dropped him off at his house, he looked about ready to give up. I didn't blame him. I think he knew more about the school charter than the school board did now. He was halfway out of the car when I reminded him, "Hey, you know if this doesn't happen, it's in no way your fault, right?" His expression told me that was the exact way he was looking at it. "Kyle, you didn't make Foster this messed-up of a town."

In a small voice, he answered, "I feel like I have." He slid back into his seat again and closed the door. "What if I never came out? What if I just shut my mouth and kept my head down? Kelly wouldn't have attacked me, and you wouldn't have had to jump in. Maybe he would be alive and you'd be better off."

I turned off the car and turned fully to look at him. "Look, there is no better place for me than right here with you right now, so get that crap out of your head. I liked guys before you, and Kelly felt like he did way before he met you. What he decided to do was his choice, and a fucking stupid one at that. You know how hard you tried to help him, and he still pulled away. That isn't on you; that is on every ass hat out there who thought it would be funny to make fun of a queer kid." Sighing, I put my hand on his. "You can't blame yourself for not being able to change everything all at once. You tried—hell, you're still trying—and if it doesn't happen, that isn't your fault."

"Then whose is it?" he asked me back.

I hated that I didn't have an answer to that.

He kissed me good night and went inside. I drove home, more determined than ever to find a way to help him.

"Stupid idea?" Kelly asked from the passenger's seat.

"Incredibly stupid," I said, not looking over. "We could have gotten through it together."

He sighed. "If the roles were reversed, if you hadn't come out and you had your shit blasted all over social media, can you tell me you wouldn't think of doing the same thing I did?"

God, is this how Kyle felt with Billy? I focused my thoughts and ignored all my guilt and fear that were sitting next to me.

When I walked into my house, I could smell dinner from the doorway and felt my stomach growl in response. I slipped off my shoes and headed toward the smell of food like a hungry dog. My mom was stirring a bowl of mashed potatoes when I walked in. "How did I guess the instant dinner was ready you'd walk in the room?" I smiled at her and then tried to look behind her to see what was on the stove. "Not a chance!" she said, kicking playfully at me. "Go wash up first."

Groaning, I turned around and went upstairs.

I tossed a clean shirt on and tried to think about Kyle's problem from a new point of view. We needed a teacher, and the only teacher who would do it would get fired if she tried. I felt a headache coming on, so I took two Tylenol before I went back downstairs to eat.

I set the table in silence while I went over and over the list of teachers in my head. Who would be so stupid to put their head in that lion's mouth, knowing how Mr. Raymond hated Kyle and me already? I must have been lost in thought, because my mom tossed a dishrag at me to get my attention.

"Have you heard a word I've said?" she asked.

I grimaced at her. "You were talking?" I saw her mouth curl up in frustration, and I added, "I'm sorry. I just have a lot on my mind and zoned out. What did you say?"

She paused, and her eyes seemed to look right through me for a second. "Well, I was asking you how school has been, but I can tell not that good. What's up?"

I sat down at the table and tried to organize my thoughts. "Was there a gay club at Foster back in the day?" She didn't look like it registered to her. "Tyler said there were rumors of a gay club when he was a student, and Kyle went to talk to Mrs. Axeworthy about it and…."

I could see by the look on her face she knew that name.

"It wasn't a gay club," my mom said carefully. "Not in any official way."

"But there was one?" I asked her.

"There was an incident," she commented neutrally. "And a couple of people got in trouble about it."

"Why?" I asked, feeling like I'd stumbled onto a murder mystery.

"Brad, I'm not sure I can talk about this with you. What happened was technically sealed. No one was supposed to talk about it." She paused and looked at me. "Did Mrs. Axeworthy say something?"

"No, Kyle wants to start a gay-straight alliance at school, and we need a teacher to run it. And when we asked her, she got really weird, almost scared."

"I can't imagine parents letting something like that be set up at Foster," she commented as she pulled out the roast.

"It's a place where kids can get together and talk about being gay or ask questions and be safe. I mean, what is wrong with that?"

"And if their questions are about sex?" she asked me. "What then?"

"Mom, do you think there is anything about sex we are going to learn in a school club that we can't find on the internet?"

She seemed to consider it as she sliced up the roast.

"So what happened?" I asked her.

"Well, we were presented with the parents' accusation, but the board never got to talk to either one of them personally. All we were told was that she had admitted she let the kids talk about sex in front of her, and that was enough." She saw the look of outrage on my face and added, "It was a different time."

"So then why not now?" I asked her, standing up. "Why can't we talk about sex?"

She stopped what she was doing and looked over at me. "Brad, there are just some things that aren't talked about in school, and gay sex is pretty high up there."

"Oh, but health class and sex education is okay as long as it's straight? Mom, gay kids have nowhere to go in this town, nowhere. If there was a place they could have, maybe Kelly might still be alive. You have to see that!"

"Nah," Kelly said, looking up from his plate, "I wouldn't been caught dead in a place like that."

I swear I almost growled at him in frustration.

She put the knife down and motioned me to sit next to her. "I don't know if Foster is ready for something like that."

And suddenly I knew what Kyle felt.

"I don't care what Foster is ready for, Mom. This is happening right now. There are gay kids out there who are thinking about killing themselves, and the fact that a bunch of old straight people have a problem with that doesn't matter to me. My friend is dead, and we all talked about making this town a better place so it won't happen again. That needs to happen now, not when Foster is ready for it."

I got up and began to walk out of the kitchen.

"Aren't you going to eat?" she asked as I walked away.

"I'm not hungry," I answered truthfully and went upstairs before I started crying again.

THE FRIDAY of the meeting, I kept expecting a miracle to happen somehow. Like there was this unheard-of rule or last-minute thing we could do in the nick of time. I know Kyle was dying to storm into the meeting again, but there was no point, since the last time they'd made it pretty clear we weren't allowed in. Jennifer and Sammy waited with us until the meeting got out, but they didn't seem to have much hope.

I hated to say it, but I knew exactly how they felt.

When the meeting let out, most of the school board proceeded past us without even a glance. As always, we were beneath their station, so they didn't need to acknowledge us or anything. Mr. Raymond followed behind them. He gave us a chilling stare as he walked by. Finally, I saw both Kyle's and my mom walk out with Jennifer's dad right behind them.

Mrs. Axeworthy was walking with them.

Kyle's mom saw us and said, "How did I know you guys would be sitting out here waiting?"

"How bad did it go?" Kyle asked, his voice laced with disappointment.

Mrs. Axeworthy looked at him and smiled. "That's a funny story."

Kyle

I REACHED across and put my hand on hers. "Mrs. Axeworthy, you can trust us."

She instantly stiffened in her seat and then gently removed my hand from hers. It didn't come across as rude, but it was very deliberate.

Out of nowhere Brad said, "You got in trouble."

The second he said it I could see it. She was afraid; her eyes kept darting to the open door, as if to see if anyone was listening in. Finally she sighed and said, "I wish I could help you, but I can't."

She stood up, indicating the conversation was done.

I stood up as well, not sure where her fear was coming from.

"I hope you find someone who can help you," she said, sounding like she meant it.

I was about to say something, but then Brad stood up behind me. "It's cool, Mrs. A, we'll just keep trying."

I was so surprised, I said, "We will?" before I could stop myself.

He gave me Smile Number Fourteen, which was his Kevin-Costner-from-*Bull-Durham* smile—a little cocky but reassuring as hell—and answered, "Damn right we will."

I honestly had no words. I had been convinced Brad wasn't even sure how important the alliance was, but here he was nonetheless.

"Thanks for talking with us," he said, nudging me toward the door.

Once we were in the hall, he asked, "So what's plan B?"

"You tell me. She was my only idea," I admitted. I really thought he had a plan for a second.

We started walking down the hallway. "Have to be other teachers out there who will help."

Okay, that's it. I just stopped and said, "You're pretty gung-ho about something you didn't even know word one about an hour ago."

He stopped walking. "Look, you think this is important so it is important. I didn't do a thing to help you with Kelly, and that was a mistake, one I am not making again."

21

His voice cracked, and he was looking over my shoulder like he was seeing something that wasn't there. I was an expert on imaginary friends, so I let him look and waited for him to come back to me.

"This is important, and that means it needs to get done."

I was blown away by the declaration. I had no idea he felt so strongly about it. "You didn't make a mistake," I told him quietly.

"Yes, I did," he responded instantly. "But never again."

The bell rang, and I knew fifth period just got out. "I need to go meet Jennifer…," I said, not wanting to leave him.

He smiled and nodded toward the parking lot. "Go. We still don't have practice, so I'll be helping Tyler out. Call me when you're done."

I nodded and then gave him a hug. "You are the best," I said, squeezing him.

"Not yet," he said, hugging me back. "But give me time."

I didn't have time to debate him on his awesomeness, so instead I kissed him and ran over to meet Jennifer.

At first I thought I had beat her to the parking lot, since her car was there but she wasn't waiting outside for me to show up. After a second, I realized she was in the car, and it looked like she was crying. I opened the door, and Amy Lee's voice came screaming from the stereo. Jennifer was so surprised by me she didn't know if she should cover her face or turn the music down, so she fumbled at both for a couple of seconds.

I reached over and turned the volume down as I got into the car.

"I really do think this car is trying to kill me," she said, wiping her eyes quickly.

"What's wrong?" I asked her, completely unprepared for her tears.

She sniffled quietly and looked at me in disbelief. "Are you kidding me?" she asked me back. I shook my head since I really was that confused. "Kyle, I love you to death, but sometimes you have no idea what is going on around you at all."

I mentally reversed in my head. "Is this about Kelly?"

She shook her head and started the car. "It isn't important. Where are we going?"

I reached over and turned the car off. "Nowhere until you tell me what's wrong." She looked at me like she was ready to fight, and I begged her, "Please, Jennifer, I just want to help."

She sighed and fell back into her seat. "Of course it's about Kelly. What else is there?" My desire was to say something to make her feel better, but I stopped myself since I wanted her to keep talking. "We're all feeling it, Kyle, and honestly I don't know how the rest of them are dealing with it. I know I'm dying inside."

She didn't say anything for a few seconds, which seemed like a good time to jump in. "It's okay to miss Kelly. It's okay to be sad about it too."

She gave a scoffing laugh and looked at me intensely. "You're not kidding, are you. You have no idea what we're feeling." The last part was a declaration instead of a question, and I felt like a complete idiot because I had no clue what she was talking about.

"What's wrong?" I implored her again.

She looked away from me and put both hands on the wheel like she was steadying herself for a response. Taking a deep breath, she finally admitted, "We're killing ourselves because of the guilt, Kyle."

"Guilt about what?" Now she was scaring me.

She glanced over at me, and it was like looking at some weird mutant clone of Jennifer instead of the real one. Where the old Jennifer was all strength and brass, this one was haunted and defeated. She had given up inside; her body just hadn't stopped moving yet. But as shocking as that was, it was nothing compared to what she said.

"We're feeling guilty because it's our fault Kelly killed himself, of course."

You ever get that feeling like you're dreaming even though you're wide-awake? It's like you become hyperaware, and everything around you is way too vivid for a few moments. I've read about oxygen deprivation, and what I felt then seemed like that. The whole world became a blur of colors and sounds before it started to fade away. That's how I felt sitting there hearing Jennifer say those words. Though I hadn't budged, the seat felt like it was falling beneath me while the whole car spun on an invisible axis. Was I asleep? Was all of this just a hallucination? Hearing the words I had used come out of her mouth made everything surreal for the few seconds I spent scrambling to get my wits back.

"How is it your fault?" I heard myself ask her, even though I hadn't consciously commanded my mouth to say anything.

"How isn't it?" she asked back sarcastically. "You told us he was in trouble, you begged us to help him, and we all did nothing." She was starting to cry again. "You had to storm out of Brad's car because he and I were so sure we knew what was best for Kelly." Huge tears rolled down her face, and she laughed through her sobbing. "Everyone always thought I was such a vapid, mean bitch who only thought of herself, and when the time came to prove them wrong, all I did was the same thing everyone else did." She shook her head as she stared off across the parking lot. "Maybe they were right. Maybe I am just a dumb cheerleader."

"Oh, shut the fuck up."

We both paused as we wondered where that had come from. I was a bit more surprised to find out it came from my mouth than she was.

"It isn't your fault Kelly killed himself, no more than it is anyone else's. He made his choice, and sucky as it was, it was his choice to make. You want to blame someone? Then blame the people who mocked him on Facebook, or blame Jeremy for posting the damn video in the first place, but don't blame yourself, Jennifer. That's just a waste of time and effort."

It was everything I needed to hear for myself but knew I wouldn't believe.

"You and Brad and half of the football team could have gone over and tried to sit on Kelly every day, and he would have made the same choice he did. Don't be upset because you think you didn't do enough—be upset about the people who did too much. Be pissed at the town that created the environment, the school that fostered the attitude, and be furious at the people who egged him on, but not at yourself. You were his friend, and he knew that. In the end, it's all we can be to each other."

I felt my own eyes stinging as the weight that had settled on my heart since Kelly had died seemed to lighten by a few thousand pounds. Jennifer had stopped crying as well. She stared at me blankly, my words sinking in past her own guilt and despair. "You really believe that? You don't blame me or Brad or anyone else for not helping you, do you?"

Now I was crying. "Did you think I would?" She nodded meekly, and I tried to laugh away a sob or two. "You guys were there in every way that counted. We all were. This isn't our fault—none of it is."

She reached over and pulled me into a hug that told me the past few days of misery were over and that it was time for a new start.

"Okay," she said, more to herself than to me. "Okay, time to stop being such a moody bitch." She sat up straighter and checked herself in the rearview mirror. "Oh God, I look like an emo raccoon who just got done watching *Titanic*." She grabbed her purse, fished out a Kleenex, and began to wipe the smeared mascara off her face. "So where did you need to go?" she asked as she reapplied her face. I felt sheepish asking her a favor after all that. "It's no big deal. Let's go see Robbie or something."

She paused and looked over at me. "No, you're trying to make things better, so let's make things better. What did you need me for?"

I made a small smile as I said, "I kinda wanted to see your dad?"

She rolled her eyes as she went back to the mirror. "Now I know I don't want to know anything else."

She drove me to the police station, and I felt my stomach do a small, nervous backflip. It was a reflex. In my mom's life, which is my life too, police were not the good guys. They were the enemy and needed to be avoided at all costs. I didn't feel that way personally, but I had an irrational fear of them nonetheless. Which is why I wanted Jennifer to go with me because there was no way I could walk into that station alone.

Jennifer parked the car and looked over at me. "So, anything I should know?"

"I think something went down in the past, and if anyone would know, it'd be your dad."

She shrugged. "Sounds good to me."

One of the few bright points about Foster was its abundant lack of anything resembling an actual crime rate. It was a quiet town, and to be honest, quiet was the way we all liked it. So it was no shock whatsoever to see a lot of nothing going on when we walked in. The lady who worked dispatch waved Jennifer and me through as she talked on the phone.

Jennifer's dad is kinda cool for an adult.

He wasn't one of those cops who took the whole badge thing so seriously that he became a dick about it. I guess growing up in Foster gave him the luxury of knowing what the town was like when he took the job, so he never had illusions that he was anything more than a small-town sheriff. He knew everyone's name and knew where everyone lived. I had never once seen him pull his gun out. Period. He didn't need to, since his expressions were enough to scare people into behaving themselves. Jennifer had once told me that her dad knew his way around a pistol, a shotgun, fifteen different kinds of rifles, and a black-powder cannon. He just didn't need to use them.

In other words, he was one of those sheriffs you wanted with you when the zombie apocalypse came.

He smiled when he saw Jennifer walking toward his office. Then I saw his smile waver a bit when he saw me walking behind her. I guess I couldn't blame him; after all, before me, this town really didn't have a body count. "Well, this is an unexpected pleasure," he said as we walked into his office. "Anything wrong?"

Jennifer sat down and gestured to me, pretty much saying this entire thing was my idea.

I sat down slowly and asked him, "Is it against the law for the school to refuse to let us have a gay-straight alliance if we asked for one?"

He didn't say anything at first, which to me was a sign that someone had brains. Only idiots, like me, went off talking without the benefit of thinking about it first, and he was not one to talk without thinking. "I am guessing your alliance thing would be an after-school activity?" I nodded. "And one that is inclusive to gay and straight students?" Another nod. "Well then, normally it would be illegal for the administration and the board to deny you one. But that's not what they are going to do."

I paused and cocked my head in question. "How do you know what they're going to do?"

He smiled and shook his head. "If you kids knew half of what you really thought you knew, you'd be running the world." I opened my mouth to retort, but he kept talking. "If you asked, they would grant you the club or alliance or whatever you'd call it and then tell you there was no faculty available to run it. I assume you know about what happened to Charlotte Axeworthy?" Jennifer and I both shook our heads. He paused for a moment, and I could see him backtrack mentally. "Okay, well, let's just say she was the only person who would want to touch that kind of thing at all, and she almost lost her job because of it. After the ruckus the kid's parent made, I have to admit I was shocked she got to keep her job."

"What did she do?" Jennifer asked her dad, now interested in the topic.

"Depends on who you ask. You ask Mrs. Axeworthy, nothing. You ask the kids, she provided a safe place to allow them to get together to talk about life. Ask the parent, and she willingly discussed the topic of gay sex and behavior with minors without parental consent." He didn't sound like he was overjoyed about the topic himself, but he kept his voice neutral. "In the end, the school board put a permanent mark on her record with the understanding that if anything, and I mean anything, was brought up in relation with her name, she would be out on the street quicker than she could pack her office up."

Suddenly her fear made a lot more sense. I sat up, concerned. "But I don't understand. Why do you say you know what they would do?"

He looked at both of us for a long couple of seconds and then sighed. "Look, guys, I hate to be the one to tell you this, but there is no way Mr. Raymond is going to let one of those alliance things be formed at Foster. He knew that Axeworthy didn't do anything wrong—that was just the excuse he used to shut it down. It was a warning to the other teachers. If they tried to do something similar, then it was just a matter of time before another parent stepped up with another 'complaint.'"

By the way Jennifer's mouth hung open, she was as shocked as I was. "But that's not fair," I complained, knowing I sounded like a five-year-old the second I said it.

He shrugged and nodded. "I agree, but a lot of life isn't fair."

"That's not an answer," Jennifer fired at him. He looked over at her with an eyebrow arched. "You know it isn't. That's just a crappy fact of life."

I saw he was about to say something to her, but I didn't really care. I had done the math in my head, and I was pretty sure where this was leading. "Who was the parent?" He slowly closed his mouth and turned his attention to me. He wasn't smiling, but I could see by the way he looked at me he was pleased I had finally caught up with the true problem. "No other teacher would volunteer to run the club because they already saw what happened to Mrs. Axeworthy. The only way a gay-straight alliance can happen is if we get whoever complained about the club to take it back. So who was the parent?"

He slowly leaned back in his chair and gave me a lazy smile. "I can't tell you that."

"Oh, come on, Dad!" Jennifer exclaimed, standing up. "Why even bring it up if you can't help us?"

I stared into his eyes as she complained, and I could see the quiet challenge in them. "He did help us," I said, cutting her off. "Thanks, Sheriff," I said, standing up myself and extending my hand out to him. "You've been a great help."

"He has?" Jennifer asked me, shocked.

"You're welcome," he said, standing up to shake my hand. "Good luck," he added with a wink.

I was going to need it.

"You ready?" I asked her as she looked at him, then at me.

She finally threw her hands up in frustration. "God, I wish I knew what was going on just once around here." She grabbed her keys out of her pocket and stormed out.

"See you at dinner," he called after her playfully.

She didn't answer him back.

"Hey, Kyle," he said as I began to follow her. "Do everyone a favor and stay away from Mrs. Axeworthy while you investigate this. Because there aren't too many people who know what happened, and they will assume…."

I held up a hand to stop him. "I got it. Trust me, the last thing I want to do is get her in trouble again."

He smiled and nodded. "Just making sure."

I nodded back and ran out the door on the off chance Jennifer had taken off without me. When I got into the car, she did not seem happy. "Where to now, Miss Daisy?"

"He can't tell us who the parent is because there was never an official complaint," I began to explain. "They made that deal to have the whole incident go away, so the fact we know what we do is something big. Now all I have to do is figure out who made the complaint."

I saw the realization in her eyes as she figured it out. "So how are you going to do that?"

"No earthly clue," I admitted, fastening my seat belt.

I SPENT the next two days feeling like I'd wandered into a wind tunnel and had to battle for every step forward. And whether I glanced at my phone or the clock on the wall or not, I never lost track of time racing by while I had to dig harder than I should have for information. If it hadn't been for Brad, I would have given up on the whole thing a couple dozen times. I don't know what had gotten into him, but he was my own private cheerleader, and it was awesome.

I spent most of my time in the library, my eyes glued to the dusty fiche reader, through which I spooled old copies of our local paper, the school paper, the published minutes of the school board—anything that might give me a clue as to the identity of the parent who'd spoken out against Mrs. Axeworthy. I found a quarter-column-sized article about it in the local paper, but all it said was that a teacher was being investigated for improper behavior at the school; it didn't mention the group or who had complained. When I pulled up copies of the school paper, as well as the published minutes of the school board meetings, I could find nothing substantial.

The only evidence that there had been a situation at all was one notation in the board minutes advising that Mrs. Axeworthy had been given two weeks of unpaid leave. But there was no reason noted. There had to be something about it somewhere. I just couldn't think of where else I could go to research. Friday came, and I knew I had failed.

Again.

Brad, Jennifer, and Sammy waited with me outside the meeting, though we knew what the outcome was going to be. Brad stopped me more than once from barging inside and starting a scene. It was a good move on his part, because we all remembered how the last time I tried to interrupt the school board went.

Finally the doors opened, and the members of the school board stalked past us. Most ignored us as adults are wont to do with kids, but Mr. Raymond locked eyes with me and gave me a scowl like he was ready to hit me. I swear the temperature dropped a dozen degrees as he passed by.

My mom walked out with Brad's mom and Mrs. Axeworthy, which kind of stunned me.

"How did I know you guys would be sitting out here waiting?" my mom asked me, smiling.

I did not feel like smiling back. "How bad did it go?"

Mrs. Axeworthy looked at me and grinned. "That's a funny story."

Dorothy Aimes

THERE ARE things in life that you can never ready yourself for.

I mean, you grow older and you see things and you think, "Well, there is just nothing else in the world that can surprise me." And then life has a way of coming along and proving you wrong in ways you can barely survive. When I was a little girl, I didn't dream only of growing up and being someone's wife; I did have other plans. However, I really looked forward to having a baby and then raising them to be a wonderful adult. What I'm saying is that I wasn't one of those women who insisted year after year that they weren't ready for children. "I'm not ready yet. We're not ready yet." That didn't even occur to me.

William wasn't as ready, but he didn't shy away from being a parent, either. The further along I got, the more he embraced it, until the end when he was easily as nervous as I was. I can tell you I had a life before that day in April when I was wheeled into Foster General feeling like I was going to explode. I had dreams and wants and friends and desires, all of them very real to me.

Right up to the point where they handed me my son, and I realized my life was just starting.

We ended up selling our part in one of the larger ranches outside of town and using the money to buy a place big enough for the three of us. From that home base, William and I set out to fit into the tax bracket we felt was ours. I wish I could tell you that trying to make friends with the women who were born into that lifestyle was easy, but I think I've lied enough for one life. I have fake boobs, fake hair, fake eyelashes, and a pretty convincing fake smile, so a little truth shouldn't be that painful.

There is a rather large group of people who live in and around Foster with money, and more than a few had children the same age as Kelly. We began to throw parties, attend fundraisers, and Will took up golfing, all in the name of our infant son. William and I told ourselves we were doing it for Kelly, that we were trying to make influential friends for his sake.

What a crock of shit.

Growing up, I had a bird named Ola. She was an albino cockatiel and, I thought, a smart bird all around. I say "thought" because one day my mother hung a mirror on the side of Ola's cage and the bird was beside herself. She would coo and chirp and preen herself, all in hopes of gaining the mystery bird's attention, never knowing it was just a reflection. I hate to admit it, but I lost respect for Ola because what was once a clever bird was reduced to looking like a self-centered fool just by adding a mirror into the equation.

I became worse than Ola once I began to socialize with the upper crust of Foster society, the people who lived just under the scale of the old money. I became vain, I became petty, and worst of all, I became a bad mother. Of course, all of this is crystal clear after the fact. There's nothing like hindsight to make you realize every single one of your flaws when it is far too late to fix them. Kelly grew up with children who had this social Darwinism bred into them unconsciously, and it made him miserable. Kelly was an emotional child. He had wild mood swings, was always on the verge of crying, whether from rage or sorrow. He walked around the house on eggshells because we had instilled such a value on the things we had purchased that he felt terrified he would accidentally break something. William pushed him into football because he thought the sport would somehow toughen him up. Again, I did nothing because I was too busy flirting with the woman I saw in the mirror and trying to find ways to make her more popular.

All in the name of our son, of course.

When Kelly started high school, everything got worse. He had already pulled away from us, something that didn't even register with me, since I was so busy trying to maintain our good standing in the community. After Halloween his freshman year, Kelly came to us and asked if he could throw a party for his friends. At first the idea seemed absurd, but he explained that Francis Patterson had let her daughter have a huge costume party that everyone had gone to and enjoyed—everyone but Kelly, who hadn't been invited. Neither William nor I caught that little detail, because we suddenly saw the value of throwing a party for the children of the people we continued to try to impress.

That first year we stayed home and chaperoned, which is a polite way of saying that I got mildly buzzed and listened to my much drunker husband make inappropriate comments to underage girls. A lot of kids had shown up, and Kelly did seem genuinely happy for once. The next year when he asked to have it again, it was no longer a matter of if he could; it was a matter of if we needed to stay home and chaperone a second time.

Trust me when I say I now realize how insane that sounds.

So we left our fifteen-year-old son alone, with money to throw a party for his teenage friends, and then caught a plane to Dallas so we could have a weekend to ourselves. It was a wonder that no one called CPS on us. There was some mess when we got back, but what it cost to clean up seemed trivial when compared to the popularity that Kelly seemed to be getting from throwing the parties.

This went on all the way to senior year, when someone taped my son admitting he had feelings for men. He shot himself a couple of weeks later.

Sorry if that seemed abrupt, but I'm pretty sure we were all thinking the same thing. I am… I was a horrible mother, and my son killed himself. I suppose everything else is just me trying to justify it.

As I was saying at the beginning, there are things in life you can never ready yourself for. Burying your son is one of them. A few years back, we bought plots of land at Foster Hills, the local cemetery. We bought three of them—one each for William, Kelly, and myself—and then another three for who we assumed would be Kelly's future family. Six plots of land so we could stay together as a family even in death.

The fact that our teenage son was the first occupant is as tragic as it is ironic.

I haven't been there since the day of the funeral. I can't bring myself to go out there and look at the tombstone yet. How can I face even the image of my son, knowing I have done nothing to atone for the numerous sins I have committed? So instead I sit in my house and try not to look at the many pictures we have hanging up of Kelly, and I wait for something to happen.

As with most things in life, karma takes very little time to catch up with you.

The thunderous declaration of "Goddammit!" came from William's study, followed by the sound of a phone being slammed into its cradle. I didn't budge. Instead I sat there and counted in my head. It took to twenty-four before he charged into the living room.

"That school is fucking us again," he roared, waiting for me to ask him how.

He would have to wait a long time.

"Don't you even want to know what they're doing?" he asked me, his anger tapering off slightly as he registered my apathetic response.

I said nothing again, which he took as a silent agreement.

"They are going to pass a set of rules about bullying and fag protection this Friday during the school board meeting. Do you know what they are calling them?" He was about to answer his own question, since I hadn't said a word so far. He froze when he heard my answer.

"Kelly's Laws."

His mouth sputtered shut and then twisted into a snarl. "You knew about this?" It was incredible how his anger could shift from targeting the school to me.

I nodded but said nothing more; there was no use.

"Why didn't you say anything about it?" he demanded.

"What does it matter?" I asked him, my voice sounding like it was coming from a machine. "Our son is dead. What else matters?"

"We still have to live here!" Spittle flew out of his mouth as he leaned toward me, screaming. Lately it seemed the madder he got, the less I was inclined to respond. I was sure he was itching for a fight, but I couldn't bring myself to care, so he kept on screaming. "You think I want our family's name associated with that kind of garbage? Liberal-loving gay protectors. It's embarrassing."

Something inside me began to smolder as he kept complaining.

"We spent all this time trying to build up a reputation in this town, and then something like this happens and that reputation means nothing."

Smoke began to rise from the shattered remains of what used to be my heart.

"I am going to have to go down there and tell those idiots that I don't want Kelly's name within a thousand miles of that crap." He looked at his watch and sighed, which was one gesture too many for me.

"Oh my goodness, I forgot. Kelly's suicide must have interrupted your plans for the day. He was always such a polite boy. I'm sure that if we'd explained to him about your schedule—" I took a breath and heard a stranger's voice coming from my mouth, rasping my next words. "—he would have shot himself on a more convenient day." I actually snarled at William, then choked down my fury.

There was no confusion on his part about what I was saying now. "Of course I knew about it. When they called me and gave their deepest condolences at my loss, they informed me that they would be taking steps to ensure nothing like this would happen again. I was so caught up in the gesture that I completely forgot to factor in how my son's death would impact our fucking reputation."

"Dorothy…," he began to say, but I had been quiet enough.

"No, William, I think I am done listening to you. I said nothing when we came home and you screamed at Kelly because somehow it was his fault that other people had spray-painted stuff on the side of his truck. I said nothing when you planned on sending him to a brainwashing Bible camp to somehow 'cure' him of his gayness. I even said nothing when you tried to stop the Tyler boy from speaking the truth at Kelly's funeral. But you know what? I am done. I told them they could use Kelly's name, and that decision is final. I cannot believe it is barely a week after we buried our son and you are still more concerned about our reputation, and, no doubt, your round of golf, but it ends now." I stood up and watched him stare at me in shock. "And you're wrong. We do not have to live here—I do. You're free to get the hell out, and don't bother coming back. Because effective right now, William, there is no 'us.'"

I waited for him to say something, but it was his turn to say nothing.

"Don't be here when I get back." I locked eyes with him. "I'm not kidding."

I grabbed my purse and left, never once looking back.

I WALKED into Nancy's and saw Gayle sitting in one of the booths talking to someone. I couldn't place him from the back, but as I walked by and took a table, I could see it was Brad, Kelly's best friend from school. Instead of sitting down, I made my way to the back and fled into the women's room before I could be seen. Tears came unbidden as I hid in one of the stalls.

Just seeing Brad had brought back a flush of memories I had been fleeing from all week, and I couldn't stop them. Brad had practically grown up in our house. For a while he was like the brother Kelly never had. We had always talked about having more kids, but it never happened. Instead we focused all our efforts on the one son we did have, which of course became a euphemism for focusing only on ourselves. I wonder, if he had a sibling, whether things would have been different.

"Dorothy?" a voice asked me from the other side of the stall.

I recognized Gayle's voice and tried to wipe the tears away quickly. "Just a second, please," I called back, wondering what a couple of seconds would accomplish. Sighing, I opened the stall and walked out slowly. I felt like a little girl getting caught by a truant officer.

"I thought I saw you rush past," she said, reaching out and pulling me into a hug. "I didn't expect to see you out yet."

I hugged her back and took a deep breath for the first time since I found Kelly.

I had known Gayle forever. I don't remember a time where she wasn't running Nancy's Diner, the center of all Foster. William had taken me here on our first date, and every Friday when Kelly got to choose where we ate dinner, he always chose Nancy's. I don't know many people from Foster who don't have a list of memories that include this diner and Gayle with it.

"I think I just left William," I whispered to her.

She pulled back and looked me directly in the eyes for a long couple of seconds. Gayle had this ability to look into your eyes and divine the truth out of them in a way that words could never quite convey. Finally she let out a sigh and said, "Good. Are you okay?"

I nodded and then walked over to the mirror. "As good as I can be. I saw Brad out there and just lost it." I dabbed at my eyes with some tissue. "I really don't think I am ever going to be okay again."

She came up behind me, put her hands on my shoulders, and gave me a warm smile. "You are okay, Dorothy. You're just going through the worst possible thing a mother can ever endure. Give it some time."

"Why?" I asked her, putting some concealer on. "Is it somehow going to miraculously get better?"

Without missing a beat, she said, "No, you'll just get better at hiding it from everyone else." It was the most truthful thing anyone had said to me since Kelly's death. "Come back to the kitchen, let me make you some food, and we can talk away from everyone."

We sat by the back door and shared a burger as we watched the afternoon sun slowly drop behind the buildings. "You hear about the school board meeting?" I asked her between bites.

She nodded. "Too little, too late if you ask me." She didn't say anything else, but I could tell she wanted to.

"Never knew you to be one to hold your tongue," I commented. "Don't start on my account."

She kept staring at her feet for a moment and then took a deep breath as she faced me. "You are grieving, and I am not going to be one of those people who use the moment to kick you while you're down. It's just good they are doing something finally instead of trying to hide the problem again."

I had no idea what she was talking about, and then suddenly I did.

"Thank you for the meal," I said politely, no longer feeling like eating at all. I opened my purse to grab my pocketbook. "What do I owe you?"

"Dorothy," she said, putting her hand over mine. "I'm not attacking you—you asked."

I slowly pulled my hand away from hers. "I did, and thank you for the honesty, Gayle." I got up and smoothed the front of my blouse. "We need to do this again."

I was being a bitch, and I knew it, but there was nothing else I could manage without tearing my own hair out. I needed to get out of there before I lost it, and thankfully she seemed to understand that.

"Anytime. You are always welcome here."

I nodded to her and walked through the back alley toward my car, beating a hasty retreat.

Thankfully it was dark enough to allow me a good ten minutes to cry hysterically in my car without anyone seeing me. After that, I wiped my eyes again and headed home.

I was in no way surprised to find William gone.

A COUPLE of days passed, and I found myself taking down things that were William's the same way a surgeon would cut away cancerous tumors from healthy flesh.

Gayle's words kept echoing in my head, but I refused to entertain them since I had more than enough pain in my life without adding to it. As I have said before, karma is not one to waste time in tracking you down. A knock on the front door made me pause, wondering if it was William crawling back with an apology.

Not that there was anything he could apologize for; I was just curious if he was desperate enough to attempt one.

Instead I opened the door and found Sheriff Rogers standing there, his hat literally in hand.

"Afternoon, Dorothy," he said in that low drawl that had always made girls smile when we were in high school.

"Stephen," I said, smiling back. "Come in," I offered, moving aside.

He did that little bowing of his head as he walked in that most boys these days never learn. It was an old-fashioned respect thing, and I was surprised to find myself sorry it had faded from popularity. "I come at a bad time?" he asked, not making the point that lately all times were bad for me.

"No, I was just—" I looked at the living room, where a small, untidy hill of William's belongings lay piled. "—taking out some garbage. I can use a break. You thirsty?" I offered as we walked into the living room.

"Anything cold if it's not a bother," he said, sitting down on the couch.

I took the pitcher of iced tea from the fridge and put it next to a couple of glasses on a serving tray. I set it down on the table as I sat in the chair across from him. "It's sweetened," I told him as he poured himself a glass.

He took a huge drink and gave me a wide smile. "That is some good tea," he exclaimed. "Tastes like your mom's."

I nodded. "The very same," I said, sipping my own. "So what brings you around?"

He put the glass down and took a moment before talking. "First, I wanted to see how you were doing. There hasn't been any time since…." His voice trailed off, and I nodded for him to continue. "But something has come up, and I thought you might want to know about it."

It's funny, I had just buried my son, but my stomach still clenched as I waited for his news. What could he say that would possibly be worse than that? "And that is?"

"I'm sure you know about the school board meeting." I nodded, and he went on. "Well, there are two or three random students trying to get something added to the agenda, and they're hitting a snag."

"You mean Kyle," I said, knowing he was the only student at Foster High who would be pushing for the administration to do more. Kyle was a magnificent boy who was the only one who'd seemed to know how bad Kelly's situation was, and we practically threw him out of the house more than once. I hadn't seen him since William chased him away from the funeral service, but I had been meaning to contact him and to thank him for being Kelly's friend at the end.

God knows I hadn't been.

Stephen nodded and gave me a half smile that told me his thoughts about the boy were as lofty as mine. "That's him. He wants to start some kind of gay and straight club at the school and thinks this is the only chance he will have of getting it pushed through."

It made sense. I would have been a fool not to understand that Kelly's death was the only reason Kelly's Laws were going to be enacted. Normally there wasn't a chance in hell that Jeffrey Raymond would let something like that fly at Foster High. "He isn't wrong," I admitted.

"No, he isn't, but it isn't going to happen," he said with a bit of regret in his voice. "I told him about the deal with Charlotte and put him on the trail. But he isn't going to find who lodged the complaint in time. It's too well hidden."

It seemed that even if I ignored Gayle's mention of the past, the Ghost of Past Mistakes was bound and determined to come back and haunt me.

"No, he won't," I admitted, putting my own glass down now. "Not after all the trouble we went through making sure everything was buried."

We sat there in silence for a couple of minutes, neither one wanting to say anything.

"And there is nobody else who will take responsibility for the club?" Even as I asked it, I knew the answer was no. We had sent a message last time that no teacher would dare ignore.

He gave me a sympathetic look. "What do you think?"

I sighed and looked out the back patio. "I think I need to go talk to Dolores Mathison."

To HELP you to understand who Dolores Mathison is means going into a small history lesson of the Foster wealthy. There are well-off people, there are wealthy people, and there are rich people.

And then there is the Mathison family.

They lived outside of Foster, but their presence in the town was overwhelming. They are old money, and their importance should never be underestimated.

Their family was the first to really strike oil in this part of the state, and when I say "strike oil," I'm saying it in a way that tells you they have more money than God. At the turn of the twentieth century, they were responsible for employing a little over 40 percent of the population of Foster in one way or another. Their money paved most of the early roads in the town, because they were the only ones to own multiple motorcars. Their money designed and installed the fountain on the corner of First Street, the first and last piece of a citywide renovation project that went nowhere. Their names are synonymous with money and power in this town, even though people don't speak about them that much. Old money works behind the scenes, diplomatically, out of the public eye.

I knew them because Dolores Mathison had approached me about Charlotte Axeworthy when I had been on the school board.

The grounds surrounding the Mathison estate are immaculate. Anywhere else their house would be called a mansion, but here in Texas we try not to use such showy words. We had enormous houses to do that for us. I wasn't too surprised that she agreed to meet with me Thursday; after all, I was the woman whose son had just killed himself. That afforded me a little pity in the eyes of the Mathisons.

Their wealth just reminded me of everything William and I wanted to give to Kelly but never quite achieved. Our money allowed us to talk with the Mathisons, but there was no way we were one of their group, and everyone knew it. We were new money, tacky money, and were tolerated only because we knew how to comport ourselves in public. The entire family had a way of making you feel insignificant without saying one word, and let me tell you, that was the true difference between new money and its loud brashness and old money and its immense, carefully wielded authority.

As I got out of my car, the man at the front door took my keys and said he would make sure my car was taken care of. I am not sure if the man's only job was being a valet, but it wouldn't surprise me if it was. Dolores met me at the front door. Her dress was tasteful while being fashionable at the same time. I knew from experience that if one was to check, there would be no label in it. The dress was one of a kind, designed and made expressly for her. She was older than me by a few years, but she was wearing those years better than I was mine, in my opinion. After all, money might not be able to buy happiness, but it can do wonders at keeping your face looking youthful, which is the next best thing sometimes.

"Dorothy," she said sympathetically while moving toward me. She gave me two air kisses and grasped my hand, which for her was positively gushing. "I am so glad you called." She was too cultured for me to know if she meant what she said. Instead, she ushered me into the house. "I've been thinking of you."

I knew that wasn't a lie—after all, Dolores and I shared an odd kind of kinship now. One that in a million years I would have never asked for.

"Thank you," I told her, walking into the stadium she called her living room. "It's been a tough couple of days."

A crystal pitcher on a silver tray put my sweet-tea setup to shame. There was more money on the table than in my entire kitchen.

"Please," she said, gesturing to her one-of-a-kind, brought from England Chesterfield. "Have a seat."

I suddenly felt like I was wearing a flour sack as we waited for her man to pour us both a drink. Once that arduous chore was done, he was dismissed, and she turned to me. "I heard the news. I am so sorry for your loss."

I nodded and smiled as I took a small sip of what was the best tea I had ever tasted. "Thank you. It's been trying."

"Anything we can do for you," she added as she held the glass but didn't drink herself. She held it like a prop, and for some reason it annoyed me.

"Well, I did come to talk to you about something," I said, taking another sip, readying myself. She didn't ask, instead raising one perfectly shaped eyebrow in question. "It's about Charlotte Axeworthy."

I saw her face darken as the past came rushing forward to overwhelm us both.

The Mathisons had three children: two girls and a boy, all of them absolutely perfect in every way possible, of course. The girls were born first, and their arrival was akin to that of royalty in the manner in which they were introduced to the town. Louise and Henrietta were given any little thing they desired and became quite spoiled because of it. They were nine when their little brother, Riley, was born, but by that time the family knew they had made mistakes with the girls.

The Mathisons had kept the girls isolated from the rest of the town, making them terrible snobs. Instead of attending public school, they were homeschooled, which prevented them from actually learning how to socialize with their peers. By the time they were old enough for junior high, they were sent to a private school outside of Dallas in hopes of instilling some kind of manners in them. But while they struggled with the girls, the Mathisons' plan for Riley was different altogether.

He was allowed to attend public school with the other kids, and the difference was immediate. If someone had asked me if there was a crown prince of Foster, I would have admitted that Riley was the clear choice. He was an adorable kid with manners and a grace that only came from a good family, and he was a town favorite. He excelled in sports and was soon quarterback of the Foster High Cowboys, a role no one was surprised to see.

What was surprising, though, was his attendance at a meeting of gay and bisexual kids during lunch with Mrs. Axeworthy.

When his mother found out, she came to the school board and made it quite clear she was not pleased with the situation and wanted it corrected immediately. And when she said "corrected," she meant stopped as soon as possible. She approached me, informing me of her son's attendance and how upset she was that this kind of thing had happened on school grounds. She said the group was confusing Riley, and that if it was not shut down and the teacher dealt with, we would be talking with her lawyer.

I knew Charlotte even then, and though she was—and is—a bit eccentric, she is a great teacher who means no harm. I calmed Dolores down, and we came to a compromise. We would discipline the teacher privately, the meetings would, of course, stop immediately, and in exchange, she would not press charges or bring suit against the school. I reminded her that any legal action would make the papers and undoubtedly include Riley.

And so with a little work and thirty pieces of metaphorical silver, the problem went away.

"What about her?" Dolores asked. Her tone of voice was the same she would use when asking about a convicted murderer.

"You need to come forward and have Mr. Raymond remove the mark on her record." I said it in one breath and without pause, because I was pretty sure she was about to throw the tumbler in her hand at me.

"I certainly do not," she countered.

"But Dolores, Riley turned out to be gay anyway. Charlotte Axeworthy had nothing to do with that." I paused a beat to let the words sink in. "Surely you can see that."

She said nothing as she looked at me like I was an insect. "Is this why you came here?" Her voice was dismissing, and I knew my time was limited. "If it was, you have wasted your time and mine." Sure enough, her man appeared with my coat in hand. I was impressed with his timing.

"Dolores," I implored her. "Kelly was gay too. It was why he killed himself. This is important."

"Riley did not kill himself," she reminded me.

"No, but don't you think the people who did kill him might have paused if there was more understanding in this town about what it meant to be gay?"

And there it was, the topic that no one broached with Dolores Mathison, and if you did, you didn't do it more than once.

Riley had gone to college out of state and ended up bringing home a boy whom he was deeply in love with. I am sure his family had been aghast, but if they wanted to be in their son's life, I am sure they didn't have much choice. It was common knowledge in town about the two, and to be honest, no one said much about it. They kept to themselves and seemed madly in love, so people respected their choice and let them be.

Until someone purposely rammed Riley with their car, killing him almost instantly in the middle of nowhere. There were quiet rumors all over town about what happened, but there was not much said out loud. The Mathison name bought a ridiculous amount of silence, and they buried their son in private and went on with their lives. It wasn't mentioned in the paper, but I knew from Stephen that the witness accounts at the time said the driver had purposely aimed for Riley and called out a pretty nasty slur about his sexuality.

In other words, the guy swerved to hit the boy and then called him a fag as he drove off.

I still saw Robert, the boy Riley had brought back to town. He ran a consignment store over on East Avenue and lived above it. I saw him in town now and again, but no one ever talked to him and he never stuck around to let them. Everyone over the age of forty knew who he was and his story; it was just none of us spoke of it out loud.

Dolores and I were sisters of a sort in grief. Both of our boys had been lost because of this gay nonsense, and I for one was done with it.

"I think it is time for you to leave," she said after a few seconds of composing herself.

"Haven't we paid enough?" I asked her, not budging. "Hasn't there been enough death for something to change? The people who killed Riley, the people who taunted Kelly to the point that he killed himself, don't you think these people need to see that as a town, as a people, we aren't going to take this anymore? We made a mistake when we shut Charlotte down, and you know it." She sat there and said nothing. "We buried our boys because of this," I cried at her, my tears now falling freely. "We held them as babies and swore we would take care of them, and then we put them in boxes and covered them with dirt. Things have to change, Dolores. You have to change them."

I sounded crazy, and maybe I was. Foster had taken the most important thing in my life, and I was angry at it. I wanted to punish it, teach it a lesson, but there was no way to do that. Kyle wasn't giving up; he was still fighting to change it, and maybe he had the right idea.

"Is that all?" she asked me.

"The school board meeting is tomorrow," I said, standing up. "If you want to find a way to respect Riley, if you want a way to make things right… you'll be there too."

I took my coat and thanked her for the tea.

There was nothing left to say.

IT WAS strangely comforting to know that after all these years, school board meetings were just as unpleasant as I remembered them.

Mr. Raymond had welcomed me with open arms, assuming I had shown up to be present when they voted Kelly's Laws into school policy. He was a spineless man who I had disliked for years. A midlevel bureaucrat, he had risen to the position of principal simply because he'd somehow managed to attain a master's in supervision and because everyone else who had had the job or might be in line for it had left for greener pastures than Foster.

Jeffrey Raymond also held deep religious beliefs, so long as his beliefs and the beliefs stated in the Bible were identical or could be interpreted that way. He used God as a shield to protect and justify his own pettiness and vengeful nature. He'd bugged the hell out of me when I had been on the board, and he bugged me now.

"Is William joining us?" he asked me as I found a seat.

I smiled at him and replied in a sweet voice, "I dearly hope not." I was rewarded by a confused look as he walked away.

"This seat taken?" a voice asked me from the aisle.

I looked over and saw Susan Graymark standing there.

"Susan!" I exclaimed, getting up to hug her.

She hugged me back. "How are you doing?" she asked me quietly.

Susan and I had been friends for years, since our boys were so close. Her husband, Nathan, was a real asshole, but then William was no catch, so I couldn't talk. "I'm here" was all I said. It wasn't an answer, but then again, maybe it was.

There was a woman behind her, and she turned and caught her left elbow to encourage her to step forward and stand beside her. "Have you met Linda Stilleno? She's Kyle's mom."

Linda gave me a sad smile and reached over to shake my hand. "Pleased to meet you."

"Your son is incredible," I told her, shaking it back. "You must be very proud of him."

I saw her blush slightly, and I could tell she was. "He was torn up about Kelly. I am so sorry."

She meant well, but I was getting tired of people telling me they were sorry. "You two want to join me?"

They took seats to the left of me, leaving me on the aisle, and we sat there waiting for the meeting to start. "I can't believe they are finally doing something about the attitude at the school," Linda said, looking around at people as they wandered in and found places to plant themselves. "I personally think the school board needs a two-by-four upside its head."

"I used to be on the school board," I said to her in a deadpan tone. She winced, looking like she was sorry for her words until I added, "And the two-by-fours are mostly shoved up their asses. I think the head slapping is done with one-by-sixes these days."

It took her a couple of seconds to realize I was joking.

We all laughed just as Mr. Raymond brought the meeting to order. "Can we have everyone's attention, please? We are about to begin." The few people who were still standing found seats, and the school board sat down on either side of him. "We have a full agenda, so let's get to it."

The next hour or so was spent going over the specific rules that were included in Kelly's Laws and how they would affect the school in general. A lot of teachers sat in the audience; they asked question after question, wanting to understand how the rules were going to affect their day-to-day teaching. Someone shifted in their seat. I was shocked to see Charlotte there. I hadn't seen her earlier.

"Is there anything else before we vote?" Mr. Raymond asked when the last rule had been picked over.

Linda raised her hand, and I saw Susan stand up with her. "I have something I would like added."

I could see the seething hatred in Raymond's expression from my seat.

"The floor recognizes Ms. Stilleno."

"I would like to propose a gay-straight alliance be added to the school to better educate the student body about different sexualities."

He didn't seem surprised by the request, and I assumed someone had warned him that it was coming. "Very well," he said, looking around the auditorium. "Does anyone have any objections?" There were none, so he went on. "I think most of the teaching staff is here. Would any teacher care to volunteer to sponsor and mentor such a group?" Of course, no one raised their hand. The teachers looked at one another and then back at him in silence.

Finally, Charlotte raised her hand. "I will."

People around the room began to talk among themselves, since no one had thought she would call his bluff. Raymond gave her a snide smile that made my hand twitch with the impulse to slap him. "I'm sorry, Mrs. Axeworthy, but as the new policy states, extracurricular activities can only be supervised by teachers not on probation. Are there any other volunteers?"

I stood up. "I move to have Mrs. Axeworthy's probation overturned."

Raymond glared at me, and I could tell he'd just seen the other shoe drop in his mind. "That is an excellent idea, but as you are more than aware, Dorothy, only the person who filed the complaint can request that, and since her pension or pay are not affected, it's not a union issue. So one more time, is there anyone who is willing to supervise a gay-straight alliance on campus?"

No one said a word.

"Then let's vote on this, shall we?" he offered.

There was silence as we all sat down.

"We tried," Susan said, disappointed.

"I hate that man," Linda whispered as she glared at Raymond.

"All in favor of passing the proposed...," he began and then faltered. Her coat flowing behind her like she was a grande dame making an entrance in a play, her stare directly focused on Raymond, Dolores Mathison swept across the stage. No one budged as she walked to Raymond's side and whispered something in his ear. His face paled, and then he nodded slowly as she pulled back and looked at him. She said something else to the panel and then walked off the way she'd arrived. She looked out and saw me sitting there. She gave me a whisper of a smile as she left.

Raymond stared at the tabletop in silence for a few seconds before he said, "I move to have Charlotte Axeworthy's probation lifted. All in favor?"

One by one the school board raised their hands. The vote passed unanimously.

"I also propose adding a gay-straight alliance to Foster in hopes of educating students about differences in sexuality and tolerance. Is there any teacher who would volunteer to run it?"

Charlotte raised her hand.

"Any objections?" he asked.

There were none.

As quickly as the meeting began, it was over. Mr. Raymond said nothing as he stormed out of the auditorium. Most of the school board scuttled after him like a herd of lemmings looking for a place to practice swan dives.

"What just happened?" Susan asked, looking around in confusion.

"Progress," I answered her as I smiled. That smile was the first real one I'd had since Kelly's death.

Charlotte walked over to us. Her expression—no, everything about her— was ecstatic. "I have a feeling you had something to do with that," she said to me.

I just smiled back at her. "It was long overdue. And because I know you won't hear it from anyone else, I am so sorry for what happened."

She gave me a sad smile. "No, Dorothy, I'm the one who is sorry."

For some reason her saying it didn't annoy me at all, most likely because I knew she was telling the truth.

"You know, Kyle and the kids are outside waiting to hear what happened," Linda reminded us.

"Well, we shouldn't keep them waiting," Susan said, motioning us toward the door.

"Tell Kyle hello for me, but I am going to pass," I told them, pausing. "I have something else I need to do right now."

Susan gave me a concerned look. "Everything okay?"

I took a deep breath and nodded. "It is now. But I need to go see Kelly. I think I'm finally ready."

There are things in life that you can never ready yourself for. People around you changing for the good is definitely one of them.

February 8
Some Nights
127 days left

Brad

BASEBALL SEEMED like a simple game when I was a kid. All a guy needed was a bat, a ball, a glove, maybe some good shoes, and he was set. I guess I'm not a kid anymore.

We had spent the whole week going through tryouts, which at this point was a formality because a majority of the team would be the same as last year. The tryouts were for the few juniors and fewer sophomores who were going to be moved up to varsity this year. The rest of us were there because "we win and lose as a team."

That's Coach-Gunn speak for "If one guy is on the field, we are all on the field."

It's a shitty rule, but let me tell you, there is motivation not to mess up when there are two dozen other guys suffering if you make a stupid mistake. It was Thursday afternoon, and the list was going to go up tomorrow, so this was the last chance to show the coach what you had in you. After four days of varsity drills, the answer from most of us was: there's not much left. The air was still cool, thank God, because once the sun came up for real in Texas, anything physical instantly involved three to four times the effort.

Most of us had been training all year, since we were varsity last year and planned on returning. Of course, up until last week it was unsure whether I was going to be able to play or not. I had broken two cardinal rules in high school baseball: I was gay, and I said I was gay out loud. Normally there wouldn't even be the smallest doubt if I would play this year, but after the school board meeting and the passing of Kelly's Laws—a name I know he would hate with an undying passion, by the way—the question went away. The school could no longer prevent students from playing sports based on their sexual orientation.

I had Kyle look it up for me to make sure.

45

On Thursday after practice, as we kind of crawled back into the locker room, I was more than a little shocked to hear Coach Gunn shout over the mumblings of the rest of the guys that I needed to come to his office once I was done showering. Well, this is where I get kicked off the team for good, I thought as I walked to my locker. My faith in Kelly's Laws and the protection they provided evaporated the minute Coach Gunn's voice boomed out.

The stipulation I had to shower separately had gone away along with, supposedly, discrimination in sports based on sexual orientation. From what Josh Walker told me, Coach and some lady who was a member of the school board had asked everyone on the team if they had a problem with me showering with all of them. No one spoke up. And I started showering with the other guys again.

So at least the guys didn't think I was going to be some weird creeper trying to hump them in the showers.

There are two types of guys in a team shower. There are the ones that are so weirded out by being naked in a room full of other naked guys that they feel the need to be loud and obnoxious to cover it. They make stupid jokes, ask asinine questions, and generally try to get everyone involved, like somehow that covers up the fact that we're all buck naked and trying not to look at each other's junk. Mostly everyone else is the quiet type. They go in, wash their hair, soap up, rinse off, and get the fuck out. They don't make eye contact, spend a hell of a lot of time looking at their own feet, and try to make the entire process as painless as possible.

I had always been a type two, since it made the whole being in a room full of naked athletes a lot easier if I never looked at them. I mean, everyone, and I do mean everyone, looked; it was just what you looked at and for how long that mattered. Guys like Kelly were the complete opposite. They went on the assumption that if they could walk around naked and have a conversation like nothing was wrong, then they were beyond suspicion. I always felt it did the complete opposite, since straight guys seemed to be more than a little squeamish when it came to other naked dudes. I had always done my best to be a rinse-and-run, but today I just stood there and stared at the wall in front of me.

What was I going to do when he told me I was off the team?

I suppose I could try to see if Granada had an opening on their team, but their tryouts were this week too, so the chance I could just walk onto their team was remote to none. They had Shayne Fuller this year, which meant they were all but guaranteed a trip to the playoffs. Also, I didn't want to throw a fit and force them to take me on the team; it would just look like I was a little bitch who was whining 'cause I didn't get my way. That wasn't an attractive image at all. The worst part was going to be telling Kyle. The second he found out I was off, he would declare a jihad on the school that would most likely end up getting us both kicked out before graduation.

I hadn't even paid attention to how long I had stood there until I realized I was the last guy in the shower.

"Awesome," I muttered to myself. "So I am off the team and look like a gay Peeping Tom all in the same day." I turned off the water and toweled myself half-dry at my locker. A lot of the guys had already taken off, knowing that if they even looked like they were trying to find out who made the cut before tomorrow, Gunn would have them running laps all night. I threw all the stuff in my locker into my bag since I wouldn't be coming back to it and made my way to the office.

Before I knocked, I took a deep breath and forced myself not to show one ounce of emotion.

I knocked twice and heard his voice come from the other side.

Gunn's office was a shrine to all things baseball. He had played himself in college, and the rumor was he had been on one of those feeder teams for the Rangers for a while but had never been moved up to the show. His wall was adorned with pictures of every team he had coached, more of them winning seasons than losing. He had three state banners on one wall, a reminder to anyone who saw them that in Texas, where baseball was a religion, being in the same office as the coach was actually standing in the presence of, at the very least, a demigod.

"Sit down, Graymark," he ordered, sliding a chair over to me. His hand was full of player stats from the week, and it looked like he was trying to put them in some kind of order. Putting my bag down, I sat, waiting for the inevitable ax to fall. "You know we got some great players this year." It wasn't a question, but he waited for an answer nonetheless. I nodded. "Not a lot of guys are going to even get on the field, which is a shame, but there are only so many minutes in a game." I felt my stomach start to sour and wished he would just get on with it. "So I have to make some hard choices, and no matter what I do, there are going to be some upset boys tomorrow."

There was at least one upset boy right now.

"But you've played since you were a freshman, so you at least deserve to know what's what." He put the papers down on his desk and finally faced me. "So here it is."

I literally forced myself not to wince.

"I am going to cut Flores, even though he is a faster runner than Walker. Josh has good heart, and I think this could be his year, but I need to know you agree with me on this, and I need to know now. I am not going to start the season by arguing with the team captain right out of the gate."

He stared at me as I tried to decipher all the words he'd said.

"Flores is a better hitter," I answered automatically. "But I'd keep Josh too."

He nodded. "Good, I thought the same thing. You have any attachment to Freeman or Paulson? Because they aren't making it either."

I shook my head. "Freeman is good, but he has no rhythm on the field." Again the words spilled out of my mouth; I had no control over them. "And Paulson might be ready next year, but not yet."

The coach raised an eyebrow at me in surprise. "You've been paying attention. Outstanding—that will make this easier." He tossed two files over to his out basket and then handed me a sheet of paper. "Anything on here you have a problem with, then?"

I took it, still not sure what was going on.

I read it, read it again, and then one more time. You know when you look at a word so much that it stops looking like English to you? Your brain is telling you the word is the word, but you are thinking, *Nope, no idea what that means.* I was stuck on one word and couldn't get past it.

"What's that?" I asked, pointing to the offending word.

He leaned over and stared at my finger. "Captain."

My face scrunched up in confusion. "What's that mean?" I asked him.

He paused and looked at me. "Team captain," he elaborated.

Shook my head. "Come again?"

"Team captain," he growled, getting upset. "You know what a team captain is?" I nodded. "Then what's the question?"

"Why is it by my name?"

He sighed and took the paper from me. "Smartass. Tell no one, and try to seem surprised tomorrow morning." He handed me a folder. "And begin to get real familiar with that. It's your job to get everyone else to understand it."

I looked down at the folder and saw the words "Team Captain: Defensive Drills."

Underneath that it said, "Property of Brad Graymark."

I just stared at it. I'm pretty sure my mouth hung open in shock.

"Any questions?" he asked when it was pretty obvious I had no idea what to say or do next.

"This is mine?" I asked him, the English language still not fully formed in my brain.

He gave me a double take to see if I was joking or not and then tapped my name on the folder. "That's you, right?" I nodded. "So then it's yours."

Nope, still not sinking in.

"But this is for team captain," I tried to explain to him.

He looked at me seriously, and his voice got dark with the slightest touch of anger. "Are you saying you don't want to be team captain?"

"I'm team captain?" I asked him, sounding like the world's dumbest guy, no doubt.

He sighed and rubbed his eyes. "Why did you think I asked you in here?"

I didn't even hesitate. "To kick me off the team."

Now it was his turn to pause and look at me stupidly. "Why would you think that?"

"Um, because I'm gay?"

And the lightbulb came on over his head.

He sat down slowly across from me. For the first time in my life, I was staring at a Coach Gunn who had gone silent because he was at a loss for words. The one man who I would have bet money on not blinking an eye in an alien invasion looked like I had punched him in the stomach. His face had gone pale. He cleared his throat and tried to talk. "What you need to understand, Brad...." And then he stopped. "I mean, the truth is...." And then he stopped again. It was obvious he was struggling with his words, and it was killing me.

So I tossed him a verbal rope to climb out of that hole with. "It's okay, Coach. It's cool."

He gave me such an odd look that I really thought he was pissed at me, even though I had no idea why. "No. No, it isn't cool," he finally said gruffly. "You're team captain." He stood up. "Study that book and get ready to drill it into the others." He turned back to his desk. "Now get out of here."

I'm pretty sure my feet didn't even touch the ground as I flew out of his office before he changed his mind.

THE NEXT day at school, I smiled like a fool because of the celebration gift Kyle had given me the night before and the fact the school was about to know I was made team captain.

A bone-rattling howl of joy roared upward from the center of the group staring at the team roster. Josh leaped up and air pumped in victory. He pushed the rest of the guys out of the way and made a beeline toward me like he was ready to tackle me. I tensed up, not sure what was going to come first.

So imagine my surprise when he hugged me around the waist and picked me up like I was made out of tissue paper. "You made captain!" he hollered as he spun us around in the middle of the hallway. Everything became a blur as he danced around in a circle with me in his arms. Last year if he had done this, it wouldn't have registered as anything but another guy incredibly happy to make the team. Now all I could think of was that my crotch was way too close to his face for me to be comfortable.

"Dude," I said, trying to catch my breath. "Little space?"

Josh dropped me and slapped my back a few times, his smile so big and genuine that it was infectious. "Come on," he practically shouted at me. "A few months ago you didn't even know if you were going to be on the team, and now you're captain. That is epic!"

I had to admit he had a point.

"It is pretty overwhelming," I admitted before giving in to the impulse to smile myself. A few guys congratulated me and themselves. A few others scowled at me and walked away pissed. There were never enough spots on the team for everyone who tried out; that was a fact of life. Those of us who made the team were good, and we knew it. The ones who didn't make it were average and had no clue they were.

I was riding pretty high at the moment, which is when, Kyle would have warned me, the bottom would fall out of it.

"Of course they gave it to him," Tony said, breaking through the din of our celebration. "His mommy would sue the school if he wasn't made captain."

We all spun around to look at him. I was not shocked to see two guys I didn't know personally from the football team flanking him. Josh used to be one of those guys until he pretty publicly quit the position during the Party over Winter Break. From the way the two of them were glaring at each other, it was obvious that neither one had let the anger go yet.

"He got it because he is the best player we got, and you know it," Josh fired back. "Something you agreed with last year, if I remember."

Tony took a step toward Josh. "That was before I knew he liked a different kind of balls."

"What the fuck?" I muttered as they argued about me without even looking at me.

"So then in your redneck mind it would be better if we field straight guys who are shitty at the game rather than let the best player we got play because he's gay? I'm curious—do you even hear the shit that comes out of your mouth, or are you stupid enough to believe yourself?"

They really did look like they were going to come to blows. Though I would have loved to see Josh beat the shit out of Tony again, I stepped between them to slow everything down. "Josh," I said but was promptly ignored. "Walker!" I screamed in his face. That got his attention. "Back off now." When it looked like he wasn't going to, I added, "You want to get kicked off for fighting before you play a game?"

That got him to step back.

I turned around and looked at Tony. "Any time you want to step out on the field and see if your superior heterosexual abilities can beat my pansy-ass gay ones, name it. Batting, pitching, catching, running—name a skill, and I will make you look like you're in junior high." He didn't say a word. "Come on, Tony, name a day and time, and I will be there and show you what real baseball looks like."

He took a step back. "Fuck this." He dismissed me with a sharp wave of his hand. "You aren't worth my time."

"Fuck you, man" came from behind me. I assumed it was Josh again, but instead I saw Scott Baker break free from the crowd of guys and stare down Tony. "You want to talk all this shit, but you can't back it up. You think he got on the team 'cause of his mom, pick a day and prove it, but if not, you're just an asshole starting shit."

Tony moved with both hands balled into fists. "What did you say to me, you little faggot?"

I was about to answer when half the guys behind me surged forward and began to scream back in Tony's face. "We said bring it, jackass!" one of them called out.

"You wanna come over here and call me that?" another snarled. I put my arms out to stop them, but it was obvious there was no way I could hold them all back.

Luckily I didn't have to.

"Tony Wright." An adult's voice cut through the ruckus like a knife. "Did you just call someone a faggot?" Tony froze as Coach Gunn walked toward us. The other kids who had been watching us parted like wheat before a thresher. He grabbed Tony's arm and yanked him toward him like the football player was a rag doll. "I asked you a question."

"I-I didn't say nothing," Tony sputtered as he realized his two wingmen had melted into the crowd.

There was a silence just before the coach tore into him again, which was when Tony's faint but recognizable voice came from the crowd. "What did you say to me, you little faggot?"

Everyone looked over and saw Jennifer standing next to Kyle, her iPhone in hand. Her eyes got dramatically wide as she asked sarcastically. "Oh, I'm sorry, was I not supposed to record that?"

Her finger hit the Replay button, and the recording of Tony screamed at the crowd.

Kyle looked over at Jennifer. "In his defense, 'I didn't say nothing' does in fact mean he said something. So not so much a lie as just bad grammar."

Gunn dragged Tony down the hall toward the office. "Congratulations, Wright, you just became the first student at Foster High to meet Kelly's Laws. If you're lucky, your name will go up on a plaque with the rest of the intolerant people who will come after you. I'm sure your dad will be so proud."

I wanted to call to Coach Gunn that I didn't want to get Tony in trouble since all it would do was piss him off, but Kyle came over and stopped me. "If we want the rules to be followed," he explained, "then we have to let them dole out the punishment." I could tell he didn't want Tony to be suspended any more than I did, but like always, Kyle was right.

An arm draped across my shoulder, and I looked to see Josh leaning against me. "So, Kyle, how does it feel to be the boyfriend of the captain of the varsity baseball team?"

For some reason his question made me blush, and I looked down in embarrassment.

"I guess it means I have to start coming to games," Kyle answered, which seemed to be the right answer.

"To the Cowboys!" Josh shouted, looking at the rest of the team. "Future state champions!"

The hallway erupted into cheering, which was deafening in the small space but felt good nonetheless.

AFTER A week of grueling practices, Coach Gunn was not impressed with our performance. So that Saturday we had our all-day ordeal, and it was brutal.

Kyle had offered to come to watch, but I told him not to bother since all he would see would be Coach Gunn screaming at us no matter what we did. As I stood in the dugout drinking water, I was doubly glad that he hadn't come to see us because it was embarrassing. You'd think by this time we would have learned that no matter how cocky we may have felt on Friday, we were going to have our faces pounded into the grass on Saturday.

Last year I resented the hell out of it because I felt like it served no purpose whatsoever: Coach would just work us until we puked. But now as team captain, I understood the logic in it. If we started the season thinking we could walk on water, then it would take at least four to five games to actually get our heads in the game, which meant we'd have to play catch-up. This way Coach Gunn broke us down and got all that garbage out of our heads so we could actually concentrate on our first game instead of how good we looked in our varsity jackets.

"Is he ever going to stop?" Josh panted as he came to a pause next to me. He had taken his water and poured it over his head, a good idea considering, but I was too thirsty to try it.

I shook my head. "He wants state this year, and so do I." He kind of smiled at me and then looked at my water. I sighed and handed it to him. "Better hurry, day is just starting."

"Get on the field!" Gunn's voice echoed throughout the dugout. If you didn't know him, you might think he had a bullhorn to be that loud. You'd be wrong.

We didn't finish until almost three in the afternoon. By that time we were lucky to be still standing, and even that was iffy.

"I sure hope you girls have more in you than that," Gunn berated us as he walked up and down the line of guys. "Because if that was the best you got, then I might have picked the wrong guys to be on the team." We all held our breath, waiting for his next words. "We're done for today. Hit the showers."

Half the team fell down into the grass; the rest limped back toward the locker room in silence. Coach walked over to me, and I forced myself not to wince from the pain I was feeling. "Here is the list of measurements," he said, handing me a sheet of paper. "Make sure you get it to Parker's sporting goods store by Monday." I glanced down at it and nodded. "Not a bad first day," he said in a lower voice and gave me a small smile.

Suddenly the pain diminished a little bit.

I stripped and lumbered over to one of the tubs we had for ice baths. One of the assistant coaches helped me sink into one—the freezing cold making my muscles go numb and the pain fade away ever so slightly. I remember when I'd first started playing and I saw older guys resting in these tubs, I thought there was no way in the world I would ever want to lie in a pile of ice. But to be completely honest with you, it had been all I could think of since about noon. I know the normal person would think that sitting in freezing cold water would wake you right up, but honestly, it's as relaxing as hell. And I had almost dozed off when Josh's voice woke me up.

"Hey, scoot over there, chief. I need some icy love."

Now, the tubs were designed for two people, but lately no one had dared get into one with me in case they might catch the gay. So I was caught way off guard when Josh dropped his towel and edged into the other side. I scooted back to give him space; we were pretty big boys, and there wasn't all that much space to share.

"Oh Christ, that's the shit." He sighed, lowering himself to his chest. I knew exactly how he felt. "They offered to set another up, but there's enough room, right?"

I nodded silently as I tried not to think that I was naked in a small tub with a guy who wasn't Kyle.

"Cool, because I was about thirty seconds from breaking down and crying, I was in so much pain." He closed his eyes and leaned back against the tub wall. "And no matter how much swag you think you got, there is no way to recover from openly crying like a bitch in the locker room." He opened one eye and looked at me. "You know?"

I nodded again, wondering why this was fucking me up so bad.

"So… how's things with Kyle? You guys hitting it off?"

His question was so random, so nonchalant that it came across suspicious as hell. No one had asked me anything about my relationship with Kyle, good or bad. In fact, it was as if we had all made a silent pledge to ignore the fact that I was gay when we walked into the locker room. So this question, this innocent question from nowhere, set off just about every alert I had.

"Why?" I asked him in a tone of voice that could only be referred to as a demand.

Both eyes opened now, and he looked over at me with concern. "I was… I was just making conversation. I mean, it's just a question, you know?"

His attempt to make his response seem innocent only made it seem that much more sinister. "A question you never asked before," I pointed out to him.

He shrugged. "And? I never asked you about a lot of things. Is that a crime?"

I decided to just play along with him. "Kyle and I are just fine. Thanks for asking," I said, waiting for the other shoe to drop.

"Cool," he said, as if trying to distance himself from the topic altogether. I tried to ease myself back into the ice and relax again. Neither one of us talked for several minutes. I had almost dozed off again when he asked, "So then, you and Jennifer are just friends now, right?"

My eyes opened slowly as I looked across the tub at him. "As opposed to?"

He blushed slightly and then looked away for a second. "I mean, it's not like you, her, and Kyle are, like… together, right?"

I tried to keep myself from laughing, but there was no way to stop.

"That's a no?" he asked when I began to snort. "Okay, I get it, it's a no, but you see why I had to ask, right?" I really think I was crying, I was laughing so hard. He muttered under his breath, "You could have just said no and left it at that."

For a few minutes, I couldn't breathe, and my stomach was cramping because I had laughed so hard. After I caught my breath, I said to him. "You watch way too much porn, dude."

From the way he looked away, I knew I was right. I didn't think much about the conversation until later.

"HE ASKED if we were all, like…?" Kyle asked, making a gesture with his hands.

I paused in front of Tyler's store. "Dude, I have no idea what that meant." I pointed to his hands. "But I am pretty sure he was asking if the three of us were banging one another."

Kyle's face got a deep red as the mental image hit home.

I pushed open the door and found Tyler sitting behind the counter nursing a Coke while he watched something on his laptop. "I know I am not paying you to watch movies, young man." He looked up at me and flipped me off as Kyle closed the door behind us.

"That didn't work coming from my dad. I have no idea why you think you'll do any better," he said, closing the computer.

"I have the uniform order," I said, holding up the piece of paper. "So you may want to be nice to me."

He rolled his eyes and looked at Kyle. "Can't you control him?"

Kyle laughed and shook his head. "I suppose I could buy a collar and leash, but he'd still jump up and try to hump people."

I looked over at him. "Hey!"

He kissed me on my cheek. "But you are the cutest mongrel in town."

I wasn't too sure if mongrel was another hit, so instead I just took the compliment and passed the paper over to Tyler. "So here are the sizes for this year."

He took it and read it over. "Seems about right."

I nodded at Kyle, who knew what I was about to ask, and he nodded back at me. I took a deep breath and asked Tyler, "So what if I wanted to change something real small on that order?"

Tyler looked up at me and then over to Kyle. "Why do I have a feeling I am going to hate this?" His voice sounded worried. And the fact that neither of us answered made him even more skittish. "Brad? I am going to hate this, aren't I?"

THAT WEEK flew by as we practiced harder and longer than we ever had before.

The pain and the discomfort became commonplace as our bodies grew accustomed to the rigor of actual season practice. That Thursday, the uniforms were delivered, and I had to admit, I had already forgotten last week's talk with Tyler in the confusion of getting ready for our first game.

"Graymark!" Coach Gunn's voice bellowed from his office. I had no idea what I had done wrong until I saw the delivery guy race out of the office as if he was on fire.

And then I remembered.

I got up, tossed my towel into my locker, and looked over to Josh. "When they speak of this, and they will, be kind and tell them I didn't look scared walking in there, will ya?"

He had no clue what I meant but nodded anyway.

When I got into the office, Gunn stood there holding one of the uniforms. "Close the door," he said, not even looking up at me. I closed it behind me but wasn't sure why—not like his voice couldn't be heard all the way to Oklahoma, door closed or not. "Is this some kind of joke?" he asked, holding the uniform up to me. I shook my head because I didn't trust myself to talk yet. "But this was your doing, right?" I nodded. "You want to explain yourself before I kick you off the team?"

I looked at the uniform and then back to him, trying hard not to show one iota of emotion. "I am pretty sure it speaks for itself."

He waited for me to say more and then threw the shirt at me. "Goddammit, Brad! I went to bat for you!" I caught the shirt as he kept shouting. "There were more than a few people who wanted you gone, wanted you off the team and out of the school, forget being team captain. I spoke up for you, and this is how you repay me?"

And there it was. It seemed like a simple question at the time, but the answer was so much more than that. I was still looking down at the uniform, tracing my fingers over the left sleeve. "No," I said in a quiet voice. "I was trying to repay him."

We both stared at the black band that had been sewn around the left arm. An identical black band encircled every left arm on every uniform, and unless he wanted to hire a seamstress to come in and pull the threads out one by one, they were on there for good. "Do you know what the school board will say? No one cleared this with them. They are going to lose their minds." I just stood there, not saying a word because I knew there was nothing to say. I had made my choice, and now it was time to pay for it.

"You're off the team," he said, grabbing the shirt out of my hand. "Clear out your locker."

My eyes stung, but I wasn't going to cry, and I wasn't going to beg him. Instead I turned around and opened the door and was shocked to find the team standing there looking up at me. They moved as I walked out. Josh put his hand on my shoulder for support as I walked by. It was a nice gesture.

Coach Gunn walked out and saw everyone standing there. "Walker, you're team captain."

Josh tensed up for a moment, looked over at me, and then looked back at Gunn. "Then I quit."

Every single person in the room froze.

"What did you say?" Gunn asked him dangerously.

"I said if Brad isn't captain, I quit." His voice gained some strength as he stood next to me.

I began to say to him, "You don't have to—" but then someone else stepped up. "I quit too."

And then another. "I quit too."

And then everyone else. "We quit."

What the fuck?

Josh took a step toward Gunn and said, "We either play under Brad, or we don't play at all."

Coach looked at them all and then back to me. It seemed to me like he was trying to figure out if he could kill me and get away with it. "Tell me this is legal," he said, holding the shirt up.

Thanks to Kyle, I did know this. "The only rule says that nothing can be added to the uniform that is distracting, and if something is added, it needs to be on all uniforms of the team."

He looked back at the stack of uniforms and thought for a couple of seconds. We all held our breath as we waited to hear if he was going to cancel the season or let us play. With Coach Gunn, either choice was just as likely. Finally he looked up and said, "Then I guess this season is for Kelly."

Without another word he turned around and slammed his office door shut. The team erupted in cheers, but I was stunned. Not from the coach's words but from the small smile I saw on his face as he turned away. I had the feeling I had missed something, but I didn't have time to think about it as someone dumped a bucket of ice water over me from one of the tubs and screamed, "To Brad!"

All my suspicions faded as I turned around and swore revenge.

It was the start of a great season.

Kyle

I AM going to be honest with you when I say I don't know who was more nervous about Brad making the team, him or me.

That Thursday I paced around his car, waiting for practice to end. He had said that he would have a good idea if he was on the team or not, even though the list didn't go up until Friday. I kept oscillating between being sure he was on the team to worrying that the school board or Raymond would keep him off out of sheer spite. It wasn't that I disliked Coach Gunn; I just knew how much trouble the teachers could get into if they went up against Mr. Raymond.

Another reason I was going to get rid of him before I left.

As I waited, I realized that Brad's "fame" as a baseball player in school had never even connected with me. To everyone else he was Brad Graymark, baseball god, but until that moment, I hadn't even cared if he never played the game again. I still didn't care, but if he wanted to very badly, I wanted him to as well. So as I paced and waited, I worried what would happen if they didn't let him play and exactly what I would do because of it.

I froze and wondered, *When did I become this guy?* Last I remembered, I was the guy who didn't want anyone to know who he was, and now I was making plans in case I had to get my boyfriend on the baseball team. I smiled because it felt good, being the guy with a plan instead of just standing there taking it. I didn't know when I became this guy, but I knew I didn't want to stop being him.

I heard the gym doors open, and the team began to pour out of the locker room.

Now, I may have never connected Brad's baseball reputation with him, but I did know the connection between jocks and being freaking hot. Football players always seemed so big and intimidating that I was never turned on by them, but baseball players were a whole other breed of beasts. They ran a lot, so they were all lean and cut, but the batting and pitching required some extensive upper body strength, which meant they had enormous arms. I don't want to sound shallow, but I was seriously loving all the extra bulk Brad was putting on. He had been hot before; now he was like something out of porn.

At least I assume, since I had never actually sat through a whole porn film.

So as the team filed out, hair slick from the shower, jeans faded and T-shirts hugging them, I had to pause and enjoy the sight for a few seconds. I mean, take Josh Walker for example; he was a good-looking guy all by himself. Dirty-blond hair cropped short, strong cheekbones, full lips—just standing still, he would have been a stud. But then add all the running and batting and sit-ups and push-ups and he became something much greater than the sum of his parts.

And let me tell you, the parts weren't half bad.

He must have seen the slack-jawed look on my face, because he grinned and nodded at me. "He's talking to the coach—won't be long now."

It took me a couple of seconds to realize he was talking about Brad. "Oh, okay. Thanks," I answered back, trying desperately not to sound like a complete spaz. God, I hated good-looking people so much.

About twenty minutes later, the locker room door came flying open, and Brad charged out directly at me. At first I wasn't sure what he was doing until he got about halfway, and I saw the huge binder in his hands. My eyes got big as I looked at him. He tossed the book onto the trunk and grabbed me in a hug that literally took me off my feet. "He made me captain!" he roared, spinning us around. I laughed with him as he put me down and looked at me. "Me! He made me team captain."

Now, I don't know about you, but I had no idea what a team captain did, but the title sounded important. I mean, if you were captain of a starship, then you got to say "Engage" and all that cool stuff. If you were, like, Captain America, you got that badass shield and got to throw it at people's heads. The only other captain who came to mind was Captain Caveman, but he didn't seem that impressive, so I pushed the image of Brad dressed like a caveman away and smiled back at him. "That is awesome! I knew you'd make it."

If you guys don't tell him, I won't.

"No one will know until tomorrow, but I want to celebrate tonight." His hug moved closer to an embrace, and I could smell the soap and cologne on him. "I want to celebrate with you."

"Any ideas?" I asked him, my hands snaking behind him and slipping between his jeans and waist.

"I can think of a few," he said suggestively.

"Yeah, I can feel a few too," I said, grinding against him.

"When's your mom get off work?" he asked, rubbing his cheek against my face.

"She closes." My heart was beating like a jackhammer.

"Let's go to your house," he whispered in my ear.

All I could do was nod back.

WE BARELY got the front door open with all the kissing.

I was walking backward toward my room as he kicked the door closed with one foot. He practically tore the shirt off over my head as we fell onto my bed. His mouth was everywhere as I tried to strip him as well. I kicked my shoes off as he tossed his shirt behind him. His chain hung down from his neck, our eighty-one cents and his silver rose tangled in front of my face. He saw me look at it and gave me a small smile. "Everything I love in one place."

My heart skipped a beat at the intensity in his eyes.

"Do you have a condom?" I asked him after a few seconds of silence.

He blinked at me a few times in confusion. "Do I what?"

I leaned up, reached around his waist, and pulled his wallet out of his back pocket. "Do you have a condom in here?" I asked again, opening the wallet and searching through its contents.

"Are you serious?" he asked, his voice almost cracking in astonishment.

I pulled the one lone condom out of the side pocket and held it up. "Does this look like I'm joking?" I could almost feel his heart pounding over me as we stared at each other in silence for what seemed like forever. Finally I gave him one of his own know-it-all grins and ordered, "Get naked, Graymark. Now."

I had never seen anyone shuck the rest of their clothes off that fast in my life.

WE LAY there panting, looking up at my ceiling.

"I'm going to need another shower now," he said, still out of breath.

Just the mention of being in the shower with him got me excited again, but I resisted the urge to roll over and attack him. "So…," I began to ask when I could catch my breath. "So, was that… normal?"

He looked over at me, and when we made eye contact, we both burst out laughing. "You're asking in general or for me?"

"Both," I said, rolling over and snuggling against his side.

"Well, for me it was thumbs-up, two thumbs-up. Like, several million thumbs-up." I moved my leg between his as I curled up as close as I could to him. "In general? I think we might have broken a record or something. You sure your neighbors didn't call the cops, thinking we were killing each other?"

He chuckled as I nudged against him. "Shut up." He nudged me back. "So then, that part, where I was…." He nodded as he got my hint. "So that was good?"

He moved his leg against mine. "That was incredible. I mean, like fireworks."

"And the part where you were…." And he nodded again. "That was okay?"

He looked over at me. "That was when you ruined me for all other men."

For half a second I thought he was serious, and it must have shown on my face because he burst out laughing and pulled me close. I jokingly tried to pull away from him, but he wouldn't let me. He said in a half whisper, "That, Kyle Stilleno, was the moment you made me your sex slave. For life." He kissed the tip of my nose. "No joke, that was incredible."

I felt the blush go all the way through my body as I hid my face against his chest.

His leg nudged my waist. "And you want more."

It wasn't a question.

I nodded into his embrace.

"In the shower?" he asked.

My face popped up with a huge smile. "Really?"

He grinned and nodded back.

It was easily the best night of my life.

I WAITED for Jennifer to show up while Brad ran ahead and waited with the guys who herded around the bulletin board outside Coach Gunn's office. That was where he'd post the list for the guys to see who made the team. She pulled up about ten minutes after we had. She still looked tired but a little better than she had a couple of days before.

She shook her head and said, "Lemme guess, he ran ahead like a kid on Christmas when he sees a ton of packages under the tree?"

I nodded as we walked toward the history building. "You know how he is about baseball."

We got about five steps, and she stopped. I looked back at her, and her eyes widened in surprise. "Oh my God, you guys totally did it!"

I'd had nightmares like this before I met Brad, but they mostly involved me being naked in front of the class and a lot of laughing and pointing.

"W-what?" I stumbled, trying to figure out how to deflect her question while simultaneously trying to figure out how she'd figured it out. "I don't know what you mean." God, that sounded lame, even to me.

She ran up to me and whispered, "You have that 'I got laid' look all over your face. Spill."

I put my hands on my face to see if there was something on it I had missed in the shower. "What do you…?" And then I sighed. "Is it that obvious?"

She put her arm around me and continued walking us toward the building. "No, Brad texted me last night, going on and on about how you rocked his world." I looked over at her in shock, and she shrugged. "What can I say? That boy is in love with you, and he wanted to brag."

Part of me was upset that he'd told someone else what we had done, but there was a larger part that kept stumbling over her words. "He said that? I rocked his world?"

She got closer and whispered, "His exact words were 'If there was ever a chance I would go back to girls, it was destroyed by Kyle tonight.'"

There was a burning heat on my face, but I had one of those rigor mortis grins that everyone the Joker ever killed had. "He said that, huh?" I said, more to myself than asking the actual question.

"He said a lot more, but he swore me to secrecy." I shot her a look of complete disbelief, and she winked back at me. "Something about a curve—"

"Okay!" I shouted, causing everyone in the hall near us to look over. In a lower voice, I said, "Okay, let's talk about something else."

Jennifer shook her head as we came on the pack of guys huddling around the bulletin board. "You, my friend, are too easy."

I stuck my tongue out at her, which made her laugh even harder.

As we got to the crowd, I pulled my phone out to record the scene. I wanted to capture the moment for Brad, who would undoubtedly play it over and over again for the rest of our lives.

We got there just in time to see Josh Walker scream, "You made captain!" at Brad and then run toward him and pick him up in a hug. I laughed and filmed as he twirled Brad around like he was a rabbit to Josh's Lenny. Brad said something to him, and he put him back down. He slapped Brad's back and said, "Come on, a few months ago you didn't even know if you were going to be on the team, and now you're captain. That is epic!"

There was such pride in Josh's voice that it took me aback a second. This wasn't ass kissing. This wasn't him just being a dude. He was really, really happy Brad had been made captain and didn't care who knew it. I looked over at Jennifer and raised an eyebrow as I nodded at Josh. She nodded back. The look on her face made it clear she was surprised too.

"It is pretty overwhelming," Brad said in his best humble voice. I knew that voice well; it was the one he used when I commented on his six-pack after his workout. He would just shrug and say, "I try to stay in shape." He was so full of shit. Brad loved the fact he was in such good shape. It was why he spent so much time working on his body. I wouldn't call it being vain so much as him thinking his body was all he had going for him. Since there was no way I could dislodge that thought from that walnut he keeps his brain in, I just let him get away with it and promised myself that I would talk to him later.

A few other guys congratulated Brad, and a few gave him death stares, which got my attention fast. Jennifer leaned over and whispered. "Sore losers who didn't make the cut. That has nothing to do with your boy."

I relaxed. I didn't know my protectiveness was so obvious to others. I could see the smile on Brad's face and could tell this was a perfect moment for him. He was truly happy. Which was, of course, the very moment fate decided to piss all over it.

"Of course they gave it to him," Tony said from behind us. "His mommy would sue the school if he wasn't made captain."

I turned, aimed the camera at Tony, and saw he was there with two meatheads I didn't recognize. Without looking away, I whispered to Jennifer. "What is with his whole Morris Day and the Time thing? He can't go anywhere alone?"

"Cowards rarely do," she said, putting a hand in her purse.

I knew what that meant—her Taser.

I was seconds away from saying something to Tony, but Josh beat me to it. "He got it because he is the best player we got, and you know it. Something you agreed with last year, if I remember."

The more he talked, the better a person Josh became in my eyes.

Tony took that angry, about-to-fight step all straight guys do when they want to seem like they are about to swing but are really just going to talk shit. It was a bunch of shit; when someone wanted to hit you, they didn't stop and give speeches. They stepped up and hit you while you fell to your ass wondering what just happened.

"That was before I knew he liked a different kind of balls," Tony shouted at Josh.

There was no way this was not going to end up with someone getting hit.

"Hold this," I said to Jennifer, handing her my phone. "Keep filming," I told her.

"Where are you going?" she called after me, but I was already pushing my way through the crowd, away from the fight.

All this reminded me of the first time I met Kelly, and he had attacked me in the quad. We had been surrounded by the same pack of savages, aching to see some real bloodshed. It was like all of this was some lame-ass reality show to them, and the two people who were about to fight were arguing about who was going to get voted off the island.

God, I hated shows like that.

It took some effort, but I was finally able to shove my way to Coach Gunn's office. I knocked on the door twice and then pushed it open. He was sitting behind his desk, the sports section in his hand. He glanced up at me with a look that said, "You better have a good reason for busting into my office."

"Fight!" I said, pointing outside the door.

He seemed confused for a moment and then pulled a pair of earbuds out and looked at me. "What?"

I was slightly stunned that he owned an iPod, but I let it go. "Fight!" I said again, pointing like I was a damn dog trying to get someone to understand that Timmy was drowning in the fucking lake.

Luckily he heard the shouting and realized exactly what I meant.

He pushed his chair back and stood in one smooth motion. Coach Gunn was more than just a man; he was like a force of nature once he got moving. He was a wide man, and I am in no way calling him fat. He was like a dwarf, a big-ass, ax-wielding, half-drunk dwarf with fists the size of human heads, and when he started moving toward something, it got out of his way.

So I got out of his way.

He barreled into the hall, and the few kids who stood near his office door scattered like roaches in the kitchen startled by someone turning on the light. He had that someone-is-in-trouble face, and no one wanted to be a handy target for all that anger. I could hear Tony talking his shit from where I stood. I pushed past another group of people to get back to Jennifer. Gunn was moving like Moses parting the Red Sea as people ran wildly to get out of his way.

"Tony Wright."

He sounded like God. No, he sounded angrier than God. He sounded like an angry dwarven god who was bent on dishing some epic vengeance. "Did you just call someone a faggot?" Tony looked to his left and then to his right, definitely searching for his backup, but they had fled the second they heard the coach's voice. The coach grabbed Tony's arm and yanked him like the football player was a rag doll. "I asked you a question."

"I-I didn't say nothing" was all he got out. He looked like a six-year-old who had gotten caught on a stool stealing a cookie.

Jennifer shook her head and pushed a few buttons on my phone's screen. I was about to ask her what she was doing when Tony's words came playing back from the speaker. "What did you say to me, you little faggot?"

Everyone stared over at us. Jennifer pretended to be all shocked and asked, "Oh, I'm sorry, was I not supposed to record that?"

Her finger hit the Replay button, and she held the video up to Coach Gunn as it played again.

Tony looked at the ground, sighing as he realized he had not only been caught cussing but had also been caught lying to a teacher.

I looked over at her and said loudly enough so everyone could hear, "In his defense, 'I didn't say nothing' does in fact mean he said something. So not so much a lie as just bad grammar."

The crowd burst out laughing, and almost instantly the tension that had accumulated in the hallway uncoiled.

Gunn dragged Tony down the hall toward his office. "Congratulations, Wright, you just became the first student at Foster High to meet Kelly's Laws. If you're lucky, your name will go up on a plaque with the rest of the intolerant people who will come after you. I'm sure your dad will be so proud."

From the look on Brad's face, he wanted to say something to the coach about not wanting to get Tony in trouble, but I stopped him. "If we want the rules to be followed, then we have to let them dole out the punishment." It was way obvious he wanted to argue with me, but he knew I was right, so instead he just sighed and silently watched Tony get pulled into Gunn's office.

I was about to suggest getting out of there when Josh threw his arm around Brad's shoulder and leaned against him. I was disgusted that they looked so good together. If someone took a picture of them, you'd assume it was an Abercrombie ad. "So, Kyle, how does it feel to be the boyfriend of the captain of the varsity baseball team?"

It was the first time anyone on the baseball team had directly spoken to me, and I was kind of stunned by it. I had always been a nonentity to these people. And now here was Josh Walker looking at me, asking me a question in front of them all.

I said the first thing that came to mind. "I guess it means I have to start coming to games."

He must have liked the answer because he roared, "To the Cowboys!" Everyone else echoed him again and again. By the third time, I was chanting with them.

It was the start of a good day.

BRAD AND I spent most of the weekend looking for a place to be alone.

It had never seemed that big a problem before because we'd spent a lot of time in each other's rooms making out. The fact that our parents were in the house never seemed to matter, but now it did matter. A lot. There was no way we were going to get naked with a chance of being walked in on, but being naked was all we wanted to do.

We ended up down at the lake Saturday night, but I was way too paranoid that someone was going to come and tap on the window, so we just sat on the hood and made out some more. By Sunday I understood all too well what a bad case of blue balls felt like. I had gone eighteen years without sex, and here it was less than a week since I'd had it, and I was dying. Brad thought I was funny as hell since he had been suffering like this since we started dating.

I gave him several hundred bonus points for not breaking up with me when I wouldn't put out.

By the time Monday rolled around, I was walking around half hard and looking for places that might double as a place to have sex. I was slowly losing my mind. I was lost in thought, trying not to think about what it felt like to have sex, when Sammy nudged me. "Are you having a stroke?" she whispered to me during class.

I looked over at her, confused. "What do you mean?"

She looked around to make sure no one was looking at us and said, "Well, I know you like school, but you've been sitting there looking like a mental patient with that smile on your face. What's up?"

I felt my face go, like, fifteen shades of red as I firmly reined my libido back in. "Just been… a lot on my mind," I explained lamely.

She didn't say anything for a while, and I settled in and tried to focus on the class. My mind began to wander to what Brad looked like naked, and she nudged me again. "See?" she whispered. "There you go again."

I sat up straight, but it was no use. I felt brain damaged.

Was this how straight guys felt? I literally already felt dumber as I walked around wishing I had lower hygiene standards so I could consider grabbing Brad and throwing him in one of the broom closets for a quickie. Did I just really think that? Broom closets and quickies? Oh God, I was, like, a pair of sunglasses away from calling other guys "brah." I needed help.

During lunch we all sat on the steps, and I tried not to obsess over the way Brad's T-shirt had hitched up under his letterman jacket and I could see the back of his boxer briefs in the gap his jeans made. When he got up to throw our trash away, I turned to Jennifer in a panic. "I need to go see Robbie." Small pause. "Like now." Her eyes were wide with surprise as I tried to release the death grip my hand had on her blouse. "Can you cut class?"

"I have prom committee, but after that, sure. Everything okay?" she asked, which was a perfectly reasonable question considering I sounded like a serial killer.

"I just need some… advice," I answered, trying to get the rest of my brain to forget what Brad's skin tasted like when he was sweating in passion….

Stop.

"I can wait," I told her, feeling like I was a drug addict waiting for my next hit.

After lunch I hid in the library and tried my best to think about anything but sex. Of course, much like someone telling you not to think of pink camels, once brought up, it was all you could think of. By the end of the period, I almost ran to Jennifer's car and waited for her to meet me.

She still had that concerned look on her face when she unlocked the doors. "You sure you're okay?"

I got in. "When you and Brad were together, was he all over you for sex?"

She paused for a few seconds. "No, not really," she answered carefully. "But then again, I recently found out that I really wasn't his type. Why do you ask? Is he pushing you?"

I sighed. "No, other way around."

"He's not pushing you?" she asked. "Or you're pushing… oh." And she got it. "Oh! You're, like, in heat, right?" I scowled at her, but she just laughed. "Okay, now I get it. Yes, the first time Brad and I had sex, he was all over me for, like, the next month or so. But that is pretty common after a guy's first time." She shook her head. "I would have never guessed you'd be all horned up."

"Me either," I said under my breath, pouting as we drove toward Robbie's store.

When we parked, there weren't any cars out front, and I wondered for the millionth time how Robbie could keep the store open when there was never any real foot traffic around. Some Broadway song was blaring when I opened the door. One of these days, someone was going to come in and rob him, and he wouldn't have a clue that anyone had been in there, the music was so loud.

He was behind the counter, singing along. Thankfully that was drowned out by the music as well.

"I am going to browse dresses while you boys have your talk," she said, patting me on the back.

I felt like such a pervert.

Once he saw me coming toward him, he turned down the music. "Oh, I was expecting this a couple of days ago. You're slipping."

His voice was laced with attitude that took me aback. "What?" I asked, stunned.

"Right. Meathead comes and tells you I was mean to him and you come running to defend his honor. How original. If he was a real man, he would fight his own fights."

To show you how messed up my mind was, it took me a full seven seconds to figure out he was talking about Brad. "What did you say to him?" I asked, my horniness now completely forgotten.

"Oh, please," he said, dismissing me with a hand. "Don't play dumb with me."

"I don't play anything," I said, pissed all over again. "Brad didn't tell me a thing, so what did you say to him?"

He blinked at me a couple of times, and then he got it. "Well, if he didn't say anything…."

"What is your problem?" I demanded, losing what little patience I had left with Robbie. "What in the hell did Brad ever do to you?"

"Well, what does it matter? Even if I had a list, you'd just deny it since your precious boyfriend seems to walk on water for you."

"I never said Brad was perfect. In fact, the only person who ever accused him of that was you."

"Oh, he's far from that," Robbie shot back.

I paused and tried to take a deep breath. "I'm curious. Is this a real something that Brad did to you, or is it another imaginary one like Tyler?"

If I ever wondered what it would be like if I slapped Robbie, I now knew.

He seemed not to breathe for several seconds before he reached over and turned the music off. "We're closing. You guys are going to have to leave."

"Really?" I asked him sarcastically. "You're just going to take your toys and go home? Very mature."

He looked over at me, and I felt like a small piece of gum that had become attached to his shoe. "You don't get to tell people what is mature and what isn't." There was none of his normal sass or sarcasm. If anything, he sounded tired. "And I can close this fucking store anytime I want. Now get out before I say something stupid and regret it for about fifteen seconds."

Jennifer came up behind me and said, "Come on. He's not joking."

There was something in Robbie's eyes that made me realize that no, he wasn't joking at all.

We left the shop, but I looked back before I let the door close behind me. He looked like he was torn between outright fury and breaking down and crying.

It was the first moment I realized that Robbie might, in fact, be human.

So THE rest of the week was brutal for both of us.

Once they posted the team roster, practices were harder and lasted longer than during tryouts. They ran drills for hours and hours, and by the time Brad got out, he was like a dead man walking. I couldn't bring myself to try to fool around with him. He looked so tired. I guess what I'm trying to say is, that week I jerked off more than when I had first figured out how to. It was the only way to alleviate my urge to throw him down and take him, even if he fell asleep halfway through it.

On the third day, he asked me for a back rub because he felt like he had pulled something and everything was sore. I didn't know much about it, but he assured me just moving over the muscles with some oil would help. I didn't need a reason to have him strip down and rub him with oil, so I said yes quickly. I watched as he pulled his shirt up and over his head, and I hated that I licked my lips automatically. He flopped down on my bed, sounding like he was already asleep by the time his head hit the bedspread.

His back felt like it was carved out of stone as I moved my hands over it. I wasn't sure how much of that was tension and how much was muscle, but he sighed contently as I pressed down. "Oh God, that feels good," he said, wincing, making it sound more like he was in pain. I remembered the way his hands felt in Kelly's shower and tried my best to replicate his technique. I moved down the line of his muscles and got a sound from him each time I did it. "You can do it harder," he prompted.

I tried not to take his words sexually.

"So how is the team?" I asked, trying my best to keep my mind off his half-naked body.

"They are… ah… they're good," he said as I hit another knot of muscle. "I think we have a real chance this year." I wasn't sure if I was imagining it or not, but his back seemed to be getting more and more relaxed the more I worked on it.

"And you like being captain?"

Another vocal emission that sounded way too sexual to me. "Oh God, yes."

"Was that to my question or the backrub?" I asked, pausing.

"Both." He chuckled. "You're really good at this."

"I'm just copying what you did," I explained, moving lower and lower on his back.

"Then I'm pretty good," he said, burying his face in my bed.

My hands kept moving lower until my fingertips touched the waistband of his underwear. I froze with indecision for a moment and then threw caution to the wind.

My fingers slipped under the waistband and went lower.

"'Bout time," he said wryly. "You can't take a hint worth shit."

I looked over to double-check if the door was locked before turning him over. "You want to see a hint?" I said evilly.

"Show me," he said, smiling back.

We figured out that night that we only needed fourteen minutes of alone time to get our business done. It was a handy number to know.

THAT SATURDAY they had an all-day practice that Brad was not looking forward to.

I had wanted to watch, but he told me to stay home because it was going to be long and not much to see. I had the impression he didn't want me to see Coach Gunn screaming at them. Either way, I was bored waiting at home for him to finish up. Sometime after three I was woken up by a knock on my door. When I opened it, there was an exhausted Brad smiling at me like a loon.

He held up a piece of paper. "I know what I want to do."

"Recycle?" I said, inviting him in.

"No. I know what I want to do for Kelly," he said, walking in excitedly.

I closed the door, concerned. "What do you mean, do for Kelly?"

He sat down and began to explain. "I've been dying to do something in his name, and I couldn't figure it out. I thought maybe we could do some kind of play or something, but I just couldn't come up with an idea. And then the coach called me in after practice and gave me this, and I know what I want to do."

He handed me the piece of paper. It was a list with a bunch of names followed by what looked like measurements. It took me a few seconds to translate them into what they were. "Are these the uniforms?"

He nodded. "I remember I looked through the catalog at Tyler's one day when I was bored. And I saw all the different types of uniforms they had. At the time I had no idea what it meant, but it just came to me. They make a uniform that has a black armband sewn into it. If I order those instead of the usual ones, we'd have to wear them, right?" He looked so eager it broke my heart.

"Brad," I said, sitting down next to him. "You can get kicked off the team for this. I mean, this isn't just a little thing. You're talking about thousands of dollars in school funds if they have to reorder the uniforms. This isn't a little thing."

"But they can't," he implored me. "There is no way they could get new uniforms by the first game. Even if they reordered, they'd have to wear these at least once. See? Either way I win."

I honestly had no idea how much guilt had been gnawing at him. "You don't win if they kick *you* off the team." I could see by his face this wasn't working, so I tried another tack. "Have you tried asking Coach Gunn?"

He got up, frustrated, and began to pace. "Kelly wasn't a baseball player, and besides, Coach Gunn ain't gonna do anything. He's like everyone else at that school. This is the only chance I have to do something."

I walked over to him. "You know you've done a lot already, right?"

When he looked over at me, his eyes were bright green, which meant he was about to start crying. "You're a lousy liar. I haven't done a thing. I need to do this. Please."

I hate it when he cries.

"At least let me look over the rules before you do something crazy, okay?" His mood brightened up instantly. "No promises. But let me look at the league guidelines and see how much trouble you can get into first."

He nodded quickly and then leaned in and kissed me. "I love you so much."

I kissed him back, but I felt like this was a bad idea.

I SKIMMED over the Foster High baseball guidelines for an hour or so. There was nothing specific about uniforms except they couldn't have advertising on them, couldn't have anything distracting, and if one had something on them, they all had to have it. Besides that, there wasn't much else to speak of. There was nothing that said a team couldn't wear a black armband on their uniform out of tribute.

According to the web, several major league teams had done it in the past, and most high school guidelines were taken from the big leagues.

"So?" Brad asked me as he bit into an apple he found in the fridge.

I closed his laptop and sighed. "Well, there is nothing that says you can't do it." Which was all he heard. "Yes. So they can't stop us from wearing them?"

"They can't stop the team from wearing it. There is no way they won't kick you off the team. You have to know that." I saw the look on his face, and it told me he did know that.

He just didn't care.

"But the team can't get in trouble for wearing them?" he asked, ignoring my question.

I sighed heavily before nodding.

"Then let's get to Tyler's."

I wanted to argue, but I knew if our positions were reversed, I'd want him to help me. So I pulled my shoes on and went with him.

We found a parking space a few doors down, and we began to walk to Tyler's. "Oh. So I'm taking an ice bath, and Josh gets into the tub."

I looked over at him. "Say what?"

"I was in one of the ice tubs, and Josh Walker got in with me," he said again.

I stopped. "I don't even know what that means," I said after a few seconds.

He laughed. "We have these big tubs full of ice water, and we soak in them after practice to help with swelling. And they are big enough for two guys. So I was taking one, and Josh got into it with me."

"Naked?" I asked, stopping his story.

"Well, yeah. You do know most guys in the locker room are naked, right?" he asked me.

"You do know that is completely different from sitting in a tub with another guy?" I shot back.

He slowly cracked a smile. "Are you jealous?"

"Am I jealous that Mr. Josh 'I have no body fat and you could cut glass on my cheekbones' Walker was naked in a tub with my boyfriend? No, why would I have a problem with that at all?" So this was what wild jealousy felt like.

He began to openly laugh. "Okay, one, I was more pissed than anything he was in my tub, and two, you do know Josh Walker is about the straightest boy in the world, right?"

I didn't say a word.

"Oh God, Kyle, seriously? Josh Walker is not my type."

I gave him a look. "So then, in shape, cut, muscular as hell, and ridiculously handsome is not your type? Now I know why you go out with me." Yeah, that sounded lame even to me.

"You're insane," he said, moving up and hugging me. "My type is tall, lanky, no body fat, smarter than the other guys, and who has sex like a porn star." I tried to look away, but he wouldn't let me. "You have nothing to be jealous of when it comes to Josh Walker." He looked at the front of my jeans. "Trust me. Nothing."

I felt like my face was on fire from all the blushing, but I still smiled.

"There we go," he said, smiling back. "So, we good?" I nodded and we resumed walking. "Okay. So, as I was saying, I'm taking an ice bath, and Josh gets into the tub." I nodded. "And he starts asking about you and me. And Jennifer."

I looked at him the same way a dog looks at you when you say more than just its name.

"He asked if you and me and Jennifer were… together," he said, emphasizing the together.

Still nothing.

"Like, together," he stressed.

Lightbulb.

"He asked if we were all, like…." I made a gesture with my hands of two people pressing against each other.

He stopped in front of Tyler's door. "Dude, I have no idea what that meant." He pointed to my hands. "But I am pretty sure he was asking if the three of us were banging each other."

I'm not sure if my mouth dropped open in shock, but I knew I was stunned enough that I was unable to say anything for a while.

Brad smiled evilly before he opened the door and walked into the store. I followed about half a step behind, jaw starting to behave again, mind in a tailspin. Is that what everyone thought? That we were all in some kind of a… thing?

Tyler stood behind the counter watching something on his laptop.

Brad said loudly, "I know I am not paying you to watch movies, young man."

Tyler flipped us off as I closed the door.

"That didn't work coming from my dad. I have no idea why you think you'll do any better," he said, closing the computer.

Brad held up the piece of paper. "I have the uniform order. So you might want to be nice to me."

He rolled his eyes and looked at me. "Can't you control him?"

I always liked it when Tyler treated me like I was the one in charge of the relationship. No one else ever did that. "I suppose I could buy a collar and a leash, but he'd still jump up and try to hump people."

Brad managed a good, fake hurt-puppy look. "Hey!"

I gave him a peck on his cheek and added, "But you are the cutest mongrel in town."

I could see he was calculating to see if being the cutest mongrel was a good thing or not. At the same time, he said, "So here are the sizes for this year," and handed Tyler the piece of paper. From where I was standing, he looked like he was working up the courage to tell Tyler the rest of his plan. His shoulders tightened, and I could see the muscles in his jaw knotting.

Tyler skimmed it over. "Looks about right."

Brad looked over at me and, though he said nothing, asked me with his eyes if he should do it. Though I hated this plan, I knew it was what Brad thought he needed to do. So I nodded at him. He took a deep breath and turned back to Tyler. "So what if I wanted to change something real small on that order?"

Even though he didn't have kids, Tyler had that spider sense all adults seem to have when kids were trying to do something sneaky around them. His eyes narrowed, and he gave Brad a look. "Why do I have a feeling I am going to hate this? Brad? I am going to hate this, aren't I?"

I laughed quietly and thought, *You have no idea.*

Out loud almost said something, but Brad shot me a look, and I closed my mouth. This was Brad's show, and I was here for moral support. "What if I wanted you to order a certain type of uniform instead of the ones the school always orders?"

The look on Tyler's face shifted, like he still hoped this might be part of a joke. "I'd ask you why in the world would I do that?"

"For me?" Brad tried.

Concerned, Tyler rounded the corner of the counter and stood, arms folded, watching Brad. "You know I like you, Brad, and you helped me out of a jam during Christmas. But this," he said, holding up the uniform order, "this isn't something small. If I were to purposefully screw up this order, next year, I assure you, Coach Gunn will go online to order team uniforms. And, if word got out, Coach James at Granada would do the same. You know how much of my business is dependent on those school orders, not just for baseball, but for every other sport."

Brad didn't say anything at first. I could see him trying to do the math in his head to counter Tyler's logic. "But what if you say I lied to you? Blame it all on me." He was close to pleading, which was odd for Brad. And I suddenly was glad I had swallowed my words earlier.

73

"So then I wouldn't be an incompetent business owner, I'd be a gullible one instead. Different opinion, same outcome. They would just stop ordering from me." He could see the urgency in Brad's expression and quietly asked, "Brad, what's this all about anyway? Even if I did tell the coach and Principal Raymond you lied to me, they would kick you off the team in seconds. And that's the best-case scenario. Worst case they bill your parents for replacement uniforms. For a whole team, that isn't cheap." His voice got a little gentler. "So what's up?"

Brad didn't say a word, but I could see his shoulders slump in defeat. "I am a complete fuckup," he said more to himself than to us. "I can't get anything right."

Bad idea or not, it was my boyfriend's idea, and I realized I wanted to back him up on it.

"It's for Kelly," I said in the silence. "They make a uniform that has a black band for mourning sewn onto it already. We thought that if we ordered those, the team would wear them, and it would be for Kelly. Like a tribute."

Tyler's resolve slipped a bit when he understood what Brad wanted to do. Everyone had that same look when someone brought up Kelly: sorrow mixed with liberal amounts of guilt and regret. "Wow. That's…," he said, choking on his words. "That's a good idea, guys. Did you ask Coach Gunn?"

"You know what he'll say," Brad said, now outright pleading. "He is just as bad as everyone else at school. He was at the school board meeting trying to get me kicked off the team too, wasn't he?"

The bitterness in Brad's voice took me aback. I had no idea he had this much anger about almost getting kicked off the team. He hid it all so well, never once complaining he had risked his chance to play for everyone else, that I had just assumed he was okay with it. But I could tell from the way he clenched his hands into fists and the harshness in his voice that he was nowhere near okay with what had gone down, and I'd had no idea. It stopped me for a moment because I wondered what else I had missed. What if I didn't know him at all?

I pushed those thoughts aside and instead concentrated on what was in front of me. I really wanted to get this done for Brad. "Look, Mr. Parker, I know you could get into a lot of trouble, but you know how much they want to sweep what happened to Kelly under the rug. If coaches try to cancel your accounts, you can make an argument that the administration and the teachers are trying to cover up the parts about Foster they don't like again. I'm sure there are a lot of people who would be on your side."

Tyler looked five years older than when we walked in as he looked directly into our eyes. "But even if people were on my side, things would have changed. Purposely placing the wrong uniform order, no matter how good the motive, isn't the right thing to do. They trust me with their money, guys, and I don't take that lightly."

Brad sighed, and I thought for a moment he might start to cry. "Well, it was worth a shot, I guess. Thanks for listening, Tyler."

He sounded completely defeated. "Will you at least think about it?" I asked the older man.

He nodded at me. "I will, I promise."

We couldn't ask much more than that.

THE NEXT day as Brad and I watched TV on the couch, his cell rang.

It was Tyler.

"Hello?" Brad answered.

Small pause. "Seriously?" he asked, his voice getting excited.

Another pause. "You mean it?" he almost shouted. He lunged to his feet, too wound up to sit.

More silence and then, "Tyler, you are the best! I owe you so much!"

He hung up the phone and turned to hug me. "He did it! He ordered the other uniforms!"

I danced around with him and smiled, but I had to wonder... what exactly changed Tyler's mind?

I didn't wonder for long, because suddenly... Brad wanted to celebrate again.

I'm not sure how we celebrated things before sex, but let me tell you, whatever it was sucked in comparison.

Coach Gunn

ONCE A Marine, always a Marine.

I'd heard that before from guys who served in the corps; a lot of them say it when people ask them if they had served in the military. I'm not sure if it means different things to different people. Maybe what being a Marine means varies from person to person, but for me that saying is pretty straightforward.

You hold up one hand and swear to God that you will live your life by a set of standards that is above and beyond everyone else's. That promise doesn't end the second you take the uniform off. For some guys a tour in the corps is a means to an end. College, training, getting out of a crappy situation—it's just a job, not a way of life.

For the rest of us, it's the only way of life. For the rest of our lives.

Honor, courage, and commitment. That's it. At the end of the day, you take those three principles and you make them your life. It isn't easy, and it isn't supposed to be, because let me tell you, anything easy is just a pile of shit with a bow on top. Easy is how most people want to live their lives these days. No work, no sweat, no sacrifice. Just a button that takes care of everything for you, like we're living in the fucking Jetsons with our robot maids waiting on us hand and foot. That's something the Marines taught me. It's also something I teach my kids every day out there on the field.

It's tough being a Marine today, and that's fine. What's hard is trying to figure out what is worth getting suited up for to fight and what you should just let pass on by.

This whole year has been one clusterfuck after another. I honestly thought I would get through my entire coaching career without having to worry about who my students want to have sex with, but it looked like I was wrong in ways I couldn't even imagine. The entire school had been brought to a grinding halt because of this crap. I'm willing to take odds that most of Foster thinks it's because of what the Aimes boy did, but that's not true. Kelly Aimes was far from the first homosexual to die inside the city limits of Foster. Hell, he wasn't even the fifth. He was just the first people couldn't ignore.

I was thinking about this whole fiasco the other day, and something struck me that I couldn't get out of my mind no matter how hard I tried.

Everything that happened was all kind of my fault.

I was the one who told Graymark that he needed to get his history grade up. I was the one who told him that Kyle was the best student in the class. From what I've heard, it was that meeting that caused them to hit it off in the first place. So no matter how I tried to work around it in my mind, I really did knock over that first domino.

That thought led me to wonder *How much responsibility do I take for it?*

The answer, of course, is not much. I mean, it's not like I set the two of them up on a date, but I was in some distant way the cause of their relationship, and their relationship was the cause of all this drama, which meant in some roundabout way that I was partially to blame for some of what happened.

Not a thought that sat well in my gut.

Also not a thought I shared with Jeffrey Raymond.

Jeffrey Raymond is the school principal and has been my friend for almost ten years now. I use the word "friend" here to mean someone I work with, have had no problem with, and have interacted with over a period of time without complaint. It wasn't like he came over for a BBQ or that we drank together or that we went to the same church.

I don't go to church anymore; that was always Rebecca's thing. But even when she was alive, we didn't go to the same church Jeffrey did. Jeffrey and Rebecca's God never seemed to agree on much. Rebecca's God was a lot like her: kind, forgiving, and understanding of the imperfections in the world around her. It was the reason I had fallen in love and married her. Jeffrey's God is a lot like Jeffrey. He's more about rules and what happens to people who break the rules. That attitude is another reason I wouldn't socialize with him outside of work.

All this and more shuffled through my brain as I watched the baseball team go through Thursday's practice. I felt bad for some of them because I had already made my mind up who was going to make varsity this year. I just liked giving all of them as much time as possible on the field so they'd realize how much work they needed to do in order to make the squad. Some of them would be back next year; some of them wouldn't. The ones who wanted it bad enough would never stop trying. Those were the ones I always paid attention to.

Which was why I had always paid attention to Brad Graymark.

The boy's father, Nathan Graymark, was and is still an asshole, but he could play football when he was young, so when he had a son, everyone assumed the boy would play as well. As fate would have it, Brad turned out to be different in a lot of ways Nathan hadn't been ready for. Though not a lot of people look for it like they look for natural talent in, say, football nowadays, Brad seemed born to play baseball. He was never going to be as big as his father, but he had enough muscle mass to make him run fast and hit hard. I first saw him when he was about thirteen and playing for Junction Middle School. At thirteen, the boy was maybe a couple of months from being as good as a few of my varsity players. All he needed was some height and some skill training and he would give a couple of the seniors a run for their money.

He tried out for me his freshman year and made the team. Oh, I heard about it; at the time, putting a freshman on a varsity team was a controversial decision. Then came game number one. In that first game, Brad's batting silenced any and all complaints from armchair coaches.

We were down two in the ninth, and it really looked like the game was done. We were up against Monterey, and they had this pitcher who was throwing fire like he was a damn volcano. This guy had struck out every senior I had without breaking a sweat. By the seventh inning, even though the pitcher had lost some of the heat from his arm, the guys were so disillusioned that they were swinging at pitches no one in their right mind would try for. So there we are, ninth inning, down by two, and freshman Brad Graymark walks up to the plate.

Now, as far as everyone was concerned, we'd lost. No one at all, not even Brad, thought he could hit off this guy. With two outs, Brad hitting was only a formality to getting this game over with, even though we had two people on base. He looked so small compared to the other players, his hat looked like it was three sizes too large, and all I could see was the thin line that was his lip as he stepped up to the plate.

People in the stands were already gathering their stuff up, and others were halfway to their car when the first pitch rushed past the boy so fast I don't even know if he saw it. Brad took a half step out of the box, took his cap off to wipe the sweat away, readjusted his gloves, and then stepped back to the plate. The second pitch had a low drop, the exact kind of pitch everyone had been striking out on all night, but not Brad. He didn't even flinch as the ball whizzed past and the umpire called ball. Taken aback, the pitcher shook his head and went into his windup, another smoker as it came barreling down the center, easily eighty-plus miles an hour.

Again Brad didn't even move, strike two.

"He's fucking frozen!" one of the seniors complained.

The pitcher smiled as he got the ball back, and you could see he thought the same thing.

He wound up, and it was pretty obvious he was going for another fastball, the same kind Brad had spaced out on twice already. I didn't see the ball move, but I heard the crack as Brad's bat connected and sent that ball flying so far that it landed out of the field and most likely one block past that. The pitcher just stared openmouthed, which would have been funny if Brad wasn't striking the same pose.

They were both completely stunned that he had hit a perfect home run, bringing the two on base home, winning us the game. The people still left in the stands exploded in cheers; the ones walking away paused to see what they had missed. Five players ran out on to the field and pushed Brad toward first, telling him to take his victory lap. The poor boy got around first before he remembered to drop the bat.

Afterward people would go on about his skill and savvy about waiting for the right pitch, but I knew that wasn't it. That wasn't why he hit that ball, not even close. I heard guys go on about how Brad had no fear of the pitcher and that he was just pulling his leg not taking the first two pitches. But they were wrong. See, the reason Brad missed the first two pitches was because he was terrified. He knew that he was going to be the guy who lost the game, even though it had taken the whole team and nine innings to do that. He was frozen with terror that he was going to be blamed for all of this. And then, against all odds, against all reason, he pushed past that fear and did what he had been training to do all year.

He hit that damn ball as hard as he could. That summer he went off to baseball camp with the rest of the team and had two-a-day practice sessions drilled into him. When he came back his sophomore year, he was easily the most improved, and by the end of that season, I was getting calls from colleges asking if he was as good as they had heard. Junior year he practically led the team to a state championship, and everyone knew it. Even though there were guys older on the team, they all looked to Brad for their cues, something a lifetime of practice couldn't teach a kid. I'd seen it in the Marines more than once—that unexplainable combination of looks, attitude, charisma, and confidence that makes people respond to you. I don't even know if Brad was aware he had it, but he did, and it could make all the difference in the world.

I have coached meatheads, guys who are just slabs of muscle with no brains in them. They can be trained to do whatever you need them to do and follow your commands like robots. They're great for tackles but can't advance further than that. The ones who stand out, the stars of any sport, are the ones who might not have been the very best at everything, but are the ones everyone else huddles around. Name a sport and then the athlete you think is the best, and I assure you there is a guy you've never heard of who is better by far but just can't speak to people worth shit. To make a long story short, what I was waiting for was for Brad to realize this and step up to be the player I knew was in him.

And I am not sure that would have happened if he hadn't come out to the entire school as being gay.

Now let me say this up front so there is no misunderstanding later. I don't like gay people in general, but that doesn't mean I have a problem with people being gay. It just isn't my thing. When talk about gay sex is put in my face, the thought of two guys bumping uglies really makes me queasy. But that said, what people do in their bedrooms is their own damn business. I served with a few guys like that, and when they were in uniform or around me, you'd never know they were any different than anyone else. I treated them as equals, and they treated me with respect, and that's all that counts. So I don't want you thinking I'm some old homophobic asshole who hates fags, 'cause I don't. I'm allowed to not like something if I want; that's my right.

What isn't my right is taking rights away from other people.

When a person puts a uniform on, raises their hand, and swears to uphold and defend the Constitution, the rights given to Americans by that Constitution become something special. If I am going to take a bullet for those damn words, those words better mean something. Not just for the people I agree with, but for everyone. I take that pretty seriously, because if my friends died just so some jackasses could only dole out rights and privileges to the people they liked, then my friends died for nothing.

I have a problem with that.

Anyway, when Brad came out as gay, I was pissed. Not because he liked guys, but because I knew this was going to fuck with my season. I knew Raymond was going to lose his shit over it when it was none of his business. By the time everything settled again, Brad was going to be lucky to still be going to school in Foster. Sure enough, everything came to a head at an emergency school board meeting. I had already been given my lines to say. Jeffrey made sure to ask me about the things he knew I could answer with all honesty. Did I think Brad should be allowed to shower with other guys? Raymond told me students had come to him to complain about having to get undressed with a known homosexual and that he was going to ask me if I thought it was appropriate.

And that was all he asked.

If I had been a braver man, or maybe if Rebecca was still alive, I might have said more. I have to admit I lost a step when she passed, one I hadn't been able to get back. Maybe I'm old; maybe I'm done tilting at windmills. Maybe I was scared that if I spoke out, I'd find out what it felt like to be Charlotte Axeworthy. In any case, I did sit down, knowing my words were going to be used to condemn a kid for nothing more than having feelings for someone else.

And then something outstanding happened.

The guy I had been waiting three years to show up, the man I knew was inside the boy named Brad Graymark, reared his head and spoke his first words.

And blew the roof off the auditorium.

I was stunned. He had taken the half measure of protection his dad had coerced out of Raymond and threw it back, demanding protection from bullying be given to everyone. Brad stopped talking for himself and began to speak for everyone. It was the moment I knew I had found this year's varsity captain. I didn't say anything to anyone, of course. Well, I might have told Becca when I visited Foster Hills, but I didn't tell anyone who could talk back. I waited and planned. I pushed Brad and the team harder than I had pushed any team before. These kids were not going to be just baseball players; they were going to be gods when I was done.

I needed them to be that good, so intense that there was no way my decisions could be questioned. If someone was going to throw somebody off that team, it wasn't going to be for playing ability, which was the only thing that counted at this level of play. This wasn't the major leagues, where you could lose a contract for cheating on your wife or picking up a hooker; there weren't million-dollar endorsement deals on the line. These were high school boys, and the only thing the baseball codes said they could get kicked off for was failing grades and my decision to cut them. There was no gray area, which meant if they did their best, Raymond couldn't come after them.

I trained them, and I waited.

And while I waited we suffered a casualty, which at any age is inexcusable, but when it is a teenager, it is so much worse.

Kelly Aimes was one of those kids that sports saved.

Boys in general are an angry sort. It's the aggression mixed with the desire to win that makes them so dangerous at times. To others, to themselves, to anything around them. The key is to take all that anger and point it at something. Kelly had that hate, that darkness in him, and thank God he found football. With his size and his problems, he could have grown up to be someone dangerous, someone unbalanced, but sports gave him an outlet to channel the pressure. I had no idea that all of that came from his trying to deny his own feelings, but once I heard, it made perfect sense.

I sat in the funeral home and listened to the service as they laid the boy to rest. There were a lot of tears and a lot of kind words, but no one was talking about the truth very much. The Aimeses were a family of means, and from what I had observed over the years, the more money a family has, the worse it is behind closed doors. The service was almost done, and I really thought no one was going to say a word until Tyler Parker stood up to talk.

Tyler was one of those kids who inspired you to root for him no matter what team he was on. He elevated high school football from two groups of teenage boys running into one another into an art form when he was on the field. I remember watching tapes of him when we prepped for the yearly Foster-Granada game, and I was always stunned at watching him play. When he ran, he did it as if there was no one else on the field with him; it was just him, the ball, and miles and miles of grass. He scored a pretty sweet deal at Florida, which ended the moment his knee was pushed in a direction knees aren't meant to bend. He had been at the school board meeting as well, and he admitted he was gay too, which was surprising. I honestly didn't think Foster could have that many gay people.

Parker stood up and said that we had failed Kelly, that as a town and as a culture, we had failed him by not letting him know it was okay to be different. He said that it was his fault for not coming out sooner, that it was everyone's fault for only now realizing there was a problem. He dared us to change; he dared us to be better. And then he stomped out, leaving me to wonder why I was so upset at his words.

It took me better than a week to realize I was pissed because he had been right.

The Monday we got back to school, I knocked on Raymond's door and asked him if he had a few minutes.

"For you?" he said jovially. "Always."

I wondered how long that attitude would last.

"I wanted to give you a heads-up. I plan on naming Graymark team captain next week."

His face went from smiling to sour in seconds flat. I found it amusing as hell, but I didn't say anything since he wasn't going to share in my mirth. "I really wish you wouldn't do that," he said when his brain started functioning again.

I pretended not to know what he was talking about and stated the facts. "He is the best kid on the team, and they respond to him. He's the obvious choice."

Jeffrey came around the other side of his desk, no doubt trying to instill some kind of personal connection between us. "You know that's not true." I refused to respond. "Jack, you have to consider the implications of making that decision."

"The only implications I have to consider are if he is capable of fulfilling the duties of the job and if he has earned the position. And he has done both with flying colors."

"I'm talking about the political implications. There are people who will not be thrilled that he is on the team at all, much less team captain. That could affect attendance." I had never noticed before how much like a rat Raymond looked when he was trying to convince someone of something. He refused to look directly at me, instead moving his body to the side as if he was protecting himself from a blow he was waiting for.

"I don't give a damn about attendance. If people are that upset, let them stay home. Because this team is going to state. I am willing to bet my job on it."

And that was the wrong thing to say.

"It might be, Jack," he said dangerously. "Are you willing to risk that?"

Once a Marine, always a Marine.

"You're damn right I am."

THE WEEK before I post the list of who makes the team is called hell week by those who have to endure it.

The kids thought they had kept the name private, but after fifteen years of coaching high school, if they called it anything less, I would be upset. By this point in the year, I pretty much already had the team made in my mind. All that was left was the one or two guys who might pull a miracle out of their asses and prove me wrong. Hell week was for them.

As hard as I was on the team, I was three times harder on Brad. I needed to know if he was in it for the long haul, which meant trying my level best to tear him down and see if he would quit.

I screamed at him that he couldn't hit hard enough, run fast enough, and every time he dropped a fly ball, he got an all-expense-paid tour of the backfield while holding a bat over his head. After the third hour of practice, I would have been shocked if he could raise his hands to even catch a ball, so he got to see the back fence more times than he saw home plate those days.

He didn't flinch.

I was married to Becca for five years before I began to wonder why we didn't have any kids yet. I assure you it wasn't from lack of trying, so we went and saw a professional. It was the hardest thing I ever had to hear. To have some stranger inform us that we were never going to have a child of our own was the closest thing to torture I had ever seen. She was devastated. There was nothing that Becca wanted more than to be a mother. We talked about adopting, but she never took a shine to the idea, and after a while I stopped pushing it. But in my mind, if we were to have a son, I would have wanted him to be just like Brad.

I admit I might not have chosen to make him a homosexual, but watching him take his tenth trip around the field without even an ugly look, I knew that inside, he had everything in his soul that made up a real man. It was that quiet resolve that made the difference. He wasn't one of these other kids whining that it wasn't fair, and I was just being mean to them. A pack of self-important idiots, that is what the internet has raised for us. In my days it was comic books—read too many and they'd rot your brain, educators warned. After that it was TV. Watch too much TV and you'd end up a drooling idiot. Now it was the internet, and let me tell you, for the first time, I believed the experts.

But not Brad.

Even after all that, I told him to pick up the mitts his teammates had dropped in the dugout before he came in. Anyone else would have at least looked at me and asked with their eyes, why them? Hell, I would have asked that. But instead he just nodded mutely and began scooping them up as he walked. And then took the two bats that had been lying there and put them away as well. I watched as he looked around the dugout to see if anything else was out of place. Not because he thought that was what I asked him to do, but because that dugout was his house, and he wasn't leaving until it was clean.

I rushed back into the locker room to make sure he didn't see me.

It was Thursday, and the list was going to go up the next day. You could feel the nervous energy out in the locker room, even though they were physically exhausted. If they ever find a way to harness teenage boys for energy, we will never go without light and heat. More than a few passed by my office, trying to seem sly as they looked to see what I was doing. I ignored them since I was the clueless adult, and they were the know-it-all teenagers. I found myself wondering how much my teachers let us get away with when I was young.

The one good thing that had come out of this whole mess was that no one cared if Brad showered with them or not. After the Kelly's Laws went into effect, I sat them down and asked if anyone had a problem with him showering with the team. I have to admit they were braver than I was, because not one said they had a problem at all.

I told him to come to my office when he was done showering. You'd think I had just told the boy to eat his last meal before facing a firing squad. Maybe he was just nervous because he knew what was coming. I had no idea what went through kids' minds anymore. I waited in my office for him to finish, stacking up the list of guys I had chosen for the team.

He knocked twice and walked in.

"Sit down, Graymark," I said, sliding a chair over to him. This was something I had always done with captains, going over the lineup before the list was posted. There are two reasons I think it's a good idea. One, it gives me a chance to see how much they have been paying attention to the other players, and two, it shows me if they are going to fight to keep the people they think are the best qualified on the team. "Not a lot of guys are going to even get on the field, which is a shame, but there are only so many minutes in a game. So I have to make some hard choices, and no matter what I do, there are going to be some upset boys tomorrow."

He looked like he was going to throw up, which puzzled me because shouldn't this be the point where he was ready to jump through the roof?

"But you've played since you were a freshman, so you at least deserve to know what's what." I put the folders down on my desk. "Here it is. I am going to cut Flores, even though he is a faster runner than Walker. Walker has good heart, and I think this could be his year, but I need to know you agree with me on this, and I need to know now. I'm not going to start the season by arguing with the team captain right out of the gate."

I knew that Brad and Josh had tussled a few times in the past, and I watched him to see if he would use the moment to get me to change my mind.

"Flores is a better hitter," he said without even pausing. "But I'd keep Josh too."

I was impressed. He didn't even blink at that suggestion. "Good, I thought the same thing. You have any attachment to Freeman or Paulson? Because they aren't making it either."

He shook his head, but he still had that dazed, glassy-eyed look on his face as he said, "Freeman is good, but he has no rhythm on the field, and Paulson might be ready next year but not yet."

That was almost exactly what I had written in my notes on them. "You've been paying attention. Outstanding—that will make this easier." I tossed the last two files onto my desk and handed him the roster. "Anything on here you have a problem with, then?"

He took the paper like it was a creature from another planet. It was just a list of names, but you could swear it was a contract for his soul the way he went over it again and again. Finally, after a good three minutes, he pointed to the sheet and asked, "What's that?"

I leaned over. He was pointing at his own name. Maybe he meant the word by it. "Captain."

He made a face and honestly asked me, "What's that mean?"

This was a kid who had been playing baseball for years; he had to know what that meant. I elaborated by saying, "Team captain."

He shook his head at me like he was disagreeing. "Come again?"

I didn't know what game he was playing, but I didn't have the patience for it. "Team captain. You know what a team captain is?" He nodded. "Then what's the question?"

"Why is it by my name?"

This was his way of making a joke. Not the best way to do it, but I just said, "Smartass. Tell no one, and try to seem surprised tomorrow morning." I handed him the folder with our drills. "And begin to get real familiar with that. It's your job to get everyone else to understand it."

He looked down at the folder with the same expression he gave the list of names. After a second his mouth fell open in what I assumed was exhaustion.

"Any questions?" I asked, wanting to wrap this up so I could get home.

He held the folder up to me, as if I hadn't seen it. "This is mine?"

I liked it better when he didn't say anything. I pointed at his name. "That's you, right?" He nodded. "So then it's yours."

"But this is for team captain," he said, like I was the one who didn't know what a team captain was.

Then it started to dawn on me—what if he didn't want the job? Had I read this kid wrong? "Are you saying you don't want to be team captain?"

"I'm team captain?" he asked me, and at any other time it would have been a pretty convincing rendition of "Who's On First."

I felt a tension headache coming on and tried to will it away. "Why did you think I asked you in here?"

"To kick me off the team."

His words were like a slap. I looked up at him and asked, "Why would you think that?"

"Um, because I'm gay?"

I swore then to myself I was going to punch Jeffrey Raymond in the face some day.

I moved closer to him and cleared my throat as I tried to find a way to explain everything that had happened. "What you need to understand, Brad…." I stopped. "I mean, the truth is…." Nope, stopped again. Goddammit, how do I tell a kid that there was nothing wrong with who he slept with and that it really had less than nothing to do with his ability to play baseball.

Then out of nowhere, he leans over to me and says reassuringly. "It's okay, Coach. It's cool."

This kid, this teenage boy who honestly had done nothing more wrong than say "I love that guy," trying to tell me, the old man who had a problem with it, that it was going to be okay.

Damned if he didn't make me ashamed to be a man.

"No. No, it isn't cool," I said, trying to clear the emotion out of my voice. I was not going to break down in front of this kid, not now. "You're team captain." I stood up. "Study that book, and get ready to drill it into the others." I turned back to my desk so I could wipe one of my eyes. "Now get out of here."

Seconds later I was alone.

"Good God, what are we doing to these kids?" I asked myself as I fell into my chair, exhausted.

"HE JUST assumed I was going to kick him off the team."

Gayle nodded as she sat across from me in the diner. I tell myself I come in here because I love the pie, but to be honest, it was the way she listened that drew me there night after night. She had the same understanding eyes Becca had. Even if she didn't know what I was going on about, she would still nod and smile and give me reassurance that everything would be all right.

"Well, what did you expect?" she said, refilling my coffee. "I mean, didn't you all try to kick him off the team once already?" I looked at her with a glance that would have made a dozen students flee in terror, but she just laughed. "And don't give me that evil eye. You let Raymond wind you up in that meeting, and you condemned the kid. What do you think he would think?"

"He could have trusted me," I grumbled as I reached for the sugar.

She slapped my hand. "There is pink, yellow, and blue in there. You don't need any more sugar tonight." I glared at her, and she didn't budge. "You want to try teaching with a stump instead of a foot, be my guest. My blood sugar is accounted for."

I grabbed three packets of the blue instead, and she smiled.

"And how can the boy trust you? Have you actually said anything to him to indicate you were on his side?" She knew by my silence that I hadn't. "So you're surprised the teenage boy went by the actions of you trying to kick him off the team instead of, what? Reading your mind? You're lucky he hadn't quit already and just gone to Granada to spite all of you."

The thought of having to face a pissed-off Brad Graymark on another team was the thing my nightmares were made of.

"You know what is even worse than him not knowing what you are privately thinking?" she asked me. Again I said nothing, because I had known Gayle long enough to know she would tell me anyway. "If he didn't think he deserved to be on the team, he must really think he doesn't deserve to be captain." She got up and put my check down. "Now I'm not an expert on male egos, but I do know that once bruised, it can take years and years to heal."

"You think he is going to blow it?" I asked her.

"I think he thinks he is going to blow it. And that makes it an almost certainty that he will." She shrugged. "But then again, I'm not a sports coach, so what do I know?"

I sighed as she walked away. Once again, she was right. If Brad had no confidence, then he was just a mistake waiting to happen. I went to reach for my wallet when I saw the note written across the bill.

"As a rule, I don't date guys who have had a foot cut off because they like too much sugar in their coffee." Under that, she had put a line through the total saying it was on her.

I threw some bills down on the table and made a hasty retreat before my mind could figure out if she was asking me to ask her out or if I was just being stupid.

I SPENT the next morning sitting in my office trying to figure out how to approach this Brad thing.

He needed to feel like he deserved to be there, earned that spot. That meant some team building, but I was worried because what if the team wasn't in the mood to follow? I didn't have any doubts that Brad was the best guy for the job, but that didn't mean the rest of the kids were just going to follow a gay captain. The worst part was that if you had asked me last year if I would have followed one, I probably would have told you "Hell no."

If they made a fuss, it was just what Raymond was waiting for to get Graymark kicked out. It wasn't discrimination if the other students complained first. I was halfway through "Ring of Fire" when my door burst open, and Kyle was standing there saying something to me.

I popped the earphones out, and he said something else, but I didn't hear him because of the noise coming from behind him.

A fight.

I got up and rushed out the door, pushing kids out of my way as I walked into the center of the argument. Which was just in time to hear Tony Wright call someone a faggot.

I took a deep breath and then proclaimed in my best Charlton Heston from *The Ten Commandants*, "Tony Wright." Even though his back was to me, I saw him freeze, which was the intended result. "Did you just call someone a faggot?" He looked around like he was going to get some help from someone, but he realized he was very much alone, literally and figuratively. "I asked you a question," I said, shaking some sense into him. Wright was one of those students who football ruined. It took a mean boy and had him work out, bulk up, and then rewarded him for hitting other people. I remembered Brad's father being the same way at this age, and let me tell you, it did nothing to raise his value in my eyes. When I was barely older than him, I was holding a rifle and being taught how to best kill a man if he got too close in combat. We were lean, we were hungry, and we were always taught that the skills we were learning should never be used on anyone who wasn't a mortal enemy. But there were always guys who wanted to pick fights—over women, over dick size, over whatever they wanted to at the time, because they knew they could beat the hell out of any three guys. I hated it then, and I hate it more now.

"I-I didn't say nothing" was all he could mutter, sounding like a damn infant too.

I was about to tell him he was in some real trouble when Tony's voice came from behind me, sounding like it was from a speaker. "What did you say to me, you little faggot?"

I looked over and saw the sheriff's daughter holding a camera phone. "Oh, I'm sorry, was I not supposed to record that?"

Her finger hit the Replay button, and she held the video up to my face and played it again.

"In his defense, 'I didn't say nothing' does in fact mean he said something. So not so much a lie as just bad grammar." It was Kyle, and he got a good laugh from the crowd.

I wasn't in the laughing mood.

"Congratulations, Wright, you just became the first student at Foster High to meet Kelly's Laws. If you're lucky, your name will go up on a plaque with the rest of the intolerant people who will come after you. I'm sure your dad will be so proud." I meant it, because his dad was no better than he was. Tony was the redneck son of a redneck asshole, and if anyone needed any proof that hatred was hereditary, all they had to do was look to Tony Jr. for that.

I tossed him in a chair and sat down across from him behind my desk. He looked like he had just eaten a bug from the look on his face.

This needed to stop, now. If I just turned this idiot over, he would get suspended, and his father would blame Brad and the rest of the liberal assholes who had taken over this school. If you ask me, Tony's dad made Brad's look like father of the year. The things that man believed weren't just wrong, they were, at times, criminal. So if Wright's dad and his friends started blaming Brad for all of this, then Tony here would get off without any feeling of personal blame. And that wasn't going to fly with me. What this needed was some good old-fashioned American guilt.

"So tell me, Tony," I said calmly. "You really don't like Graymark, do you?"

I saw the conflicting feelings on his face. He knew if he said he had no problem, that it would be a bold-faced lie, and that would make two he had said to me within five minutes. But if he admitted it, then wouldn't that be worse? I let him stew for a few seconds before continuing.

"Don't answer that. I can tell. You have to know yelling at him in the hallway is a waste of time, right? I mean, come on, in the end all you do is get in trouble, right?"

He nodded slowly.

"So then, how about this. How about I keep him after practice one day, and the rest of the team is gone. Then you can come in there and 'talk' with him," I said, making air quotes. "Sound like a plan?"

He nodded slowly again.

"I mean, no witnesses, no evidence, just you and him and an empty gym. You can do that, right?"

A small smile and a nod.

"That's what I thought. Now, I have bats there. You can bring a tarp, right?"

He stopped nodding and smiling all at once. "A what?"

"A tarp," I said again. "For his body." Another pause. "We are talking about killing him, right?"

Tony's face went white as he moved farther back in his chair. "I don't want to kill him," he said loudly, almost in a panic.

"Don't you?" I asked, keeping my voice calm. "I assumed because it was this same kind of harassing shit that got Kelly to kill himself, and I just thought you were going to try to steer Brad in that direction too." I got up slowly. "I mean, what did we learn by Kelly putting a pistol in his mouth and pulling the trigger? That you can only mock and attack fags for so long before they kill themselves? I was just trying to cut to the chase, give you a chance to do it yourself. You know, feel the blood splatter as you beat him to death."

His eyes were wide, and I think he might have been shaking.

"Because what other reason would you have for screaming and calling him a faggot in front of everyone if you weren't trying to drive him to kill himself? We just got done burying one of them. You couldn't have forgotten this quickly, so I assumed this was your plan." I walked over to him, and he pushed back in his chair even more. "I mean, you do have a plan, right, Tony? You aren't just out there spreading hate because you're bored or because you're jealous. You can't be openly mocking a guy for the same reasons a friend of yours killed himself, without thinking the same thing could happen again. So, Tony…." I put my hands on the arms of his chair. "What is your plan?"

He was looking up at me, terrified. Not at me, but at my words. I could see his brain connecting the dots, and the image it was painting was not a good one. "Between you and me, Tony, don't you want him to kill himself?"

"No, sir!" he said, pleading. "I don't."

I let my voice go and bellowed at him. "Then why would you keep calling him a faggot?" He flinched and then began to break down in front of me. "Why would you come all the way down here just to mock him on the day he was named captain? I can't figure out a reason, Tony, other than you want him to kill himself just like Kelly. That you saw Kelly's death as a good thing and want more of it. Because there is no other reason here, son."

I paused as he openly sobbed.

"I know you love your dad, and you should. But your old man has some thoughts on things that are wrong, Tony, dead wrong. And I don't say that from opinion or from guessing. I say that as someone who passes Kelly's grave every week when I go see my wife's. Those words and those actions kill— they kill. And if you aren't trying to get someone to die, then you need to stop saying them."

I knelt down in front of him. "Do you understand what I am saying, son?"

His face was a wreck as he blubbered something and nodded.

"It's okay not to agree with the lifestyle, Tony. But it's their life. You have to let them live it."

He leaned forward and threw his arms around me. I froze, surprised, and I heard him continuing to cry. "I just… I just keeping thinking if they just kept their mouths shut, Kelly would still be here." He clung to me and just cried. "I miss him so much, Coach…. Why do I feel this way?"

I pulled back, and though I wanted to say something that would make him feel good, I needed to tell him the truth.

"You feel this way because you feel guilty, Tony. Because you know you were partly responsible for his death." He didn't say a word, but I could see the guilt in his eyes. "You can't keep hating Brad for this. You need to forgive yourself. You know that, right?"

He nodded as he wiped his nose. "Am I suspended?"

I shook my head. "No, but you need to realize you can't keep doing this. It isn't their fault."

"I know, Coach," he said miserably. "I just miss Kelly so much…."

Neither one of us knew what to say, so after a while I let him go to class.

It got me no closer to figuring out the Brad problem.

IN THE old days, it would have been easy.

If I had doubts about a team rallying behind their captain, I would simply go on a warpath and start training them mercilessly. There would be general bitching, but no one would say anything, at least not to me. That technique solved two problems. The first was that it gave them a common enemy: me. Nothing unites people more than a bad guy to bitch about. The second, and more important, would be that sooner or later one of them would go ask the captain to talk with me about easing off some. Though they weren't conscious of it, the team would acknowledge that the captain was their leader and ask him to speak for everyone in telling me I had gone too far.

It's a shame that wouldn't work now.

I had gotten the report of what happened in the hallway after I'd pulled Tony away, and from what I heard, it was encouraging but not in any way proof Brad was home-free. It took people a bit too long to fight back against Tony's bashing. It was only pride in the team that motivated the other kids to fight back. I needed to know their acceptance of my decision wasn't just a reflex from being grateful they had made the team. They needed to really bond around Brad, or when things got bad—and every season, they did—they would turn on him, and in turn, themselves.

I just had no earthly idea how to do that.

I had settled in for a quiet Saturday night, after a week of practices with the new team, when my phone rang. I must have been one of the few people left in the country who still had a phone connected to a wire, but I didn't care. As far as I was concerned, it was a step forward that the phone had buttons instead of a dial.

"Hello?"

"Coach Gunn?" a male voice asked. It didn't sound like a student from the tone, but it held the same reverence I was used to hearing in kids.

"You got him," I answered, trying to place the voice.

"This is Tyler—Tyler Parker?" I wasn't sure if the boy thought there was a list of Tylers who would call my house on a Saturday night, but I gave him the benefit of the doubt.

"What do you need, Tyler?"

He cleared his throat, and I smiled as I heard the nervousness in his voice. I was never his coach, but he had spent more than enough time in sports to know that most of us liked to be spoken to with a certain regard. "I was wondering, if you weren't busy, if you could come down to the store."

If he was this hesitant when talking to other men, it was no mystery why he was still single.

"Is there a problem?" I asked him, knowing he wouldn't have called without there being one.

He paused, which told me he was trying to find the right words to use. "I just think you should come down here if you can."

I was tempted to ask what would happen if I didn't, but I refrained. "Give me twenty minutes," I said and hung up the phone.

I hadn't been downtown this late on a weekend since… well, let's just say for a while. There was more traffic on First Street than I would have guessed, the majority of it around Nancy's. It was crowded with what looked like a full range of couples enjoying a meal. The sight of so many people in love made me feel cold for a moment as I remembered what having someone to sit across from was like.

"Jack?" a voice called from the alley next to the diner.

I squinted and was barely able to make out Gayle, sitting outside finishing a cigarette. I trotted across the street toward her. "I didn't know you smoked," I said, my voice sounding harsher than I intended.

She shook her head as she took one last drag. "I don't. At least, I didn't. It's a stress thing, I suppose. I don't even inhale anymore. I think it is just the ritual that calms me down." She tossed the butt down and ground it into the street with her heel.

"Stress?" I asked, surprised I was actually concerned.

She sighed and leaned against the side of her diner. "Dorothy Aimes came by. She's filing for a divorce."

I wasn't sure how to react to that since her husband was a first-class idiot. "That's a… bad thing?"

She laughed. "I suppose. Lord knows, after Kelly, things haven't been ideal, but I think it was the last straw. She told him tonight, and he went off on her, so she came over here to talk, and it just got to me. I mean, here she is, a strong-willed woman who used to be such a go-getter, and to see her crying because she wasn't sure if she wants to leave that ass of a man… it just gets to me to see a strong woman tore up about a man who doesn't deserve her. When did we as a gender become so scared of being alone that staying in a loveless relationship was better than leaving?"

It was the most I had heard her talk about herself, and I had nothing to say back. It wasn't that I didn't agree or have opinions. I was just struck by how, out there, with only part of her face lit by the streetlights, she looked a thousand times more delicate than she normally did. If you were to ask anyone in town what would be around after a nuclear war, the most popular answers would be cockroaches and Gayle. And I am willing to bet you that she was a thousand times more resilient than the bugs. But seeing her right there, right now… it reminded me that she was a woman too.

"Look at me blabbing away," she said, standing up. And just like that, her mask slipped back into place and she was good, invulnerable Gayle. If I hadn't seen it with my own eyes, I would have not believed it was true. "What has you out this late?"

Why was I there?

"Oh," I said as my brain finally found a gear. "Needed to head over to Parker's for something." I stood there for a second, feeling like I was sixteen again and nothing in my body worked liked it was supposed to. "I don't know how long it's going to take, and I can tell you're busy in there, and you probably aren't even hungry, so it's not a thing, but I was…."

She reached out and put a hand on my shoulder. "When you're done, come over here, stop in, and we'll have a coffee."

The smile on my face felt foreign as I looked back at her. "I'd like that."

We stood there just looking at each other for several seconds before she said, "Well, go on over there and get whatever it is over with already. I'm not a young woman, and I don't have time to dawdle."

I chuckled as I turned and jogged back across the street.

"That's some good hustle, Coach," she called after me.

Damned if I didn't feel my face get red as I walked into the store.

Parker was sitting behind the counter. In front of him was a catalog, and beside it was the uniform order. "You asked me down here to verify a uniform order?" I asked him, closing the door behind me. The implication was that we could have done that over the phone.

"No," he said, standing up. "Well, yes and no." He sounded conflicted and gestured to one of the stools. "You want a Coke?" he offered as he walked into the back room.

I thought about the coffee that was waiting across the street and waved him off. "I'm good. So what's this about?"

He came back in with a bottle of Coke in his hand. In this light he looked like his father when he was younger. "Were you aware how tore up Brad was about Kelly Aimes's suicide?"

It was the first time I had heard someone refer to the boy's death as a suicide, and it was as shocking as I imagined it would be. "The whole town was affected," I said, not sure where this was going.

"Yeah, but Brad and Kelly had a history," he said, sitting across from me. "They were friends for a long time, and he is harboring a lot of guilt over the death."

That made little to no sense to me. "Why? Wasn't like Graymark was one of the kids riding Aimes about being gay. Why would he blame himself?"

Tyler sighed. "Because he is a teenage boy, and everything in the world is about him. It's worse than anyone really knows."

I nodded, accepting his words but still not getting any closer to figuring out what this had to do with me or my uniforms. "Okay, so Brad is upset. That was what you wanted to tell me?"

"He is so upset that he wants to find a way to make it up to Kelly. Something that would settle his guilt and make him gain some closure."

Again I had no idea where this was going, and then my eyes fell to the uniform order. "What did he do?" I growled.

Tyler got up and tried to calm me down. "He didn't do anything. He asked me to do something, and I told him that I wouldn't. But I think you should know about it."

"What did he want to do?" I amended my question.

Tyler turned the catalog toward me and pointed to the open page. "He wanted me to order those." I looked at where his finger was and read the description.

I couldn't pull my eyes away from the black armband. "They make these?"

"I was surprised myself," he admitted, sitting back down. "It's based on the Texas Rangers' tribute to Danny Thompson in '77. I looked it up, and they are completely legal for play, but I told him I wasn't going to go behind your back and order them." I nodded in agreement. "Instead I decided to bring you down here so I could beg you to order them."

I looked up at him in amazement.

"I know we don't know each other well, and you don't owe me a thing. But I am begging you, on behalf of every single person who is still mourning the loss of Kelly, to order these uniforms and let them wear them. These cost more, but I will personally pick up the difference. I'll mark them down to cost if you want. Just, please, let the team wear them for the season."

His voice was nothing but emotion. It was obvious he was not used to asking for things.

"I can't make a decision like this," I said, knowing that was a half lie even as I uttered it. I could make a decision like this; I just shouldn't because Raymond would lose his ever-loving mind. He wanted nothing more than for this whole incident to go away, and dedicating our entire season to Kelly, wearing tribute uniforms, was the furthest thing from going away you could get.

Tyler sighed and looked down. "I understand, Coach. Look, I don't want to get Brad into any trouble. He was just trying to step up and do something for Kelly. I'd appreciate it if you didn't punish him for this."

I could do this; I could tell him to order these, and it would be another nail in my coffin at Foster. Raymond would have it out for me, and anything less than a state championship would mean I was gone, and even a win didn't guarantee anything. It was too risky, not for something that was just symbolic.

I looked out the windows and saw the diner. Gayle was talking to someone as she took their order, and I suddenly felt ashamed. When did I become this scared man? Was he born when Becca died? And if the man I'd been was gone, then what was left? I traced a finger over my Marine Corps ring and saw our motto shine back at me.

Semper fidelis: always faithful.

Tyler was still talking, no doubt trying to convince me to change my mind, but I hadn't heard any of it. I was tired of being scared, and it ended now.

"Order them," I said, cutting him off. "Order them, and tell Brad you did it, but don't tell him you talked to me."

He paused as he tried to figure that out. "Why?" he finally asked.

"Because they need a bad guy," I said, smiling. "They need something they all agree with to rally behind, and they need someone to stand up to. Order them, Tyler, and I will pay the extra cost for them. Just don't tell Brad we talked. Let him think he talked you into it."

"But... but he should know what you did," he sputtered as I stood up. "I mean, he should know you're on his side, Coach."

I continued smiling at him. "And he will, after I spend the entire season seeming to be upset about his choice. Then I will slowly get wore down until I can admit to him that he changed my mind." I looked Tyler right in the eye. "He needs a win—they all do. The kids at Foster need a real, solid win. And I plan on giving it to them."

With that, I turned around and began to walk out. "Now, if you'll excuse me, I am keeping a lady waiting." I tipped my imaginary hat to him and walked out to cross the street.

It was time to stop being afraid of a lot of things in life.

MARCH 26
EVERYBODY TALKS
81 DAYS LEFT

Brad

I RUSHED into the classroom, trying to make as little noise as possible.

"Mr. Graymark," Mr. Powers called from the front of the room. "I know the baseball team is on a seven-game winning streak, but that does not mean you can walk into my class at any time you wish." This was a dick move, because he was wasting more time bitching about me wasting his time than me coming in late did.

"I'm sorry, Mr. Powers, won't happen again." I used my humblest voice and even gave him a quarter of my aw-shucks smile. I have been told it gives me the appearance of a scolded puppy and makes it almost impossible to continue to berate me.

He sighed. "Take your seat, and make sure it doesn't happen again."

Chalk another one up for the patented puppy eyes.

I moved to the back of the room and sat next to Jennifer, who was rolling her eyes at me. Her expression grew innocent, and she pantomimed sniveling a bit. "It w-won't happen again, Mr. Powers." I flipped her off as I pulled out my book. "One of these days that stare isn't going to work, and you are going to be in actual trouble."

I shook my head and pretended to look at the board. "Never happen. The power of the puppy eyes is foolproof."

She laughed and pretended to watch Powers talk. "So let me guess—you're late again because you were making the sex with Kyle?"

I looked over at her and said quietly, "I really think I created a monster."

Jennifer paused. "Kyle?"

I nodded. "All he wants to do is have sex. I mean, all the time." I looked around to make sure no one could hear us. "Like all, all the time."

She gave me a strange look. "And this is bad how?"

"I'm tired!" I explained.

97

I was tired and sore. We had won seven games straight, but not without a cost. We had paid for every single run with hours of agonizing practice that left me with about enough energy to kick off my shoes before I passed out. I had never been so tired in all my life, but I had no time to rest. As soon as we were alone, Kyle would start kissing me, stripping me naked, and next thing I knew, we were having sex.

And I was even more tired.

And sore, but I am not going into that.

Jennifer covered her mouth as she began to laugh at me. "Shut up!" I hissed at her. "This is not funny." Of course, that only made her laugh more. "I'm serious. Do you know what it's like to have someone wanting sex every second of the day? I love him to death, but God, I need a break."

She snorted out loud. The entire class stopped as she put her head on the desk and began to laugh insanely. "Is there a problem back there?" Mr. Powers asked us.

"We're fine," I said quickly. "Everything's fine. How are you?" I asked and winced as soon as I realized I had just quoted *Star Wars*. I swear to you I was cool before Kyle corrupted me.

"Try the look," Jennifer snorted between laughs. "That always works."

I jumped up out of my seat and pushed her to her feet. "We need just a second. Won't take long," I said, leading her toward the door. "Just go ahead. We'll catch up."

Before Mr. Powers could say a word, we rushed out of the class and into the hallway. The second the door closed, Jennifer burst out laughing even louder as she leaned against a locker door to draw breath. "Are you kidding me?" I muttered as I led her toward the quad. Last thing we needed was all the teachers in the building coming out to see how a wild hyena got locked in the hall.

"It's not that funny," I told her the second we hit outside.

"Oh, it is," she protested, finding a bench to sit down on. "It is in so many ways funny."

I sat down next to her, trying not to see the humor, but if it was anyone else, I would have been laughing too. "I must be the only guy complaining about too much sex, huh?"

"Welcome to the 'God, sex again?' club. Most of the girls around here are in it. We have T-shirts and everything."

I chuckled and all my anger drained away. "It's not that I don't like sex," I mused. "I just need a break now and then."

Jennifer began to giggle all over again. I nudged her, and she tried to sober up. "Okay, okay. I can do this," she told herself. "Have you tried talking to him?"

I hadn't, but I had a good reason for that.

"You know how Kyle is," I began to explain. "He doesn't take criticism well. If I say something, he'll overthink it to death, and by the time he's done, we won't even kiss anymore. I need a way to bring it up without him thinking I'm saying everything he does is wrong."

She thought about it for a moment and then nodded. "Yeah, I can see him doing that."

"Trust me, he will," I added, not bringing up the two-day bout of silence that came from me saying I didn't understand his cowboys in space TV show. I just didn't understand what it was about. Kyle took it to mean I hated everything he liked, including movies and television shows and, it turned out, even kissing. I finally had to watch a few episodes on Netflix before he would let it go.

I still don't understand what the hell that show is about.

"Well, you can always say you have a headache," she said, giving me a grin. "Worked for women for ages now." I gave her a not-laughing stare. "Okay, well, you can't use the 'time of the month' excuse, which means you're left with faking a disease or telling him the truth. Or you can just get used to constant sex."

"Man, I never thought I would be bitching about too much sex," I complained, lying back on the bench.

"Have you tried not being so hot?" she asked sarcastically. "Because it's hard for us mere mortals to resist."

"I hate you," I said, looking up at the sky.

"Tell me something I don't know." She smiled back. "Talk to him," she said, standing up. "Kyle is a smart guy. He can be reasoned with."

As she began to walk away, I called out, "You should try dating him for a week, then. You'll have a different opinion."

"And apparently a sore ass," she yelled back.

"I hate her," I mumbled to myself as I closed my eyes.

AT LUNCH there was no way I was going to bring anything negative up to Kyle.

He had three books open on the music hall steps, and he was scribbling notes on index cards in what I hoped was some kind of code, because if not, Kyle had suffered a stroke and could no longer write actual English. He had barely said three words to anyone, and before going back to his books, he finished in one gulp the Pepsi I had brought him. The only response I heard was a small burp.

"Why is he crazy?" Sammy asked me after a few minutes of this.

"He's worried about the SAT tomorrow," I explained, trying not to sigh as I said it.

Both Jennifer and Sammy seemed to ponder my words for a second. "You haven't taken the SAT yet?" Jennifer asked Kyle.

"He's taken it three times," I answered for him, since he was still hip-deep in the rabbit hole that was his brain. "This will make number four."

Sammy looked shocked. "He failed the SAT three times?"

Again I struggled at trying to keep the annoyance out of my voice. "No, he has scored a 1475 three times and thinks he can do better."

"It was 1473," Kyle said, not looking up. "I want a 1500 at least."

Both girls looked at me and asked me silently if he was kidding. I shook my head, indicating Kyle was so far from kidding that he was bordering on crazy.

"What's a perfect score?" Jennifer asked.

"A 1600," Kyle answered as he scribbled something else down.

"Well, now my 1310 feels real stupid," she said, taking a bite of her sandwich.

"You got a 1310?" Sammy asked. "I liked you better when I just thought you were a pretty, mean girl."

Jennifer gave her a wide smile and looked at me. "What did you score?"

"A solid 1280," I said, not ashamed at all. "More than enough for a sports scholarship."

Sammy finished her Coke. "Okay, now I don't feel that dumb."

I flipped her off, and we both laughed.

"Kyle," Jennifer asked, drawing nearer to him. "You do know your score is great, right?"

He stopped and looked over at her. "Great isn't enough. I need perfect. I need outstanding. I need to have the best SAT score in the school if I even have a chance of my colleges looking at me. Minus starting up the alliance, I have zero extracurricular activities, and I would need Hillary Clinton to write me a recommendation to make a difference, and I don't know Hillary Clinton. Do you?" She shook her head. "Then I need a better score."

And he went back to his studying.

Jennifer raised both eyebrows and backed away from him. I could see in her face she now understood part of my problem. We got up to throw our trash away, and she pulled me closer. "Okay, forget everything I said before. Don't say a word to him. In fact, new plan. Just put out and enjoy it until the SATs are over, because that boy is one bad day away from snapping."

I tossed our trash. "Tell me about it. I mean, his score is insane. I can't figure out why he is in such a panic."

Jennifer looked over at him and sighed. "Brad, Foster has been a life sentence to him so far. Those SATs are his only chance at parole. Let him be a little crazy. He's earned it."

I nodded, as I knew she was right. "I just wish I could get it across to him that he doesn't need to worry."

Jennifer paused. "He does have to worry, Brad." I gave her a confused look. "Most letters of recommendation come from the teachers. One word from Mr. Raymond and they'll say they never had him as a student. It wouldn't matter if he was Stephen Hawking—no school would touch him."

I had no idea who she was talking about, but I understood everything else she said. "Raymond wouldn't do that, would he?" Jennifer gave me a look, and I sighed. "Yeah, he would."

The bell rang. "You're going to be late," I called out.

Kyle scrambled to pick up his papers in one huge rush.

"I'm gonna go help him," I said, jogging over to him.

She may have thought I was talking about his books, but I meant more. Way more.

THE NEXT day when I came to pick him up, he looked like he hadn't slept a wink.

"Please tell me you closed your eyes," I said as he got into the car.

He tossed his backpack in the back seat. "I passed out around four, I think. That was the last time I saw." He sounded like a robot as he buckled himself in.

"What time is the test?" I asked him.

"Third period," he answered. He looked forward like he was in a daze.

"Then let's go by Nancy's, eat some, and get about a gallon of coffee in you. Because if you pass out during the test, I'm pretty sure that won't improve your grade."

He looked like he wanted to complain, but once I brought up that his grade wouldn't improve, he couldn't argue. A sure sign he was tired, because if he was awake, he could have found a dozen ways around that excuse. "Fine, sounds good" was all he said.

His agreeing saved me the trouble of kidnapping him and making him eat something.

We got a table and ordered a ton of food. I looked around for Gayle, but she wasn't working—that was a first for me. When I looked back, Kyle had slipped his index cards out of his hoodie. I reached over and took them from his hands.

"Hey, I need—" he began to protest.

"You need to turn your brain off and relax for five minutes," I said, putting the cards in my pocket. "You ever see *Bring It On*?" He shook his head. "Well, neither did I, but I heard there was a scene where they got to finals, and they were hearing some girls out on the lawn practicing. One of the girls opened the window and screamed out at them, 'If you don't have it yet, you don't have it!'"

He looked at me blankly.

"Kyle, there is nothing you are going to learn in the next hour that you don't already know. Just relax and enjoy breakfast, okay?"

He nodded and took a sip of his coffee and then looked up at me. "If you didn't see the movie, how do you know what they said?"

I looked over to see if our food was ready. "Drink your coffee," I told him.

I WALKED him to the student union for the test.

"Okay, you got this," I told him, rubbing his shoulders. They felt like they were carved out of rock, he was so tense. "Relax, you are Kyle Stilleno. You own this test. I have complete faith in your superheroic brain."

He turned around and smiled. "You do?"

"Hey, only one of us can look this good," I said, gesturing around my face.

"Ah," he said, grinning back. "The moneymaker, if I remember. And how much money has it made you now?"

I leaned over and kissed the tip of his nose. "It scored me a superhero boyfriend, so I'm ahead in the game."

He blushed and kissed me back. "You'll be here when I get out?"

I cocked my head. "I got a game today, remember?" From the look on his face, he didn't. "I won't be back until tonight."

"I am a horrible boyfriend," he said, sounding upset. "All I've been stressing over is my test, and you have a winning streak—"

"And you have a test," I said, putting a finger over his lips. "Go kick its ass, and I'll call you when I get home."

He nodded as the guy announced last call for the SAT.

Kyle dashed into the room, turning once he was inside and giving me a small wave.

I did not think it was possible to love him more than I did at that moment.

WE WERE on the bus to Archer City when Josh came and sat next to me.

"You seem out of it," he said once I pulled my earbuds out.

"I am," I admitted. "Kyle is taking his SATs, and I'm nervous for him."

"You're worried for him?" he asked me with a grin. "Dude, I'd be worried for everyone else at the school who has to put their score up against his. Talk about score envy."

I shrugged. "He has to be the best at what he tries to do or he loses his mind."

Josh pulled out a can of chew and offered me a pinch. I tried not to make a face as I declined. "Yeah, I can see that in both of you," he said, spitting into an empty Coke can.

That brought me up short. "Both of us?"

He nodded as he watched the countryside pass by our window. "You guys aren't, like, superachievers in everything, but what you guys set out to do, you all have to be the best at." He looked me in the eyes. "It's admirable."

I was kind of stunned. No one had ever said anything I did was admirable before. "Thanks, dude" was all I could respond with.

He nodded and went back to looking out the window.

I checked the time on my phone; the test was still going on, and they automatically failed anyone who had their phone out. I sighed and opened up my binder, going over for the hundredth time the cheat sheet we had for Archer's players. Baseball was the only thing that could take my mind off Kyle, and even then just barely.

THE GAME passed in my mind as a blur.

It felt like one minute I was getting off the bus to stretch and the next the guys were rushing out of the dugout to celebrate another win. My mind began to unfocus like it did every time we finished a game. My body let out a huge breath I didn't even know I was holding, and I laughed as we ended up falling on our asses as more guys ran and tried to hug each other. It took almost five minutes for everyone to untangle from one another and regain some composure. At first, the crowd didn't seem too taken with our win, but I couldn't blame them. If someone came to our school and kicked our butt this bad and then spent five minutes cheering on our field about it, I would be pissed too.

But they could get over it. I saw Coach Gunn walking onto the field and knew our celebration was about to be over.

"You all want a penalty for showboating?" he asked in an angry tone. "Because if you idiots don't get off the field, that's what you're going to get."

I wasn't sure what kind of penalty we could get once the game was over, but I didn't want to know.

"Okay, come on, guys," I said, getting the team's attention. "We can finish this on the bus." There was another roar from my guys before they hustled toward the locker room. Gunn was standing there looking at me, and I felt like I had been caught coming in after curfew. "Sorry about that, Coach. We're just happy."

"I don't care about that," he said absently. "Come with me."

As with every other time I have heard those words, my stomach felt like I was about to puke, and all I wanted to do was run. Instead, I nodded and pulled my cap down lower so the fear in my eyes wouldn't show. The crowd was mostly gone now; the only people left were talking to the other team's players and shooting me dirty looks as I followed Coach Gunn toward the stands.

I wanted to ask him what this was all about, but to be honest, I was too afraid of the answer, so instead I just walked.

There was an older man sitting near the third baseline. He had a blue windbreaker on over a dark-red polo shirt. He had an iPad in his hand and looked like he was typing something on the screen when we walked up.

"Frank," Gunn said to the man, trying to get his attention. The man held up one finger and intently pushed the screen a few times. I had never seen anyone in the world tell Coach Gunn to wait with just a gesture, but for this guy he didn't seem to mind.

I could hear cheering coming from the device—it sounded like part of the game. He pushed the screen and the noise stopped. "Got it," he said, looking up at us. "Sorry, but I barely know how to work this thing as it is. Sometimes I feel like I'm fifteen, sitting in my dad's car, just knowing it's too much machine for me." He looked at me, and I felt like he was looking right through me for a moment. "And you're Brad, right?"

I nodded.

Coach Gunn looked over to me. "Take off your damn cap," he growled. "Show some respect."

I yanked the offending article off my head so fast I might have taken some hair with me. "Sorry," I mumbled.

Frank smiled. "It's okay, I know how it is. Sometimes you forget you're even wearing it." That made me smile, since I had walked into class wearing a cap so many times that most teachers didn't even bother to tell me to take it off anymore. "So, good game?"

He was asking it as a question, but I had the feeling he already knew how the game went and wanted my opinion. I looked at Coach, and he nodded but said nothing. I took that as my go-ahead. "We got lucky in the fifth inning—their shortstop was sleeping and didn't set up the double play. If he had, we would have been tied until the eighth, which might have changed the game completely."

The man cocked his head with a bemused smile, and I felt like he found my answer funny.

"How would you have it changed it?" he asked.

"By the eighth inning they had already given up because of our lead. If it was tied, they would have fought harder and might have gotten lucky."

"Lucky? So you don't think they had the skill to beat you guys?" Again I felt like he found all this hilarious.

"No, they aren't as good. Their pitcher is the only guy out there who had game, and he killed his arm trying to move us off the plate. By the sixth he was done. I would have taken him out then. Their right fielder shouldn't even be out there with that throw, and I think this was the third base guy's first game, because he didn't understand the signs the coach was giving him." It wasn't the nice thing to say about another team, but it was the truth.

He looked at Coach Gunn and chuckled. "You were right" was all he said.

"I usually am," he said back.

"And your game?" Frank asked me, and I could tell this was another test.

"I fell for the pitcher's curve in the first, but I had it by my second time at bat. And there was no way I could have got that homer in the eighth off a fresh pitcher." I had a much longer list of what I had done wrong, but I was pretty sure that was all someone could see from the stands.

"You almost ate dirt rounding third in the fifth," he commented, arching an eyebrow.

Fuck.

"Yeah, I was looking to see if Bart was going to make second and lost my footing." Damn, was this guy watching me the whole game?

"Fair enough," he said, looking back at the iPad. "You know what your best moment of the night was?"

"The homer in the eighth?" I guessed.

He shook his head. "No, you had the game won by then. It was this." He turned the iPad around, and sure enough, it was a video of the game. It was a paused image of me standing at the dugout, watching Josh get ready to go to bat. I remembered the moment because it was when I told him that the pitcher was losing his arm, and he should take a step back from the plate so when he tried his fastball, Josh could tee off on it. From the third baseline, it wasn't easy to tell what I was saying, but somehow this guy had figured it out, which was freaking weird. "You told him how to hit it, didn't you?"

"Josh is a good player," I said neutrally.

"Didn't say he wasn't, but he crowds the plate, and every pitch before that moment, he struck out. You told him how to hit it, didn't you?"

"I just gave him a pointer."

He laughed and looked at the coach. "I know guys who would have claimed he taught the other guy how to walk and talk, much less hit the ball." He looked at me. "The second Josh hit that ball, the pitcher knew he was tired, and from that moment on, he was already beaten. You broke his confidence a good two or three innings before he would have on his own." He closed the video. "That changed the game."

"Josh hit the ball by himself," I added quickly, not wanting to take anything away from the other guy.

"No, he was just holding the bat," Frank said, putting the iPad in a satchel. "You hit that ball and in doing so, won the game." He stood up and put his hand out to Coach Gunn. "Tell me he is just being modest."

Gunn shook it back. "Nope. That's pure Graymark there."

Frank patted his windbreaker for something as he told me, "Well, Brad, you played a good game, and you're right. The other team gave up too quickly, which allowed you guys to take it from them. And I agree they could have gotten lucky and caught up with you, but I doubt they could have beaten you."

"Thank you?" I said, confused.

He checked his pants pockets and nodded in response to my words. "Wasn't a compliment, just the truth, but you're welcome. Dammit, I swear I brought my cards."

I looked at Coach Gunn, who shook his head slightly and gave me a "just wait it out" look. So I said nothing and stood there.

"You're good," Frank said, putting his satchel down on the bench. "With some work, maybe great, but I'm not sure yet." I opened my mouth to respond, but Coach put his hand on my shoulder to stop me. "But I am sure of one thing." He unzipped his windbreaker, and the dark-red polo wasn't dark red at all. It was maroon.

Aggie maroon.

As in Texas A&M.

As in the only college I really wanted to play for.

Frank pulled out a card and handed it over to me. It had an A&M symbol in the middle with his name on it. Under that was Baseball Recruitment Agent. "Keep up the work, don't let the streak shake you, and if anyone else comes to you before we do about college, call me first."

I took the card and held it in shock. I was pretty sure this would be the same way I'd react if someone had handed me a golden ticket from Willy Wonka.

"Thanks again for the heads-up, Coach. Good luck on the season." He picked up his satchel and walked off, leaving me and Coach Gunn standing there, silent.

Gunn didn't say anything for a while before he shook his head and began to walk toward the locker room. "If you're not on the bus when we're ready, I will leave you here."

I waited until he was at the dugout before I jumped up and screamed as loud as I could. I even threw my cap up in the air for effect. It was easily one of the happiest moments of my life.

So, of course, there was no way it could last.

IT WAS almost midnight by the time the bus pulled into the parking lot.

Most everyone had nodded off after the half hour of celebratory bragging that seemed to follow every win. Once things had gotten quiet, I tried to call Kyle but got his voicemail. I left him a message and then waited for a reply. After thirty minutes of that, I tried calling again. Finally I tried texting him, asking where he was. About five minutes later, I got back a message.

WE NEED TO TALK WHEN YOU GET BACK.

No matter how happy I had been seconds before, it was nothing in comparison to how worried I was now.

I have always been a worrier. From the day I could talk, I always thought I was in some kind of trouble with someone. At first, even though I had done nothing to think that, I would be petrified that I had screwed up somehow and was going to get punished for it. I never knew what would set my dad off, and my mom usually only cared when she could use it as a weapon against him.

I'm glad things aren't like that now, but the effects still linger.

By the time I hit junior high, I had given up trying to do the right thing. If I was going to get in trouble no matter what I did, I might as well do something to earn it. And though I covered it with a smirk and a nonchalant attitude, my stomach was still a wreck leading up to the moment I got caught.

So even though I couldn't figure out what might have happened, I was too upset to sleep as we hurtled toward home. Part of me wanted to get there and find out what was wrong; the other part wished we'd never get back to Foster.

The bus parked outside the locker room, and Coach Gunn told us we had played a good game. That was high praise coming from the man, who began walking our equipment into the building with the assistant coaches. I shouldered my bag and headed to my car, wondering if I was supposed to go over to Kyle's house or try to call again.

I was so preoccupied I didn't even notice him by the driver-side door, waiting.

Now, I had seen Kyle upset before. I had seen him indignant, defiant, and once, outraged. But until that moment, I hadn't even caught on that I had never seen him truly angry. At least not at me. His arms were crossed, and he glared at me like I had killed his cat or something.

"Hey," I said, surprised to see him. "What are you doing out here so late?"

He came off the car and began waving his finger at me as he asked, "Did you tell Jennifer about our sex life?"

My mouth moved way faster than my brain. "No!"

As I said it, I knew it was the wrong thing.

"So you didn't tell her you disliked having sex with me?" The tone of his voice was just different tones of rage and hurt.

"I didn't say I disliked it," I countered.

"So then you did talk to her about our sex life?" he asked again.

Stupid mouth.

"I was just telling her that—" I began to explain.

"Why would you tell her anything?" he roared, cutting me off. "What we do in the bedroom is between us only. Why would you think that was okay? Wait, let me guess. You didn't think." His face was red, and he looked like he was about to cry.

I knew how he felt.

"Do you know how embarrassed I was?" he asked, looking like he was fighting the urge to hit me. "How horrible it is to find out your boyfriend doesn't like sex with you from someone else?"

"I didn't say I didn't like it!" I broke in. "I just said I was sore."

"Why would you say that to her?" His voice echoed across the parking lot.

I looked over and saw a few of the guys looking at us as they got into their cars.

"Can we talk about this somewhere else?" I asked him quietly.

"Why? You don't want them to know?" he screamed at me. "You would hate to have your private business told to others without your permission?" I saw him look over at the other guys, and I could see the hurt in his eyes.

"Please don't," I implored him. "I know I fucked up, Kyle, but please… don't do this."

He looked back at me, tears rolling down his face. "You know, that was exactly what I was thinking when Jennifer started to tell me. Please don't do this."

He took off his ring and tossed it to me. I caught it as my body went numb with shock.

"Well, now you don't have to be sore at all." He turned around and walked away.

It was the second time this ring had been given back to me. And as with the first time, it was all my fault.

INSTEAD OF home, I drove to Jennifer's house.

I was in luck because her dad's cruiser wasn't in the driveway, which meant he was working. I say I was lucky because I was so pissed that even if he was there, I might have pounded on the door, and most likely he would have shot me. I stormed up the walk and raised my hand to knock, but then the door opened.

She stood there with puffy eyes, obviously crying herself.

"I'm a horrible bitch and don't know when to keep my mouth shut and fucked it up for you." She walked back into the house. "If you have anything you want to add to that, come in."

Turns out I did.

"How could you?" I roared, slamming the door. "How could you even bring it up to him?"

She spun around and yelled back. "I thought you had talked to him." She paused and took a breath. "By the time I realized you hadn't, it was too late. I didn't think he would get that crazy."

"He's crazy," I said back. "I told you he was crazy. In fact, you told me before I left not to say anything because he was crazy."

She swallowed a sob. "I know, and I fucked up." She grabbed a tissue and wiped her nose. "How bad is it?"

I reached in my pocket and pulled out my ring. "The only thing missing was a bucket of Coke dumped over my head."

Her eyes were wide as she realized we had broken up.

"I can fix this," she said urgently. "We can fix this."

I collapsed into a chair and sighed. "I hope you have a plan, because minus a time machine, I don't see how."

THE NEXT day was Friday, which meant if I didn't do something to change Kyle's mind now, I would be stuck with him ignoring me the whole weekend.

I sat on the edge of my bed and had a feeling of déjà vu. It took me a while to realize this was how I felt the first day Kyle and I were supposed to go back to school after the kiss. My normal routine of picking up Jennifer and hanging out before class was gone, and I'd had no idea what to do. Now my routine of picking up Kyle and spending the morning with him was gone, and I felt miserable. If I had slept, I didn't remember it. All I could think of were ways to get Kyle back somehow.

The clock moved closer and closer to eight, and I knew time was running out.

I drove to school, my mind forcing my heart not to drive to Kyle's and beg him to take me back. He was upset, and me trying to change his mind about that was just going to piss him off more. I knew from experience he needed time to decompress and let his logic work through his emotions before I could even try to apologize and have it mean something.

I parked and walked toward the music hall steps, wondering if I was allowed to sit there anymore. I had no idea what the protocol for this was. I supposed I could go eat with a few guys from the team, but I didn't want to. I wanted to sit on the steps and laugh with my friends. My eyes stung as I walked toward the quad. I was terrified to see what happened next.

The steps were empty.

I was more depressed by that than I would have been if Kyle had ordered me to go away. I walked over to the steps and sat down with a sigh. It felt like the gravity had been increased by, like, 1,000 percent, and just standing was too much effort. I looked around and watched people go through their morning routine like I was a ghost. No one looked at me. No one talked to me. It was as if I wasn't even there.

"Is this what it was like for him?" I asked myself out loud.

"Talking to yourself is a sure sign you're crazy," Jennifer said, sitting down next to me. I looked over at her, and she shook her head at me. "He isn't coming to school today. He texted me so I wouldn't worry."

"What if I can't fix it?" I asked her, the tears rolling down my face.

She didn't have an answer and let me cry on her shoulder.

IT WAS the longest weekend of my life.

Normally a weekend that lasted longer than two days would be a blessing. Without Kyle, time seemed to just crawl, and the world was just a series of muted colors that I couldn't care less about. By Sunday I was so bored I actually cut the grass without being asked just so I'd have something to do. Jennifer had said she'd tried talking to him, but he avoided the topic entirely, so she'd let it drop.

Sunday night my mom knocked on my door.

"You still up?" she asked me.

I paused the movie I was watching. "Yeah, just finishing this up."

She came in and sat on the edge of my bed. "So, something is wrong." It wasn't a question.

"I screwed it up with Kyle," I told her, trying not to get drowned as the emotions came rushing back.

She gave me a sympathetic smile. "Well, I knew something had to be up because you didn't mention this." She held up an envelope.

"What's that?" I asked her, confused.

She told me, and my world stopped moving.

It was almost ten at night as I knocked on Jennifer's door.

Her dad answered after a few minutes. "Brad? Son, you have to know how late it is."

I nodded as I tried to keep calm. "I know, sir, and I wouldn't normally bother you, but I need to talk to Jennifer for just a second...."

He didn't move from the door for a long moment. Finally he arched an eyebrow and asked, "You still gay?"

The question stopped me cold for a moment. "Um, yeah. Last time I checked."

He didn't blink as he scrutinized me like I was a lab experiment. Finally he sighed and took half a step back. "Then I guess I can trust you up there for five minutes. Any longer and I will remind you I have firearms in the house."

I nodded as I flew up the stairs to her room.

I had wanted to tell Kyle, of course, but there was no way he was answering the phone from me right now. I thought about calling Josh, but since I had never once called him, it seemed like a weird thing to start on a Sunday night. I knocked on Jennifer's door. She had a robe on as she opened it slowly. "Brad? What the hell...."

I rushed in and took a deep breath. "I had to tell someone before I exploded."

She didn't close the door the whole way, obviously knowing her dad had let me up here on a pass.

"Tell someone what?"

I handed her the letter and waited for her to read it. Her face paled as she looked up at me with questioning eyes. "Is this for real?"

I nodded.

We stood there for a long time, neither one talking as we tried to figure out what came next.

Kyle

Do you know what the difference between adumbrate and sketch is?

How about evince and express?

And my personal favorite: What is the difference between fecund and fertile?

111

The difference is your entire life.

See, in one life, where you do know the difference between those words, you score near-perfect on your SATs, colleges across the country sit up and take notice, and one of them is kind enough to offer to pay your way to attend their school. You obtain a degree in something that you want to do as a career, you enter the workplace at the very least equal to if not ahead of the rest, and if you are very, very lucky, you made some contacts along the way to help you get a job. Because you have a real career, you are free to pursue a lifestyle in which you have more choices than absolutes, more free time than work, and are ensuring that you have a future so when you're old and tired, you have the luxury of not working.

In the other life, where you don't know the difference, you score a higher-than-average score on the SAT. If you're lucky, maybe one or two colleges will offer you a limited scholarship that will reduce the cost of an education but in no way ensure that you will be able to actually get a degree. You end up having to take at least one job so you can have such luxuries as food and shelter, and in the end probably end up dropping out and moving back home. You end up working at a gas station while you attend community college, and if you're lucky, you will one day be able to be an assistant manager at Better Buy. You are stuck in the same town you were born in, and it is most likely where you will die.

What a difference a couple of words make, huh?

This was what had been running through my mind the past few weeks as the final opportunities to take the SAT drew near. I had taken it three times so far, and the best I'd scored was a 1473. I know to most people that would be a great score, but I was not most people. There was no college fund put away for me, at least not anymore. If there had been such a stash of money in the past, it had long been spent by my mom to maintain our luxurious lifestyle. Since I had spent the first three years of my high school life being a social ninja, I had exactly zero extracurricular activities on my record, which was the equivalent of a death sentence for most students.

The one thing I could say I had done was blackmail the school into starting the gay-straight alliance, but since we hadn't even had our first meeting yet, it wasn't going to count for much when weighing my application against other people's. So I had no money, no fancy activities, I hadn't been active in student government, and the closest I had been to the school theater program was painting backdrops for *Our Town* the year I was forced to take drama as an elective. The only thing, and I mean only, was the fact that I had an oversized brain. Up to this point in life it hadn't helped me much, but I was hoping it could come through and pull a rabbit out of that SAT hat.

A 1473 was not a rabbit. It might have been a bouquet of flowers or maybe a dove or two, but it was not a rabbit. And I needed a big white floppy-eared bunny, or I might as well get "Resident of Foster, Texas" tattooed on my arm because it was going to be true as long as I was alive.

No one else seemed to understand how important this test was to me, but they decided to fall on the side of caution and let me be crazy in silence.

I had spent days at the library copying every question in the practice SAT books onto index cards so I could have a portable version of the test on me at all times. Then I broke the questions down into three categories. The first were the ones I knew the answers without thinking. The second were ones that seemed too easy for their own good. These included math word problems that asked dodgy questions, math equations that asked you to solve for more than one variable at the same time, and words that looked too much like other words. The last pile were the ones that were so daunting that if most people ever got that far into the test, they would just start picking random answers and hoping the urban myth about picking C was right.

These questions became my own Legion of Doom.

Every spare second I had went to going over my cards, drilling the salient facts into my brain one word at a time. Okay, so not every second, maybe every other second I used to study. The other seconds I saved up and spent with Brad. I could see in his eyes that he thought I was worrying about nothing and that my scores were more than sufficient. He was wrong, and one day, after baseball practice, I pulled out a folder and began to explain it to him.

"Look, I want to go to UC Berkeley, and their average acceptance score is 1300. That is just for them to look at you, not an automatic scholarship or anything. That is, like, almost 40 percent higher than a normal college, and their acceptance rate is 14.8 percent. Fourteen point eight!" He still didn't seem to get it. "That means even if you have over a 1300 and your application is perfect, out of every one hundred applications they get, only fifteen people get in."

"Yeah, but you're different," he said, giving me the smile that could melt ice at twenty feet. "They'll take one look at you and say 'We need to get that guy in here!' You know that, right?"

It was sweet he thought getting into college worked like that.

"You do know they aren't even going to look at me period if I don't have a much higher score than the one I have now, right?"

He just laughed and pulled me across the bed toward him. "You worry too much."

I let him draw me into a hug because I needed one. "UC Berkeley costs on average sixty-five thousand dollars a year for a nonresident. Four years is over two hundred fifty grand. I have to worry because I don't have that much money."

He twisted one of the drawstrings of my hoodie around his finger as he teased, "Have you thought of doing porn? That's easy money."

I nudged him as he laughed out loud. "You gonna do it with me?" I teased back. "Because I refuse to have you pimp me out on the side."

"Aw, but I wanted a huge purple hat and a cane!" I turned around and pounced on him as he burst out in hysterics. "I could be all 'Bitch, where's my money!' and I could get a big ole boat of a car to cruise in."

"You'd do that to me?" I asked him, pinning him to the bed.

"Nope," he said with a bright smile. "I don't share you with anyone. No matter how much money they offer."

I leaned down to kiss him. "Good answer."

Just as our lips were about to touch, he added, "And I didn't even need a stack of cards to come up with it."

I pulled back and looked down at the smirk on his face. "You are so dead," I warned him.

Turns out I didn't get any studying done that night at all.

THE NEXT day I spent studying to make up for lost time.

I had less than twenty-four hours before the test, and I needed to cram as much as I could in that time. Thankfully I was caught up in my classes, so I could afford spending a period or two going through my cards over and over. At lunch I spread out my books to go over some of the hardest questions and made notes on my cards to help me out. Brad put a Pepsi down next to me, which I downed in one gulp because I needed the caffeine in a serious way. If there was an intravenous way to ingest caffeine, I would have long ago hooked one up to my arm and forgone sleep altogether.

They were talking about me and my obsession with getting a better score. I kept one ear listening as I tried to look up if "upbraid" meant what I thought it did.

I heard Brad sigh as he said, "No, he has scored a 1475 three times and thinks he can do better."

"I got a 1473," I said, not looking up. "I want a 1500 at least."

I found "upbraid" and cursed whoever came up with such an incredibly lame word as Jennifer asked me, "What's a perfect score?"

"Max is 1600," I answered as I wrote a definition on my card.

They kept talking about their scores, which was when I zoned them out. I shouldn't have let Brad lure me away from studying last night. I was going to have to go over the math all night, and that meant little to no sleep.

"Kyle," Jennifer asked, drawing nearer to me, "you do know your score is great, right?"

I might have answered her in a more hospitable way if I wasn't so damn tired of explaining this to everyone around me. "Great isn't enough. I need perfect. I need outstanding. I need to have the best SAT score in the school if I even have a chance of my colleges looking at me. Minus starting up the alliance, I have zero extracurricular activities, and I would need Hillary Clinton to write me a recommendation to make a difference, and I don't know Hillary Clinton. Do you?" She shook her head. "Then I need a better score."

I went back to my notes, hoping it was the last question I got on this for a while.

I'm not sure how much time had passed, but when Brad called my name to get my attention, most of the quad was empty. I looked over at him, and he had a worried look on his face. "The second bell just went off. You're going to be late."

"Fuck." I began to scoop my books up and throw them into my bag. "If they insist on making our entire life depend on this fucking test, the least they could do is give us time off to study for it." The cards fell out of my hands, and I let out a cry as they fell to the earth, their order forever lost as they hit the steps and went everywhere. It was like looking at my future crumble into ashes as the wind snatched a few of them and swirled them across the quad.

I dropped my bag and went racing after them. It was a metaphor for my entire life in one idiotic gesture.

I began to scoop up the cards on the steps when the wind gusted again and took more of them into the air. The cards flew higher and higher, out of my reach, and I gave up. The imagery of my life literally blowing away from me caused something to short circuit in my brain. I made the same sob a drowning cat would and sank to the steps. Who was I kidding? I was never going to get out of this town. This place was worse than the Matrix, because if I was in a computer-generated reality, at least I'd have cool superpowers or something. Instead, I was a nobody teenager in a nowhere town doing nothing.

"I got as many as I could." I looked up and saw Brad, out of breath, with a handful of my cards. His face was flushed, and he had the same smile I would imagine on a really happy golden retriever if they had human faces and liked chasing things as much as Brad did. "Don't be sad anymore. Please?"

He was the best thing that had ever happened in my life.

"You don't give up, do you?" I asked him, taking the cards.

He sat down on the steps and leaned close to me. "I refuse to give up on two things. Baseball and you." He looked over, and I saw the green in his eyes flicker as his bangs fell into his face. "And if you want to know a secret, baseball is a distant second."

I was late to fifth period. I didn't care.

AFTER SCHOOL, I met him by the locker room like I always did before practice.

"You wanna go somewhere when I'm done?" he asked, nodding to one of the guys as they walked past us.

"I can't." I saw the disappointment in his face, and I hurriedly added, "I only have tonight to study, and all I am going to be doing is freaking out over this stupid test, and I don't want to put you through that because I will be—"

He shut me up by kissing me. My whole train of thought got derailed, and he said, "I'll pick you up for school tomorrow, then."

"You're not mad?" I asked, trying to regain my equilibrium.

"You can make it up to me." He had an evil look on his face, and I understood exactly what he meant.

"You are going to want a back rub," I said rather than asked.

"No," he answered, looking innocently at me. "I am going to want a lot of back rubs."

That made me laugh. "Okay, fine, go play ball and stuff. I'll text you if I get a break in studying."

"Text me even if you don't take a break."

I nodded, and he jogged into the locker room. I had a long night ahead of me, and none of it was going to be fun.

I WAS four hours into Trig when I let out a soul-crippling sigh.

"I cannot do this," I said to myself.

"So then quit," Myself said back.

"Fuck." I put my head down. "I can't be this tired."

The personification of everything negative and self-loathing in my mind stood up from the seat in the corner of my room and began to walk leisurely around my bed. "Bitch, you are as tired as tired can get. You're like Sleeping Beauty up in this hood. You're…."

"I get it," I barked, cutting it off. "What do you want?"

Billy spun around and looked at me and said,

"Hold up, you just gonna let that one slide?"

"What?"

"Calling me Billy and not explaining it to the people at home?"

Oh, for Christ's sake…. I call it Billy because it looks like Billy Porter. Happy?

"No, I'm stuck in Texas hell with you. I am nowhere near happy."

"You were saying?"

Billy thought for a moment. "Line?"

Sighing, I repeated myself, "What do you want?"

"Right," it said, getting back into character. "No, my dear boy, it is what do *you* want?"

I swear to God I knew it was going to say that.

"Well, of course you did!" it snapped. "I am you! Don't make this anymore meta than it needs to be. Just answer the question. What do you want?"

"I'd like to stop having long, drawn-out conversations with myself for one."

"Not gonna happen, next?"

"I want to pass this test."

"And nope, you've passed this test. Three times."

"I want to ace this test," I amended.

"And bullshit, you honestly don't care about the test."

I glared at it for a long time. "I care about the test insomuch that it gets me out of Foster."

"And there it is, the truth."

Sighing, I threw my hands up. "Fine! I want to get out of Foster, but I need the test to do that."

"And we've gotten into the talent portion of the competition where Kyle Stilleno will be dazzling us with his incredible skill at bullshitting. So Ms. Stick So Far Up My Ass Splinters Come Out When I Hiccup, tell us how that test is your only way out of this town."

I sat there staring at it.

"Explain to our studio audience how there are laser grid towers set up all around the city limits and that the only way to move past them is to show them a scholarship. Describe the bullshit *Fifth Element* knockoff uniforms the armed guards wear to keep any noncollege attendees from leaving. And while you're at it, explain to them how the best job you think you can manage is assistant manager at Better Buy. Because I am sure there are a lot of people who do not possess a photographic memory and haven't memorized the entirety of Wikipedia, and they are asking themselves, if that nerd can't score a decent job, then what chance do I have."

It turned around now and held out a thin, wand-like microphone. "We're waiting."

"There aren't a lot of decent jobs around here."

Billy snapped the microphone in half. "Then move, you fucking idiot!"

"Um, what?"

Billy looked just as confused. "She was looking kind of dumb.... Oh, for fuck's sake, wake up so I can stop singing this horrible song!"

I opened my eyes suddenly, realizing my alarm was playing Smash Mouth. I had fallen asleep in the middle of my cards and books, which got even more messed up as I tried to get up. I kept seeing something out of the corner of my eye, but whenever I tried to look at it, it'd move with me. It took me a few seconds of waking to realize I had an index card plastered to my cheek.

I silently thanked God Billy hadn't been around to capture that moment of genius.

My phone beeped, and I saw I had missed two calls and five texts from Brad, a new record even for me. I texted him back that I was getting in the shower and began to gather all the supplies up off my bed.

I looked down to see Brad's reply text: *While you're in the shower send pics!*

That made me laugh as I stuffed my books and folders into my backpack. My cards were shuffled back into a neat pile, and I took a second to raise my arms over my head and stretch the last dregs of slumber out of my system. For a moment, my whole body felt like it was energized as I extended everything from my fingers to my toes....

And then fell face-first onto the bed as the exhaustion I was trying to con myself out of made even keeping my eyes open a chore. I swore I closed my eyes for only a second, but the next thing I knew, my mom was knocking on my door, telling me Brad was outside waiting for me. I looked at my phone, and sure enough over thirty minutes had passed, and I was instantly late.

"Crap," I said, jumping to my feet, shucking off my shirt. "I'll be right there."

My mom laughed. "I'm sure he'll wait for you."

I didn't even answer as she closed the door. I broke a new speed record changing my clothes and threw some water on my hair before I raced out the door. I opened the passenger-side door and tossed my backpack in the back seat. "Please tell me you closed your eyes," he said.

I was barely aware I was fastening the seat belt as I answered him. "I passed out around four, I think. That was the last time I saw."

"What time is the test?" he asked me.

My eyes burned, and all I wanted to do was close them for hours. "Third period."

"Then let's go by Nancy's, eat some, and get about a gallon of coffee in you. Because if you pass out during the test, I'm pretty sure that won't improve your grade."

I opened my mouth to argue but decided I didn't have the energy to bother. "Fine, sounds good."

I honestly think I might have dozed off as we headed down East Avenue toward First Street. The car stopping woke me up, and I saw Brad looking at me with worried eyes.

We found a booth, and Brad ordered us enough food to feed a small country. Sitting still for more than thirty seconds without doing anything felt wrong, and I pulled my cards out of my hoodie. I didn't even get a chance to arrange them before Brad reached over and took them out of my hands.

"Hey, I need those," I protested.

He gave me a serious look from across the table. "You need to turn your brain off and relax for five minutes. You ever see *Bring It On*?" The question was so out of the blue, all I could do was shake my head. "Well, neither did I, but I heard there was a scene where they got to finals, and they were hearing some girls out on the lawn practicing. One of the girls opened the window and screamed out at them, 'If you don't have it yet, you don't have it!'"

While he was talking, my brain started to drift off.

Brad likes the movie *Bring It On*, which is eighty-six minutes long. If Brad has three and a half hours of free time, how many times can Brad watch *Bring It On* before his boyfriend pukes all over him?

I'm not sure if he noticed my space out, but he explained, "Kyle, there is nothing you are going to learn in the next hour that you don't already know. Just relax and enjoy breakfast, okay?"

I took a sip of water, desperately looking around for some coffee or iced tea. And then something clicked in my mind. "If you didn't see the movie, how do you know what they said?"

Now he looked away and told me, "Drink your water."

His reaction made me laugh, and I reached across the table and grabbed his hand. "Thank you," I told him, which got him to look back at me. "I love you." His face broke into a wide grin. "Even if you are like a thousand times gayer than me now for admitting that."

He pulled his hand back and flipped me off.

As I laughed, I felt some of the exhaustion fade away. My day had just started.

I MUST have drank half a pitcher of iced tea with a pound of sugar to wake me up.

By the time we got to the student union, my sugar rush was just starting to kick in. I saw the proctor standing at the door, and my stomach suddenly clenched in anxiety.

Brad was behind me and put his hands on my shoulders and rubbed. "Okay, you got this. You are Kyle Stilleno. You own this test. I have complete faith in your superheroic brain."

I turned around a little, surprised. "You do?"

"Hey, only one of us can look this good," he said, giving me his Zoolander impression.

"Ah," I said, grinning back. "The moneymaker, if I remember. And how much money has it made you now?"

He leaned in and kissed the tip of my nose. "It scored me a superhero boyfriend, so I'm ahead in the game."

I felt my entire body react and forced myself to ask, "You'll be here when I get out?"

"I got a game today, remember?" Oh fuck. I had been so worried about this test, I had forgotten his schedule. They were away against... *oh, come on, Kyle*.... Archer! He had to see the confusion in my face, because he added, "I won't be back until tonight."

I felt like an ass. Here he had been busting his ass to make sure I was all right, and I completely forgot about his thing. "I am a horrible boyfriend. All I've been stressing over is my test, and you have a winning streak...."

"And you have a test," he said, putting a finger over my lips. "Go kick its ass, and I'll call you when I get home."

The proctor announced last call for the SAT.

I rushed in the door and turned around to give him a small wave. He was the last thing I saw as they closed the doors.

"Okay, Stilleno," I said to myself. "You have him convinced you're a genius. Time to prove it."

"Oh goody," Billy said from the empty seat across from me. It had on a pair of thick black glasses, complete with a piece of tape in the center, short-sleeved white button-up shirt, pocket protector and all. "More tests."

I ignored it and pulled my calculator and pencils out of my backpack. We were told to open our tests and start. I was blurring through the first ones when Billy remarked, "You forgot a problem."

I glanced over my answer sheet and shook my head.

"Oh, yes you did," it said, trailing off.

I checked a second time and then it hit me.

I had forgotten a problem, but not the test. There was a small lake's worth of tea in my bladder and it was moving through me like a Karen looking for the manager. I was most likely going to piss myself right here in the middle of the test, but if I got up, I would lose valuable time.

"Told ya," Billy said, snapping its gum.

I scribbled faster as I crossed my legs under the desk.

By the time the test let out, it was lunch, and I was exhausted.

I know there is no way I could do what Brad does at practice every day, but I never let that get to me because I know he couldn't do what I just did in that test. Though I had no empirical evidence to prove otherwise, I just knew in my bones I had crushed that test. There was nothing I came across that was foreign or unsolvable, and my response time was way faster than the last times I took it. There was no way to be objective about it, but I just knew this was the last time I was going to see that test.

Sammy was waiting on the steps when I got out. She had a can of Pepsi waiting for me as she cheered for me as a conquering hero. Normally someone making this big a scene in public would have made me feel self-conscious, but this time it didn't. I may not have thrown a ball farther or ran faster than someone else, but I damn well was smarter than a whole bunch of people. And that deserved a pat on the back.

And an entire Pepsi to keep me standing.

"So how did you do?" Sammy asked me as I sat down.

I wanted to scream at the top of my lungs that I fucking killed it but instead went with a more muted "I think I did all right."

She rolled her eyes at me. "You did all right the last three times. You think you got what you were after?"

I smiled and nodded.

"I knew you could do it," Sammy said, giving me a hug. "Hey, I need to ask you something—"

Before she could, Jennifer stomped up the steps and plopped down next to us. The dark cloud of her bad mood surrounded her like stink lines on Pigpen.

"Hey, I got you a Pepsi," Sammy said to her, handing her a can.

She mumbled a thanks and drank half of it in one gulp.

"Thirsty much?" Sammy asked under her breath.

Jennifer looked pissed, but I wasn't sure about what. "How was the test?" she asked me after a few seconds.

I sighed. "I don't know. Between having to go to the bathroom every ten minutes and feeling guilty, I barely noticed the test."

"Guilty?" she asked with a small smile. "Guilty about what?"

"I am a horrendous boyfriend, and I need to make it up to Brad."

I expected her to ask about what, but instead she just shook her head and said, "Don't worry about it. He's more tired than sore. It's not like he isn't enjoying it."

I paused as her words penetrated my exhausted mind. "Enjoying what?"

"The sex," she answered, confused. "He told me that he was worn out and didn't know how to bring it up to you. I'm impressed that he did."

I could feel my face redden as my heart began to jackhammer under my skin. "Brad said what now?"

She fumbled and coughed. It was obvious that she was trying to find something else to say. Finally she just asked in the fakest tone I have ever heard, "I mean… what were you guys arguing about?"

I was tired as hell, so it took longer than it normally would have, but I got there. "Brad is enjoying what?" I asked, as pissed as I had ever been at someone besides my mom.

"Nothing," she said lamely. "So, how was the test?"

"You already asked that," Sammy said from behind me.

I felt what little patience I had fade with each word I spoke. "What did Brad tell you?"

She began to blab the same way you saw people in cop movies do when they were confronted with their lies. "He said he was worn out because you guys have been having sex all the time lately and that with the practice and the stress over the test he was just beat. But he said he was enjoying it."

Of course he told her. Why wouldn't he? Sure, it was just our sex life—why not tell anyone he could find about it? I wanted to scream, but of course, what good would that do? Brad wasn't here, and if he was, he'd have the same stupid look on his face Jennifer did right now.

Sammy asked her in a shocked tone, "He told you that?"

"He's my friend," Jennifer snapped back at her. "We've slept together, for God's sake. It's not like he's sharing state secrets."

I half stepped in front of Sammy, reminding Jennifer who she was actually arguing with. "He told you about our sex life? He complained to you about us having sex?"

I couldn't tell if she was mad or upset or anything. It was like a mask had slammed down over her face, making her emotions impossible to read. "He was just talking, Kyle. It's not the end of the world if your boyfriend wants to talk to someone about their life. It's just what friends do."

It was weak logic, so I decided to use it against her. "Do you like your nipples played with?"

She blinked twice and asked, "What?"

The second she hesitated, I pressed the point. "Do you like your nipples played with in bed? How important is foreplay? We're friends, so it's no big deal for you to share these things, right? Or it would be okay for Brad to tell me that stuff, right?"

I saw the hurt in her eyes, and I felt like shit. I was mad at Brad, but since she was in front of me, she got the anger.

"Ask him whatever you want, Kyle. He told me as a friend, and I am sure he didn't think he was betraying a trust." She knelt down to grab her stuff and turned to the both of us. "I have prom committee. Talk to you guys later."

I wanted to say something to her, but honestly, I had nothing but more bile in my head.

"Kyle, I am so sorry," Sammy said, putting her hand on my shoulder.

"Not as sorry as Brad is going to be."

AFTER MY last period, Jennifer pulled me aside and apologized thoroughly for even saying anything.

I tried to explain my thoughts, but after all the cramming for the test and lack of sleep, I just forgave her and said we could talk about it later. I walked home, going over in my mind what I was going to say to Brad. I couldn't just explode at him like I had at Jennifer. I mean, he deserved to get yelled at, but if I was going to make my point, I needed to use actual words instead of just volume. Half an idea formed by the time I walked into my room. I wanted to explore it, but I saw my bed and fell face-first into it.

Time ceased to exist for me for a while.

My phone woke me up around nine.

It was Brad calling, and for half a second I almost picked it up. And then I remembered. I rejected the call and let it go to voicemail. I sat there waiting for the message to end, and every second I got madder and madder. This was typical Brad through and through. His discomfort was the only thing he thought about, not the fact that I might not want our sex life shared with other people or that maybe, just maybe, if he had a problem, he should have talked to me. Nope, instead the only thing that mattered was what his problem was and how bad it was for him. The phone beeped, and I deleted the voicemail.

"For real?" Billy asked.

I ignored it and got into the shower. I still felt like shit, but better shit than when I got home.

The hot water helped wake me up, but it did nothing to affect my mood. It was like a spiral of anger that kept feeding off itself the more I thought about it.

"See, you wanna be mad, but that's not what this is," Billy said from outside the shower.

"Go away," I said, trying to banish my own thoughts.

I got out and started drying myself off.

"So you're really going to do this?" Billy asked as I walked past it and into my room.

The phone rang again, Brad calling.

Declined it and tossed it on my bed.

"This has nothing to do with him telling Jennifer anything," Billy said, standing in front of my closet door.

"Move," I said, pushing it aside and grabbing some clothes.

"Why do you even care? You were the one who told me this was a mistake."

"Um, actually that was me," my pessimism said from the other side of the room.

I shook my head and started to pull on some clothes.

"See, my objection at the time was that you were going to get hurt because of the statistical chance of a guy like Brad liking a guy like us. But as time has passed, my objections have changed," pessimism kept explaining on a white board.

"See, though Brad does like you and seems honest with his intentions, the fact that you and him are nothing alike is troublesome. You clearly know this but have resisted the urge to talk about it with him, which makes the underlying problem even worse."

"What problem?" I asked.

"The one where you two graduate and go to different colleges."

I froze as I realized we hadn't talked about college plans at all.

"Um, actually," pessimism pressed on, pushing up its glasses, "you two have talked about it, but you never really listened to him."

"I listen to him," I protested.

The whiteboard changed to a monitor, and it was an image of Brad and me in his room, pretending to study. It changed from an image to a memory in a flash.

"So, what do you want to do this weekend?" he asked me, his eyes twinkling under his ever-present baseball cap.

"Hang out, eat pizza, and then sex," I said, reaching for the cap.

"Hey!" he exclaimed, jerking back, "Watch it. That's my lucky hat!"

I took it off his head and he watched me like I was holding his baby. "What's ATM stand for?" I asked, slipping it on my head.

"What? Are you serious?" he asked me.

"Um, yeah. Is it a bank thing?"

He looked like I had called his mother a bad name.

"That hat is maroon red."

I looked at him, confused.

"Aggie red?"

More confused.

"A&M! The only college I ever wanted to play ball for," he said, taking the cap back. *"My dad bought me this freshman year, after I won us a big game. I've worn this cap ever since, hoping it can get me into the school."*

"You do know that hat has nothing to do with it, right?"

He put the hat on his head, and he went from cute to hot in seconds flat. There was something about the way that beat-up hat rested on him that made him look so jock-like that it was crazy.

"Don't knock the hat," he said, moving closer to me. *"It's gotten me this far."*

I rolled my eyes and kissed him. Who believes in lucky hats?

Pessimism stood in front of the monitor. "You want to change your answer?"

"I hate having a photographic memory," I muttered to myself.

"He wants to go to A&M, which is in College Station, which is in Texas. You are pushing yourself to go to Berkeley, which is in…."

"I know where the fuck Berkeley is!" I snapped.

"Well then, that is my objection. You two may be fine now, but come graduation, you two are heading in opposite directions."

I sat down, stunned by the revelation.

"You had to have had a plan for this, right?" Billy asked me.

"He was planning on pushing Brad away so it would be easier for them to break up," my passive-aggressive nature commented from the bed. I glared at it and it shrugged. "What? It's been in your subconscious ever since you realized you loved him."

Billy looked at me. "It has?"

I had to admit it had.

"Look, what do you want me to do? Follow him to A&M? Stay stuck in Texas for four more years? Or am I supposed to tell him to kill his dreams and find somewhere on the West Coast to play ball? That isn't fair to either of us. So yeah, I've been looking for a back door so I could break up with him and let him go find what he wants."

Billy knelt down and made eye contact with me. "Honey, what if he wants you?"

My phone rang again, and I realized I needed to stay strong and get this done. Rip the Band-Aid off instead of a slow, horrible breakup. Just cut it off and let him go.

Billy stood up and looked over at pessimism and passive-aggression. "You two bitches can talk shit all you want, but this isn't about letting Brad go, and it isn't about letting him find what he wants."

"What is it, then?" I asked Billy.

"This is you wanting to end it now because you still don't believe that boy really loves you, so you're willing to blow this shit up now rather than risk what could come next."

I said nothing for a long time. Finally I sighed. "It's not going to work out."

"It's not going to work out because you are going to blow it up! You can't just let...."

ENOUGH!

My room was empty and completely silent.

I sat there until midnight, steeling myself for what I had to do. I needed to break up with him and stick to my guns. That was better for both of us in the long run, and I needed to keep that thought in my mind at all times. I threw on the rest of my clothes and made my way to school to meet the bus when the team got back. I waited by Brad's car and kept reminding myself no matter how miserable I felt, it was for the better. It was for the better.

After a while I began to believe it.

I checked my phone and saw a dozen missed texts from Brad. I texted him that we needed to talk when he got here and nothing else. I wasn't surprised he didn't text back. I don't know how much time passed, but my thoughts went into a daze as I kept my warring emotions locked away. I needed to be of a single mind about this. I had no time for the clown car of emotions that made my life hell to chime in with their opinions. This needed to be done.

Really.

The bus pulled in, and I felt a little nauseous. I just kept chanting *It's for the best* in my head over and over. He came over to his car and froze when he saw me. He looked like he was about to hurl as well.

"Hey," he said, surprised. "What are you doing out here so late?"

I pushed myself off the car and asked him, "Did you tell Jennifer about our sex life?"

Like a five-year-old, he instantly said, "No!"

That just made me madder. "So you didn't tell her you disliked having sex with me?"

His voice sounded like he was denying a murder. "I didn't say I disliked it."

"So then, you did talk to her about our sex life?" I knew the answer. I was just leading him to say it out loud.

"I was just telling her that...," he began to explain.

That was what I needed to hear.

"Why would you tell her anything? What we do in the bedroom is between us only. Why would you think that was okay? Wait, let me guess. You didn't think." I could feel my emotions getting crazy, and I could feel tears starting to form. "Do you know how embarrassed I was? How horrible it is to find out your boyfriend doesn't like sex with you from someone else?"

"I didn't say I didn't like it!" he broke in. "I just said I was sore."

My mind went red with rage. "Why would you say that to her?"

"Can we talk about this somewhere else?" he asked me quietly.

I saw most of the team standing by their cars looking at us. And once again he was more concerned about being embarrassed than how he made me feel. "Why? You don't want them to know? You would hate to have your private business told to others without your permission?" I looked over to the guys like I was going to tell them everything.

"Please don't. I know I fucked up, Kyle, but please... don't do this."

The tears were falling now as I realized everything I had been thinking was true. He really had no idea how he had made me feel.

So I decided to explain it to him. "You know, that was exactly what I was thinking when Jennifer started to tell me. Please don't do this." I took off his ring and tossed it to him. "Well, now you don't have to be sore at all."

The pain on his face was like emotional acid, and all I wanted to do was hug him and wish we could do this day over again. But it wouldn't make any difference, because no matter how many times we tried to change it, it would end the same every time. So instead, I walked away and forced myself not to look back at him.

It was the hardest thing I ever had to do.

THE NEXT day, I was not going to school.

I didn't care if stormtroopers came charging in my room to carry me down the street to class. There was no way I could face Brad without caving instantly. It felt like something had been punched inside my chest, and every time I thought about him, it ached like a bruise. A bruise that was never going to get better. My mom was still asleep, so I left a note on my door that I was sick and staying home.

Then I texted Jennifer so someone knew I was all right. I knew how this would go: Brad would tell her we had broken up, she would say she hadn't heard from me at all, images of me swinging from a rope would fill her mind, and she would rush right over. And talking about it was the last thing I wanted to do.

She almost instantly texted me back. *Do u hate me?*

I sighed and wished I could explain to her how so little of this was actually her fault. *No, not at all. We broke up and I can't face him.*

Her response was predictable. *OMG u broke up?*

Yes, I responded. *will call u l8r*

I turned off my phone before she could respond.

I buried myself under the covers and fell back asleep. All I could dream about was Brad.

WHEN I woke up, it was afternoon, and I could hear sounds coming from the living room.

My mom was on the couch, watching TV. She looked over and smiled when she saw me walk out. "So it lives," she commented.

"Why are you home?" I asked, confused. She usually worked Friday afternoons.

"It's nice to see you too, son, and I switched with Sharon for the day off." She gestured toward the kitchen. "There's some McDonald's on the counter for you."

My stomach made a sound in response.

I grabbed the bag, pulled a Coke out of the fridge, and sat in the chair. "So what's all this about?" I asked as I shoved some fries in my mouth.

"What, I can't take a day off and make sure my son is okay?" I gave her a look, and she shook her head. "You take a day off from school and Brad isn't here hovering, I worry." I must have made a face because she leaned forward and asked, "You want to talk about it?"

I began to cry as I shook my head.

All in all, it was a lousy day.

THE NEXT day, the impossible happened.

I went to get the mail from the large bank of mailboxes the apartment complex used, and there was a letter waiting for me. An impossible letter. A letter that in no way could exist. I sat there staring at it for what must have been ten minutes with the mailbox open and my mouth agape.

I slammed the mailbox shut and ran back to the apartment.

I picked up my phone and went to call Brad before I remembered the last forty-eight hours. Suddenly, my letter seemed less miraculous. My mom was at work, so I couldn't call her. Last time I talked to Robbie I had bitched him out, so he wasn't going to be sympathetic. Instead, I texted Jennifer and asked if she could come over. I couldn't open it by myself. In fact, I wasn't sure if I could open it at all.

Ten minutes later she knocked on my door, a worried look on her face. "What's wrong?"

I handed her the letter silently.

She glanced at it, not getting the significance at first. Then she saw who it was from. "Is this for real?" she asked. I nodded, not even sure if I was breathing anymore.

She tried to hand it back to me, and I shook it off. "I can't open it. I think I'm going to have a stroke."

"You want me to open it?" The tone in her voice made it clear she thought I had lost it. All I could do was fall back on the couch and nod. She sat across from me and carefully picked at the envelope's seal, like she could ruin its contents if she did it wrong. She paused when it was halfway open. "You're sure?" I nodded again. She ripped the rest of the way and opened it, revealing the piece of paper inside.

We both stared at it, half expecting it to jump up and do tricks.

She pulled it out and unfolded it. I saw her eyes scan the contents briefly, and she gasped halfway through it.

"What's it say?" I asked her.

When she answered, I knew nothing was going to be the same.

Jennifer

I REMEMBER the very moment I knew I wasn't like the other girls.

Maggie Hayes had thrown a slumber party at her house, and only those of us considered cool were invited. Now, I'm unsure what criteria of cool we were using in junior high, but I am sure it had something to do with which Winchester brother was hotter and our love for Katy Perry. Either way, I was invited, and it was supposed to be one of those epic events that bonded us together as friends for years to come.

That didn't exactly happen.

Maggie's older sister was a cheerleader at Granada and the girl everyone our age wanted to grow up to be. She was pretty without looking like a slut, she was popular without being a tease, and I remember thinking that when I got to high school, I wanted to be just like her. Maggie's popularity really came from Penny's rep, but none of us ever said it out loud, because just being friends with the most popular girl's sister was better than most people were doing. So after a double feature of *Moulin Rouge!* and *Slumdog Millionaire*, the conversation turned to what it always turned to when six teenage girls got together anywhere, but especially in a room with the door closed.

Boys.

I know that guys are supposed to be the ones who think about sex, like, every ten seconds or so, but I also know junior high girls think of boys at least three times in that same ten seconds. The problem was that, in a town as small as Foster, every single boy had been scoped out and observed since he was ten. Everyone knew everybody, so there was this weird kind of pairing ritual that took place where we would claim certain boys, even though none of us had ever once talked to them in a romantic setting. My dad had heard us do this once. He said it sounded a lot like a fantasy football league, where we were trading boys back and forth between one another without ever asking the boy what he wanted.

Leave it to my dad to make everything about sports.

So anyway, there we were, talking about boys, when Penny came in. She was drunk, which at the time made her seem so much cooler than being drunk actually is. The difference between a thirteen-year-old girl and a seventeen-year-old girl may seem vast to those on the outside, but when you're the thirteen-year-old, it looks like science fiction. There was no way the thing people called my chest would ever develop into breasts that looked like Penny's, and I was pretty sure my face was going to look chubby until the day I died. She seemed so cool and sophisticated that it hurt to know I would never, ever be that cool.

So she sat down and asked what we were talking about, and as soon as she realized it was boys, she put her hands out to quiet us and said, "Do you guys want to know the secret to getting a guy and keeping him?" It was a stupid question, because we all sat up liked trained dogs and waited breathlessly for her to feed us treats of her hard-earned wisdom. "The secret is being hot," she slurred, stuffing a handful of chips into her mouth. "Once you're hot, they'll be tripping over themselves to do anything for you. And you know how you get hot?" Again a stupid question, but since she had a captive audience, she was going to milk it for all it was worth. "Some will tell you it's exercise, and some will tell you eating right, but that's crap. The secret? Eat whatever you want… just afterward—" We all leaned forward, just knowing the wisdom was about to flow. "—you throw it all up." No one said a word; they just gazed at her like she had hung the sun and moon. "I carry around a toothbrush, and before class… I just stick it down my throat and… lunch is gone."

The silence in the room was palpable as we all absorbed her words.

"Now I bring some mouthwash, 'cause no one wants nasty puke breath, but others use gum…."

And I burst out laughing.

I mean, not just a chuckle or a giggle but a loud, sidesplitting laugh that was the equivalent of a record scratching to silence in a movie. Everyone looked over at me, wondering what exactly I had found so funny. Penny specifically looked like she wanted to hit me. When I became aware that no one could figure out what I was going on about, I blurted out, "Are you fucking kidding me? Puking? That's your secret to getting boys?" More silent stares. "Have you just tried, I don't know, being nice to them or something?"

In a tone of voice that could have kept meat chilled, Penny said, "It's not that easy, little girl." I'm sure the "little girl" part was supposed to be an insult, but honestly, she had lost any power over me the second she brought up the mouthwash.

"Seriously? You all are buying this? There's not a boy alive who is worth blowing chunks for. I can tell you that now."

"Get the wrong guy and you'll be stuck in this one-horse town forever," Penny argued. "Trust me, when you're older, you'll do whatever to get the right guy. Anything."

That confused the heck out of me, and I asked with all honesty, "Why do you need a boy to leave? It's not like we can't leave by ourselves." Less than five minutes later, I was on the phone, asking my dad to come pick me up. It was the last slumber party I'd ever attend. Not that I wasn't invited; I just never bothered to go because I had learned everything I needed to from Penny. There was what girls in this town thought they were supposed to want, and there was what I wanted.

Rarely did the two meet, much less overlap.

Nothing makes a person more popular than not wanting to follow a crowd. My reluctance to define myself by what boy I was dating made me something of an enigma to my friends. On one hand, they could sense a strength that they seemed to be lacking. On the other one, I was a freak who refused to play by their rules. The summer before high school, I got my breasts and lost my facial (and other) baby fat. I went from being a little girl to a young woman. My dad began to hover around me, wanting to know where I was all the time, and God forbid a boy should say hi to me on the street. There's nothing better than a dad with a badge and a handgun for scaring off boys. I spent a lot of time rolling my eyes whenever I was with my dad.

"This was the part your mom was supposed to handle," he told me as we bought new school clothes. "I'm not wild about you wearing a bra already."

Dad rarely brought up the topic of my mom. She had passed away when I was five. Mom was a face and a voice that came to me in my dreams, but I didn't have any real memories of her. I suppose being raised by the town sheriff should have made me a total tomboy, but I liked girly things just as much as any girl in town. I just never understood why someone would think she had to be defined by the guy she was going out with. Most of the girls I knew didn't even consider the idea of college or having a career. They mostly talked about staying in Foster and starting a family, just like their mom and their grandmothers. I didn't find anything wrong with that plan; it just was never for me.

My dad had never treated me like a "girl," I guess. He didn't understand the difference between the genders enough to change his parenting style. Instead, he had raised me with the same beliefs the boys in town were taught. I could be anything I wanted to be; all I had to do was work at it. I guess with all the world open for me to learn about and make a choice, staying here in Foster and being someone's wife seemed small.

And then I began to understand how high school worked.

Being independent and strong sounded good on paper, but the truth was that "different" in high school was not appreciated and celebrated like it was in my house. Different meant weird, and weird meant exclusion, and exclusion meant never being talked to again. There's a reason people use solitary confinement as a punishment. No one likes being forced to be alone. They may be able to handle it or even not be that affected by it, but when isolation isn't a choice, it becomes unbearable. So between exclusion and conformity, I picked the easier of the two evils. Notice I say easier and not lesser, because I really think making people be who they aren't is the worst thing you can do to another human being.

That was a lesson taught to me by Robbie after I told him Brad had come out of the closet.

I guess this is the place where I could say I always suspected Brad, but I can't. I was so preoccupied with pretending to be someone I wasn't that it never occurred to me he was doing the same thing. In a year, I had transformed myself from a freethinking person into just another one of the pretty girls who cared about nothing but which boy she could capture. It made me sick at times, but after a while I just went with it, since the only other option seemed like a fate worse than death.

I had known Brad since we were kids, but I had never thought about actually dating him until the day of the Monterey game in freshman year.

We were down two runs at the bottom of the ninth. It really did look like we were going to lose. I had made the cheerleading squad, but since I was also a freshman, the only thing I had done so far was carry equipment and memorize cheers. I had been bored silly, since I hadn't cared who won or lost when the game started. But by the last inning, I found myself drawn in. I didn't want us to lose. Brad walked up to the plate, and for some reason, I paid more attention.

Brad was still a couple of inches short of his current height, and I remember thinking he looked so tiny compared to the rest of the guys who had been playing. I could see intensity in his eyes burning from beneath the batting helmet's visor, and I knew all he wanted was not to look like a complete idiot in front of the entire school. I saw his back foot dig in, and he crouched slightly as he brought his bat up. The pitcher drew back into his windup, and I held my breath as he let the ball fly.

The sound of the bat hitting the ball was like a thunderclap.

He hit that ball so hard that it was out of the park before I could even follow its movement. Brad was still at home plate, his bat in hand as he tracked the ball's arc out of the field, his mouth open in shock. I remember it so vividly, the half second of silence that shattered against the explosion of cheers. I could hear someone behind me in the stands mutter a hushed "Goddamn!" The Monterey third baseman threw his glove to the ground in disgust.

It wasn't until the whole place erupted that I realized he had just won the game. From the way Brad looked around at everyone yelling at him to run around the bases, he hadn't figured it out either. Overnight he went from one of the many boys who were tolerably cute in Foster to The Hottest Boy Ever. He was one of the few freshmen to play varsity baseball, and every single girl in our class suddenly knew his name. I remember being interested in him not because he won the game, or because he was popular, but because of the look on his face when it finally sank in he had hit a home run. The goofy grin broke out across his face as he almost tripped halfway to first. There was no swagger and no ego, just unbridled joy in the game and the contentment of a prayer answered.

One of that year's seniors set us up at a team party out at the lake. I was one of the only girls who hadn't thrown themselves at him. That worked to my advantage, because he was obviously looking for a way to duck some of the attention that came at him from all directions. I remember the voice in my head listing everything positive about him as we talked: he was cute; he was in shape; just underneath a thin layer of bravado, he had an alluring shyness; and—the best part—he didn't leer at me like a creeper. When we talked, he seemed to listen, and I never once caught him looking at my chest.

We ended up dating more out of convenience than anything. Neither one of us wanted to be the first to name what it was. That summer he gave me his class ring, and I wore it dutifully. Even then I knew something was missing. We fooled around because we were both teenagers and were more curious about sex than we were about actual emotions. I thought the sex was good, but it was nothing like I had imagined it would be. Like every other girl I knew, I kept him on a short leash when it came to getting some, because if I gave it up too easily, I'd be a slut. If I never gave it up, I was a prude. I kept him more than content, and he never strayed with other girls. It seemed like the perfect setup for both of us.

If only we had been in love with each other.

Now, I'm not going to be one of those girls who says "I always suspected something was wrong" just to save face, because I didn't. Brad was the least gay guy I had ever seen. Of course, before this, besides Robbie, all the gay guys I had seen were on TV and in the movies, but still. By that I meant he never once gave away what he was feeling inside. I suppose if I had been more aware, I might have noticed that he didn't pressure me for sex as much as the other guys did their girls, or that he seemed more interested in sports than me, but that was just Brad. He'd acted the same since the first time we talked. I had no idea he was anybody but the boy I was going steady with.

Until the day he kissed Kyle in the quad.

I had known he was failing history, but that was nothing new with Brad. He put exactly the least amount of effort into schoolwork that he could get away with. No more, no less. The fact that he had spaced out in history because he assumed Coach Gunn would cut him a break shocked no one. I tried to warn him, but he ignored me. I tried to help him study, but he blew me off. When he ended up failing a test, Coach Gunn told him how close he was to being cut from the team, and it was then he started to do something about it. He had said he had a line on a tutor, and I thought that was that. I had no reason to suspect, even when he introduced me to Kyle during lunch. I thought I knew how the rest of this drama called high school would play out, and I assure you, it didn't involve him kissing another guy in front of everyone.

I wasn't there when it happened, but I heard about it soon enough.

Practice was halfway done when the whispering started. That was nothing new. Foster is a small town, and not everyone had cable. The only reliable entertainment was gossip, and thankfully, there was more than enough to go around. Gossip was a lot like playing spin the bottle with a bunch of gross people. You could laugh and laugh when it landed on someone else, but sooner or later it would be pointing at you.

From the way people were staring and laughing at me, the bottle had indeed landed on me this time.

The key to facing a pack of mean girls is basically the same as facing a pack of wild dogs. Never turn your back on them, show no fear, and whatever you do, try to remember they are mindless beasts and are probably just hungry. Of course, it was Maggie who walked over to bring me the news. She spent most of her time talking about me behind my back, laying the foundation of succession when/if I ever lost popularity. She wanted to be the queen bee and was willing to sting me to death to get there.

"So," she said, her face contorting to her pre-sneer look. "How are you and Brad getting along?"

There were packs of girls standing around us, some of them holding back laughter while others looked at me like I was the last one to know I had cancer. "Fine," I answered, trying to figure out what in the hell this was about. "Why do you ask?"

She held up her phone, and there was an image of Brad kissing Kyle.

"So then you knew about this, right?" She put a hand on her hip and waited for me to lose it.

I shrugged and tried to keep my face impassive. "So Brad lost at gay chicken. Wouldn't be the first time." It was a bullshit answer, but I was willing to bet she didn't know anything more than I did. Someone sent her that pic, most likely with the following text: *OMG look at this*. There was just no way anyone knew more than the fact my boyfriend was kissing another guy. "You act like the guys around here don't try to make everyone else freak out on a daily basis." Another bullshit answer but more truth than fiction. We live in a town where cow tipping is an actual event, not a concept or an urban legend, but an honest-to-God activity that some people do on weekends. It was not outside the realm of possibility that one of the guys would kiss another guy just to make people squirm.

I saw the hesitation in her face, and I knew I had bought myself a few minutes.

"Seriously, Maggie, if you spent as much time practicing as you do minding my business, we'd be national champs by now." It was an ugly thing to say, but the only way I was going to get her off my back was by attacking. People laughed at my joke, and she slowly retreated, falling back until she could get more dirt on me.

As soon as people went back to their routines, I ran toward the locker room and changed into my street clothes. I wasn't going to admit it out loud, but I had a sinking feeling that my world was about to fall apart around me.

Turns out I was right.

By the time I got home, my phone was filled with texts and missed calls from people wanting to know if I knew. While I am sure a couple of them were actually worried about me, all I saw were vultures circling overhead, waiting for me to stop twitching. I called a couple of girls I trusted and asked them if they had any idea what had happened. Finding out the truth took time, since a lot of what people knew was second- and thirdhand. From what I gathered, Kelly had bullied Kyle, and Brad had stepped up and kissed him, daring Kelly to say something else.

How did I know Kelly would be involved?

Kelly and Brad had been friends since they were kids, but they were never really friendly. There was always an odd tension between them, which I always took as Brad being turned off by Kelly's neediness. Even though he was popular enough, Kelly always did what Brad said, like he was Brad's servant almost, and it was annoying as hell. Maybe this wasn't what it looked like. Maybe Brad was just trying to mess with Kelly somehow, though I wasn't sure how kissing another guy did that. After a while I just sat in my room and ignored call after call.

None of them was Brad.

I suppose I didn't call him because calling was the quickest way of finding out the truth, and the truth was something I was not interested in. I expected everything to be a mistake, a bad joke, something that would clear itself up over the weekend. My head spun a thousand scenarios of what could have happened to make Brad kiss a guy, but my gut seemed to know better. My gut told me this was exactly what it looked like. If I called him, I'd have confirmation in a matter of seconds.

I didn't want anything confirmed. I wanted to keep living the life I had twenty-four hours ago.

That may seem like a pretty oblivious statement, but it was a weird thought for me. I hadn't been happy with my life since I started high school. I had become someone I honestly didn't like, and the thought that I would rather stay like that than be forced to face the truth was as disappointing to me as Penny's revelation all those years ago.

Only an idiot or a masochist would have gone to school that Friday.

There was no way in hell I could face the pack of hungry bitches that was no doubt stalking my locker. Instead, I said goodbye to my dad and ditched school altogether. I drove around town trying to find something to do until the Vine opened. My best bet was catching a movie and wasting time until it got later. Robbie's shop wouldn't be open until he dragged himself out of bed, which could be anywhere from ten in the morning to two in the afternoon.

After a slow and drawn-out breakfast at Starr's, I cruised down First Street, making sure the Vine was open. I parked my car around the corner so my dad wouldn't see it when he did his rounds and began to walk toward the theater. I bought a ticket and scrolled through social media instead of watching the movie. Once the movie was over, I got up to grab a drink or to stretch my legs.

Which was when I saw Brad walking out of the other theater, looking at me like I was a ghost.

I don't know what made me madder—that he had ditched school and didn't bother to call me, or that he had taken my hiding place first. Either way, I was plenty pissed when I confronted him. "Hiding?"

He took half a second and then answered with "Thinking."

More typical Graymark bullshit. He couldn't even admit he was hiding and had to find some way to make himself look better. "Do you have any idea how horrible today has been?" It was such a selfish thing to ask him, but it just came rushing out of my mouth like vomit. "I am the laughingstock of the school. People whispering behind my back, everyone looking away as I pass by. What am I supposed to do now?"

"I don't have any answers." He sounded so depressed, so not Brad, that I took a mental half step back.

"Is it true?" I asked him, even though I knew it was. "Because if you were just sticking up for the lame kid, you can tell people that, and they'd believe you." Where was this coming from? Was I asking him to lie now? Was I willing to lie just to keep my status?

"One, he isn't lame," he fired back, pissed. It was more passion than I had seen in him in the three years we had been dating. We always seemed to be circling each other in some weird emotional cat-and-mouse game, neither one of us wanting to be real before the other one. But this, this was the real Brad, and it nailed home that everything I had heard was true. "Two, you think today has been any easier on me? You think I can just do something like that and not be—" He took a half beat as he searched for the right word. "—concerned about how it will affect my life? You can't be so conceited that you've made this all about yourself?" I felt my face get warm, knowing that was exactly what I had been doing. "And three, you had to have some clue. After all, wasn't the reason you went out with me in the first place because you didn't want to have some guy trying to get up under your skirt every five seconds? We both know I was the safe choice. Maybe I wanted you to get up under it more." But it wasn't true. He was right. One of the things I liked about dating Brad was that he didn't paw over me like I saw the other guys do to their girlfriends.

"Well then, maybe you should have dated someone who was into you!" If he had reached out and slapped me, it would have hurt less. He regretted it the second he said it, but it was too late. There was no way for him to take his words back, and even if he did, the fact that he had been telling the truth remained.

Possibly for the first time since we met.

"Jennifer, that wasn't what I—" His apology made me madder than the actual comment. I grabbed his Coke and threw it in his face, and I yelled, "Fuck you, Brad!" before following it with the empty cup. While he sputtered from the shock, I pulled his class ring off and threw it at his head.

Hard. I then turned around and ran out of the theater.

As worst-case scenarios went, that was near the top of the list.

I ran to my car, yanked the door open, crashed into my seat, and slammed the door shut. I was crying, even though I wasn't sure why. Was I crying because of what he said? Because of what he was now? Because of what it meant for me? I had no earthly idea. All I knew was I was crying, and I couldn't stop. Through blurred vision I drove to Robbie's, the only place I would be safe, because no one else I knew would be there.

I had been shopping at Twice Upon a Time since it reopened a couple of years earlier. It used to be nothing more than a thrift shop before Robbie took it over. He had bought a few stores' worth of clothes from New York and brought them back in what I can only assume was his attempt to infuse some class into Foster. Most people still thought of it as an old folks' store, which was good for me since I always scored the best stuff.

"What the hell is wrong with guys?" I screamed as soon as I walked in.

Robbie, who had been putting a jacket up on a rack, froze and gave me a weird look. "Are you talking in general or someone specific?"

Tears were running down my face, and I hated that I couldn't stop. "All of you! You're all so fucking useless! You just take and take and never care about anyone else, and then once you're done you… you…."

And I broke down, unable to say anything else.

"Whoa," he said, putting the jacket aside and seeming to glide over to me. Normally I would have asked him why he was on roller skates, but right now I just didn't care. "Where is this coming from? What happened?"

"Brad," I said through my wailing, wishing I had some small control over how I felt.

"Brad?" he asked, confused. "The moose?"

I hated that he called Brad that, but since right then I was calling him so much worse in my head, I just nodded.

"What happened with Brad? Did he break up with you?" I shook my head. "Did you guys fight?" I nodded. "About what?" he asked and then gasped. "Did he cheat on you?"

I looked up at him and nodded. The pain and the anger I was feeling were out of control now.

"With who?" he asked, sounding like someone asking what she'd missed on the last episode of *Real Housewives*.

"Kyle," I blurted out, falling into racking sobs again.

He paused and cocked his head in confusion. "Kyle? You mean Kylie? Or Kelly?"

"Kyle!" I screamed.

"That sounds like a boy's name."

I know he said it more to himself than to me, but I still reacted like he had been telling me the most obvious stupid fact in the world. "It is a guy! He's fucking gay! He came out in front of everyone yesterday!"

He didn't say anything for a long time as I just cried and cried. I finally forced myself to breathe and grab for some control. After about three minutes he asked me, "Is he okay?"

I gaped up at him, mouth open in complete disbelief.

"Is he okay? Is he fucking okay? Are you kidding me?" I raged at him.

"Well, yeah," he answered calmly. "He just came out to what, at best, would be a hostile crowd, at worst a casting call for extras in *Deliverance 2: Scream, Pig, Scream*. I know you're feeling shitty, but you're beautiful and will get another boyfriend. Brad, on the other hand, might just get the shit beat out of him—or worse." His tone didn't vary one iota from pleasant, but I could sense the anger and something else behind his words. "So let me ask again, is he okay?"

When I could control my jaw, I snapped my mouth shut. When I opened it, I hissed, "I can't believe you." I backed away from Robbie as if he were a stranger. "No, wait, I can. Of course you're going to take his side. What was I thinking? Now he's fair game for you, right? Free to swoop in and grab yourself a new boy before the rest of the town—"

He caught up with me in one long stride and grabbed my hands firmly. In a voice barely above a whisper, he said, "I know you're mad, so I am going to ignore everything you just said. Let me make a few things clear. One, you're out of line, way out of line, and you know it. Two, you're pissed because you think Brad coming out makes you look like a fool, and you're probably right. Three, I am not kidding when I say he is in real danger. And four, if you feel like verbally vomiting all over me again, do not think I am above slapping a hysterical woman. Like my mom always said, if you want to act like a crazy person, you get treated like a crazy person."

"Let go of me," I said, hauling in a futile attempt to free my hands.

"You're upset right now, so this isn't going to make much sense, but I am not mad at you, and when you have calmed down, you can come back any time you want."

I tried to pull away again. "Screw you. I am never coming back here again. I can't believe—"

"Right. Just remember, everyone has at least one free crazy. This is yours. When you want to talk, I'm here."

He let go, and I almost fell on my ass, I had been pulling so hard. I glared at him and wanted to scream and cuss him out so bad, but somewhere in the back of my mind, I knew I was really pissed at Brad, and Robbie was just an easy target.

Instead, I turned around and stomped out, sure I was never going to step foot in there again.

What I did next I am not proud of.

Somewhere between Robbie's and home, I had decided that I was the victim, which made Brad the attacker. So, when I got to my room, I did a lot of things quickly. I changed my status on Facebook and then unfriended Brad. I wrote an ugly post about how people who lie and pretend to be something they aren't should be shot. The post got a dozen likes in thirty seconds, which meant it was the response people had been waiting for.

That weekend I spent with "friends," bad-mouthing Brad everywhere I went.

People lapped it up in a way that would have been disturbing to me if I hadn't been so preoccupied with my own mood. I heard exactly what I wanted to hear: that I had done nothing wrong and that they had known Brad was an asshole the entire time. Of course, this was from people who had practically waited on him hand and foot since he was a sophomore. Again, I ignored the irony because what they were saying was exactly what I wanted to hear. The one I was really shocked to hear from was Kelly. He seemed to have a lot more to say than everyone else. He explained to anyone who would listen that Brad hit on him the summer they both went to football camp and that Kelly had had to fight him off.

That didn't sound right at all, but at the time I said nothing because I wanted to hurt Brad in any way I could. When I showed up to school Monday, I acted like I had been saved from a kidnapper. Everyone hated Brad, and not one person blamed me, which I thought was awesome at the time. My satisfaction lasted until lunch. I held court at the Table, telling people the shock I'd felt when I heard about my one true love being gay.

"Well, we took care of him for you," Tony announced smugly as people laughed at my story.

I smiled at him before my brain engaged. "You did?" I asked brightly, trying to ignore the dread that was settling into my stomach.

He nodded and looked at everyone else. "Yeah—Josh, Cory, and me taught him a lesson before gym."

People cheered, and I felt the smile on my face go from genuine to fake in one second flat. I forced myself not to react since I was in public, but inside my mind was racing. "What kind of lesson?"

He gave me a smile that looked predatory. "The kind that he limped away from."

Robbie's voice echoed in my mind. "I am not kidding when I say he is in real danger."

"Yeah, and from what I hear, they are going to have some meeting so they can kick him off the team," Cory chimed in. "Can't have some fag watching me while I shower and stuff."

My mouth moved faster than my mind. "Did he watch you before?" Everyone looked over at me, and I mentally backtracked. "I mean, did you catch him before or something?"

"Fuck no," he answered quickly. "If I did, I would have put him down a long time ago."

That was doubtful since Cory was at best a Walmart version of Brad. "But he practically won state for us last year." Again I wanted to know what the hell was wrong with my mouth.

"Yeah," he agreed slowly. "But now he's a fag."

Everyone else murmured in agreement.

"I have to go," I said quickly, startling Tony, who had been high-fiving Kelly.

"What, why?" he asked. I could see the rest of the Table was wondering the same thing.

"My dad," I began lamely. "My dad wanted to know the whole story. You know, 'cause he's pissed." I was lying outright; my dad didn't know a thing about what had happened. There was no way he was hearing about it from me.

"Oh my God!" Lori said, covering her mouth. "He could, like, be guilty of fraud and stuff, right?"

She had just said what was easily the dumbest thing I had heard since the last time she'd tried to think and speak, but I couldn't say a word about it because she was on my side. Instead, I nodded and smiled. "Maybe. I just want to be sure."

They all smiled at me as I tried not to run away from the Table.

I was pissed at Brad, sure, but not because he was gay. I hated him because he'd hurt me, lied to me. But would I want anyone, much less an ass hat like Tony Wright, beating him up? Not on a bet. Never. Tony beating up Brad had nothing to do with me, and I knew it. Tony beating up Brad was Tony's little mind at work. And the fact that his dad was a huge homophobe, and Tony was a bully.

One weekend had passed, and things were already spiraling out of control.

I tried not to peel out of the parking lot before I raced to Robbie's place.

The door slammed open, and I rushed into the shop. Robbie screamed in fright from behind the counter and lobbed a well-worn copy of *Under the Rainbow*, which hit me in the chest. That hurt. I picked up the book and gave him a look. "Why the hell did you throw a book at my boob?"

He paused for a moment, his hand still on his chest. "You come barging in, almost breaking my door, and the first thing I think of is Carole Baskin is here to rub sardine oil all over me. I did what any self-respecting homosexual would. I threw my copy of Liza Minnelli's biography at her—well, you—in self-defense and screamed for my life." He took the book back and slipped it behind the counter. "It was just a bonus that I hit your boob."

"Okay, well, that makes no sense. Don't you own a gun?" I asked him.

He cocked his head and sighed. "Yes, little Miss Texas, like everyone else in this state, I was issued a gun and three complimentary packs of ammo when I left civilization to move here." He gave me a scornful look. "Of course I don't have a gun. Did you see how I reacted with a paperback book? If I had a gun, you'd be on the floor bleeding, and I would be hyperventilating." He emerged from behind the counter. "So what happened to never coming back?"

"Thought I had one free crazy. I am redeeming it as of now," I said, trying not to blush at the memory of my previous actions.

"Done," he said, smiling. "Consider it redeemed. So seriously, why are you here? I expected you to wait at least a week or so or until you missed an episode of *Drag Race*, before you came crawling back."

That made me smile. "I am not crawling anywhere, and I am here because you were right."

He nodded. "I am always right." Then he paused. "Wait, right about what?"

"They beat up Brad, and they are going to throw him off the baseball team."

His face went pale, and he put a hand over his mouth, but I could tell that was a reflex at being shocked. His actual reaction was to stare off over my shoulder as his expression hardened in anger. "Well, of course they did," he said with more spite than I had ever heard used in any sentence before. "Is he okay?" he asked me after a few seconds. In that time he went from an expressionless robot back to his normal, over-the-top self, which only solidified in my mind that the over-the-top thing was all an act.

"I don't know, but we need to do something," I replied quickly. "If Brad gets kicked off the baseball team, it'll kill him."

Robbie stared at me for a long time and then let out a sarcastic laugh. "Only in Foster, Texas, would someone be more concerned about a boy playing baseball than him getting physically attacked." He rolled his eyes and looked up for a moment. I could swear under his breath he said something about "Riley" and then took a deep breath. "Okay, so what do you think we can do?"

I wanted to ask who Riley was, but I could tell he wanted to ignore he'd ever said that, the same way I wanted to ignore my little outburst a couple of days earlier. A free crazy is a free crazy, so I let it go. "Okay, I meant you need to do something about it."

He gave me a look. "Like what? I know I may act like I have magical powers, but I assure you I don't have an invisible jet out back. And even if I were Wonder Woman, which I am not denying, the people at Hick High still wouldn't listen to me. You do know that, right?"

I did know that, but Robbie was the only adult I knew of who could help. "But you're a grown-up." I paused as his look bored into my eyes. "I mean, you're technically a grown-up." He nodded for me to continue. "They have to listen. I just know no one else will show up to speak for him. It's just going to be a lot of uptight assholes saying the queer can't play baseball."

"Good," he said, walking away from me. "I mean, why would anyone even want to play that horrendous game? Sure those pants are hot, but only in a stripper way—no one could ever wear those for real. It's grown men running after balls. Brad's better off without it."

This was the part about being friends with Robbie that drove me crazy. He just didn't get how things worked in Foster, and he had no desire to learn. I walked over to him and turned him around. He wouldn't meet my stare, so I knew the big guns were necessary.

"Are you going to send Brad to college?" He stared at me in surprise. "Are you going to come up with a ton of money so he can go to a college?" He said nothing. "Then Brad needs to play baseball so he can get a scholarship and go to college. I don't care what you personally think of baseball. Unless you are willing to pony up at least a hundred thousand dollars, we need to help him."

That seemed to get his attention.

"Running around chasing balls—that's a skill you need to get into college," he said, walking back behind the counter. "You think Tim Gunn got offered a scholarship for design? You think Michael Kors got a full ride when he graduated? No, but if he could hit a ball the farthest, then he was a shoo-in." He sat down and sighed. "I swear, I hate everything in the world right now."

"Will you go?" I asked him.

He looked up at me, and I could tell the answer was no before he even spoke. "Sweetie, I would love to help, but those people are just going to laugh me out of the room, and in the end, it will do more damage to Brad's case than help. I am an outsider here, the token fag for this one-horse town, and the only way they tolerate me is if I stay on the outskirts and shut up." In a lower voice, he said, "Trust me, I've seen what happens when you try to be gay and happy in this town."

I couldn't believe what I was hearing. "So that's it? You're just going to do nothing?"

"I'll talk to some people," he said, which sounded like so much bullshit I wanted to scream. "But I have a sinking feeling that Brad is on his own."

And that was where I left it, pretty sure Brad was screwed.

But that next week a story started to circulate, a story no one really believed. They said—and isn't it always *they* who talk, no one with names, always the faceless they—they said that Brad had been offered his place on the team because his dad had come in and threatened to sue the hell out of the school. They said that Brad had gotten a free pass to play if the subject was just dropped and ignored. They said that it was a perfect deal for Brad and that anyone in their right mind would have taken it.

And then they said Brad refused it.

This was where the stories got blurry, but it seemed that Brad, instead of taking the deal and pretty much solidifying his chance to play baseball, instead demanded the school give the same protection to everyone. He said that the way people were treated in Foster was horrible, and the school just let people do it. He said it had to change, and if it didn't, then he would play baseball somewhere else.

And then he walked out.

They had no idea what to do about it. On the surface it sounded like Brad had walked away from a cush deal that would have saved his ass, but that was just on the surface. Deeper… it sounded like he'd stood up for every single person in the school who had been picked on. The long and the short of it was… they had no fucking idea how to react to it.

But I thought I did.

I spent the time talking to Robbie and trying to get over how pissed I was at Brad for using me like that. I didn't think random people had the right to beat him up, but that didn't mean I forgave him instantly. Robbie explained to me how hard it was for a guy to come out and that the fear they feel of someone finding out their secret was deadly sometimes. Brad hadn't just been lying to me; he'd been trying to hide himself from the entire town. It wasn't about appearances; it was about safety. It was about survival.

After a while I began to understand what he meant.

One day I woke up, and I wasn't mad anymore. I still remembered the shame and anger, but I wasn't feeling the actual emotion. I was just too tired. Keeping the anger alive demanded too much energy, and it began to fade. That was when I decided to take a real look at Brad and Kyle without feeling like a dagger had been shoved through my heart. I watched them eat on the music hall steps, and it was so obvious they were in love—like a neon sign flashing over their head obvious—that I had to accept what Robbie had been telling me was true. Brad had forced himself to like me to hide who he was because he had never, in the entire time I had known him, looked at anyone that way. Now that I was seeing it for the first time, I also realized that Brad was truly happy.

After that, I said screw it and decided to be their friend.

Which catches us up to the week of Brad's away game and the SATs.

Watching Brad try to deal with Kyle's crazy was cute because it was pretty obvious he had no idea why the test was so serious to his boyfriend, but he never hesitated to back Kyle all the way. Kyle was desperate to get out of Foster, and I had to silently admit I knew how he felt. I couldn't imagine having no prospects after high school and having to live with the knowledge that the rest of your life was going to be spent between First and Main Street. Brad, on the other hand, never once thought about the possibility that he wasn't going to get out of Foster, as far as I knew.

One of the things that made Brad equally adorable and annoying was his ability to ignore reality while trying to will things to be the way he wanted them to be.

Here we were on a seven-game winning streak, and it was hard to argue that Brad had not willed it into existence. He had more than stepped up as team captain. He owned the role. There were zero whispers about him not doing a good job or that he was screwing up somehow by being gay. In fact, most of the talk about his sexuality had vanished altogether, which was as surprising as it was a relief. No one much cared that he was gay or straight; he was Brad, and he was dating Kyle, and that was that.

Of course, I wasn't privy to most gossip anymore, since I had all but abandoned my previous life.

I still showed up to prom committee, because I hadn't spent the last three years doing every piece of grunt work I needed to become the chairperson, then quit. No way would I give up running it because I was sick of mean girls. I refused to resign, which drove the other girls that tiny inch over the edge into crazy. I have to admit, I loved watching them squirm while trying to find a way to ask me things with a smile on their faces. They would have loved me to step down so they could all fight to see who would run prom, but I hadn't, so they were forced to deal with me. And forced to do it nicely, which was killing them.

Watching them squirm with that was the high point of my day, to be honest.

So the day of the Archer away game, Brad came slinking into class looking like death warmed over. He told me that Kyle and he had finally moved into the having-sex stage of their relationship. I really expected to hear complaints from Kyle since I knew how bad Brad could get if he went without too long. But it seemed Mr. Graymark had met his match, if not his better, in sexual appetite from the way he looked. I didn't say anything to Brad, but it didn't surprise me that much. Quiet ones like Kyle were the ones with the most surprises. I didn't mean to laugh. I really tried not to, but I kept leaking snickers, you might say.

Brad took me out of class and tried to explain his problem to me, once I'd controlled my laughter. By the time he'd finished, it was pretty obvious to me that he needed to talk to Kyle before things got out of hand. I'm not sure why I thought Brad would actually try to do that, since I knew from personal experience that he hated conflict and would do anything to avoid an argument. His standard move had always been to apologize, even if he had no idea what I was pissed about, and hope I would forgive him. After a while I counted that as a win and let the situation die since the apology was the best I was going to get out of him.

Kyle was not me, though. And the better I got to know Kyle, the more apparent it became.

He would stress and worry about it until he imagined things to be much, much worse than they actually were. The longer Brad waited, the bigger it would get, so he was better off just saying something and cutting it off at the pass. I felt that way until I saw how crazy Kyle was over the SATs, and then I realized, the last thing Kyle needed was one more thing on his plate; he was about to explode. I pulled Brad aside and told him just to do whatever Kyle wanted because the alternative was him ending up on the ten o'clock news being referred to as "the victim."

I honestly thought that was the end of it.

The next day I saw Brad walking Kyle to the SAT, and they looked as happy as ever. I can't say that seeing them that much in love didn't hurt a little. I mean, I wasn't spiteful; there's just nothing that highlights how alone you are like seeing another couple in complete love.

I couldn't wait to get out of Foster. I stopped where I was and said that sentence out loud.

I realized I hadn't felt like that in a long time. Before I got to high school and started dating Brad, getting away was all I thought about when I looked ahead at my life. Getting into a good school or going somewhere like Dallas or Austin and going to junior college: I had a thousand dreams back in the day. Those dreams all went away when I started playing the popular game. I felt good, to be honest, like I was waking up from some kind of mind-control programming that made me giggle at jokes that weren't funny and go to the bathroom as part of a group.

"They are disgusting, aren't they?" a voice commented from behind me.

I spun around, surprised. Josh Walker was standing there looking three different kinds of hot in his letterman jacket. Only problem was that Josh knew how hot he was and used it like a bludgeon to impress anyone around him. I must have looked confused about who was disgusting, because he nodded toward Brad and Kyle.

"Are you calling my friends disgusting?" I said, balling my hands into fists.

He did a quick double take as he tried to figure out why I was so pissed. "Yeah, I mean… wait, no!" he said, holding his hands up. "I didn't mean disgusting like that. I meant how much they are in love. It's disgusting to see when you don't have it yourself."

It was an eerie echo of what I had been thinking, but I didn't cop to it. "I think expressions of affection are sweet. Not enough people have the guts to show how they feel these days." That was half true. I mean, I agreed seeing someone like those two in love when you were single sucked, but having someone who would be willing to make you the center of their universe no matter how many people were watching… that's hard to find.

"You do?" he asked in a stranger tone. "You always seemed a little more low-key."

Maybe it was the fact that I was acutely aware of how single I was. Maybe it was the fact that I had been pretending to be someone else for so long around here, that no one knew a thing about me, so having someone express how they thought I would act pissed me off. Maybe I was just being a bitch, but his words just hit me the wrong way.

"I always seemed?" I asked him angrily. "Did you learn that from your Sherlock Holmes-like skills of observation? Or from the countless hours we've spent not talking to each other? Or is it just the first thing that popped into your head, so of course you said it out loud?"

He was silent for a few seconds and then said, "Um, C?" in a halting voice.

"It's not a multiple-choice question!" I raged and stalked away from him.

"What did I say?" he asked as I stormed off to class.

If you had asked me, I couldn't tell you what he'd said that pissed me off so much. I just knew that I didn't need to be there anymore.

I was in a pissy mood all the way till lunch. It felt like I had pulled a thread loose in my mind. Now my defenses were unraveling against my will, exposing something I didn't want to face. When I got to the music hall steps, Sammy and Kyle were already there, deep in conversation. For some reason even that irritated me.

"Hey, I got you a Pepsi," Sammy said as I sat down.

I mumbled a thanks and drank half of it in one gulp.

"Thirsty much?" Sammy asked under her breath.

I felt my temper start to flare, but I forced myself not to say anything rude to her because I was 99.9 percent sure it was not her I was pissed at. Instead I looked at Kyle and asked, "How was the test?"

He rolled his eyes and sighed. "I don't know. Between having to go to the bathroom every ten minutes and feeling guilty, I barely noticed the test."

"Guilty?" I asked, intrigued. "Guilty about what?"

"I am a horrendous boyfriend, and I need to make it up to Brad."

That gave me pause. Brad had actually said something? Maybe I was wrong; maybe he had grown up some. "Don't worry about it. He's more tired than sore. It's not like he isn't enjoying it."

I finished my Pepsi and saw Kyle looking at me oddly. "Enjoying what?"

"The sex," I answered, confused. "He told me that he was worn out and didn't know how to bring it up to you. I'm impressed that he did."

"Brad said what now?"

The tone in his voice brought me to a screeching halt. Time slowed down as I realized that Brad had not said a word to Kyle and that I had just said the absolutely wrong thing. I mentally tried to backtrack, but it was way too late. "I mean… what were you guys arguing about?"

"Brad is enjoying what?" he asked again, his tone growing cold as his face contorted in anger.

"Nothing," I said lamely. Shit, shit, shit, I thought to myself in a panic. What the hell did I just do? "So, how was the test?"

"You already asked that," Sammy said from behind him.

"What did Brad tell you?" Kyle asked, every syllable sharp enough to cut glass.

I panicked. There was no good answer to that question, and all I wanted to do was to get the blame off of me.

"He said he was worn out because you guys have been having sex all the time lately and that with the practice and the stress over the test he was just beat." My words tripped over themselves as I verbally threw Brad under the bus. "But he said he was enjoying it."

Silence like I had never heard before surrounded us. Kyle looked right into my soul with those eyes, and Sammy stared at us in shock. "He told you that?" she asked in the gap of silence.

"He's my friend," I snapped at her, my emotions exploding over themselves as my lips suffered from some form of emotional diarrhea. "We've slept together, for God's sake! It wasn't like he's sharing state secrets."

"He told you about our sex life?" Kyle asked, drawing my attention back to him. "He complained to you about us having sex?"

Abruptly, I knew what it felt like on the *Titanic*. The deck is tilting, you know the ship is sinking, and you're just desperate to grab on to anything and hold on. "He was just talking, Kyle. It's not the end of the world if your boyfriend wants to talk to someone about their life. It's just what friends do."

"Do you like your nipples played with?" he asked out of nowhere.

"What?" I stuttered, dazed. The sudden shift in the conversation made me feel like I'd hit a brick wall.

"Do you like your nipples played with in bed? How important is foreplay? We're friends, so it's no big deal for you to share these things, right? Or it would be okay for Brad to tell me that stuff, right?"

I had heard Kyle rip people to shreds before, but hearing it and having it done to you are two different things. Hearing it, you have a dozen thoughts in your mind, and you're cheering him on. But when he's in front of you doing it, your only thought is to run.

"Ask him whatever you want, Kyle. He told me as a friend, and I'm sure he didn't think he was betraying a trust." I gathered up my stuff and turned to the both of them. "I have prom committee. Talk to you guys later."

They said nothing to me as I walked away. I'm not even sure I wanted them to.

EVERYTHING HAD faded into a small buzzing sound.

Not that I paid a ton of attention at these meetings anyway, because usually the first twenty minutes or so were spent gossiping and backstabbing by the Bitches of Eastwick, as Robbie called them. They prattled on about whoever they hated that week, and I sat there wondering why I'd ever opened my mouth. Of course Brad hadn't said anything to Kyle. Why would I think differently? I hadn't just made things worse between them, I made things worse for all of us.

"Yeah, it was a total passive-aggressive slip. I didn't even know until later that I wanted to say that."

I looked up at Stacy, the girl who had been talking, with a glare, thinking she had been talking to me. Instead Patricia, the girl she had been talking to, nodded and said, "I know! I always do that when I'm pissed. I don't mean to say mean stuff, but then it comes out anyways, and later that night I realize I wanted to start shit with that bitch. My mouth just figured it out first."

They cackled like the hags in Macbeth, and my blood turned to ice water.

Was that what I'd done? Did I say that to Kyle knowing it was going to cause a fight between them? Maybe I had been fooling myself this whole time. Maybe deep down I was nothing more than a shallow bitch who only cared about herself. I had just commented that seeing them that much in love reminded me of how lonely I was. Did I really sabotage them on purpose?

"I need to go," I said, interrupting their talking.

"Um, what about the prom?" Stacy asked.

"What about it? We picked the theme. We have the colors. What else is there to talk about?" I grabbed my purse and headed toward the door. "See you next time."

If they said anything to me as I left, it fell on deaf ears.

I NEARLY pounced on Kyle as he walked out of his last class.

"We need to talk," I said as I grabbed his hand and pulled him out of the building. I had no illusions that if he didn't want to go, he couldn't have stopped me, since I wasn't gripping him very tight. But he came along, which meant he was at least willing to hear me out.

That was a good thing.

Once we got out toward the quad, I let him go. "Okay, look, I'm going through a lot of crap in my head right now, and it's possible I might have said what I said because I am incredibly jealous of what Brad and you have. That makes me a raging bitch, and you need to take that into account when being mad at him."

He didn't say anything for a few seconds. At first I thought he was thinking about it, but then he let out a huge yawn.

He apologized by covering his mouth. "Sorry, I am completely burnt. I'm not mad at you. I'm just mortified that Brad would tell someone else about our sex life. I don't know why I expected more from him, but I did, and I am just sad. You didn't deserve me attacking you. I'm sorry."

The words lifted a great weight off my shoulders, but I still felt lousy for getting Brad in trouble. "Look, Kyle, you should give him a break. He's new to this whole thing."

He looked at me with bloodshot eyes, and I really began to grasp how tired he was. "Jennifer, do us both a favor. Don't try to jump in front of Brad to save him on this. He screwed up, and I don't want any reason to be angry at you. Okay?"

I understood what he meant. I had been seconds away from never talking to Robbie again because I had thought he'd been trying to justify what Brad had done to me. Even though what Brad had said was no big deal to me, it was to Kyle, which meant it was now a huge deal between the two of them. "Okay, but try to take it easy on him. We both know he didn't mean anything by it."

"No, we both know he didn't think before he said anything."

He was right, and there was nothing I could say to that. "You want a ride home?" I asked, since he looked like he was about to fall over.

He shook his head. "The walk will do me good."

It felt like he was blowing me off, but the only thing I could do was give him some space. "Okay, well, call me later. Let me know what happens." He nodded and tromped off toward home.

I had a sinking feeling this was about to get much worse.

I WENT through several bouts of crying waiting for a phone call from Brad.

The team had gotten home a little bit ago, according to some of the guys' tweets. Which meant it was a countdown until Kyle laid into him. My dad was working, which meant I didn't need to hide behind a closed door, pretending I was asleep. I expected Brad to call or to text, but instead I got him showing up at my door.

Thank God for both of us my dad wasn't there.

I swung open the door and started to ramble before he could start to scream at me. "I'm a horrible bitch and don't know when to keep my mouth shut and fucked it up for you." I walked into the house. "If you have anything you want to add to that, come in."

I didn't have to wait long. He slammed the door. "How could you? How could you even bring it up to him?"

I was done being yelled at today. Maybe tomorrow I could summon up the courage to be a punching bag for one of these guys, but tonight, I was done. I spun around and screamed back. "I was trying to help you. I thought maybe if I eased into it that it would make it easier for you two to talk. I didn't expect him to get that crazy."

"He's crazy," he said back. "I told you he was crazy. In fact, you told me before I left not to say anything because he was crazy."

I choked back another round of crying. "I know, and I fucked up." I wiped my nose. I had to look like a complete wreck. "How bad is it?"

He showed me his ring, and my breath caught in my throat. "The only thing missing was a bucket of Coke dumped over my head."

It was so much worse than I thought it was. "I can fix this," I said quickly to him. "We can fix this."

He finally stopped pacing and fell into one of the chairs and sighed. "I hope you have a plan, because minus a time machine, I don't see how."

"Look, Kyle loves you. He's just been crazy the past few weeks because of everything. He has the alliance, the SATs, and college. Trust me, once he gets some sleep and works it out, he'll be fine."

He looked up at me with the saddest eyes I had ever seen. "I don't think so."

I wanted to argue with him, but in the pit of my stomach, I felt the same way.

THE NEXT morning Kyle texted me.

Skipping school today.

Damn, I was really counting on having all day to wear him down about the whole Brad thing. I texted him back. *Do u hate me?*

I held my breath as I waited for a response. This answer would determine the rest of everything, really. If he hated me, there was no one except Sammy to plead Brad's case, and she wasn't his biggest fan. The only chance we all had of things going back to the way they were was if Kyle didn't hate me.

Even though he had every reason to.

No, not at all. We broke up, and I can't face him.

The last thing I wanted to do was tell him I knew they had broken up already. He was mad enough about Brad telling me stuff; admitting he had told me more wasn't going to help anyone. So I typed back. *Omg u broke up?*

He texted back: *Yes. Will call u l8r*

I sighed as I headed to school to tell Brad that things were as bad as he thought they were.

When I got to school, Brad was sitting on the music hall steps alone, looking like someone had run over his dog. I walked over to him and heard him muttering something to himself.

"Talking to yourself is a sure sign you're crazy," I said, sitting down next to him. He looked at me hopefully, but I shook my head. "He isn't coming to school today. He texted me so I wouldn't worry."

I saw the tears well up in his eyes as he asked me, "What if I can't fix it?"

I pulled him into a hug because I honestly didn't have an answer.

SATURDAY AFTERNOON I walked into Robbie's shop.

He arched an eyebrow at me and commented, "You look like someone just told you everything Bernadette Peters sang was Auto-Tuned."

I had no idea what he was talking about. "Kyle and Brad broke up."

He paused for maybe half a second. "Well, that didn't take long," he finally said, going back to folding.

I tried not to gape at him. "Why would you even say that?"

He tried not to sigh but failed miserably. "Did I ever tell you about John Black?" I shook my head. "He was the boy I was going to marry. He had dirty-blond hair, these incredible hazel eyes, and a body that most of the boys in West Hollywood would kill for. He was tall and lanky and did all that sports stuff like every boy in the world did. From the moment I laid eyes on him, I was utterly smitten."

"What happened?" I asked.

"Well, we ended up talking once in detention and became quasi friends. Which here means 'friends that no one else knew about.' He came over a few times, and one night he admitted he was curious, and we fooled around. It was like tripping over a muse who roller skates." I gave him a confused look, but he just waved it off. "It was incredible for a little while. Then you know what happened?"

"Something bad?" I offered.

"No. Life happened. It was high school, and life happened, and what seemed to be the most important thing in my life became a footnote in the long and highly entertaining story of the rest of my life so far. We all have Johns, my dear. In this case, you and Kyle have the same one."

He gave me a sad look, but I ignored it. "What happened to you that made you incapable of seeing true love when it is in front of you?" If I had thrown a piece of dog shit at him, I would have gotten the same look back. "I mean, you can't look at those two and see they are meant to be together?"

He rested his hands on the counter, and I could see the fake and always catty Robbie go away, leaving a deadly serious one who seemed devoid of any emotions. "I am fully capable of seeing love, Jennifer. I just happen to know there are things that it can't defend against. Things like life, distance, confused lust, and speeding cars can kill love in a split second. Brad and Kyle were sweet together, and I am sure they thought they were going to make it to the end together, but the truth is neither one of them is the person they will become. What if those two people don't like each other? Are you the same girl you were when you started high school? You think you're going to be the same after college? Are you telling me the guy you panted over at fourteen is going to do it for you at twenty-two? There's a reason they're called high school sweethearts. No one expects them to last past their expiration date."

It was the most cynical thing I had ever heard uttered out loud. The thing was, I don't think he meant a word of it. I mean, technically he did, but inside, deep inside where you could only see it in his eyes, I could tell he was just saying what he thought was safe. I had never seen such pain in an adult before, and seeing it now in someone who pretended to be as invulnerable as Robbie—it was horrible and overwhelmingly sad.

"What happened to you?" I asked hesitantly.

And just like that, he was gone, replaced with the caricature of him. "What hasn't, sweetheart? Trust me, they will both find better when they are out of this town."

"You don't believe that," I said, like a bloodhound on the scent of prey. "You're just saying that because it's easy. Robbie, what happened to you?"

He slammed his hands on the counter, startling the shit out of me. "Life happened," he roared. "A messy and completely merciless life happened, and it sucked, and you know what? There is nothing anyone can do about it. Not me, not you, and not your precious Kyle!" He seemed as shocked as I was and took a second to smooth his hair with fingers that trembled. "It seems so easy when you're young, but trust me, life has a bitch of a learning curve, and there are no second chances. It's better they learn now how hard it can be."

I waited a few seconds before replying, "You're upset right now, so this isn't going to make much sense, but I am not mad at you, and when you have calmed down, I'm here if you want to talk."

It took him a few seconds to realize I was paraphrasing his own words. He gave me a mirthless smile and waggled a finger at me. "Nice try, my dear, but I am immune from my own spells. I do give you an A for effort."

"Brad and Kyle belong together," I said like I was reciting an oath. "You know it as well as I do. If he comes in here, will you try to talk some sense into him?"

He laughed. "I think he found all the sense he needs."

I practically sprinted to the counter and grabbed the dog tag chain he wore around his neck. "If you are a decent human being, you will talk to him and try to keep whatever emotional cancer you have out if it. Those two were born to be together. I'm sorry some kid was mean to you in high school, but this is different, and you know it." He said nothing as he stared back at me. "I'm asking you as a friend. No, I'm begging you. Please keep your own shit out of it and help him."

He just nodded.

I let him go. "Thank you."

He straightened the chain, and we stood there in uncomfortable silence for almost a minute before he said, "So you done going all She-Ra on me?" I nodded. "Fine. There is new stuff on the rack. Go look and let's never speak of this again."

I couldn't have agreed more.

I WAS halfway home when Kyle texted me. *Can you come over?*

It was the first actual sign of life I had seen or heard from him, so of course I pulled over and texted him that of course I could. Ten minutes later I was knocking on his door. He answered, and I asked immediately, "What's wrong?"

He handed me an envelope without saying a word. I felt like he was giving me a ransom letter for a few seconds. He nodded at it, and I read who it was from. It was from UC Berkeley. It was still sealed shut. "Is this for real?" I asked, even though I knew it was. He nodded, and I suddenly felt sick to my stomach. I tried to hand it back to him, but he shook his head.

"I can't open it," he said weakly. "I think I'm going to have a stroke."

"You want me to open it?" He practically collapsed onto the couch and nodded. I sat across from him and began to carefully open it, afraid that if I tore it open it might explode or something. I got halfway and asked him again, "You're sure?" He nodded again. I ripped it the rest of the way and opened it, revealing the piece of paper inside. I unfolded it and peered inside the envelope, wondering if fireworks were going to come screaming out of it.

He leaned back and closed his eyes as I began to read it.

I gasped as I got to the middle of the first paragraph.

"What's it say?" he asked me anxiously.

"You got in," I said, not believing what I was reading. "They're offering you a full scholarship, including room and board." I turned the paper over. "There is a web address. They want you to go and register." He seemed to have stopped breathing. "Kyle, you just got into college!" I screamed, throwing the paper up in the air. I rushed over and hugged him, but he didn't move, frozen in shock.

"Did you hear me? You just got a full ride to Berkeley!"

He looked at me and blinked a few times before nodding. "I got into college." I felt like cheering. "In California." I couldn't contain my smile anymore.

I went to hug him again, and he stopped me, and we locked eyes. "Don't tell Brad."

That was when I knew this wasn't all good news.

AFTER A while I went home in a daze. I had never seen someone so depressed about good news in my life. Luckily I had my laptop in my trunk so he could log on and verify that the letter was for real. The amount of the scholarship was insane.

He seemed confused since the SAT score that got him in was one of the ones he was trying to beat, but it seemed he had more than enough to qualify for Berkeley. He wouldn't go into why I couldn't tell Brad.

I fell asleep with an upset stomach, knowing I should say something.

That day my dad and I went to church and then took in a late breakfast at Nancy's. We began to talk about what was new, and I told him about Kyle's letter.

"That's impressive," he admitted after a few seconds. "What about you?"

I shrugged. "What about me?"

"Have you applied anywhere?"

"No. It's not like we're rich or anything. I was thinking community college or something. Maybe I could get a job at Robbie's."

I looked away because it wasn't what I wanted in the least, but it was realistic. My dad didn't make a ton of money; there was no way he could afford a real college.

He put his hand on mine. "Jennifer." When I didn't look at him, his voice got sterner. "Jennifer." I looked up. "You think I haven't been ready for this? You think I haven't been planning for this since the day you were born? Do you want to go to college?" I nodded, my eyes beginning to sting. "Then how about you apply to where you want to go and let me worry about paying for it."

"You don't have the money for—" I began to protest.

He put up one finger, stopping me in midrant. "Me, grown-up. You, child." I gave him a look. "Okay, fine—you, young woman. Me, worry about money and finances. You, worry about boys and whatever you think about."

I rolled my eyes. "It isn't that easy."

He didn't even blink. "Yes, it is. I want you to have the life you want. Let me give it to you."

I hated that I began to cry.

"Okay, I'm going to take that as a yes," he said, leaning back in the booth. "Let me ask you a question." I looked up. "What do you think of Dorothy Aimes?"

I looked up, and my tears stopped as I smiled. "Oh… really?"

He blushed and looked away. "Forget I said a thing."

I didn't say anything more, but I think my dad has a crush on Kelly's mom.

I WAS almost ready for bed when someone banged on my bedroom door.

I tossed on a robe and cracked the door to see Brad standing there out of breath. "Brad? What the hell…?"

He came barging in my room, oblivious that I was a little freaked-out he was there that late on a Sunday. "I had to tell someone before I exploded."

There was no way I was shutting the door. Gay or not, Brad was a boy, and my dad was not going to let a boy be in my room with me, so instead I sat on the edge of my bed in clear view of the hall. "Tell someone what?"

He handed me a letter, and I felt a sense of déjà vu, my first instinct that it was some kind of joke. "Is this for real?" I asked.

He nodded, and I knew it was for real.

It was a letter of intent from A&M saying they were willing to negotiate a four-year scholarship for him to play ball. I looked up and saw my dad standing there. "Is this a scholarship?" I asked him.

He walked in and looked over the paper, but Brad answered. "No, my dad says they're just saying they are interested in offering me something, but I need to say I'm going to sign with them before they make a deal."

My dad looked up. "You know you can tell them to go to hell, right?" Brad looked a little shocked as my dad handed the paper over. "They're asking you to do this because they don't want to haggle with anyone. It's a preemptive strike to make sure they get you."

Brad smiled and folded the letter back up. "My dad said the same thing."

My dad looked around and said, "Well, congratulations and all. Let's wrap things up, okay?" He looked at me, and I nodded.

As soon as my dad walked out, Brad gave me a desperate look. "I need to ask you a favor."

Oh God, this could be happening.

"Sure," I said neutrally.

"Please don't tell Kyle."

Oh, I was wrong. It was much, much worse than that.

APRIL 9
TONIGHT, TONIGHT
67 DAYS LEFT

Robbie

SO ONCE upon a time there were these two boys who fell in love.

Now, you would think that in a world as vast as ours, with so many people and choices out there, two people making any kind of connection at all would be celebrated. Like winning the lottery or finding a magical box that takes you back to 1975 so you can see opening night of *A Chorus Line*, things like two people making a connection should be as valuable as they are rare.

But people who win the lottery usually don't possess all of their teeth, and they blow the money before they actually get it, and with my luck if I was to find such a magical box, it would have been taken over by angelic statues that would end up trying to eat me. So what I am saying is, just because two people find each other in this world doesn't mean it's always a good thing.

Sometimes it leads nowhere. Sometimes it just peters out. And sometimes one of them is killed, and the other is left to wonder how to manage getting up each morning without chemical aid.

I digress.

So there are these two boys, and they fell in love. And as boys are prone to do, they screwed things up. As boys are prone to do. Boys, and I am referring to emotional boys—my criticism is not limited to chronological age—boys are stupid, stupid creatures. They spend an inordinate amount of time trying to be what they think society wants them to be, because the worst thing in the world a man can be called is a girl.

Which is offensive on so many levels I can't even begin to explain.

Now, call a girl a boy or a man or even a tomboy and she will shrug and roll her eyes because one, it is a stupid insult, and two, there is nothing really offensive in the statement. Which I think is funny, since guys are so stupid you'd think being called a guy would be an insult, but it isn't, and I can't explain why except to say

158

that up to this point it has been a man's world, which explains why it is in such a crappy state, if you ask me.

Which you didn't, so let me continue.

So the boys, being boys, screwed it up and then made it worse. One of the boys, who was a big baby and fearful of anything that resembled actual human emotion, ran away from his feelings and refused to hear the other boy. The other boy had done everything but fall to his knees and beg the first boy to take him back. It was an impressive display of nonboyness, if you ask me, since the second boy could have easily dated anyone he wanted, but he fought for the first boy's heart.

Which of course just scared the first boy to death.

So for two weeks this went on, the first boy running and the second boy chasing, while their friends looked on in confusion. I'd seen it before. A group of friends are close, and then a couple breaks up and suddenly it's like a messy divorce, and the kids have to figure out who they want to live with. No one knew who they wanted to live with yet; they were still under the impression the two boys might make up.

I was not under that impression at all.

You see, teenage love bored me. In fact, most love bored me these days, but let's not stray, shall we? We're talking about the boys. Teenage love is like glitter. Don't look at me that way. I have logic on my side. Glitter is a wondrous thing. It is sparkly and beautiful, and it can be entrancing in the right light. Glitter, on the surface, seems to be one of the best things in the world, especially in a club as you kiss that boy at midnight and it is falling all around you, making even the nastiest dive look magical.

But then that's it.

It falls to the ground, and it gathers under your feet and just makes a huge mess. It doesn't look so nice later in the night, and everyone tries to ignore it, and the people whose job it is to clean it up? I assure you they hate glitter in a biblical way. So then you go home, you change, you shower, you wonder how all that crap got in your hair, and you go to sleep. The glitter is in a trash bag and the night is over. In the end, it served no purpose at all outside of being a momentary flash of magic in an otherwise mundane life.

The only other time glitter matters is months later, when you pull a shirt out and you see some embedded into it. And you wonder how it got there, and then the memory of that night drifts through your mind, and through the filter of time passed, the whole night becomes magical retroactively. Then you shake your head, wonder whatever happened to that guy, brush it out of your shirt, and get ready for work.

And that's it. A moment of magic and then the memory of it later. Glitter and teenage romance—equally useless, equally disposable.

So in my mind, the fact these two boys had decided to end things sooner rather than later was a good thing. They both had their real lives coming up, and it was time to leave high school life behind. Or as it has been said: When I was a child, I talked like a child, I thought like a child, I reasoned like a child. When I became a man, I put the ways of childhood behind me. See how I said that and nothing began to smoke or sizzle? I was under the opinion it was time for these two boys to become men.

But all you have to do is look at nearly anything in the world and see my opinion does not mean much outside my own head.

And even then, not that much.

So when the first boy came to me for advice, as all young and naïve commoners do in fairy tales, I wanted to tell him to stay the course and just wait it out until he graduated. It was a sensible plan and, I think, the right thing to do. Of course, though, I had made other promises. I had already sworn I would help get the two boys back together, so help I would.

The next time I saw Kyle, I dropped a not-so-subtle hint I needed some work done at the shop and I had just gotten some new shirts in that would make perfect payment if some skinny twink-looking bitch wanted to help me.

Complete lie, I was still unpacking shit from the last time I visited my mom and sister, but he didn't need to know that.

He accepted with a sigh, which I took more about his relationship status and less on his enthusiasm for helping me. Because everyone loves helping me. I'm a pip. Of course all he did was stand there, fold things and sigh once in a while. Luckily for him I was once a sullen, moody teenage bitch and knew all he needed was a change of topic.

"So, big day Monday, huh?" I asked Kyle as he folded the pile of clothes in front of him.

He didn't say a thing as he just kept folding.

"Bueller? Bueller?" I droned, getting his attention.

"Huh?" he asked. He looked like he had forgotten I was there.

Can you imagine anyone forgetting I was in a room? Trust me, it was a first.

"I said, big day Monday?"

He nodded and went back to folding.

God save me from teenage queens and their funks.

I grabbed the sweater out of his hands, and he looked up at me in confusion. "If you're going to be helping me, I need you to actually be here and not be moping because you're too stupid to take your boyfriend back."

There was a momentary glimmer of the stubbornness I knew was inside him. "I'm here."

I held up the sweater. "You've been folding this for twenty minutes now. Unless you're going to turn it into a swan or something, I think it's safe to say you're distracted."

He sighed and went to grab another piece of clothing.

"I swear to you, if you put your grubby little hands on one more piece of merchandise in hopes you can use it to ignore me some more, I will personally shove it so far up your ass you will hiccup fabric swatches."

A small smile flickered across his mouth, and I knew my declaration had done its job.

Finally he admitted, "I just thought he'd be there with me the first day."

"Then answer your phone one of the fifty times he calls you every day and take him back. Problem solved." I began to fold the sweater myself.

"It's better this way," he said, sounding the same way you'd say it's better for Fluffy if you put her down because she is just in pain. It's not something you want to do, but once you make the decision, you just can't look the cat in the eye again. Kyle didn't want to look Brad in the eye again because if he did, he'd crack, and all this drama would be forgotten. "I mean, it was never going to work anyways."

My hands paused as I heard my own words coming out of his mouth.

It was one thing to hear that kind of defeatist dogma come out of someone who was… I was going to say older, but let's use wiser. It was one thing to hear myself drone on about it, but to hear it from his mouth… well, that was too depressing for words. I put the sweater down and looked him right in the eye. "Well, if you jump out of the boat at the first sign of trouble, then yes, you're right; you are going to get wet. Of course, if you know you're going to lose before you play, then you don't ever have to go to Vegas, and if you know you're going to die eventually, you don't need to live. So you have that whole life thing wrapped up there, my young friend."

He said nothing for a few seconds and then asked, "How did we get to Vegas boats?"

It was a nice feint, and with anyone else it might have worked. "Nice try, but it's far too late to start playing dumb when you don't like the conversation. Sure Sporty Spice fucked up, but instead of trying to work it out, you just blew up the whole thing in seconds flat. Now, I am not his biggest fan, but I do know there are way worse things than talking about your sex life to someone else. It's not like he posted it on Facebook for the world to see, and you know what? I think you know that. So what is this really about?"

Kyle and I had danced around the subject of the breakup for two weeks now, and up to now I had backed off out of respect and all that garbage. Okay, fine, I backed off because I honestly didn't have the heart to go the ten rounds it was going to take to get Kyle to admit what the real problem was. That, and I suppose deep down I was hoping he would fix it himself.

"I just realized there was no way it was going to work between us," he said, taking a shirt to fold.

"And you based this on your years and years of experience of dating and healthy relationships?" He paused and glared at me. "No, really, explain it to me, because what do I know? I've only dated more men than are named in the Bible, so what do I know? Educate me, Kyle. Tell me why it wasn't going to work out."

He dropped the shirt and stood up. "I don't think I need to explain myself to you."

It was a pretty good imitation of me, but it lacked the pizzazz it needed to have any effect. "You're right. You don't need to say one word to me." He nodded and grabbed his coat. "But don't you think Brad deserves one or two?"

I saw him stiffen for half a second, and I knew. If I hadn't just sunk his battleship, I had at the very least scored a direct hit on it. "See you later," he said, walking out without turning back.

"Dammit," I said out loud. "I couldn't have waited to alienate him until he finished with his stack?"

AN HOUR from closing, someone new walked in my door.

Now, I am not an expert on all things Foster, and I will admit I don't have a picture directory to keep all the names and faces together, but I do know a pretty face when I see one. The town gets bunched up into categories in my mind, where they are stored for memory's sake. There are old people, which there are a lot of. There are hicks, which there are more of. There are kids, a word that spans from babies to Kyle. There are guys I wouldn't touch with a ten-foot pole, and there is Tyler.

Tyler gets his own space because no one in the world deserves to be shelved next to him.

The guy who walked into the store fell into none of those categories.

He was bigger than the average Foster boy, and I don't mean fat. He was wider, huskier, and I suppose, in the right light, handsome. He wasn't my type, but then lately nothing was my type. He was my age, which was odd because I thought I had a working knowledge of everyone who could turn my head in Foster.

Normally I would have thought he was a new resident, but from the clothes he had on to the way he carried himself, I knew he grew up here.

"Help you?" I asked cheerfully, trying to keep any suspicion out of my voice.

"Just looking around," he said distractedly. "Do you guys sell jackets?"

"Back corner." I pointed, noticing he had a pretty nice jacket on already.

He sorted through the racks slowly, almost too slowly for my taste. Oh sure, tell me I'm being overdramatic, but I knew sooner or later someone would come into the shop meaning me harm. True, I expected them years ago, but it doesn't change the fact I did not trust anyone from this town at all. I panicked slightly as I realized I didn't have a weapon to my name, so I put my hand on Liza's book and waited.

He continued to browse for a length of time no straight man has ever browsed before. My mind shifted from paranoia to suspicion as I took a careful inventory of him. His clothes at first glance looked like they were normal for Foster, but as I checked his ass, I could tell this wasn't true. Everything he had on was designer in some way, yet still managed to look like he got it from Walmart. His hair was cut short, which seemed to be the cut guys around here favored, but there was product in it, which reminded me of someone, but I couldn't place who. It wasn't until he walked to another rack that I had him.

His shoes were to die for.

Most guys around here either wore disgusting work boots that looked like they had been salvaged from World War II, or tennis shoes that some Indonesian kid earned half a cent making before they ended up on clearance. These were leather, John Varvatos chukka boots that were two hundred bucks if they were a dollar. This guy was rocking some decent hetero camouflage, but I'm sorry, sweetie, your shoes just clocked you as a 'mo. Which meant he wasn't here to beat me to death... so then, who was he?

"You new to town?" I asked, trying to make the question sound as innocent as possible. I had long ago found that nearly anything that came out of my mouth was either taken as sarcastic or flirty, depending on how much alcohol I had imbibed, so I had crafted a voice that to me sounded nothing like either extreme.

He looked over at me with an odd expression. Finally he shook his head and went back to looking at clothes. "No, I grew up around here. I just moved back, though."

"Oh," I said, actually surprised. The thought of someone willingly moving back to this town seemed ludicrous to me. I mean, it had taken Riley months and months to talk me into giving up the real world to come back and settle down in Mayberry, and even then, it was a hard sell. He had argued for days and days that the town was nothing like what I thought it was and that we would be deliriously happy here.

My sister also once convinced me that the Easter bunny only hid eggs that he found in the house he was visiting and talked me into hiding a dozen eggs under my bed a week before to help him out. Of course I forgot about them, and a month later the smell began to seep out under my bed and permeate everything I owned. My mom lost her shit when she found out what the smell was and punished both of us severely.

I was seven years old at the time, and that decision was about as dumb as moving here.

"Family problems?" I asked after a few seconds. He looked up at me again. This time the look on his face was even more confused, so I added quickly, "I just can't imagine many reasons for someone to move back here willingly."

A smile flickered over his mouth, and I had to admit, for not my type, he was kind of cute. "I don't have to ask if you're from Foster or not."

I held a hand to my chest. "Moi? What gave me away? Lack of livestock? Complete sentences? My keen fashion sense?"

"Actually, the spiked hair and eyeliner kind of cinched it," he said with a grin.

"I'm Robbie," I said, extending a hand to him.

"Matt," he said, shaking it before going back to the clothes.

"So what brings you in?" I asked, now definitely curious.

"I was just looking to see the lay of the land," he explained as he continued to poke at the rack. "Just trying to catch up with the town and everything. I remember this place being a bit more...."

"Golden Girls?" I prompted him.

He nodded slowly. "I was going to say Maude, but same difference."

"I bought it a few years ago and decided Foster was ready for actual fashion." I pointed at him. "Kind of like your shoes."

He looked down at them and then back up to me. Damned if he didn't blush. "Shit," he said more to himself. "I thought I had done so well too."

"From afar, you did," I said, almost laughing at his expression. "But in this town, you could have had a matching clutch and not have been as obvious as those shoes."

"Can you blame me for buying them?" he asked with a sparkle in his eye.

Was he flirting with me? For real?

"No, but then again, they aren't my style."

He shrugged. "Well, to each his own." He grabbed a couple of shirts and walked to the counter. "I'll take these."

I folded them and then rang them up. "So, Matt moved back to town. Care to tell me the real reason you came in here?"

I saw his hands freeze as he unfolded his wallet. This guy was cute, but if he came in here to flirt with the only gay guy in town, then it was my obligation to tell him he was a tree or two away from the one he should be barking at. He slowly pulled a credit card out. "That obvious, huh?" he asked, handing it to me.

"To the casual observer?" I said, swiping the card. "No. But when someone your size comes in, looks through five racks, and bags two shirts that wouldn't fit over your chest, I begin to wonder what's going on." I handed him the bill to sign.

"My size?" he asked with what I assumed was mock offense. "You calling me fat?"

I took the receipt and closed the drawer. "No, fat is not the word that comes to mind. Healthy, fit, built like a brick house? More accurate."

He put his wallet away and took a deep breath. Here it came, the eventual ask out that I was going to have to shoot down. Poor guy.

"I'm dating Tyler."

"I'm sorry, but…." And my brain locked up. "You said what?" I asked before I was even aware.

"My name is Matt Wallace, and I am dating Tyler Parker," he repeated a little slower. "I had heard about you and wanted to see you with my own eyes."

A coldness emanated from my chest outward to my extremities. It felt like the reverse of having an IV of morphine, where the warmness moves through your veins eventually to your heart, taking you to a most magical place where things like pain have no power. This was the complete opposite of that feeling. Instead of numbness, I felt raw pain, as for half a second, I felt everything from that night Riley died replay. Someone associated with Tyler being this close just broke past the paper-thin walls I had separating me from my memories, and I hated it.

"He too chickenshit to come in himself?" I asked, venom spewing out with each word. "He has to send his boyfriend to see if the coast is clear?"

"He doesn—"

"Shut up. You tell Tyler I have nothing to say to him, and if I did, I sure wouldn't say it to his closet case of a boyfriend. This isn't high school. He doesn't need to slip me a note in my locker. Tell him to be a man and—"

"He doesn't know I'm here!" he shouted over me.

"Well, of course he doesn't," I replied. "Because the only thing Tyler Parker knows how to do is run. Run and hide like a little bitch. I don't know you, Matt, and I don't want to, but take my word. That man is not to be trusted, and he will bring you nothing but pain."

Matt waited for me to take a pause. "He came out." When he saw I had no response to that at all, he repeated it. "He came out at some kid's funeral, and it was because of what happened between you and him. He hates himself for what happened, and you can't think that he doesn't feel like shit for what he did."

I let a few seconds of silence settle between us before I asked him, "And?"

That took him back a second. "And what?"

"And nothing," I said. "I don't care if he died and came back as a whole other person. He is still Tyler, and he still hasn't said one word to me since that day. Not one. So it doesn't matter if he grew hoofs and a horn and became a unicorn. He is still the asshole he always was. So you two have a nice life together, and when he fucks you over, and he will, just assume an 'I told you so' from me."

He looked like he wanted to say more, but the expression on my face made it pretty clear the conversation was over.

"For what it's worth," he said, leaving the bag on the counter, "I'm sorry for your loss."

I picked up the bag and threw it at him as he opened the door. "You forgot your beard."

He caught it and looked at me with an incredibly sad expression before walking out.

My heart was pounding, and I could feel my breath coming like the DJ had just played the *Grease* megamix and I just had to dance it out. I looked at my wrist and nodded. "Just as I thought," I said to myself. "It's vodka time."

"CAN YOU believe the nerve?" I said into the phone.

"Fuck off and die!" my sister responded, shouting. I waited for a few seconds before she added, "Yeah, it does seem kinda immature."

I took another drink of my wine as I flipped through Netflix for something to watch. "It's bullshit. Passive-aggressive bullshit."

"Awww, poor baby gonna suck a dick and cry?" she called out. I waited for her actual response. "Well… yeah, I guess that's one way of looking at it." Before I could respond, she exclaimed loudly, "Then stop fucking playing, noob!"

I guess I should explain a little about Nicole, my little sister.

Nicole was the only person I had ever met who could be a spy. She looked like a typical just-turned-twenty pretty girl who liked nothing more than partying. And though that was true to a point, Nikki hid a double life that no one else had guessed.

She was a secret nerd.

She lived to log in to first-person shooting games and head-shoot teenage douchebags while taunting them over voice chat. Now, normally the sound of an actual female voice in one of those games would be like dropping a naked Channing Tatum in the middle of Fire Island, but in this case it was different. Nicole was viciously deadly and had a reputation online already about her expertise with a virtual rifle. Most thought she was an urban legend, a girl who played video games; others assumed she was, like, five hundred pounds and owned cats. Both were wrong. For fun, Nikki would wander into Best Buy and ask the tech guys what was a good computer and stuff, all the while twirling her hair and batting her eyelashes. If the guy tried to sell her crap, she knew he was an asshole and shut him down quick. If he knew what he was talking about and tried to do her right, she would eventually drop her number.

It was sad to see so many straight boys trip themselves over quad processing.

So when I called her to tell her about Matt's little adventure, she was in the middle of a session of "head shot Saturday," as she called it, so if I wanted to talk, she would have to multitask while she killed people.

"What's another way of looking at it?" I asked cautiously.

She sighed, which was directed toward me, and said, "Crybaby," which was directed to some poor jerk who just got his game ended. "I can't see this Tyler person sending his boyfriend in to feel you out."

I almost did a spit take. "You don't even know this guy!"

"No," she said calmly. "But I do know guys, and what is there to gain from it? If he sent his boyfriend in, then why would said boyfriend give himself up and tell you?" Before I could respond, she shouted, "Sit the fuck down, bitch!"

I hated the fact she was smart. I really hated the fact she was smart and younger than me.

"Maybe he's an idiot," I threw out, already feeling the holes in my argument start to widen.

"Yeah, he's a guy, so that means he's an idiot," she said, the sound of plastic being tapped rapidly accenting her words. "But he wouldn't go through the whole browsing show if he was that stupid."

Did I mention I hated the fact she was smart?

"Okay then, Veronica Mars, why did he come in?"

She paused a few seconds before answering, which meant she was actually thinking about her response. That didn't bode well. "He came in there for the very reason he said he did. I think he was telling the truth."

"Then what are you arguing with me about?" I looked over at the bottle of wine. It was a little lower than I expected.

"We're arguing because you said you were pissed because Tyler sent this Matt guy in to spy on you. I don't think he did, and I think you don't think that either."

Yes, I had drunk a little too much wine, because it took me three times to get that sentence down. "So if I did know that, then why am I upset?" I was no longer sure if I was arguing with her or actually asking her.

There was silence, real silence on the other line, and I realized she had paused her game. That meant I really wasn't going to like what came next.

"I think you're pissed because you thought he was flirting with you, and for a couple of seconds you liked it." I heard her put the controller down. "And I think you think that somehow you're cheating on Riley. So you're mad at Matt for making you think that, and you're mad at yourself for liking feeling that way."

My eyes were stinging as I put the wine down.

"What are you still doing there, Mario?" she asked, using the nicknames we used when we were much, much younger. "You know the princess is in another castle."

I bit, literally bit, my lip to stop myself from sobbing. "Maybe I don't have any lives left."

"Come home," she said, tears in her voice now.

"I need to go," I said, turning the TV off.

"That's what I've been saying."

"Thanks for the chat. Be nice to the boys," I told her gruffly as I tried to cough away my emotions.

She sighed in resignation. "Call me later."

I didn't reply as I hung up the phone.

I WAS nursing a pretty sizable hangover the next day as Kyle talked to me.

I wish I could say I was paying attention, but the truth was, the salient facts of what he was saying were lost on me as Nicole's words bounced around my head. Painfully bounced, I might add. I should have just kept the store closed and gorged myself on *Ab Fab* until this feeling of darkness passed.

"So what do you think?" Kyle asked me.

I looked up at him and realized a good chunk of time had passed, and I hadn't said a word in response. I opened my mouth as I prayed for something to happen to save me from having to explain to this poor boy that I hadn't been listening to him.

They say when God is feeling puckish, he answers wishes.

The door swung open, and I felt the whole shop tilt like I was in the Batman show from the '60s. I literally stopped breathing as she walked into my shop and looked around with casual arrogance. It seemed Matt was only one of the spirits that were going to haunt me.

This was the ghost of Christmas Past, Dolores Mathison. Riley's mother.

"Oh my God, it's her," Kyle whispered to me.

I felt two things simultaneously. One, relief because he could see her too, which was followed by immediate shock that he recognized her. "You know her?" I asked in the same whisper.

He nodded. "She was the lady who came to the school board meeting to get the alliance approved. Everyone made it seem like she was a big thing."

"A big thing" wouldn't even begin to cover it.

She looked over at me, and I felt that same sickening feeling in my stomach, as if just standing there, I was a disappointment to her. I almost succumbed to the impulse to flee in the face of true evil before remembering that this was my shop, and there was no way Cruella de Vil here was going to give me attitude within these four walls.

"Kyle," I said loud enough for her to hear, "go in the back and fold something." My eyes never left her.

"Fold what?" he asked, confused.

I looked over at him and jerked my neck. "Anything. Just go in the back."

He nodded and turned around, making sure to walk as far away from her as humanly possible.

"Robert," she said, knowing damn well I hated being called that.

"Dolly," I said with a huge fake smile, damn well knowing she despised that. "What brings you down off the mountain? Running out of virgins to sacrifice?"

I saw the small twitch around her mouth and knew I had scored.

"Charming as ever," she said, giving me a smile that made me feel even smaller than I already did. "So this is your place?"

"Be it ever so humble," I replied, waiting for the dig.

She looked around again and then back to me. "It's far too fashionable for Foster. I can't imagine how you stay in business."

I didn't have a response to that because I couldn't tell if it was an insult or not.

"You look well," she said, walking up to the counter. "How have you been?"

"Alone," I said, each letter frozen in acid like bile.

She looked at me, and I could see the pain in her eyes. "I know the feeling."

Neither one of us said a word, since we were both looking at the invisible corpse of Riley lying there between us. My head was pounding, and I knew it wasn't the damn hangover. I decided to get this over with and just pull the trigger. "So what brings you in?" I asked her, not caring one bit why she was there.

"I was…," she began to say and then paused. "Nowhere near this neighborhood," she admitted. "You don't happen to have something to drink here? This is far more difficult than I had expected."

I slid open the bottom drawer under the counter and pulled out half a bottle of tequila and two shot glasses. There is absolutely no reason for me to explain how or why they got there; suffice it to say they were there and move on. I poured us each a shot of the amber liquid and held mine up. She looked at hers, and I wondered if she was going to chicken out. Finally she shrugged, picked it up, and tapped my glass. "To Riley."

That I could drink to.

It burned going down, and I winced as I swallowed. She didn't so much as blink as she threw it back. She looked at the glass for a moment in contemplation. "Quaint," she commented and held it out. "Again."

I poured, knowing that at the very least it would deal with the hangover.

After the second shot, she grabbed one of the stools by the wall and sat down across from me. "I was serious. This place is far too progressive for most of the residents. I can't imagine the kids buy enough to keep you solvent."

I nodded and poured myself another one. "It's a labor of love. I sell enough to keep the lights on. Everything else is already paid for." I held the bottle over her glass, and she thought about it for a few seconds and then nodded.

"Riley's settlement," she said as I picked up my glass. "Right?"

I gripped the shot glass tightly, and a few drops fell onto the counter. "Yes." I was surprised I got the word out with my teeth clenched shut. The family had given me a pretty sizable chunk of cash when Riley had died, and all I had to do was never talk to them again, which suited me just fine. It was a nice way to get cash if you could stomach watching the most important man in your universe die in front of you.

"Good," she said, tossing the shot back like it was water. "He would have liked this place." She put the shot glass down. "He would have liked to see you happy." She looked at me. "You are happy, right?"

I took my shot and nearly broke the counter as I slammed the glass down. "Of course I'm not, Dolores. How can I be?"

Her mask slipped a bit, and I saw the unabashed pain in her expression as she nodded slightly to me. "Arthur asked me if I was happy the other day, and I said those exact words."

"How is Arthur?" I asked, the warmth of the booze dispelling my hesitation. "He still threatening to sue anyone who says his son was gay?"

Her face paled as she froze in place. After a second she looked away. "I deserved that. We were horrible to you after what happened. That was inexcusable." I hated how she could make everything she had done to me sound like a lapse of manners instead of a systematic plan to destroy me because she blamed me for Riley's death. Only the very rich and the very evil could pull that off convincingly.

I opened my mouth to hurl a dozen biting and completely insulting comments at her, and something in my mind stopped me. Instead I heard myself ask in a very neutral tone, "What did you come here for, Dolores? Forgiveness? Absolution? Fine." I made the sign of the cross at her. "Go forth and sin no more. Anything else?"

She looked like she was going to stand up and be insulted, but instead she just sat there, looking like the frail old lady she really was. She had always been this juggernaut of a person to me; the fact she was composed of actual skin and bones seemed ludicrous. I would have believed she had been sent from the future to kill John Connor before I acknowledged she was a human being.

Because human beings don't do what she did to other human beings.

"I am done hating you," she said, opening her purse. "I blamed you for his death, wished you were dead, and now I realize I was wrong. Riley was Riley, and his death was nothing more than a horrible incident in a series of horrible incidents that make up a life. I lashed out at you, and that was wrong, and I wanted to make it right."

"If you are going to offer me money, I swear I will knock that wig right off your head." I was shocked to hear the venom in my voice as I threatened her.

"No," she said, pulling an envelope out of her purse. "I'm not going to offer you a thing besides my apology. Trying to buy your forgiveness would be as useless as it was insulting." She held the envelope out to me. "This is not from me. It's from Riley."

I looked at the piece of paper like it was a snake.

"Arthur got a ruling, and there is no legal reason that I should be giving this to you." When it was obvious I wasn't going to take it, she put it on the counter. "However, there are a thousand other reasons to give it to you, the least being my son loved you with all his heart." I saw her eyes well up with tears. "And for that I thank you. I never could make Riley happy, no matter how hard I tried. I'm glad you were able to."

She stood up and smoothed her dress. "I expect we won't be doing this again, so let me say this and I will be gone." She took a deep breath. "I was wrong, and I am sorry." I could see her wondering if there was anything else to add, but instead she just nodded to herself and walked out the door.

It wasn't until Kyle walked out of the backroom looking like he just saw a murder that I realized she was really gone. "What was that?" he asked, looking out the door to see her driving away.

"I have no earthly idea," I admitted, looking down at the envelope.

"What's in it?" he asked, walking up to the counter.

"Do I look like I have X-ray vision?" I snapped at him. "How the hell am I supposed to know?"

He sat on the stool and stared at it with me. "So open it," he prompted.

I looked up at him. "You open it."

"Okay," he said almost instantly and picked it up.

"Wait!" I said, stopping him. He froze, looking at me. "No, go ahead." He began to tear it open. "No, give it to me." He handed it to me. I just stared at it. "No, you open it."

In a flash he tore it open, and an envelope and a piece of paper fell out. It was a check, and from the way the blood rushed out of Kyle's cheeks when he looked at it, there were a lot of zeroes on it.

I didn't care about the check. As far as I was concerned, it was blood money. What I was terrified of was the letter. I could see my name in Riley's handwriting on the front, and I began to have a panic attack. Last time I was this bad was after he died. My vision began to pinhole as I struggled to breathe. The world began to spin as I screamed at myself not to faint in front of the fucking kid.

I don't even remember hitting the ground.

THERE IS nothing in the human experience like losing time.

I mean, normally when people talk about passing out, they make it sound like they went to sleep for a little bit, which is not unconscious. When you fall asleep, you're in an altered state of consciousness. If you're aware you were sleeping, you were in some way conscious. If you are one second sitting up having a panic attack and the next find yourself lying down somewhere else, that is, my friends, a blackout. I have had more than a few experiences with them over the years, so I speak with confidence that there is a vast difference between what it is and what people think it is.

But then, life itself is a lot like that. The contents resemble nothing like what is shown on the package when you buy it.

So when I woke up, which is a phrase I loathe, I found myself still in some kind of nightmarish dream state, where the worst things my mind could summon up were presented to me like a waiter offering up the daily special. I knew this because I had to be trapped in some nightmare; otherwise, that would mean Tyler was standing over me, holding a cold cloth on my forehead.

With more strength than I would have expected, I batted his hand away from my person. "Get off," I said, trying to sit up to get away from him.

That was a mistake.

Seems my body hadn't gotten all the blood where it was supposed to be yet, because my head spun like a country fair Tilt-A-Whirl as I fell back into what I realized was a pile of clothes. "Happy?" Tyler asked, his face an expression of distaste that had to be mirroring my own. "You want to hiss and claw, wait until you have some balance back first, kitten." He dropped the towel on my face and looked to Kyle. "He's going to be fine."

One plus one equaled a dead teenager.

"You called him?" I asked the shocked-looking Kyle, sitting up slightly. He nodded mutely, taking a half step back. "Why would you do that?" I roared, ignoring Tyler completely. It wasn't that hard. I had a couple of years practice already.

"Because you tipped over and slammed into the floor pretty hard," Meathead explained instead. "He wasn't sure if you were having a heart attack or just doing a pretty fair Judy Garland impersonation."

I looked over to him. "Get out" was all I managed to say.

He shrugged and looked at Kyle. "Told you so. Make sure he eats something, and call him a cab when he's ready to go home." Tyler looked over at me momentarily. "He's nowhere near as fine as he is going to try to convince you once I am gone."

"Get the fuck out," I repeated.

"I'm going, I'm going," he said, holding his hands up in defense. "Let me know if he lives, Kyle."

There was silence as I waited for him to get out of my shop. As soon as the bell rang from the door closing, Kyle began babbling. "You just fell over, and I didn't know any adults to call because you don't know anyone, so I called him instead of 911, because if they took you to the hospital you'd just bitch that I was overreacting, so before you bite my head off, that's why I called him."

I counted backward from ten in my head as I closed my eyes.

"I am not mad at you, Kyle. Just go home, and we'll talk about it later," I said in the most neutral tone I have ever used in my life.

"He was worried about you too," he added, apparently thinking my lack of explosion meant I wasn't as mad as he thought I would be.

Boy, did he read that one wrong.

"Go home, Kyle. Now." I knew I sounded like an ungrateful bitch, but if this kid kept poking me, I was going to lose it again.

He hesitated for a few seconds and then looked to the front of the shop. "Can I at least call you a cab?"

"I don't need one," I assured him.

"Says the guy who can't stand up," he muttered under his breath. "I am going to call you a cab, and you can tell the guy to go away if you want."

He began to pat himself down and paused. He had forgotten that he'd returned the iPhone Brad had given him last Christmas. I took the pause to drive my point home. "I am fine. I don't need a cab, and I don't need any help."

I saw him seem to teeter back and forth on his decision before he just sighed and gave up. "Fine, but if you die, it's not my fault."

He grabbed his backpack and headed toward the front door. "I'm going to flip the sign and lock the door," he called back to me before walking out.

I fell back into the pile of clothes and took a deep breath. It was not my day at all.

"So you passed out, yelled at a kid who called you a cab anyways?" Nicole said later that night. "Wow, you're a dick."

The Valium I had taken when I got home had kicked in, so I wasn't as upset at her words as I should have been. "Aren't you supposed to be on my side?"

"I'm on your side when you're right or when I don't care. Past that you have to convince me, and after that story, you are a dick."

I had caught her in a rare break from gaming, which meant I had her undivided attention. I was not quite sure that was a good thing. "He called him!" I pleaded with her.

"Oh, please," she said, sighing. "Tyler is not He Who Shall Not Be Named. Let me ask you this. Have you even bothered to tell Kyle the reason you loathe the man so much? Or did you just warn him to stay away from him without adding one specific reason why?"

"I hate you," I said, taking a sip of wine.

"No, you hate being wrong and I just happen to be right." Her voice grew more concerned. "Look, Mario, if you insist on staying in that godforsaken town, then why don't you actually take someone into your confidence? Of course, in this case, it's a high school kid, and normally I would be all Chris Hansen on you, but you need to talk to someone about this, and since you are acting like the target demographic for a Disney family series, maybe Kyle is your best bet."

"I have friends." I tried to argue with her.

Huge mistake.

"No, you don't. You have people you drink with at the place where your boyfriend was killed, and you have people you talk to when you are medicated enough to go out and gather supplies, but you haven't had one friend since Riley died, and you know it."

I put the glass down and leaned forward on the couch as if she were in the room. "Actually, the last friend I made watched as Riley died in the middle of the road, so maybe I have a good reason not to make friends."

I could hear her moving, which meant she was probably doing the same thing. "If you were that concerned about trusting people and making friends, then you would have moved away from there instead of haunting the goddamned town like a hag in a horror movie. Look, either kill the damn kids who go up to Crystal Lake, make friends, or move. Those are your three choices, O brother of mine. Anything else and you are just slowly torturing yourself for no reason at all."

We both sat there glaring at each other over the phone, each glad the other one couldn't see it.

Finally, after almost a minute of silence, I asked, "Did you see *Drag Race* this week?"

"God, what is wrong with those people?" she asked loudly.

We eased back into talking about nothing, but she had been right, and we both knew it. But even that wasn't my problem. My problem was the still unread letter on the coffee table and my inability to see what was written inside.

THE NEXT day I called Kyle at home and told him to come down to the store. It was a Sunday, which meant the store would be relativity quiet until church let out. Which would give us a chance to talk.

I had left the envelope at home because if I had it around me, all it would do was give me another panic attack, and I did not have enough Valium to keep passing out indefinitely. I straightened up as I waited for him to get there, practicing my speech the whole time. Finally I turned on some music and let my mind relax.

He walked in the door slowly, looking like he was expecting me to throw something at him. Once he saw I wasn't rabid, he came inside carefully. "Everything okay?"

"Oh, stop it," I said, turning the music down. "You act like I have an oven in the back to cook innocent children."

He took his backpack off and sat down. "I assumed you kept it at home."

I gave him a withering stare. "You know, I was seconds away from treating you like an actual person instead of a smartass teenager...."

"Okay, okay, okay!" he said quickly. "Do actual people find out why calling Tyler is such a bad idea?"

I hated the fact this kid was so smart. And then it hit me: he reminded me of Nikki a little.

Well, okay, a lot.

"Look, do you want to hear this or not?" I asked him.

"Well, technically I don't know what this is," he said, using air quotes. "But if it explains what happened to you yesterday, then I'm all ears."

Kyle already knew the basics of the outcome, so I explained more in depth how I had met Riley, we got together, moved here, and tried to be happy. I went into how Riley and Tyler knew each other from school, and the way we invited him to be friends with us since he wasn't out of the closet yet. I skimmed over how close the three of us were and how much I liked seeing Riley and Tyler together because it was like being able to see Riley before we met in a way. They were both overgrown kids in muscle-bound bodies, and listening to them argue over sports cracked me up for some reason. I shied away from going into detail on Riley's and my attempts at setting Tyler up with single gay friends we knew. And when I got to the end, the part that Kyle knew but hadn't heard the particulars about, where Riley got hit by a car full of drunk homophobes and lay dying in the street, we were both crying.

And through those tears, I told him, once again but more specifically, how I'd seen Tyler in his car look me dead in the eyes as I screamed for someone to help… and then drive away in the night out of fear. Neither one of us talked for a while after that. Finally Kyle got us some tissues and asked, "You're sure it was him? I mean, you know he saw Riley… um, hurt and drove off."

I wiped my eyes and dug through my pile of CDs to find some upbeat music somewhere. "No, Kyle, I am sure he saw Riley was dying, and he drove off. And I never heard from him again. Not a call, not a note, he didn't even show up to the funeral. He just vanished like the coward he is, and it was as if we never knew each other."

I slipped in the soundtrack to *Mamma Mia!* If there was anything that could dispel a bad mood, it was ABBA. Lisa Stokke began to sing "Honey, Honey" and I felt some of the darkness recede for the time being. "So calling him was the very last thing in the world you should have done, but you didn't know, so all is forgiven," I said as cheerfully as possible. "But if you do it again, I will cut that pretty face from ear to ear." I saw him pause as I leaned over the counter at him. "All you'd need is white face paint to go as Heath Ledger's Joker for Halloween. We clear?" He nodded mutely. "Awesome. So, you hungry?"

I pulled out a stack of takeout menus from under the counter. "Pick a cuisine from Foster's own illustrious restaurant row." I fanned the menus out like a deck of cards. "I'm buying."

Since three of the menus were from Nancy's, it was no surprise we ended up with burgers for lunch.

A COUPLE of days passed, and I had heard nothing from Kyle.

His gay-alliance thing was Monday, and I had been curious about how it went over. The whole thing sounded like some weird gay-superhero thing to me, but the boy had insisted it was a huge first step for Foster High, so I was as supportive as I could be for something that sounded like an excuse to cosplay. By the time Friday rolled around, I had almost forgotten about the whole thing and had gone back to obsessing about the envelope.

Stop—don't judge me. Of course I hadn't opened the damn letter yet. It was like a ghost reaching back from the past, and I was simply too terrified to take its hand. Also, it was the last new thing Riley ever said to me. I know it sounds stupid, but after he died, I refused to change our voicemail message because his voice was on it. I still hadn't deleted the videos I had taken of him on my phone where he yelled at me to stop filming him. I had memorized every second, every minute detail of those moments like I was afraid if I didn't, they would just fade away.

That letter was the last new thing I would hear from him, and I didn't want it to end.

I know it ended, but shut up, it's complicated.

So anyways, by Friday afternoon, the envelope had crept back into my thoughts, and I felt myself rolling into a weekend with Prince Valium. I thought of sending the letter to Nicole FedEx and having her read it to me over the phone, but that seemed too chickenshit even to me. So instead, when Monday arrived, I sat behind the counter and stared at it, willing it to jump and roll over or do some other trick besides making me miserable.

So imagine my shock when Tyler came barging into the shop.

"You have some fucking nerve," he said, his face red with anger. "You just can't leave shit alone, can you?"

I slipped the envelope into my back pocket as I mentally donned my armor. Yes, it does resemble the armor Wonder Woman wore in *Kingdom Come* and there is nothing wrong with that, and why don't you pay attention to the story instead of what's going on in my mind, huh?

"Excuse me?" I said, standing up, letting the stool fall behind me. "You did not come crashing through my door all Hey! Kool-Aid style, screaming like I owe you money. I told you last time to get out, and I meant it."

"You know, if you hate me, hate me," he said, ignoring my words completely. "I get what I did was wrong, and there is no way to fix it, but do you have to poison everyone else on me too?"

"How would you know there's no way to fix it?" I shouted back at him. "You never tried! You just ran away and then lived your life like it never happened. And I have no idea what you're talking about." It was true; I had no earthly clue why he was yelling at me, but I knew I wasn't going to let him.

"You made it clear you wanted me out of your life, Robbie, so I gave that to you." His voice was husky with emotion, and he looked as upset as I was, which was impossible. "I fucked up that night, and I did what you wanted. I left you alone. I never said a word, good or bad, about you to anyone else. I never warned anyone about you. I let them come to their own decision about you, and I thought you'd do the same about me."

"I made it clear?" I tried to catch my breath, but I was too far gone now. "How in the fuck did I do that, Tyler? Telepathy? Smoke signals? Did you get a telegram from me? You know, if you have absolved yourself of the sin of what you did that night, fine, but don't come in here yelling like you were being the bigger person by ignoring me. I didn't out you, did I? I didn't scream from the rooftops that you were a fucking fag just like me, though I should have. I didn't bring you up to the cops when they asked if there was anyone else there who saw a thing. You did what you did for the same reason you do everything, Tyler. To make yourself feel good. That's it, and if you think it's going to be any different with your little spy of a boyfriend, you're nuts. Because you are incapable of loving anyone else, because you're too busy hating who and what you are."

"Do not bring Matt into this," he warned me.

"Why? Maybe he could get hit crossing First Street, and you could look up and see me drive off instead."

It was easily the worst thing I had ever said out loud. I mean, to even make light of that, much less make a joke? Well, suffice it to say there are many reasons I'm going to hell besides liking men.

"I'm sorry," he said after a few moments of silence. "It was wrong, and I was stupid. But you have to get past your hatred of me because it's affecting the kids."

I looked at him three different kinds of confused for a second. "Are you trying to be funny, or did we have offspring at some point?"

"Brad and Kyle, jackass," he threw back at me. "It's bad enough they're in a fight, but you whisper in Kyle's ear about me, and he charges into the store and confronts me on it." I paused because I hadn't thought about it even for a second. "So now he hates me. Is that what you wanted?"

It wasn't at all, and he could tell by the look on my face.

"He is in a bad place, Robbie," he said, his voice imploring me. "I don't think he's going to take Brad back, but I do know there is no chance of them working it out if they end up fighting about us too. I'm not saying we need to bury the hatchet or become friends, but we need to find a way to let them know we can agree that they should be together." He paused. "You do agree they should be together?"

I had no idea what to say to that.

Tyler opened his mouth to press the point, but his phone beeped before he could. He read the text and looked like he was going to throw up. I opened my mouth to ask him what that was about, but then my phone went off too. I glanced at the text and knew instantly.

I wanted to throw up too.

"Come on," he said, shoving the phone in his pocket. "My car is faster."

I followed him out and locked the door behind us. "What exactly do you think we can do?"

Tyler stopped before getting into his car. "I don't know. I'll figure it out on the way."

I got in the passenger seat and closed my eyes as we pulled out of the parking lot.

It was the first time I had prayed since Riley died.

Brad

FML.

I know it isn't eloquent or as descriptive as most people would like, but seriously? Fuck my life. Here I am, inches from going to the state championships, an offer from A&M for a full ride, all the popularity I had lost when I came out back tenfold, and I was miserable. That word doesn't really get how bad I feel right now, so you'll have to trust me on that.

In fact, if you had asked me, like, four years ago for three wishes, I would have said a perfect baseball season that would lead to state, a chance to play ball at A&M, and to be the most popular guy in school. I have to be honest with you—fourteen-year-old me was a pretty sucky guy. I mean, who the fuck cares about baseball or a stupid college when you can't share it with the most important person in your world? I guess I can't fault fourteen-year-old me too badly; if I had a fourth wish, I might have gone with being the fifth ninja turtle or owning a Charizard.

But all of this was nothing to me, because Kyle kept ignoring me.

Jennifer at first assured me he needed space, and sooner or later he would come around. Well, it was later, and he had enough space to fit the Astrodome in, and still nothing. I should have known it was going to be worse than I thought when, that first Monday back at school, Sammy came and gave me Kyle's iPhone back, box and all. She said she was sorry it had come to this, and it looked like she meant it, which was something. When I turned the phone on, the lock screen was empty; he had deleted the picture of us I had put on it.

That one action made me cry more than all the times I had bawled during *Field of Dreams* combined.

That week we lost our first game, and it was my fault. I mean, if I had been on their team and infiltrated our team as a spy, I couldn't have done as much damage as I did in that one game. I dropped balls, let easy pitches sail past me, and worst, I just sat in the dugout without trying to cheer my team up once. It was a quiet ride home that night. Even in my funk, I knew they were all glaring at me in the dark. When we got back to school, I waited because I was pretty sure Coach Gunn was going to kick me off the team or something. Only Josh talked to me afterward. He patted me on my shoulder and said quietly, "He'll take you back. Be patient."

It was hands down the nicest thing a straight guy had ever said to me.

Coach Gunn didn't even look at me as he walked past me into the locker room. "Go home, Graymark. We lost. Nothing you can do about it now."

"You aren't mad at me?" I asked him, shocked.

He paused in the door and turned around. "Son, I have gone to state and won. I have had perfect seasons, and I even went to college. Nothing you do on that field is going to change that. If you were waiting for a lecture from me, I am fresh out. What you should be thinking about is the fact that the rest of that team follows your lead, and if you don't care to play anymore, they won't either. You may not care if you get into college or not, but I'm betting some of them do." My eyes stung as he leveled a look at me. "I am not the person you should be playing for—it should be them."

He closed the door on me, leaving me to sit in my car, screaming at myself as tears rolled down my face.

The next day at practice, I put a wall up around my heart and ignored my problems.

We won the next game and the game after that. I put all my effort into winning and tried to forget that something inside of me was dying. I had a job to do, and damned if I wasn't going to do it. Even with my newfound zeal for baseball, I had a lot of extra time on my hands, time I spent with Tyler in his shop. He didn't mind the help or the company, so it was a good fit.

What wasn't a good fit was his new boyfriend, Matt.

Matt wasn't thrilled to have me hanging around Tyler all the time, though he never said a word to me about it. It was just the way he acted when he came in and I was there, a coldness that made me feel like I was doing something incredibly wrong. When we were alone in the shop, I asked Tyler about it, and he nodded and looked embarrassed. "It isn't you," he assured me. "Well, it is you in the fact you are young, in great shape, and are stunning for your age…." I felt my face grow warm at the compliment. I had no idea Tyler even knew what I looked like outside of help around the shop. "I am not hitting on you," he added when he saw my reaction. "I'm just saying why Matt is so standoffish. He just came from a world where a lot of guys my age would jump at the chance to date someone like you. Straight guys get red shiny cars and try to date strippers when they hit middle age. I guess some gay guys go after young guys in an effort to prove they still got it."

He shook his head, obviously disgusted with the entire concept.

"So he thinks we're fooling around?" I asked, kind of shocked that someone would think that.

"No," Tyler said, getting up to get us a couple of Cokes. "He's just insecure about where we are, so it's messing with his mind. Don't stress about it, Brad. He'll come around."

His words did nothing to cheer me up as I mumbled, "Yeah, you said that about Kyle too."

He gave me a sympathetic look as he handed me a Coke. "Don't give up faith yet."

I tried to ignore the "yet" in his sentence. I didn't know what to do with his "yet."

I GOT home one afternoon and found my dad talking to a stranger in the living room.

"And here he is in the flesh," my dad said, a smile that I had never seen plastered on his face. "Bradley, put your stuff down and come in."

Bradley? Since when did he call me anything but "boy"? I put my practice bag down and kicked off my shoes before walking into the room. "Sorry if I still stink. We've been practicing so much I lost track of clean clothes in my locker," I said, hoping I was still on the right side of ripe. The truth was, Kyle had taken it upon himself to remind me to grab my clothes after practice, and I had spaced it out by myself.

I tried to ignore the pain in my chest as my dad introduced the man.

"This is Mr. Perkins. He is from A&M." My dad's eyes locked with mine, and I could hear the "Don't fuck this up" even if it was silent.

"Coach Perkins?" I asked, taking his hand. "You played for the Mets with Nolan Ryan!" I had this guy on a baseball card under my bed, and now he was in my living room.

He looked over at my dad and chuckled as he shook my hand. "Okay, you were right. Almost all kids his age have no sense of history anymore." He looked at me. "Pleased to meet you, son. I've heard a lot about you."

I fought the urge to ask him to hold on as I ran upstairs to grab his card to get him to sign it. Instead I just nodded and thanked him as we sat down.

"Your dad here tells me you've always wanted to play for A&M."

I nodded as I pointed to the pictures on the bookshelves. "There's a picture of me dressed up as an Aggie for Halloween. I still have that cap."

Perkins smiled and nodded. "I saw it. We like that in our new students. We have a rich history and tradition that has been passed down year after year. We don't like to think of ourselves as just another school. We are something different."

"I know," I answered quickly. "I've dreamt of going to Midnight Yell forever."

"Well, we sure would like to make that dream come true," he said kindly. "I've been talking with your dad, and we were talking about you coming by the campus for a tour. Something you'd be interested in?"

I literally jumped up out of my chair. "Seriously? I'd love it, sir!"

Perkins shook his head and laughed. "Okay. Nathan, I owe you a drink. You were right about your son."

I paused, not sure my dad knew anything about me that wasn't bad.

"I told him you were practically an Aggie already," my dad explained. "I bet him a drink that he had never met a kid who wanted to get into his school more than you."

I had no idea what to say to that. It almost sounded like my dad was proud of me.

"Okay then, so this weekend good?" Perkins said to my dad.

"Sounds great. We'll drive down Friday and get a room in College Station." They both got up and shook hands.

Perkins handed my dad a card. "Call this number when you're in town, and one of the recruiters will be by to show you around." He looked at me. "Next time we meet, Brad, I might just be your coach." He held his hand out, and I felt my control slip.

"Can you wait one second while I go get my baseball cards? I would love for you to sign your rookie card."

My dad sighed as I ran upstairs in my socks, trying not to holler in joy as I went.

THAT NIGHT at dinner, my dad brought the cruel reality crashing in on my dream.

"They say this is to show you around the school, but what they are really doing is checking to see if you're the type of person they want to waste a couple hundred thousand dollars on. So you need to be on your best behavior. No, scratch that, I've seen your best. You need to be better than that."

He accented every word by waving around a chicken leg, which made him look even more pompous as he declared what was going to happen. My mother, as always, tried to lessen his effect. "Now, Nate, if they didn't want him, they wouldn't have offered to show him around."

"It's not true," my dad went on, as if I wasn't sitting at the table. "Plenty of kids out there with a good arm and a fast hustle. Trust me, they have a dozen guys lined up for this one spot. He needs to knock them out."

"I'm sure he will," my mom said, giving me a smile.

"That makes one of us," my dad mumbled under his breath.

BEFORE I was just anxious; now I was anxious and panicking as the week slipped by. The team was crazy for the news, especially Josh, who had taken up the role as my de facto best friend since Kyle dumped me. It was nice because no one else brought up the fact that I was suddenly single. At least Josh talked with me about it.

"So, nothing?" he asked as we ate lunch in the student union. Since Kelly, no one really wanted to eat at the Table anymore. It was like without him there, it wasn't the same. So most of the group gathered into smaller groups that ate in other places. A lot of the team had decided on the student union as their home base.

No joke intended.

I shook my head as I looked out the window toward the music building. I could see Kyle, Jennifer, and Sammy eating there, talking—everything we used to do. My sandwich tasted like ashes in my mouth. "I called three times last night.

His mom finally said he went to bed at eight. Kyle hasn't gone to bed at eight since he was in diapers."

"That's cold," Josh agreed as I looked away from the window. "But still, A&M, dude. That has to be exciting."

I shrugged. "Between my dad and no Kyle, I have a bad feeling about going."

"I would hit my grandmother over the head with a snow shovel for a chance at what you got, man." I looked up at him, and he added hastily, "I meant the scholarship, not the Kyle part."

That made me laugh. "You're good, man," I said to him. "You have to have offers so far."

He nodded as he took a sip of his Coke. "Yeah, but none of them are A&M." I couldn't argue with that.

The rest of the week plodded on as my nervousness about the weekend grew worse. My mom kept trying to convince me it wouldn't be that bad. My dad did nothing to make me believe her. Thursday before practice, Jennifer was waiting for me by the locker room.

"Hey, stranger," she said, smiling warmly. At least it would look like that to anyone else. I had known her too long not to know when something was wrong. I suppose I had always had that ability, the difference being, before I would just find reasons to be elsewhere until it passed. As I walked up to her, I marveled again on how much of an asshole I used to be.

"Hey," I said, putting my practice bag down. "What's up?"

"Nothing," she said way too quickly. "I just hadn't talked with you in a while, and so I thought—"

Yeah, she was really bad at this.

"What's wrong?" I said, interrupting her. "It's not that I'm not interested. It's that if I'm late to practice, Gunn will make me run extra laps, and at this point I have run enough to get to Africa and back."

She sighed and looked away, which meant she wasn't sure how to start.

"Is this about Kyle?" My heart paced faster as I asked.

"Okay, look. He has been in a mood lately. A bad one. A seriously bad one. At first he was just short with people, and then there was the meeting...."

"How did it go?" I asked her. I had purposefully stayed away from it because I knew Kyle didn't want me there.

She rolled her eyes. "Think about the worst-case scenario and then multiply it by a thousand."

"It couldn't have been that bad?" I asked, disbelieving since I hadn't heard about anything happening. In fact, I hadn't heard of one person outside of Kyle,

Jennifer, and Sammy showing up. If one of the guys had dropped in to cause some shit, I would have heard about it by now.

"Trust me, there was yelling and screaming, and Kyle losing his shit...."

"About what?" I asked, shocked.

As she opened her mouth, the locker room door opened, and Coach Gunn glared at me. "You really like running, don't you, son?"

Fuck.

I grabbed my bag and gave her an apologetic look. "I have to bounce. Call you after practice?"

She nodded and gave a half smile to the coach.

"Miss Rogers, nice to see you again," he said.

Jennifer gave me a half salute. "Sir, yes sir," she said and took off toward her car.

As I walked in, Coach Gunn said in a low voice, "You know how I know you're really gay?" I looked up at him in confusion. "Because you didn't ask that girl to marry you. It was the only possible excuse." He smiled, and it made me chuckle.

"Yeah, she is great," I said, watching her get in her car as the locker room door closed.

What was wrong with Kyle?

I FOCUSED on practice and let Kyle slip from my mind for the time being.

I love how that makes it sound like I actually stopped worrying for a while. Truth was, my body was on autopilot while I thumbed through all the things that could be wrong with him. I wanted to think it was me, or the lack of me, since it was the lack of him that was fucking me up. But if he was that upset because of our breakup, why wouldn't he just take my call? When I heard the coach's whistle blow twice, signaling the end of practice, I was ready to skip a shower and race over to Kyle's house and make him talk to me.

I got a couple of steps before I saw my dad standing next to Gunn, the two of them laughing about something. My dad looked up at me when I got closer. "Hey, get changed. Your mom packed you a bag of clothes so we can leave tonight."

My mind stumbled over itself. "Like, right now?"

My dad's smile dimmed a bit as he answered. "Yes, like right now."

I tried to calculate the chances of him taking me by Kyle's before we left. I had a better chance of finding pirate's gold on the bottom of my locker. Instead I walked past him into the locker room, pissed that life kept getting in my way. I tore my uniform off and threw each piece, balled up, into my locker with force. I was nearly nude when Josh walked up to me slowly. "Whoa," he said carefully. "What did those cleats ever do to you?"

I realized I had one of my cleats in my hand and was about to hurl it into my locker with the rest of my uniform. Instead I dropped it and sat on the bench. "I really think I am never getting back together with Kyle."

Josh sat down next to me. "Hey, don't talk like that. You can't give up on it now."

"Something is wrong with him, and he won't talk to me, and now my dad is here, and I won't be back until Monday, and this sucks," I raged.

Paul, one of the younger players, walked by and saw Josh and me sitting together on the bench practically naked and gave us a look. Josh looked up at him and growled. "Hey, noob, you keep staring, I'm suddenly going to remember you didn't get initiated to the team last year." Paul took off like his hair was on fire.

"Did we initiate anyone last year?" I asked him.

"Yeah, dude, we made them strip down and do something humiliating because we're trapped in a bad '80s teenage movie." He shook his head at me. "Of course we didn't initiate anyone, but he doesn't know that."

That made me laugh despite how upset I was.

The doors from the field slammed shut, and I saw Gunn and my dad walk toward his office. "Fuck, I need to change."

"How about I go talk to him?" Josh asked.

"My dad?" I asked, grabbing my towel and shower bag.

"No, Kyle, you idiot," he said, following me into the shower area. "While you're gone, I can go by and make sure he's okay. Maybe talk you up some? You never know, might do some good."

I turned on my shower. "Or you could make things ten times worse by just showing up."

I lathered up my hair and heard him say, "I'll stay out of it, but no offense, dude. How much worse can it get?"

WE WERE about an hour out of town when my dad asked me if I was hungry.

I shrugged as I watched the nothing outside my window.

"What's up?" he asked. "I'd think you would be bouncing off the walls, you've wanted this so long."

I glanced at him and gave a weak smile. "I am, Dad, really. I just have a lot going on right now."

186

He looked back to the road and then back at me a few seconds later. I couldn't read the look on his face, but it wasn't good because he pulled the car over. He turned it off and shifted to face me fully. My stomach soured as he began to lecture me. "No, in fact you do not have a lot going on right now," he informed me sternly. "In fact, you have nothing else in your life besides this interview, period. Your entire life, everything is wrapped up in this weekend, and I don't want your mind somewhere else." He let a few seconds go by before adding, "Or with someone else."

I looked up, and I knew he knew about Kyle and me.

"Breakups suck, Brad. That is a fact of life. The thing is, you get angry, cry, and move on with your life. You don't let your future tumble out of your grasp because of it. So you have tonight and some of tomorrow morning to get over it, but when you walk onto that campus, you had better have gotten over it or better at hiding it. Either way, it's done. Got it?"

I nodded, knowing there was no way I could argue with him about this.

"There's a Whataburger up ahead. You hungry or not?" he asked as he started the car.

I nodded.

"Fine," he said, pulling back onto the highway.

After another few minutes of silence, I asked him, "You ever have a breakup screw up your entire life?"

He didn't look over at me as he drove. "Sure," he said, thinking about it. "It was when your mom broke up with me when I told her I was going to school out of state." In a much more subdued tone, he said, "Heck, that was the reason I got drunk and kicked out of college." I was shocked, since I was pretty sure my parents barely tolerated each other. "Anyway, I do know how a bad breakup can fuck up your future. So I am speaking from experience when I say don't let your heart ruin your life."

He took the next exit, and we got Whataburger, but neither of us talked much.

THE NEXT morning, I had put Kyle out of my mind the best I could.

My dad was right; this had been my dream forever, and I needed to be fully here, not half here and half wishing he would take me back. So I got dressed as I mentally told myself that I couldn't mess this up. It was bottom of the ninth, and the winning run was on second. It all came down to me hitting this ball as hard as I could.

My dad called the school, and less than twenty minutes later, there was a knock on the door.

I answered it and found myself face-to-face with the tallest guy I had ever seen in my life. I mean, he was six foot six if he was an inch. He stood there wearing an A&M sweatshirt and a pair of khakis. I just blinked as I tried to comprehend that they made guys this big.

"You must be Brad," he said in a deep voice that made him seem even more imposing. "I'm Danny." He held his hand out. I took it and tried not to notice the way his palm completely engulfed my own like I was a child. "Howdy," he said with a huge smile.

I smiled back, because I had been waiting my whole life to be howdied at A&M.

"Howdy back," I said, moving a step into the room. "This is my dad."

Danny ducked slightly as he walked in. "Pleased to meet you, Mr. Graymark." He shook my dad's hand, and I could see the same awe in my dad's face as he just shook it back mutely. "Welcome to A&M," he said when he was done. "You guys have breakfast yet or you wanna jump into the tour?"

"You go to school here?" I asked incredulously. It was stupid question, but I was still trying to wrap my mind around that guys came in that size. "I mean, you play baseball here?"

He shook his head. "Basketball, but the baseball team is pretty busy with playoffs, so they asked me to show you around. That okay?" he asked casually. I realized if I could get used to standing next to a guy who was taller than a building, I would have found him attractive. He had black hair and blue eyes that made it look like he found everything funny. It was like someone took a normal cute guy and then stretched him to supersize.

"Yeah, it's great," I said quickly. "I was just trying to imagine you playing baseball, and it didn't work."

"Couldn't do it," he answered as my dad and I grabbed our coats. "The balls are too small."

He said it so deadpan that it took me a second to realize it was a joke. I burst out laughing as we walked out of the hotel room.

"How about we swing by the dining hall, which is called Sbisa to everyone else, and grab some breakfast?" He had a golf cart that was painted A&M maroon. When he got in, it looked like a clown car. On the seat was an A&M cap. "That's for you," he said to me casually as my dad got in the back. I picked it up with reverence, like it was priceless.

Danny chuckled. "I had that same face the day they recruited me and handed me a cap. I must have worn that all summer before my freshman year."

I realized that I looked like an idiot and slipped it over my head.

"Looks good on you," he said with a smile.

I was not going to blush over a straight guy complimenting my cap. "So, food?" I asked, getting into the cart.

"Food it is!" he said as we took off toward the campus.

WE SPENT the next few hours walking around the A&M campus as Danny informed us of the history of each building or statue. It was hard to hear all those stories and not feel a sense of reverence as we walked; this place was a Texas tradition. By the time we got to Olsen Field, I was feeling a little overwhelmed by all of it. As we walked up to the building, Danny said in a low voice, "Don't worry, my first time I was kind of awestruck too. It takes some getting used to."

As I looked up and saw the three arches, I said, "There is no way I will ever get used to this."

"And this is where I hand you off," Danny said as three men walked out of the building toward us. One was Coach Perkins, but he was following the other two men a couple of steps behind. It was kind of obvious they were important.

"I hope Mr. Devin here was a good guide?" the man in the middle asked.

"He was great," I said truthfully. "If I wasn't obsessed over this place before, I sure am now."

"Thank you, Danny," the man said. "You can go."

The basketball player nudged me and gave me a quick wink. "Good luck, man."

I shook his hand. "Thanks for the tour, man."

"I'll be seeing you later." He waved to the three men as he walked off.

The middle man walked up to me. "So you are this Bradley Graymark I've been hearing about. I'm Rodney Peterson, head of athletics here." I shook his hand mutely. "This is Bud Freeling from our alumni association, and you know Coach Perkins." I nodded and shook each man's hand. "We have a lot to discuss. Why don't you and your father follow us?"

"Nice place you got here," my dad said as we walked into the huge stadium.

The alumni guy smiled and answered, "We try to live up to the motto 'Everything is bigger in Texas.'"

My dad began to joke with them casually, as if my entire future didn't depend on it. "Well, that tour guide of yours must be fourth-generation Texan to be that big." The other men laughed, and I realized this was what my father did for a living. He was a salesman, and right now he was selling me.

Not going to lie, I was a little unsure how to feel about that.

"If I remember, Danny is a military brat, but he did go to high school in Texas, so I think we can claim him," Mr. Peterson said as we walked into a conference room. There were drinks on a table to the side and a counter from Blue Bell with a dozen flavors under glass. I wasn't sure if I was in a baseball stadium or Willy Wonka's. "Have a seat. Either of you need anything?"

I shook my head, but my dad took a bottle of water. Once everyone was sitting down and situated, Mr. Peterson got real serious. "From what I have been told, we have had our eyes on you for a while." He looked over at Coach Perkins, who nodded. "Since your sophomore year, I believe."

"Coach Gunn told us about you pretty early on," Perkins added. "We were going to come to you with an offer before the season, in fact."

My dad asked casually, "Then why didn't you?"

Mr. Peterson cleared his throat. "I think we all know why that didn't happen."

Perkins and the alumni guy looked away, and my father's face got red as he clenched his jaw. It was a classic sign that he was about to lose it. I, on the other hand, was completely clueless. "I don't get it," I asked in the uncomfortable silence. "What did I do?"

All three men looked at me, none of them wanting to say whatever it was out loud.

Then I got it. "Oh, I came out," I said, more to myself than to them.

"Yes, that," Mr. Peterson said. "That changed a lot of things."

"Why?" my dad asked, his voice gruff with anger. "Does who my son decides to sleep with change the way he plays ball? And by the way, if it does, then you should pray your team is gay as well."

"Dad," I said trying to calm him down.

"Shut up, Brad," he snapped at me. "Are you saying that my son isn't getting a scholarship because he is gay?"

Mr. Peterson seemed unaffected by my dad's anger. "No, I am saying that if we were to offer your son a chance to go here, there would need to be conditions."

"Like?" my dad asked before I could.

"For one, he cannot be vocal about his sexuality to anyone. Not the press, not publicly, period. For the next four years, as long as he is on the team, he does not comment on his preference at all." My dad looked like he was going to say something, but Peterson kept talking. "Two, we are giving him a scholarship, not his boyfriend or his future boyfriends. If he is going to date, he can do it off campus and away from where people can see. If he wants to pursue a relationship during the summer, away from here, I don't care. But while he's here, that is a nonstarter. And three, if for any reason he does violate these conditions and is released from his scholarship, he is going to sign a nondisclosure agreement not to discuss why he was let go. I am not going to put the school into jeopardy by having its name dragged into the press over this."

The alumni guy broke in. "Look, it's nothing personal. It's just a lot of our budget comes from donations from alumni, and they are not ready in any way, shape, or form to embrace a gay athlete being an Aggie. No one at this table cares what you do on your own time. We just can't risk making certain people upset."

"So this is about money," my dad said after a few seconds.

"It's about reputation," Peterson corrected him.

"Right, it's about money." My dad looked at me and then back to the men. "Can I talk to my son for a moment? Alone."

The three of them got up. "Of course, take all the time you need. We'll be across the hall in my office." They all gave me a half smile as they passed. Coach Perkins paused and said, "This isn't as bad as you think, Brad. You aren't the only gay athlete out there, trust me. They all played under this rule."

I nodded, and he walked out.

Once the door was closed, my dad looked me straight in the eye. "At the end of the day, this is going to be your decision. I can't make it for you, Danny can't make it for you, no one can. You have to make the choice and be able to live with it." I nodded, overwhelmed by it all. "But if you want my advice, take the deal." I opened my mouth to say something, but he talked over me. "Look, you're broken up with Kyle, and you were never vocal about this before. All you have to do is keep your head down, play ball, and you have the best education money can buy on their dime. You feel lonely, then maybe you find someone on the side who can keep it quiet or we invest in more porn for you. But I am telling you, Brad, you are not going to get another deal like this. I was wondering why there weren't more people knocking at your door, and this makes sense. No one is ready to sign a gay ballplayer yet. It just won't happen."

His words were like someone was punching me. Not hard, not enough to knock me out, but enough for each one to hurt. One by one they were nothing. All together they were devastating. "You want me to just lie?" I asked him, trying not to show how hurt I was.

"Why not? You spent eighteen years doing it," he countered. "It was just the last six months that you felt the need to express yourself, and look how that turned out. If you had lasted eighteen years and six months, you'd be beating schools off with a stick."

"But—" I began to explain.

"Look, Brad, I said it was your choice, and it is. But if it's not this, then what? You going to work at that sporting goods shop while you go to junior college? How gay do you think you're going to be able to be in Foster, working a part-time job? You want out of that town, and I don't blame you. This is the only way you got right now."

I honestly just wanted him to stop talking.

"Okay, fine," I said bitterly. "I'll take the deal." I felt a part of my soul shrivel up and die, because I knew, the second Kyle heard word of what I did, he would never, ever talk to me again. And I can't say I'd blame him. "I just don't want to talk about it anymore."

I saw my dad's face blanch at the tone of my voice, and he leaned over and put a hand on my arm. "Brad, life is making hard choices and doing things you don't want to get to things you do want. It's part of being a man."

I looked him squarely in the eyes and asked, "You mean like coming back and raising a kid with a woman you left behind?" I was rewarded by his face going even paler. "I said I'd take the deal. We don't need to talk about anything else."

He slowly took his hand away. "You can be mad all you want," he said, standing up slowly. "But this isn't my fault. You can hate me for a lot of things, but the advice I just gave you? That's not one of them."

Before I could respond, he walked out to get the men back in there.

I missed Kyle.

So THE deal was, they were going to write up a contract for me to sign the next day. In the meantime, they said, some of the guys on campus were having a party, and I was welcome to join them to experience what college life was like after class. I didn't feel like going anywhere, much less a party, but my dad reminded me that this was still an interview, and if I refused, it gave the impression I was rocking the boat.

God forbid the boat is ever rocked.

So around nine there was a knock on the hotel door. I wasn't that shocked to find Basketball Danny standing there. "You ready for some trouble?" he asked with a devilish smile.

I was wearing a button-up shirt and khakis, not sure what the proper dress code was. "This too much or not enough?" I asked him.

"As long as you don't mind having beer spilled on them, it doesn't matter." He laughed at his own joke when he saw my dad lying on the bed behind me. "Oh, hi, Mr. Graymark, didn't see you there." He scratched his head as he tried to find a way to cover himself. "I didn't mean actual beer. I was talking about...."

My dad waved him off. "I'm not completely ignorant to what goes on at a college party. Go and have fun," he told me. What he meant was go and don't draw attention to myself as a problem child. I grabbed my letterman jacket and followed Danny.

"Your dad is a lot like mine," he said as we got into his jeep.

"Your dad is a raging asshole who's distant and unavailable?" I said, buckling myself in.

He gave me a sideways glance as he started the car. "Okay, then. I guess they aren't that alike."

He took us by the campus, and the school looked completely different to me now. Instead of this great institution where Texas history had been made, it looked like a huge beast waiting to devour me. All the joy of the place had been drained out of me. Now it was just another jail that I was willingly committing myself to.

"So how did the meeting go?" he asked me, turning down the music. "They all slobbering on you to get you to sign?" It would have been easier to dislike this guy if he wasn't so freaking cute. I don't mean to say I was attracted to him; I'm just saying he was ridiculously cute for a guy who was taller than most field goals.

"No, nothing like that," I assured him, not wanting to get into it.

"Ah, well. I don't know how the baseball department works," he said, making a turn. "I had UT, USC, and Arizona after me, but I wanted to play here."

"Must be nice," I grumbled, trying not to sound like a complete bitch.

"There are going to be some baseball players at this party. You can ask them how they were courted. It's different for everyone." We pulled in to what looked like an apartment complex. "Welcome to Northgate," he said as we parked. "One of the best places to live off campus."

There were cars parked everywhere, and I could see people milling around, some heading out to party, some heading in to do the same. It was exciting, despite my mood. I'd never been to a college party, but this reminded me a lot of when I was asked to a varsity party when I was a freshman. I followed Danny, who waved to a few people as we passed by. "I was going to pass you off as a new student, but the letterman jacket is a giveaway," he said as we went inside. "If anyone gives you shit, let me know, but shouldn't be a problem. Most of these guys are my bros."

We walked up a couple of flights of stairs. When we got to the third floor, Danny opened the door, and the sound of the party came crashing out. As we walked down the hall, I saw nearly every door was open, and there were people everywhere. It was insane. I was thinking of, like, a party at a house or something, but this was the entire floor. "A few of us on the team got the same floor, and we lucked out since just about everyone else here are either jocks or cool with partying," he said over the music. "The RA is a huge basketball booster," he added, smiling. "Well, more correctly, he is a wannabe, so he lets us get away with hell." We got to the common area, where there was a keg set up while a crowd of guys sat around a big-screen TV playing COD against each other. With each death, the guys either cheered or groaned. I instantly cheered up.

It was exactly what I pictured a college dorm to be like.

"You want a beer?" Danny asked, pausing to hear my answer.

I had been one of the popular kids too long not to know when I was being tested. "Yeah, whatever there is."

His smile got wider, and he walked away to grab us some drinks.

I walked around, taking the whole scene in at once. There was an energy that reminded me of the parties we used to throw after games. There was no organization or pattern; it was just a bunch of guys getting together with an excuse to get drunk and have fun. This was what Kelly's parties were like before....

I sighed as I realized Kelly would have loved this place.

"Whoa, whoa, whoa," Danny said quickly as he walked toward me with two red cups of beer. "You almost looked like you were going to smile there for a second. Quick, take a drink!"

I took the beer and downed almost half of it as I tried to drink myself out of my misery. Danny finished his in one gulp and looked at me and my half-full cup. He moved his head as if to hurry me along, and I laughed. "Are you trying to get me drunk?"

He leaned closer and whispered, "I'm trying to get that gigantic stick out of your ass and get you to have some fun, dude. Drunk just happens to be the quickest way to do that."

He looked like he was joking, but I knew he wasn't.

I finished my beer in one shot and held my cup out again. "Hit me," I said, swallowing hard.

"There it is!" he cheered. "Come on, let me introduce you to some people."

I followed, trying my best to be happy.

SEVEN BEERS later, I was feeling no pain.

Danny had introduced me to a few of his teammates, all of them older than both of us. They were nice enough, but since I wasn't being recruited for basketball, they weren't too keen on getting to know me. That was okay, because being surrounded by a group of guys who consider six foot four short was a bit intimidating. I did meet a couple of guys on the baseball team, and they seemed very cool, but I could tell talking up a potential recruit at a party was not their thing.

A couple of hours in, Danny brought us back two more red cups of beer and two girls. I began to break out in a cold sweat as he introduced girl one and girl two to me. It seemed girl two was meant for me, because she moved next to me and gave me a drunk smile. I didn't know her, so I could be wrong about that, but I do know at the very least she gave me a pleasantly buzzed smile. "I like your jacket," she said, putting a hand on my chest and letting it trail downward.

I took a step back and spilled beer all over my slacks.

"And we have a winner!" Danny roared as I jumped up quickly. The people around us laughed as I tried to wipe the beer off my lap. "What did I say? You're dressed fine," he said, raising his beer in a salute.

Girl number two moved over to me and whispered in my ear. "You want to get those pants off?"

"No!" I screamed in reflex. She froze as everyone within earshot looked over at us. I had forgotten what being consumed by peer pressure felt like. "I mean, it's good," I added quickly. "I just need another beer now."

"We can get you guys some," girl number one offered, taking Danny's now empty cup.

Girl number two stared at me for a few seconds before taking my cup. She was way too drunk to know what was going on, but she wasn't so stupid as not to sense something. "I'll be right back. Don't take those off without me," she said with a slur.

"I won't," I said, chuckling at the nonjoke.

As soon as they were out of range, Danny moved closer to me. "Look, dude, just play along right now. It's easier if someone sees us talking to some drunk chicks before we jet."

"Say what?" I asked.

Danny couldn't answer as one of his teammates walked over with a girl on his arm. "Hey, we're heading to IHOP. You guys wanna bring your dates?" he said, gesturing to girls one and two, who were standing in the line at the keg.

"Maybe," Danny said with a sly grin. "But I doubt it."

The other guy broke out laughing and held his fist out for Danny to bump. "Tear it up, my brother." Danny nudged his fist. "Nice to meet you, Barney."

"Brad," I said, correcting him.

"Who?" he asked back.

"Never mind," I said, as the beer began to dribble down my legs.

The guy gave me a quick "Whatever" and said to Danny, "Call me tomorrow, big guy."

Danny nodded, and about a dozen guys walked out with girls. They looked like a band of giants who were taking their female captives back to their lands. I shook my head as I realized I was a bit more buzzed than I had figured.

"Okay, good," Danny said as soon as they were gone. "Come on, before they get back." He grabbed my arm and pulled me through the crowd.

"Who?" I asked, following the best I could.

"One skank, two skank, red skank, blue skank," he said, nodding back the way we came. "Come on before someone sees us!"

I let myself be pulled down one of the halls simply because I had no idea what was going on anymore. We stopped at a closed door, and he pulled a key out of his pocket. "The party is winding down. They'll assume we left with the other guys." I nodded, not knowing what that meant as he opened his door. "Get in here already."

I hurried in as he slammed the door. I turned around to ask him what was going on, but as soon as I opened my mouth, I found his on top of mine.

I stood there frozen as he kissed me.

Seconds passed, and I didn't move.

After more nothing from me, he pulled back slightly.

He stared at me for a second. "You okay?"

I nodded.

He leaned in to kiss me again.

"Whoa," I said, pulling back. "Why are you kissing me?" The room was ridiculously small—even more so when occupied by a guy his size.

"Why?" he asked, pulling his sweatshirt over his head. "I've been wanting to attack you since this morning." His T-shirt had ridden up, exposing a body that was just this side of perfect. He had an eight-pack, and I realized there wasn't an ounce of fat on him. He was huge and defined. I instantly hated everything about his genetics.

And then my brain stopped being a horndog. "Wait, you're gay?"

"Bi," he said, pulling the T-shirt off. "It's cool, dude. I know about you," he said, advancing.

I took another step back. "You do? How?" If this guy was going to try to force the point, I really didn't think I could stop him.

He chuckled as he slipped his shoes off. Jesus Christ, his feet were huge. "Why do you think they sent me to walk you around? I'm in the same boat, man. Trust me, it's all good."

His hands went to his pants, and I called out, "Okay, stop!" He froze as I tried to ignore the fact I could see he was already aroused through his boxers and slacks. "I can't do this."

The top button of his pants was undone, and I could see the Adonis cut of his torso flex. I honestly didn't know they made guys who looked like this. "You can't? Dude, we're covered. The guys saw us with those chicks. As far as anyone is concerned, we fucked them silly and then crashed."

"No," I tried to explain, shaking my head. "I don't.… Look, can you please just sit down and talk for a second?"

He stopped walking toward me and looked down. "Are you not into me? Because you've been staring pretty hard for someone who isn't attracted."

I sat on the edge of his bed as he straddled the chair at his computer desk. "Do I think you're hot? Yes. But I am not going to fool around with you."

He got a confused look. "Why?"

I honestly didn't know what I was going to say when I opened my mouth, but the moment the words came tumbling out, I knew they were the truth. "I'm in love with someone else."

He put his head down and let off a pretty convincing growl. "I. Have. The. Shittiest. Luck."

"I'm sorry?" I offered.

He looked up and sighed. "It's cool. You want me to take you home?"

I sat there for a moment and thought about it. "I'd rather you tell me what it's like to be an athlete in the closet."

He didn't say anything for a few seconds, and I really thought he hadn't heard me. Finally he said, "What's it like? Crap. You can't tell anyone what you're really thinking. You can't be with the person you really want to. I'm dating a girl that I have zero interest in, which is a shame because she's an incredible person. I feel like a dog that has a piece of steak on his nose, and the world is just daring me to eat it. So how is it? Well, if I had a choice between this and having a guy come in every day and kick me in the balls, I'd invest in ice packs and industrial-strength cups."

He sounded miserable, but I think he felt better after unloading all that on me. I went back over his words, and something clicked. "Who is he?" I asked.

He looked up at me. "Who?"

"The person you really want to be with," I answered.

He didn't say a word for a long time and then just deflated in his chair. "Who cares? I screwed it up with him anyways."

"Me?" I asked, pointing a finger to my chest.

He chuckled a bit. "Okay, I guess it's true. All jocks are self-absorbed idiots. No, not you. You just happened to be hot, and I knew you were into guys. The guy I screwed up with was... different."

"Different good?"

He nodded and added, "Different incredible."

I knew the feeling. In fact, I knew the exact feeling. The words I said next weren't so much to him as they were to my own lazy ass. "Then go get him. Go after him, and don't let anything stop you. Look, you love basketball the same way I love baseball, but look at us now. We're fucking miserable. Sports isn't going to make our lives instantly perfect, and they aren't going to give us everlasting joy." I leaned toward him. "And we both know that playing any kind of ball isn't going to make us like girls. So you… we have a choice. We either keep being miserable because we sacrifice the things we really want for the things we think we should want, or we stop being pussies and man up. Go get the thing in life that is going to make us complete, and fuck the rest of the world. If they aren't ready for a gay athlete, then someone else will be. Because I'd rather be a happy me than a miserable someone else." I stood up. "And I'm tired of being someone else."

He looked up at me, his face kind of stuck between a smile and something else.

"You're right," he said slowly. "You are absolutely right. If I want Sam, then I should go get him."

I had no idea what that meant, but I chimed in. "And I want Kyle, and I am going to go get him." He looked at me and smiled.

He stood up, and I instantly felt like a reject from the lollipop guild. "Fuck yeah!" he roared.

"But not right now," I said, quieter. "Because it's, like, three in the morning, and any guy we call and proclaim our love for will think we're just drunk-dialing them."

He thought about it and agreed. "Yeah, good point. Then tomorrow, I'll go get him." He looked down at me, and I again tried not to stare at his eight-pack. "I'm glad I met you, Brad. You're a serious bro." He did a quick one-shoulder hug and patted me on the back. "Seriously, man, your guy is a lucky dude."

I smiled at him. "Thanks, man, and I'm sure Sam is just as lucky."

He pulled down his shirt and grabbed his keys. "Not yet, but he will be."

WHEN DANNY dropped me off at the hotel, I wasn't surprised to find my dad asleep in his bed.

I didn't turn on the lights and just slipped my clothes off in the dark. I was digging through my bag for some sweats to sleep in when I heard him ask, "So, have fun?"

I pulled on the pants and slipped my shirt over my head. It reeked of smoke. I tossed it in the corner and felt my way over to my bed. "Kinda," I answered, sitting on the edge. "Dad, I came to a decision." The room was dead silent as I waited for him to speak. I heard him rustle in his bed, most likely moving to turn the light on. "Please don't turn that on," I said quickly. "I need to say this, and it is going to be a lot easier if I don't have to see your face."

I could hear a half sigh escape his lips. "Fine. No lights."

He was waiting for me, and I was waiting for courage. Not finding any, I took a deep breath and said, "I don't want to take the scholarship, and here is why. I know it's a great opportunity, but they want me to pretend I'm someone I'm not, and I can't do that anymore." I heard him move from the other side of the room, but I kept talking. "Okay, no, I could do it. I just don't want to. You don't know how it was, Dad, lying to everyone, keeping secrets, making sure I didn't look too long or say the wrong thing. I didn't even know it until Kyle, but I was dying inside. Something inside of me was in agony, and I can't go back to that. If I did, I'd either end up binge drinking or just blowing my head off, because I can't go four years lying to every single person I know. I just can't."

He said nothing.

"So if you want to be mad and kick me out of the house and whatever, fine. But I am not going to go to school here, period." I waited for him to scream or to start bellowing. Hell, part of me was expecting him to come leaping out of the shadows to hit me.

Instead, he turned on the light on the nightstand. He was sitting on his bed across from me. "You done?" I nodded. "Okay, then let me say a few things." I mentally prepared myself to be torn into a million tiny pieces. As my eyes got adjusted to the light, I could see a half-empty bottle of something on the nightstand with a glass next to it. Leave it to my old man; he wouldn't pay the minibar prices, but he wasn't going to let that stop him from getting his drunk on.

"If you don't want to go here, then don't. I told you it was your choice, and it is. Do I think it's the right one? No, but then again, I'm not gay, so I have no idea what you're going through. I think you're wrong, though. I think you can get through it. Not because I don't think it's that difficult. I think you can get through it because you're my son, and I have never seen you back away from a fight in your life." My eyes stung as he kept talking. "I know we haven't always gotten along, and that is because I couldn't afford to be your friend, not while I was pushing you so hard to succeed. I put you in sports because it changed my life, and I knew it could change yours. When you wanted to play baseball instead of football, I didn't stop you. Hell, I didn't care what you played as long as you were the best."

He paused like he thought I was going to say something, but I was too stunned to even breathe.

"I don't know if you'll ever be a father, but if you are, try to remember this. It's your job to make sure that kid gets across the finish line. Whatever race they decide to run in, you have to support it, and then not let them back out of it, because that's what kids do. They start something and then whine when it gets too hard and never see it through. As a father, I made sure you saw things through, so that when you were there and had to make a choice, you could make an informed one. You made it here. You have A&M offering to pay you for four years of college. That is because of you and your talent. If you don't want to take it, that's your choice, but it's a choice that you made because you got here. You didn't stop in junior high because you hated running or freshman year because you didn't like playing under a Texas summer, and that's because I made you play. But you're here now. You're a man. If that's your choice, I'll honor it."

There were tears going down my face because this was the closest my father had ever come to giving me a compliment.

"I know I was rough, and I know the shit between your mom and I affected you. But seriously, Brad, you are as good as I knew you could be, and that's why I pushed you. So you could sit here and tell one of the biggest colleges in the south to go fuck themselves."

I rushed over and hugged him like I had never hugged him before.

"Thank you, Dad," I said as he hugged me back. "Thank you for everything."

He chuckled. "Well, not everything, but most of it."

I sat there crying. I couldn't have agreed more.

MY FATHER did the talking as he told Mr. Peterson that he could go jump off a cliff.

"That is regrettable," he said, not sounding the least bit upset.

That was when my inner Kyle jumped out. "No, what is regrettable is the way you treat athletes who generate millions of dollars for your school, sir." All three men looked at me like I had grown a third eye. "Bad enough that you license their likeness and names without giving them a cent, but to make them live a life that is a lie is the worst." I looked at the alumni guy. "If the people who donate money here have a problem with gay athletes, then they should get used to losing a lot, because in the future, more of them are not going to take it anymore. My sexuality has nothing to do with how I play baseball, and anyone who thinks so is welcome to try to prove it at a batting cage any day of the week." I looked at Coach Perkins. "I'm sorry I won't be playing for you this or any year you're coach here." I pulled his baseball card out of my pocket and put it on the table. "I don't need this anymore. My heroes don't stand by and let shit like this happen."

I looked over to my dad and nodded. "I'm good."

He smiled and put his arm around me. "Good luck with your season," he said cheerfully and walked me out.

As we made our way to the car, he asked, "You sure?"

I gave him a smile as I opened my door. "Never more sure of anything."

As we buckled up, he reminded me, "You do know you still have to figure out what you're going to do."

He started the car. I nodded but didn't say a word. I knew exactly what I was going to do.

I was going to get Kyle back, no matter what.

WE TOOK a detour to Arlington instead of going home because the Rangers were playing the Mariners, and my dad said he wasn't ready to head home yet, and I never needed a reason to see the Rangers play in person. I felt like a kid again as we walked into the stadium, and I begged my dad for something to eat. He shocked the hell out of me by coming back with a basket of hot dogs and nachos and two beers. I was about to tell him he forgot my drink when he handed me one of them. I took it and looked around guiltily.

"I can't drink this," I said, whispering for no reason whatsoever. "I'm not legal."

He gave me a smile. "I know how old you are, and we're in the middle of a baseball game. Just drink the damn thing and try not to pretend that it's your first one."

I couldn't help looking around before taking a long drink. On a hot day like this, it was the best beer I had ever had.

"I remember my old man took me to see the Oilers play back in the day, and he bought me a beer." He was looking at the field, but I knew he was looking backward in time. "I remember thinking that if I started drinking, I'd end up like him. Turns out I didn't even need that. I turned out to be an asshole all by myself."

It was weird seeing my dad as another person, with thoughts and wants and all that. I mean, you know your parents were once kids like you and all, but you get so used to seeing them as these things… these parental units that you forget they're human.

I put my hand on his, and he looked over at me in confusion. We were never the touchiest of families, so he was a little bewildered by the action. "You may have been rough, but I just turned down a scholarship to A&M, and it's because of you." He gave me a look, and I laughed. "That didn't come out right. I mean, I wouldn't have gotten this far without you pushing me. I'm not going to pretend you were always my favorite person, but you were a decent father."

I could see my words had touched him, and I let them linger there for a moment. "This whole hand-touching thing is weirding you out, isn't it?"

"Little bit," he agreed.

I laughed and went back to drinking my beer.

It was a great day.

We also won 11-3, just saying.

WHEN WE got back late Sunday night, I realized there was no way to talk to Kyle until tomorrow at school.

I thought about calling Jennifer for a moment and then changed my mind. Calling this late was risking the wrath of her dad, and that was nothing I wanted to risk. So I forced myself to lie in bed until I finally passed out. The next day, everything changed. I just knew it would.

THE DAY started the same as every other day: too early for my taste.

I took a shower and got dressed, thinking only of Kyle and getting him back. I wasn't even hungry as I ran out the door. I texted Jennifer and asked her if she needed a ride. She wasted no time saying "Hell yes." She was waiting outside when I got to her house. She handed me a Pop-Tart as she got in the car. "Someone is up early."

I almost finished the pastry in one bite. "I have a mission," I said as she buckled her belt.

"How was A&M?" she asked.

I waved my hand at her. "They offered me a full ride, and I turned it down, but that isn't important."

She almost choked on her food. "What? Since when?"

"Doesn't matter." I began driving to school. "I need to get Kyle back," I said with conviction.

She didn't say anything for a couple of blocks. Finally she piped up. "Wait, so they gave you a scholarship and you turned it down? Why?"

"Because they didn't want the gay me, just the me that played baseball." It was weird that I had no malice about it as I explained it to her. It was a choice. I'd made it, and I was at peace with it. I really didn't think that would happen. "They wanted me to sign all this crap that said I wouldn't date a guy or tell anyone I was gay, and I said no. I'm not that guy anymore, and I don't want to be him again."

She didn't say a word all the way to school. In fact, when we pulled into the parking lot, I saw she had just been staring at me. "What?" I asked, thinking I had food on my face or something.

"Did you give up A&M for Kyle?" she asked me, her voice half-concerned and half-sad.

"No," my mouth said without thinking. No? I didn't? Then who did I turn it down for? "No, I didn't do it for him." My mouth kept talking without my help. "I did it for me. I did it because I wasn't willing to pretend to be the perfect little jock they wanted. I am who I am, and if they don't want that, then they don't get the rest."

I honestly think I just impressed myself.

"We need to talk about Kyle before you talk to him," she said as we got out of the car. "This isn't a normal 'Brad rushes in and says a bunch of stuff and wins the day' kind of situation. Kyle is in a bad place, and I think you just professing your love might make it worse."

"What's wrong with him?" I asked, pausing before closing my door. "You never got a chance to tell me Friday."

The first bell rang, and I realized she wasn't going to have time now either.

"In class," she promised me as she turned to the building. "Don't do anything until then."

I gave her a salute, which made her laugh.

I LOST it before I got to Mr. Powers's class. When she walked in, I almost jumped her.

"So what's wrong with Kyle?" I asked her before she even sat.

She put her purse and books down. "Chill—you're going to have an aneurism."

"I'm going to have worse if you don't tell me what's wrong with him."

She pulled her stuff out, and I could tell she was composing herself as Mr. Powers took roll and began to go over the homework. "The first meeting didn't go too well," she whispered cryptically.

"Bad how?" I asked, more worried than ever.

"Well… see, Sammy had this idea…," she began to say.

Which was the exact moment gunshots echoed out across the school.

We hit the floor instantly, more than a few people screaming in terror.

"What the—?" I asked out loud.

"Shhhh," Mr. Powers said, kneeling on the ground. He was moving toward the door to lock it. "No one say a word."

I looked over at Jennifer, and I could see she was worried but not panicked. It was easy to forget sometimes she was a sheriff's daughter. She pulled her cell out of her purse and began texting someone. It was a great idea, and I pulled mine out as well… but had no idea who to text.

She sent one text and began texting someone else. She looked up at me and mouthed the name "Tyler."

I pulled his name out and typed as another gunshot came from outside. It didn't sound close, but it echoed across the quad like crazy. More screams, and I winced. Jennifer didn't even stop typing. I sent my message.

Shooting @school

Before I could Send, there were two blasts over a loudspeaker, alarms began to whine, and a recorded voice over the PA system announced we were in lockdown and no one was to leave their rooms.

I finished the text.

In lockdown. Am worried.

I sent it and wished for the millionth time Kyle hadn't given his phone back to me.

And then it hit me. Kyle was out there alone.

Kyle

DO YOU know what Fate does to really screw your life up?

I mean, when you've pissed him/her/it off royally, and it wants to teach you a lesson you'll never forget? You'd think it would be something obvious like killing someone you care about or destroying something you value, but you'd be wrong. Those are minor-league curses that befall nearly everyone during their lives. I assure you that Fate doesn't even get out of bed for those kind of afflictions; it has a whole staff to handle the small stuff. No, when Fate has had enough of you and your life, it does the last thing you'd think would be horrible.

It grants your every wish.

I used to wish that people would know who I was, that I would fall in love with a great guy, and that I would eventually get a college scholarship to get out of this fucking town. And here I was able to say that every single one of those things had happened, and my life was worse than ever. People knew who I was, sure, but I guess I forgot to wish that they would like me as well. Outside of Jennifer and Sammy, I had no friends, and since Brad and I broke up, even that had been strained. I met the perfect guy, and against all odds he said he loved me also, but again, I forgot that I wanted to fall in love with a guy I could share my life with instead of what was left of this school year and then nothing. And yes, I did get a full ride to UC Berkeley at the cost of the previously mentioned perfect guy, making what should have been my golden ticket feel more like a lottery ticket that was one number off from winning the jackpot.

And now I had a gun pointed at my head. That, by the way, I had not wished for.

Your mind does strange things when you realize your life expectancy could be represented with single digits. You'd expect to think things like what you regretted not doing, or maybe you'd watch your whole life flashing before your eyes or whatever. But nope, none of that happened. All that went through my mind as I stared down the barrel of what looked to me like an awfully large caliber gun was the lyrics to "West End Girls" by the Pet Shop Boys.

That song was on one of the many '80s CDs I had confiscated from my mom's collection before they got lost or destroyed by her lifestyle. Most of the music was a combination of catchy tunes mixed with cryptic lyrics that had to have been written under the influence of at least one controlled substance. But "West End Girls" was different for me, and I never knew why. There was something dark about it that betrayed the synth-pop sound it was trying to pull off. Like "Pumped Up Kicks" from Foster the People, the music hid a darker undertone that unless you were paying attention you wouldn't catch. A version of the song was wandering around my head for some reason.

"... better off dead there's a gun in his hand and it's pointing at my head."

I mean, it's about a guy who's going to kill himself, yet he seems just as confused as the listener is. Thinking these were going to be my last thoughts, I wondered if he was as confused as I was about what he'd started.

It would be easy to say this all came about because of Brad's and my breakup, but that wouldn't be fair. If I was being honest—and I mean, if you can't be completely truthful with a gun to your head, when can you be?—everything that was happening was all my fault. I had laid the seeds for this minute to happen from start to finish. I could look at the events that led to here and, like a greedy little pig, claim them all for myself. I'm sorry if this is making little sense to you. I'm a bit stressed at the moment. Please forgive my rambling.

I have a feeling it's about to be cut short anyways.

Brad had spent the couple of days after our breakup trying his best to make things right between us. Since I had found the one transgression on his part that he couldn't defend, he thought the breakup was all his fault. Of course, he didn't know I was going to Berkeley in a couple of months. Though I knew geography wasn't his strong point, he would know that College Station, Texas, was nowhere near Berkeley, California. He wanted to play baseball for A&M, and I wasn't going to let me deter him, even for half a second.

The same way I wasn't going to let him affect my decision either.

I know I sound like a dick, and on several levels I am one, but let me explain.

Brad and I have had the same dream for as long as we could remember: get the fuck out of Foster. He took to baseball and became the best he could be so some school, hopefully A&M, would pay the ridiculous cost of a college education as long as he hit a ball better than most other guys his age. I, on the other hand, decided that if I got the best grades I possibly could, that I could get one of the thousands of colleges out there to pay for my education based on my SAT scores. I had succeeded, and I knew if I told Brad, it would have made him think about changing his mind.

And that wasn't fair to either of us.

I knew Brad and the type of person he was. As many issues as I had with self-worth—and trust me, there were several—they were nothing compared to the litany of problems Brad suffered from when he looked in a mirror. He would think it was his duty or job or whatever to make the sacrifice and move to California with me. Which on paper sounds incredibly romantic and all that. But sooner or later it would affect him. He would see himself going nowhere while I got a college education. He would see me pursuing my dream while he worked a dead-end job so we could make bills, and then he would see me graduate and know for the rest of our lives that it would fall on me to be the breadwinner.

He'd start to resent me. And that would lead to him hating me.

He'd wake up at twenty-two, with no chance to regain the time he'd lost, and realize he'd flushed his dream down the toilet because he wanted to do the "right thing" when it came to me. So, instead of putting us both through the whole wasted years I saw for him, I ignored his attempts to get back together and did my level best to not see him at all. I even had Sammy deliver the phone he gave me for Christmas back to him. I made sure to send myself all the pictures that were on it and kept them in my email, because I knew someday I was going to want to look back at this and cry like a bitch. And then I erased everything that was in the phone.

Pushing the Erase key hurt like I was carving my heart out with a spoon.

So instead of thinking about how much of a mistake I was making, I threw myself into the gay-straight alliance. I worked with Mrs. Axeworthy to come up with a place that was inviting and welcoming to all. We set up topics like tolerance and civil rights, and drew up talking points for both sides and then practiced them on each other. For an adult, Mrs. Axeworthy was pretty cool. She owned a giant black cat that she called Little Eddie, hence her fascination with all things black cat, and he didn't like me at first. She explained that she hadn't had many visitors since her husband passed away and that Eddie had grown used to being the only man in the house.

The next time I went over, I brought tuna. After that, the cat loved me, and I had to admit, for a cat he was pretty cool as well.

Jennifer and Sammy took turns trying to convince me to talk to Brad. I knew they were just trying to be friends, but they were driving me crazy. I had to work nonstop to keep my own traitorous mind in check, but them coming up with perfectly rational reasons to forgive him was not helping. The more they pushed, the more I retreated. The more impassioned their pleas, the harder my resolve became, until finally it became too much.

The Friday before the first meeting, I was nervous as hell.

Not for the meeting, but because I was sure no one was going to show up. I had passed out fliers and put up a few on the bulletin boards, but none of them lasted more than a day before they were torn down. I found one of them shoved in my locker; across it was written: Fags Meeting This Monday!! Whoever it was had horrible penmanship. The only thing that would have been worse than no one showing up was a lot of assholes showing up and causing a scene. It was hard enough to get people to admit that being gay wasn't a federal offense, but if I had Tony Wright and his douchebag friends heckling us, it was going to be over before we began.

So at lunch I found myself picking at my food and reevaluating the choices I had made in my life.

"So, heard from Brad?" Jennifer asked coyly, knowing damn well I hadn't.

"Yeah, I called him last night, and we made up. He asked me to marry him, so that's a thing now." I hate to admit it, but I kind of liked the way she choked on her Pepsi as she looked over at me in shock. "I wish you'd stop bringing him up," I said, trying to sound as nice as I could.

"He's miserable," she exclaimed as passionately as any defense attorney trying to save their client from the death penalty. "You do know this is killing him, right?"

The fact that it was killing me too, obviously hadn't registered with her yet, because it was the third time this week she had brought it up.

"Yes, I'm sure he's crying all the way to the state championships." My stomach had soured, and I tossed my untouched sandwich into my paper bag. "I made up my mind, Jennifer. I wish you'd just let it go."

She looked sad as she finished her drink. "I just think you need to talk with him," she said softly.

"I said everything I needed to when we broke up. Going back and picking at the wound isn't going to help anything." I looked over at Sammy. "Please tell her to stop."

She glanced at Jennifer and then back to me. "Actually, I've been wanting to ask you about the meeting and who can come."

That was the last straw. "Seriously?" I snapped at her. "You too? Look, we went out, we broke up, and it's over. Completely over. So I don't want to talk to him, call him, see him, and I certainly don't want him showing up at that meeting. This is not a chance for us to be in the same room and then suddenly make up, and if either of you two bring him, I will lose my shit." I paused to make sure my words had sunk in. "You got it? Shit. Lost."

Sammy scowled at me and tossed her lunch onto her tray. "You know what, Kyle? I don't know if it's the heartbreak or you needing to get laid, but you've become a raging asshole." She stood up and glared down at me. "Not everything is about you."

Before I could answer, she turned around and marched off.

I looked over at Jennifer, who held her hands up in defense. "Okay, okay. I won't bring Brad. You've changed my mind."

And here comes Pet Shop Boys again. *"I think he's mad, too unstable."*

Right. Still a gun at my head. Getting there.

So that weekend I spent getting my ducks in a row. Not that I possessed a lot of ducks; in fact, my duck population had dwindled considerably since I'd been single. Nonetheless, there were ducks to get straightened out. I spent most of Saturday going over my talking points in detail in case there was something I had missed the forty-three times I'd reviewed them before. Sunday I went over to Mrs. Axeworthy's house, because I had pretty much convinced myself that everything I had planned on bringing up at the first meeting was crap and we needed to call a bomb threat in or something to make sure it wasn't going to happen.

She found my panic absolutely delightful, which is one of those things grown-ups do that piss kids off something fierce. Instead of responding to my self-made emergency like a proper teenager would, she instead put out a plate of cookies and a pitcher of juice and told me to eat something. It is chemically impossible to be mad at someone when you're eating a cookie. Don't believe me? Try it.

"You need to calm down about this," she chided as I finished my third cookie and wondered if we were splitting the plateful or if they were all mine. "You've done everything you can to prepare. Now you have to let the chips fall where they may."

"What does that even mean?" I asked, throwing caution to the wind and grabbing a fourth. "I mean, I get it's a casino reference, but don't you roll dice? I never got that."

"It's not a casino reference," she said, leaning back with her drink. "It's about woodcutting." Confused, I looked at her and, less confused, back at the last cookie. She smiled and nodded as she began to explain. "It's about obsessing over the small stuff when you have more important things to worry about. If you are carving something, you shouldn't worry where the wood chips are going to fall—you should focus on the job at hand. There is always time to sweep up the little stuff later."

I stared at her, kind of stunned that she knew that off the top of her head.

"I know this alliance is important to you, Kyle, but I can't help but feel it isn't the task you should be concentrating on." I looked away from her penetrating gaze to study the worn patch on my jeans. "I haven't seen Brad since you two stopped by my office that day. Everything okay?"

My jeans got a thousand times more interesting.

"You guys get in a fight or something?" Her voice was kind and inviting, which made me clam up even faster. "Okay, I don't want to pry, but let me give you some advice." I looked up at her, and she seemed to know exactly what was wrong. "Liking someone is a fleeting emotion. It can be like being hot or cold—it happens and then it fades away. But when you meet someone you fall in love with, that is a whole different kind of creature." I found myself leaning forward as she elaborated. "Love is something you can't get over, even if you want to. Once a connection is made, a real connection, it's usually forever. And you can try to do a lot of things to get rid of it. You can run, you lie, you can even try to pretend that it's for the best, but in the end, real love will find a way."

I sat there staring at her, wondering if I was so obvious that someone who didn't really know me at all could see so much so easily. "How do you know when it's real love?"

"When you close your eyes and all you can see is that person? That's real love. When you wake up in the middle of the night from a bad dream, and he's the first person you want to talk to you? That's real love. And when your life flashes before your eyes and you think this might be the end, the one person you wished you could talk to one more time—that's real love."

I did everything I could not to think of Brad.

In fact, I was doing everything I could right then not to think of him, but damn, the only thing I could think of, besides Pet Shop Boys, was that I really, really wanted to talk to Brad one more time. The funny thing was, I didn't even want to talk to him about anything real. I didn't want him to apologize or to take him back. I just wanted to tell him about my day and how shitty fourth period was now, knowing I wasn't going to see him at lunch. I wanted to ask him if he'd seen the new TikTok dance or if he was ready for the playoffs. I didn't even care what it was about. I just wanted to talk to him one more time.

The sound of a gun's hammer being pulled back shouldn't have been as loud as what I just heard.

I was explaining how I got to the point where a gun and I were staring at each other, and I got sidetracked. I'd spent a lot of time on the weekends at Robbie's, trying my best to stay away from Brad until graduation. Robbie had made no pretense about how he felt about Brad, so I thought his store would be a safe place where I wouldn't have to listen to someone encouraging me to patch things up. I could fold clothes peacefully and stay out of sight.

Of course, that wasn't what happened at all.

Robbie was dealing with his own drama that week as well, which probably saved me from his version of an encouraging lecture. It had something to do with the creepy woman who walked into his shop and gave him a letter from his dead boyfriend, something that was just a bit too wild to be believed. Then he'd passed out.

It turns out when someone actually faints, it is nowhere as funny as it seems on TV.

For one, on TV they put their hand on their forehead and just wilt away, their knees slowly buckling as they drift back onto the ground. They're performing more of a dance move than an actual loss of consciousness. If they do that thing with their eyelashes that makes them look like they're having a seizure, I laugh every time.

When someone really passes out, they go down, like, in a flash. The second they no longer care about standing up, gravity takes them and sucks them to the ground in less than a second. There is no slow fall or bent knees; there's a thud when they hit the ground that is unmistakably painful.

The sound Robbie's head made when he hit the floor was bone chilling.

I ran behind the desk and shook him to try to wake him up but realized how stupid that was. I mean, he wasn't trying to get out of going to school. He had been hit by a panic attack and passed out. I considered slapping his face but then thought better of it on the off chance it did wake him up. I had a feeling he wouldn't take me slapping him as a good thing. Throw some water in his face? No, he wouldn't be thrilled with that either. I was starting to panic because I had no idea what to do.

I needed an adult.

If you're an adult, you may think that thought a pretty obvious one, but to a teenage boy, it is literally the last resort. Asking a grown-up for help is the antithesis of everything we learned growing up, and it's a hard habit to break. We're taught that we have to deal with problems ourselves, man up, and look trouble in the face, and most important, don't be a little bitch and whine to your mommy. As a teenage boy, I can safely tell you that there are days I'm firmly convinced I can do whatever I put my mind to, and if everyone over the age of twenty-one were to vanish one day, I'm under the impression that I would be fine in the new *Logan's Run*-like future.

However, as I looked down at Robbie's unconscious form, it dawned on me that I might not be as prepared as I thought I was.

I could call my mom, but that seemed like a bad idea. She already distrusted Robbie. In her world, an older gay guy giving advice and clothes to a teen boy meant the old gay guy was a predator. Calling her and saying Robbie had passed out would have unleashed a whole new set of suspicions. Was he drunk? On drugs? Was he trying to get you drunk? Forget that. I could call Gayle at Nancy's, but she would call an ambulance, and so far I wasn't sure Robbie needed that. I went through a whole list of adults I could call, but it came down to one name, the person I knew wouldn't narc me out or panic.

Tyler.

I grabbed the store phone and dialed the sports shop's number from memory. It felt like a million years ago when I would call up and talk to Brad over winter break. When did time get so messed up? I was eighteen years old, but I felt like I was a hundred.

Tyler's way-too-chipper voice answered the phone. "Parker's Sporting Goods."

"Tyler, it's Kyle," I said quickly. "I need some help."

"What's up?" he asked casually, probably thinking I was calling to ask him about Brad.

Nice try, sir, but not even close.

"I am at Robbie's shop, and he had a panic attack and passed out. I don't know what to do." I tried not to sound as scared as I felt, but I'm pretty sure I was screwing that up.

There was silence on the other end of the phone, and I wondered if he had hung up. The only way I knew he hadn't was the sound of his breathing. After what seemed like hours of nothing, he said, "Call an ambulance."

"Tyler!" I called out over the phone. "What if he doesn't need one and is charged for it? You know it will be all over town the second he ends up in the ER." The time it took a rumor to reach from one side of town to the other was best measured in picoseconds. If picoseconds is too nerdy for you, one picosecond is a trillionth of second.

"What do you want me to do, Kyle?" he asked, knowing damn well what I wanted. "If I show up over there, he will lose his fucking mind. Call someone else."

"Like who?" I was close to losing my own mind. "Give me a person who I can trust not to blab that the gay recluse who lives on the edge of town passed out in his shop and I will call them. One name, go for it."

211

Again with the silence, and finally a defeated "I'll be right over."

I don't know how he did it, but the way he hung up the phone made it sound angry.

Less than five minutes later, he walked in the door, looking as angry as his hang-up had sounded. I pointed behind the counter, and he walked over and knelt down. He put a hand on Robbie's forehead, then down to the vein in the side of his neck, checking Robbie's pulse. "Go to the bathroom and get a damp washcloth." He scooped Robbie up behind his knees and shoulders, took a breath, and rose to his feet, carrying Robbie like he weighed nothing. Because Tyler wears comfortable clothes and has that easy way about him, it's easy to forget that he's also in great shape. When he carried Robbie to the backroom as if he was a mannequin, I had to admit, for his age Tyler was kinda hot.

I ran to the bathroom and got a washcloth.

I handed it to him and watched him apply it gently to Robbie's forehead. "What's wrong with him? Why won't he wake up?"

Without looking at me, Tyler asked, "Do you know who Riley was?" I didn't want to tell him how much I knew, so I held my hand out and waved it back and forth indicating "kind of."

"After Riley died, Robbie checked out for a while. His mother came to town and took care of him. He was prescribed Valium for panic attacks." He looked over at me. "What set it off?"

I wondered how much I should share and then thought better of it. I mean, I had dragged Tyler in there even though he didn't want to come. The least I could give him was the truth. "Some Cruella de Vil woman came in and gave him an envelope. I think she was Riley's mom."

"Dolores?" he mused out loud. "Holy shit, I'd pass out too."

"Why?" I asked, wanting to know more of the story.

He paused, obviously wondering how much to share with me. "It's complicated. Let's just say after Riley died, she was a bitch to Robbie."

"And he hates you why?" I asked, hoping he would answer automatically.

He looked over at me and grinned. "If he hasn't told you by now, there's no way I am going to."

Crap.

I was about to try a different approach, but then Robbie began to come to. Both Tyler and I quieted down as we watched him and wondered if he was okay.

He slapped Tyler's hand off his forehead. "Get off," he ordered, trying to sit up and failing.

Tyler looked down at him and asked, "Happy? You want to hiss and claw, wait until you have some balance back first, kitten." He dropped the towel on Robbie's face and turned to me. "He's going to be fine."

Robbie looked over at me and asked, "You called him?" in the same manner someone would ask if I had kicked their dog or possibly killed it. "Why would you do that?" he yelled at me pretty angrily.

"Because you tipped over and slammed onto the floor pretty hard," Tyler jumped in. "He wasn't sure if you were having a heart attack or just doing a pretty fair Judy Garland impersonation."

I swear the temperature dropped thirty degrees when Robbie said "Get out!" to Tyler.

Tyler shook his head and rolled his eyes at me. "Told you so. Make sure he eats something, and call him a cab when he's ready to go home." Tyler looked at Robbie momentarily. "He's nowhere near as fine as he is going to try to convince you once I'm gone."

"Get the fuck out!" Robbie roared.

"I'm going, I'm going," he said, holding his hands up in defense. "Let me know if he lives, Kyle."

As soon as the front doorbell rang and I heard the sound of the door clicking shut, I confessed. "You just fell over, and I didn't know any adults to call because you don't know anyone, so I called him instead of 911, because if they took you to the hospital you'd just bitch that I was overreacting, so before you bite my head off, that is why I called him."

Robbie closed his eyes and seemed to be trying to regain his composure. "I am not mad at you, Kyle. Just go home and we'll talk about it later." He honestly sounded like a serial killer, he was so calm.

"He was worried about you too," I added, trying to help Tyler the best I could. He did do me a solid.

Now all the anger was there in Robbie's voice. He pointed at the door. "Go home, Kyle. Now."

I bit my tongue as I wondered if I should push the moment. "Can I at least call you a cab?"

Robbie answered way too quickly. "I don't need one."

"Says the guy who can't stand up," I muttered under my breath. "I am going to call you a cab, and you can tell the guy to go away if you want." I reached for my phone and then remembered I had given it back to Brad. Suddenly I was sad all over again.

Robbie seemed to sense my hesitation and assured me, "I'm fine. I don't need a cab, and I don't need any help."

I would have almost believed him if his eyes weren't having so much trouble in their attempts to remain uncrossed. However, I knew we were just wasting time; he was going to argue the point forever if I let him. I grabbed my backpack and growled, "Fine, but if you die, it's not my fault. I am going to flip the sign and lock the door."

I walked out. From the payphone half a block from the store, I called Robbie a cab. I didn't care if he got mad or not.

The next day Robbie sat me down and told me the rest of the story. He explained how Tyler had driven off, leaving Riley and him there. How Tyler acted like he never even knew Robbie in public and that he'd never apologized or even tried to talk to Robbie again.

I was stunned.

I felt like I'd found out someone you thought you knew through and through was actually a superhero and had a whole other superhero identity. No, that's not right. It's like thinking the person you knew was real and finding out that person was really a supervillain in hiding. I didn't say anything in front of Robbie since it looked like it had taken a lot out of him to tell me the whole story. Instead I ate lunch with him and left, faking a smile and a wave.

And headed straight for Tyler's shop.

He was closing up when I threw the door open. His boyfriend was behind the counter, and they were laughing about something. The laughter stopped as if it had been lopped off when I barreled in.

"No wonder you didn't want to come over," I said, feeling pissed and betrayed all at the same time. "If I had done what you did, I wouldn't have dared walk into that shop. Hell, I wouldn't stay in the same town if I was you."

Tyler's face fell, and his entire posture changed. His shoulders slumped a little, and it looked like someone had hit him in the gut. "Be glad you aren't me, then."

"I am," I declared, getting even madder. "I'm damn glad I'm not you, because I would not know how to live with myself. So is this what you're teaching Brad? To be some closet jock who cuts bait and runs at the first sign of danger? Or does he even know what you did?"

Matt stood and stepped out from behind the counter; clearly, he was pissed too. "Hey, you little snot, back off! You have no idea what you're talking about."

Suddenly all the rage and emotion I had been stifling over the breakup came busting out as I screamed back at the man. "I know exactly what I'm talking about. I'm talking about someone watching another person die. Leaving that person behind, even though he was a friend. Leaving someone else to clean things up. And why? Because he was too chickenshit to take the risk that people would figure out he was gay." I glared at Tyler. "Was it that important? You happy with your choice?"

"Of course I'm not," he said in a voice barely above a whisper.

"I think you should get out," the boyfriend ordered, standing between Tyler and me.

"You know, if Brad is supposed to grow up like you, I'm glad I broke up with him!" I screamed as this huge guy took a step in my direction. He wasn't going to actually throw me out, but he could crowd me out of the shop one step at a time.

"Stop talking," Matt said once I backed out the door. I opened my mouth, but he cut me off quickly once we were outside. "Things are incredibly easy to see when you're a teenager because you think you know everything. But trust me, kid, if you think he hasn't spent every day regretting what he did or didn't do, then you are as stupid as you're acting. When you get to be our age, pray that there isn't some punk there to rub it in. Because you're going to struggle with the same thing I am right now."

"And what's that?" I asked, not really caring about the answer.

"Wondering if popping you in the mouth is worth a couple of nights in jail." His hands clenched into fists, and I could see the real anger in his face. "Do not come back here just to make him feel like shit again. You got it?"

I wanted to argue, but he really did look outraged. So I just nodded.

"Smart boy," he stated before slamming the door shut and locking it.

Fuck him and Tyler. And Brad too for that matter. The three of them deserved each other!

At least I tried to convince myself of that as I walked home.

The next day was Monday, which meant the first meeting. I didn't remember falling asleep, I was so nervous. That meant, as far as my mind was concerned, I hadn't slept at all. I ate something and headed to school, the sense of dread growing in my stomach with each step. The closer I got to school, the more I felt like the old me: the me who wanted to be invisible and forgotten, the me who had done his level best to be ignored and who'd felt that standing up in the middle of a group of people and talking was the worst thing in the world.

It was an odd sensation as I mentally regressed more and more until I was literally standing on the edge of the school parking lot, afraid to cross that line, like a vampire who hadn't been invited in. I thought about running home and feigning illness until people just assumed I had died. I'd almost turned around when I realized people were counting on me. No one had pushed me into anything. The idea to form the damn club was all mine. No matter what I did, the obligation to see the alliance through was all mine.

I realized part of the reason why adults looked miserable most of the time.

My mind would not engage during my first classes. I was too busy preparing myself for everything that could happen during the half-hour meeting ahead of me. Of course, my own imagination took over, spinning different scenarios from dumb to just ridiculous as my paranoia bloomed. I was pretty sure aliens wouldn't invade during the meeting, but if they did, I had an evacuation plan, just in case. When I walked out of second period to go set up for the meeting, I felt like throwing up.

Mrs. Axeworthy was already waiting for me in the library when I walked in. "Well, good morning, Kyle. You ready to make history?" she asked brightly.

"Only if by 'being ready' you mean ralphing all over the room," I muttered, setting my backpack down on one of the chairs.

"Oh no," she said, making me stop. She pulled the chair out at the head of the table. "This is where you sit."

I honestly felt bile rising in the back of my throat.

"But that's where you sit," I protested weakly.

She shook her head and gestured to the desk behind her. "I am the faculty advisor. I am here just to keep order, but this meeting is yours. You lead it."

Why, oh why, hadn't I run home when I had the chance?

I plopped my pack down next to the chair but refused to sit. It looked sinister to me somehow, even though it was identical to the other chairs in every way. Something about it was hungry. I knew I was imagining everything, but I was still terrified of the chair and the sitting down and the leading a meeting.

She put a hand on one of my shoulders and squeezed. "You'll do great. I know it."

That made one of us.

Lunch period started, and Mrs. Axeworthy opened the door, indicating the meeting had begun. Jennifer was standing there waiting. Her smile made me feel a tiny bit better. She walked in, grabbed a seat, and whispered, "This is so exciting."

I nodded and tried to keep breathing.

Two more people poked their heads in, looking around to see what an alliance meeting was all about, no doubt. "In or out," Axeworthy chided them. "This isn't a staring zoo."

I didn't recognize the two guys. They were obviously freshman, and it was the first time I looked at someone who went to this school and thought of referring to them as kids. They looked at each other, silently questioning if they wanted to enter. After about thirty seconds of silence, one of them nodded, and they both walked in and sat down. I tried not to stare in amazement at their presence.

Andy, Jeff, and Mike walked in, their binders of Magic: The Gathering cards in hand. They waved, which made me smile as they sat down too. Andy looked over at me and whispered, "If things get weird, we can pull out our foil cards again."

That made me laugh for the first time in forever.

We waited another couple of minutes, and then Mrs. Axeworthy closed the door.

Everyone turned toward me and waited for me to say something.

I took a deep breath and began reciting the speech I had memorized.

"Welcome to the first meeting of the gay-straight alliance for Foster High. I'm Kyle, and I am gay." A couple of people smiled as I nodded to them. "This is a safe room. Nothing that is said inside of it leaves. It is the first and only rule of this club—what is said in here stays in here."

Mike said quietly, "The first rule of gay club is there is no gay club."

Everyone laughed nervously, which broke the tension.

"This is a place for everyone, not just gay people. It is a place of welcoming, and no matter who you are, you're always welcome here."

Which is when the door opened, and Sammy stood there.

I smiled, and I nodded for her to walk in.

"No one is turned away," I continued as she took a few steps into the room…
…and Jeremy walked in behind her.

Something in my mind snapped. "Get the fuck out," I snarled. I couldn't ever remember feeling the rage I felt at that moment. Both of them froze as I glared at Jeremy. "Don't stop. Turn around and get out." I did my best to keep my voice level, but the anger had begun to seep underneath the words and escape into the library.

My raw rage crashed across the distance between me and the door. Between me and Jeremy. His jaw dropped open, and he took a slow step backward.

"Kyle!" Sammy interjected. "He's sorry and wants to…."

"Sorry?" I roared, striding around the table toward them. To Jeremy, I snarled, "You're sorry? Oh well, then that makes it better, doesn't it?" Sammy looked like she was thinking of stepping between us for a second, but when she saw how pissed I was, she backed away. "It doesn't matter what you did as long as you say 'sorry' at the end. Is that how it works?"

Jeremy's mouth opened a few times, and he looked like a fish trying to breathe on land. "I-I just wanted…."

"I don't care what you wanted, you dick!" I could hear people moving behind me, but I ignored them. "You didn't care what he wanted, right? So why should anyone give a flying fuck what you want?"

His face went white as he realized what I was talking about.

"Kyle," Mrs. Axeworthy asked quietly from somewhere just behind me. "Kyle, what's going on?"

"Jeremy was leaving," I said, not breaking eye contact with him.

217

"I thought anyone could be here," Sammy argued. "Wasn't that what you were just saying?"

I looked over at her in complete shock. "Really? You want him to stay?" Before she could answer, I looked back to Jeremy. "Sure, he can stay. He can stay as long as he wants. As soon as he tells everyone what he did." I heard both Jennifer and Sammy gasp. "So go for it, Jeremy. Share with the rest of the class and you can have a seat anywhere you want."

"Please don't do this," he pleaded.

"Leave, or I will tell them what you did." My voice sounded severe even to me.

I tried not to imagine a dog that had been kicked as he turned around and walked out the door. I forced myself not to care about his feelings as he marched out of the room looking like he had a gun to his head. As soon as the door closed, I glared at Sammy. "Why in the world would you bring him here?"

Now it was her turn to sound outraged. "I tried asking you. I've been trying for weeks now, but you've been so busy being an asshole because you broke up with your boyfriend, you haven't had time. He's hurting, Kyle. He's talking about killing himself, he's so torn up about all this. He needs a place like this. He needs friends."

"Then maybe he shouldn't go around bullying people into killing themselves," I shot back.

No one breathed. I teetered on the edge of a razor blade, seeing myself from the outside. Every muscle in my body knotted in order to keep me in one place.

"Okay," Mrs. Axeworthy spoke into the silence. "I think we're done for this week. I want to thank everyone for coming. Obviously this is a work in progress and we…."

"So he doesn't deserve help? Because of what he did, he is forced to wander through life without friends, period?" Sammy asked me, both of us ignoring the adult in the room. "Because he was a dick once he never gets forgiven?"

"Something like that," I spat back.

"You sound exactly like Robbie," Jennifer said behind me. I felt a chill go up my spine as I turned around to confront her. "So Jeremy isn't gay enough to help? He doesn't pass your test, so you just hope he kills himself? Really? I thought you were different."

I wanted to tell her that was not what I had been saying, except that was exactly what I had been saying.

And I didn't care.

"We're done," Mrs. Axeworthy said in her best authoritative voice. "Everyone except Kyle, please leave. We will meet again same time next week. Thank you for coming." She made it clear the topic was closed, and they were all leaving.

One by one they got up and filed out of the room. The library crew wouldn't even meet my eyes, and I heard the new guys I didn't know say to each other, "I had no idea it was going to be that exciting. We are so coming back next week."

At least someone enjoyed themselves.

Sammy looked at me like I was a monster. "I know you're upset because of Brad," she started, voice shaking, "but what you just did, the Kyle I know would have never done. Because if he could have, I never would have become friends with him."

I looked over at Jennifer. Face unreadable, she shrugged and said, "We'll talk later."

Silently, both Jennifer and Sammy left the library without a look back.

Which left me and Mrs. Axeworthy alone.

She went and sat down at the desk, a look of extreme disappointment on her face. "When you came to me about this, Kyle, I really thought you wanted to make a difference here. I honestly believed that your intentions were good." I began to protest, but she kept talking. "However, if you formed this alliance just so you could be in charge and dictate who is and who isn't worthy of membership, then you are sadly mistaken." She picked up some papers off the desk and began to look them over. "We'll try this again next week," she said, not looking at me. "If the Kyle I just saw intends on showing up again"—she looked up at me—"don't bother coming."

I moved to start putting the chairs away, and she said, "I'll get someone to do that," dismissing me completely.

I grabbed my backpack and stormed out of the room. I'd always thought that "a haze of red" was just an expression. It's not. It's real. And it had dropped over the entire world. I started to head to my next class, because following routine had always been a good thing for me. Suddenly, out of nowhere, I said, "Fuck it," and walked off campus. I charged home, muttering to myself like a crazy person the entire time. I felt equal parts betrayed and confused. How could Sammy do that? She knew what Jeremy did to Kelly. She knew what he was responsible for. Did she really expect me to forgive and forget?

I opened the door to the apartment and froze when I saw Tyler and his boyfriend sitting on the couch.

My mom turned around in the chair and looked at me, confused. "What are you doing home?"

I closed the door and made straight for my room.

"Kyle!" my mom called after me. "You aren't even going to say hello?"

I was almost to my room when I heard the boyfriend mutter, "Told you this was a bad idea."

Dropping my backpack, I turned around and looked at him. "What was a bad idea?" I asked furiously. "Coming here or threatening to hit a teenager in the face?"

The looks of confusion on both my mom's and Tyler's faces told me the boyfriend hadn't shared our conversation. Tyler looked at me and then asked his boyfriend. "Did you say you were going to hit him?"

"Actually he said he wondered if popping me in the mouth was worth a couple of nights in jail, to be accurate." I wished I had remembered this guy's name, because it was pretty obvious he wanted to beat the shit out of me at some point.

"You said that to my son?" my mom asked him point-blank. I tried not to smile as I saw him squirm.

"When someone barges in with only one thing on his mind, and that would be making Tyler feel like shit for something that happened years ago, I don't care much how old they are. An attack is an attack, and if the kid can't learn to watch his mouth now, then I assure you someone is going to come along and teach him that lesson."

"Matt," Tyler said, obviously trying to control his voice, "you can't go around threatening to hit kids. You know that."

Matt stared coldly at me. "Tell me you had a reason other than making him feel like shit when you walked in there."

If he thought I was going to wilt away at the question, he was dead wrong. "He watched a man die," I spat back. "He should feel like shit."

Matt surged to his feet; he had obviously had enough. Tyler stood also and stopped him from coming at me. My mom just looked at me with a confused look on her face. "Why in the world would you talk to Tyler like that?"

"You don't know what he did," I responded, trying my best not to whine. "You don't know—"

"I know exactly what happened," she said quietly, cutting me off. "And I am willing to bet you don't." My mouth fell open as I wondered how she could forgive him for such a thing. "I honestly thought you were a better person than this, Kyle."

"Better than what?" I could not believe I was suddenly the bad guy.

"Better than to torture someone with something they did in the past. Wasn't that the whole lesson you were trying to teach with Kelly?"

My words sputtered out in amazement. "You're chastising me?" I pointed at Tyler. "After what he did, you are going to look at me and say I did wrong?"

The look of disappointment on her face was devastating. "Just go to your room." When I didn't instantly move, she snapped, "Go to your fucking room. I don't think I can look at you right now."

I wanted to fight some more, but it was obvious Tyler, Matt, and my mom were against me. All I was doing was making things worse for myself. Without saying a word, I bolted into my room and slammed the door. I grabbed my pillow and screamed into it until there was so little oxygen to breathe that my world grew fuzzy. When had everyone turned against me? Exactly when did life stop making sense?

No answers seemed to be forthcoming, so I just passed out.

You know how they say hindsight is 20/20? Which means looking back, it's easy to see what you missed the first time around. There I was with a gun at my head, and suddenly I could see it perfectly clearly. I was a complete asshole. I mean, it was easy to say with some time and the threat of my life ending and all, but I just couldn't see it when it was actually happening. I really thought I was right and everyone else was wrong.

Which, by the way, should be a warning sign for everyone out there. If everyone you know is telling you the same thing, you are either wrong or everyone else has been taken over by aliens, which means you're screwed anyways. There are no aliens in this story, so that means I was dead wrong.

Sorry, the dead part was unintentional.

It should come as no surprise to anyone to find out that the next day at school, instead of calmly talking to Sammy and telling her what I felt she had done wrong, I came at her that morning like a raging bitch.

"What the hell were you thinking?" I asked her as she sat on the music hall steps.

She looked up at me with utter shock and disdain on her face and glared at me for a few seconds. "Really? You still don't see how much of a dick you're being?"

"You brought Jeremy! Why are you even talking to him?"

She stood up, her anger growing. "Oh, are you going to tell me who I can and can't be friends with now? His dad called me and told me Jeremy was miserable trying to find a way to make up for what he did. He is losing his mind over Kelly."

"Good!" I shouted back at her. "He should spend the rest of his life stark raving mad for what he did. He can never make it right!"

"So he shouldn't try?" Jennifer asked from behind me.

I hadn't heard her approach and was startled to find myself suddenly surrounded. "Let him try somewhere else."

"Where?" Sammy asked. "The alliance is a fucking gay-straight club, Kyle. It's the very place he should be talking about it, and you know it."

I did not know it. In fact, I thought the exact opposite at the time. "He isn't walking into that club as long as I am there." It was an ultimatum, and both of them knew it.

Sammy grabbed her purse. "I never thought I'd say this, but I miss Brad being around. He was much better at dealing with your insanity."

"I'm serious," I called after her as she walked away. "Tell him to stay away."

She turned around and shouted back, "I don't think you have to worry about anyone showing up, you asshole." To accentuate her words, she flipped me off.

I glanced over at Jennifer with a look that asked her if she believed her attitude.

There was an attitude she could not believe, but I didn't think it was Sammy's. "Kyle, I know you're upset about Brad—"

"This isn't about fucking Brad," I snapped, cutting her off.

She paused for a moment, either thinking of her next words or trying to calm down. "You're out of control. I think you need to talk to him."

"I don't need anything." The tardy bell rang, interrupting the argument. "I didn't before I met all of you, and I don't now."

It was quite possibly the stupidest thing I have ever said out loud.

She gave me a look of pure pity and shook her head. Without a word she turned around and walked away from me.

Everyone had walked away from me. Fine. I was alone before Brad fucked up my life. I could be alone again. I didn't need anyone.

Right?

Right?

Yeah, I didn't have any answers either.

The rest of that school week was the longest four days of my life. Each class seemed to drag out for hours of torture. I spent lunches alone in the library, avoiding any chance I might run into anyone I used to know, the whole time thinking they had abandoned me. As we headed into the weekend, I heard Josh Walker telling a couple of people that Brad wasn't at school because he was taking a tour of A&M over the weekend.

Josh's words stripped away the illusion that somehow things would end up for the better. I don't know how, but I guess that in the back of my mind, no matter what, I'd believed that things were going to fix themselves. The reality was completely different. In a moment of pure horror, when I realized just how bad things were, Brad was out looking at his dream college and everything I had been dreading was coming true. This year was going to end, and I was never going to see Sammy or Jennifer or Brad—"Brad," I murmured, too stricken to care how I sounded—again. This life, the whole existence I had cobbled together for the past eighteen years, was going to end, and I was expected to make a new one thousands of miles away—alone.

It was the most morose weekend of my life.

I couldn't get away from my sadness. The multitude of emotions that berated me in my room were endless. There was no point in talking to them; all I could do was ignore them. My mom barely spoke to me. She was still pissed about the way I had talked to Tyler, so I more or less expected that. I didn't leave my room except to eat and use the bathroom, and the next forty-eight hours were spent staring up at my ceiling, wondering when it all went so wrong.

Sunday night my mom said I had a call, and my heart felt like it was going to burst out of my chest like something from *Alien*. Leaping out of bed, I ran to the phone, knowing in my heart it was Brad. I needed to hear his voice. It felt like my soul was riding on saying I was sorry to him and making all this right.

"I knew you'd call," I said, picking the phone up off the kitchen table.

Mrs. Axeworthy's voice came from the other side. "Yes? Well then, you must know what I am going to ask."

My mouth went dry as I realized it wasn't Brad and things were not going to be fixed.

"I need you to tell me we aren't going to see a repeat of last week tomorrow." Her voice was stern and lacked all the empathy she'd had when we talked before. Looking back, I can't blame her. She'd taken a huge gamble when she volunteered to mentor the club, and I had lost my shit. But that is looking back and literally down the barrel of a gun.

At the time I could understand none of that. "I am sure things will be different," I assured her, since I knew Sammy wasn't going to show her face, which meant no chance of Jeremy showing up either.

"I hope not. Because, Kyle, this is important, more important than me and you. It has the ability to change people's lives, and we can't risk that for personal problems."

My mouth opened to argue that this wasn't a personal problem, and that Jeremy was responsible for someone killing himself, but I refrained, knowing it would go nowhere. I just repeated that everything would be fine and hung up, knowing that "fine" was so far away it was pathetic. I looked at the phone and wondered if I should call Brad myself. Just give in and call him and make up and just stop all of this nonsense.

And then I saw the admission packet from Berkeley on the kitchen table and knew there was a reason I was doing this.

Not a good reason, but a reason nonetheless.

Which brings us to Monday. Today. Right now.

We opened the door. The two freshmen and a girl I had never seen before came in. I waited to see if anyone else would show up, closed the door, and began the meeting. I was halfway through my whole speech about everyone being welcome and that this was a safe room when the door burst open and Jeremy came barging in.

Immediately, I went into attack mode. I stood up in a rage and came around the table at him. I honestly think I was ready to hit him. It would have been the first time I had ever hit someone physically unprovoked before.

Jeremy pulled a nasty-looking handgun out of his jacket, pointed it at me, and fired.

Someone should all the police! There's a madman....

APRIL 30
SPECTACULAR, SPECTACULAR
46 DAYS LEFT

Jeremy

GROWING UP, everyone had a PlayStation.

It was the game system of the moment, and everyone I knew owned one. I had just started first grade, and it was all anyone could talk about. They talked about what games they owned, what score they got, and what level they had unlocked. Like any normal kid, I was instantly jealous of this toy and wanted one for myself. I begged and begged my father that I needed one and that I would die if I didn't get one.

My dad is one of those guys who doesn't take hyperbole well at all.

His father, my grandfather, was a bastard of a man who believed that kids were a cheap form of labor and that their preferences didn't count for much. So my dad and his four brothers grew up working the land outside of Foster and hated it. I don't know how much you know about farming today, but let me sum it up for you in a way you can understand.

There are people who work in the hot sun to grow the things you eat, and they don't make shit in the way of money for it. They almost literally work themselves to death just to say they own a piece of land and, through pure force of will, create something to thrive on it, and then sell it for less than it had cost to plant. It is a losing battle against an enemy you can't fight, and most farmers, the ones who know they are slowly dying, can be very angry people.

And now you know everything you need to about my grandfather.

My two older uncles left the farm almost at the same time. They both joined the Army and decided they'd rather get shot at than be forced to live in Foster, Texas, anymore. That left my dad and his two younger brothers to take up the slack for their missing kin. Since he was the oldest, it fell on my dad to do the lion's share of the work. He ended up dropping out of high school when he was fifteen and never again stepped foot inside a place of learning.

When my grandfather fell over dead from a heart attack, my father had to step in and take over the farm's financial business. What he found almost sent him to a grave as well. The farm was not just broke, it actually owed money to the bank. If the next day gold bars grew on the vines, there still wouldn't be enough money to cover the debt that had been left. The farm was foreclosed on, my grandmother took my dad and my uncles to live with relatives over in Odessa, and my dad was now a nineteen-year-old high school dropout with no marketable skills whatsoever.

When the Mathisons bought the land where my grandfather's farm was, they offered my dad a job as a field worker. It was more money than he had been making working as a night stocker at the local H-E-B, and it allowed him to move out and away from the crowded house that had become his home. He leased a crappy little shack from the company and spent twelve hours a day under a sweltering Texas sun, working the land we'd once owned. He loathed it as much as anyone had loathed anything before. My dad found himself trapped in a life defined by the mistakes of his father, and it was dawning on him that he was never going to escape it.

And now you know everything you need to know about my father.

My grandfather's policy was if you worked like a man, you could drink like a man, and my father thought he was enough for three men. Which basically meant that my dad drank enough for an entire bar full of sailors a night. Sitting alone in that empty box of a shack, he started his slow devolution from a man into the creature he'd one day become.

That was when he met my mom.

She had been born and raised in Foster as well, and unlike the herds of women who found and married their true love out of high school, my mother graduated single and alone. She had two sisters, both married and pregnant by twenty, and it was expected by this time she would be on the same track. What her parents and her sisters didn't know was my mom had something they were all lacking.

A brain.

Not enough of a brain to get her out of Foster with a scholarship, but enough of one to know the trap of a wasted life when she saw it. She worked at a secondhand store and was saving her money up to move away from Foster and never look back. Her one weakness was books. She loved to read. As much as she wanted to flee this flyspeck of a town, she wanted to be transported in her mind somewhere else more. I am convinced if she hadn't bought so many books, she would have saved more than enough money to move at least a year earlier.

Which would have meant never meeting my dad.

Now, I've heard the whole list of reasons why love is a good thing. I was spoon-fed the same list of Disney movies you were while growing up, but they had a completely different effect on me than they did for everyone else. Where everyone else saw a world of wonderment where bluebirds sang to you as you looked for your one true love, I saw a horrifyingly powerful spell that made smart people like my mom marry dumb people like my dad.

As long as I live, I will never understand what she saw in him. Every memory of him I have is him being a bitter and broken old man who hated life. Before I even had words for it, I knew they should have never been together, and instead of some grand and wondrous fairy tale where beauty tamed the beast, this was real life, where the beast wore the beauty down until all that was left was a shell of the woman she once was.

I knew none of this when I asked for a PlayStation, of course. I just knew everyone else had one and I needed one.

My father taught me that day the difference between want and need in the most physical way possible. For example, I learned that while I may have wanted him to stop hitting me, I needed him to let go of my arm before he broke it. I may have wanted him to stop slapping my face and calling me a spoiled brat, but I needed him to stop kicking me once I fell down before he cracked my ribs. The difference is slight, but let me tell you, it makes all the difference in the world.

The thought of getting a PlayStation was effectively squashed in my mind, and I resolved myself never to speak of it again. If my father was trying a Pavlovian experiment associating negative stimuli with the thought of a PlayStation, he had succeeded beyond his wildest dreams. So that Christmas when I found a console-sized box under the tree, I wondered if this was just a test to see if I would jump at it. A silent nod from my mother gave me the courage to unwrap it.

Again I would like to cite that my expectations were influenced by those same crappy Disney movies that told me good things happened to those who deserved it. The world where a prince wanders through a forest to kiss a sleeping maiden is the same world where mice make things for downtrodden damsels in need of an outfit change, so the thought that somehow a PlayStation was under the Christmas tree for me was not that crazy. When I pulled the wrapping paper free, though, the true irony of the situation was revealed.

The moment I laid eyes on the box, I knew what had happened.

My mother had no doubt pleaded that I be allowed at least one present I'd asked for on Christmas, and if it was a video game I wanted, then I should be allowed to have it. Of course, that was the beginning and end of my parents' knowledge of video games. What everyone possessed and talked about was a

PlayStation, made by Sony, and was the top-of-the-line system for the moment. What I had unwrapped was a used Sega Dreamcast, a system as useless as it was obsolete the moment it had been released and no doubt procured from a pawn shop.

I had a scant second to shove my disappointment down and give them both a look of radiant gratitude. They had no idea they'd saved for nothing, that their scrimping and saving had literally been for shit. To them, they had done the right thing and given their son something he wanted for Christmas, when in fact all they had done was cement my fate as an outcast forever.

No one wanted to come over and play with me. The games I had didn't work on their systems. After a while they stopped even asking me if I had a PlayStation and just ignored me altogether.

By the time I was in third grade, I was officially a nobody.

That system became a symbol for my life. On the surface I was the same as the rest of the kids, but when you looked closer, nothing was alike. Sure, I was a human boy born and raised in Foster, Texas, but I was nothing like the rest of them at all. I didn't go with anyone. I didn't fit with anybody else. I was an anomaly in a town that thrived on community. Because I never had friends, I never played with them during recess, and because of that, I never had the physicality to go out for sports. During the summer, when kids were off playing football or baseball, I was sitting by my mom's side, reading books with her and trying not to show outwardly that it affected me.

It affected me.

I began to convince myself that they were horrendous people, and that I didn't want to play with them anyways. Stuck-up, superficial punks who only valued things like sports and looks while they completely ignored the things that really counted in life. I was a real person, and they were just cardboard cutouts of stereotypes. I wish I could say I was invisible and that they just ignored me, but I can't because they didn't. I stuck out like a nasty-looking weed on a perfectly groomed lawn, a volcano of a pimple on the otherwise perfect face of our town. I wasn't so much picked on as I was downgraded to less than human.

Like the Morlocks from *The Time Machine*, I was barely considered a person and treated as such. Random shoves in the hallway were expected, followed by long, donkey-like laughs from the douchebag who had done it. People slamming my locker shut as I tried to change books out between classes was also a popular pastime, once again followed by resounding glee from onlookers. Sometimes it got worse. Sometimes they would slap the books out of my hands as I walked down the hall, a few times I had random pieces of food tossed at me during lunch, and once someone put a fresh pile of dog shit in my backpack.

I'm sure they thought that last one was especially clever.

Since I was considered the enemy, I began to act as one. Since I didn't have the brawn to make someone cry, I used my words instead, with devastating results. A war of wits with a jock is a lot like a modern-day Marine unit attacking a Civil-War-era squadron; it is over pretty fast, and it could be days before anyone knows what actually happened. I tried to focus my attention on academic studies, since I knew it was the only arena I could actually compete in. And until junior high, I thought I was easily the smartest person in Foster.

That was when I became aware of Kyle Stilleno. We had a social science class in seventh grade, and I had assumed it was going to be one of those topics I dominated in, showing up the rest of the small brains who actually had brains. It was a softball question about the Emancipation Proclamation asking how many slaves did it free? The Civil War was one of those things I had obsessed about over the summer, so I was more than ready for this kind of question.

"Over four million slaves were freed," I answered, not even waiting to be called on.

The teacher paused, giving me a small smile and then asking the class, "Anyone disagree with him?"

I didn't even bother to turn around. I mean, who would even dare? It wasn't like anyone here actually knew....

"Kyle," the teacher exclaimed brightly. "Okay then, what is your answer?"

I spun around to stare at the idiot who was about to publicly announce how little he knew in front of the entire class. Of course, it was one of the random good-looking assholes, this one with shaggy hair, no doubt trying to pretend he was a skater or something. I smiled darkly at him, trying not to appear happy when he crashed and burned.

"None," he said, sounding smug to my ears.

"None?" the teacher asked him back, sounding a bit surprised. "You sure you want to go with that?"

She was giving him an out! How predictable. The cute ones always got special treatment. I scoffed under my breath, knowing he had just had a public, epic fail.

"Well, technically you can say around twenty to fifty thousand were freed on the day it went into effect, but there is a pretty strong case that Lincoln didn't have any authority over them at the time, so the official answer is none."

Now I laughed out loud, waiting for the teacher to tell him how wrong he was.

"Who thinks Mr. Stilleno's answer is right?" she asked the class.

Almost half the class raised their hands, which made me smile even more. Of course they were going to vote for one of their own; lemmings follow in a pack.

"Well, those with their hands up are right."

I was about to give this idiot a well-deserved laugh when her words penetrated. Instead I turned to her and demanded, "What? That's wrong."

The teacher gave me a patronizing look and said, "No, Jeremy, it isn't. The proclamation was more a political move than an actual social one and in fact only freed slaves in the rebel states, where Lincoln had no power. Though I'd like to know where you got your other number from, Kyle."

I sputtered out noises that weren't quite words in protest as Kyle explained a *nonsensical* answer that made even less *sense* than before. "Over four million slaves were freed by Lincoln!" I exclaimed. "You can't deny that."

Before the teacher could answer, this Kyle person said, "Actually, the slaves weren't freed legally until the Thirteenth Amendment was passed, and he did that by making the lame duck Congress do it. That wasn't until after he was reelected."

I stared at him in shock.

"Very good, Kyle." The teacher beamed at him. "You have a run for your money, Jeremy."

The class laughed at her words, which made me sink lower into my chair. The idiot behind me kicked my seat, whispering, "Dude, you can't even be a good nerd!"

That was when I became obsessed with Kyle Stilleno.

I could say that was when he moved onto my radar and I began paying attention to him, but I don't see much reason to lie now. At first he seemed to be everything I wanted to be, and it infuriated me. He was cute, seemed to be in shape, and he moved through the world without anyone bothering him at all. I never once saw someone pick on him, berate him, or even laugh in his general direction. School seemed to come easy to him. He always had an answer on the tip of his tongue, and if he had ever gotten a question wrong, I wasn't there to see it. As junior high progressed, I realized he wasn't everything I wanted to be; he was something far worse.

He was everything I wasn't.

Instead of being this superman that I was trying to become, he was a totem of everything in the world I wasn't. I would never be liked, I would never be considered cute, I would never be accepted, I would never be him, and it began to make me a little crazy. I was running an academic race against a guy who didn't even know he was in a competition. His graduating GPA from junior high was perfect—not near perfect but absolutely perfect—where mine wasn't. I had lost points in gym class because of not participating, which is an overall useless class anyways, and I lost half a grade in science for bad attitude, which again had nothing to do with my brain. Mr. Diego had said I was combative and antisocial when working in groups, and even though I had aced every test, he was not going to reward my behavior.

Mr. Diego was the first person I put on my list to make pay later.

That summer I begged my parents to let me go to Granada. I knew that Kyle was headed to Foster, and the last thing I wanted was another four years watching him mentally lap me in each class. I needed a place to thrive, a place where I could invent myself again, become someone else. I laid out my reasons carefully and clinically to both of them.

That was when they told me my mom was dying.

Of course, they didn't put it to me that way. They explained she had been diagnosed with pancreatic cancer and that they were going to treat it as aggressively as possible. They told me not to worry and that things would be okay. My mom would give me a sickly smile and say that everything works out the way it is supposed to and that I had to have faith in that. That was June. By August she was dead. My father reeked of booze as they handed him her ashes. He shook his head, and they gave them to me instead. As we drove home, he told me he never wanted to see the urn again. It was the last time we talked about my mother.

Because I was cursed, of course I ended up having to go to Foster High instead of Granada, and my Sisyphean torture of following Kyle Stilleno began all over again.

It was freshman year when I began stealing my dad's smokes. Though I wasn't fond of the habit, taking the time between classes to light up in the alley was the closest thing I could find to a hiding place from the galloping herd of zombies who made up my peers. It was there, between third and fourth period, struggling to not cough as I inhaled, that I met Sammy.

She was the only other freshman in the alley, and it was obvious no one was talking to her either since every other smoker was older than us. She gave me a small smile, and I nodded back, and that was how it started. Every day I would go out to smoke, she would be there, and we'd nod and smile at each other. I know it doesn't sound like much, but when all you've known is open disdain, a smile and a nod is like winning the social lottery.

It took us a week before we talked to each other, and even then it was just her asking me if I had an extra smoke she could bum. From there we worked up to names, how we both hated the school, and by extension the town. She told me she had decided to join the drama club to escape the endless press of small-minded people and that I should look into it.

It was the closest thing I ever had to a friend asking me to join something.

It turned out that the drama club was Foster High's secret island of misfit toys. It was a hodgepodge collection of losers and nerds who were seeking asylum from the jock culture that ruled our school. We were all high school pariahs who possessed little to no social skills, which made fitting in even harder than it normally was. I fit in almost instantly, and within a month or so was practically running the place, which was also something new for me. The drama geeks became the center of my universe for two reasons. One, because having people listen to me was intoxicating, and two, Kyle had nothing to do with drama club.

I began to worry less and less about my academic standing and more and more about being in control of drama club. I passed freshman year easily, but not with the GPA I had become accustomed to in junior high. I didn't care because that summer I had a group of friends to hang out with, and that made all the difference in the world. None of us was old enough to drive, so we spent the majority of our time at each other's houses watching bootleg anime and hating on everyone who wasn't us. I learned all the lines to *Rocky Horror*, discussed *Buffy* in great detail, and tried my best not to dwell on the fact my mother was dead.

My dad finally relented and let me turn our basement into a bedroom, which pretty much meant that the only time I had to see him was when I ate or went to the bathroom. That summer everything changed for me. I embraced the fact I was a freak and would never fit in to normal society. I had a pack now, a group of like-minded individuals who felt the same way I did, and that made me strong.

Which made going back to school that much easier.

I stopped caring about who was popular or what people were saying to one another. My days were measured in how much time I could hide in the drama department and away from everyone I hated. Though I never once stood up on stage and said a line of dialogue, every production Foster High put on was mine. The thought of standing in front of a crowd and acting made me want to throw up. I was much more relaxed behind the scenes, calling the shots. I watched jock after jock stand up on stage and make a fool out of himself with *each* play, *each* time making sure that if something went wrong with the production, it looked like it was their fault.

Sammy became my best friend, and we ended up doing everything together. She was with me the night the Vine played *Donnie Darko*, and we both sneaked in bottles of schnapps to drink during the movie. Afterward, when we stumbled out onto First Street, we wandered into a group of equally drunk jocks who saw us and thought it was open season on drama fags. They threw empty beer bottles at us while they mocked the way we dressed. It was that night that I met Brad Graymark.

Of course he was cute, and of course he was in perfect shape. I mean, what jock isn't? He had done something impressive on the baseball team that other people seemed to like and had instantly been propelled from normal hot brah to superstar overnight. He began dating the sheriff's daughter, and people around here thought he could walk on water. They had even made a sign for his lawn that proclaimed him MVP and everything.

I could have produced a play that cured cancer and there wouldn't have been so much as a flier made for my front lawn.

Facial features that made him look like a character from a CW show were distorted into ugly hatred as he hurled his half-empty beer bottle at me. Though the pack of them seemed like rabid dogs, Brad's hatred was a bit louder than everyone else's, his loathing closer to the surface than his friends'. It was something I should have noticed at the time. It's important to point out that Kelly Aimes was there that night too. Though Brad was taking center stage as he normally did, Kelly was there throwing bottles and cursing me out with as much gusto as the rest of them. I didn't notice because I was too busy dodging flying glass, but I just want to point out, he was there in the parking lot that night.

As Sammy and I walked home, I honestly thought to myself that this was the worst Foster had to show to me, that those boys in their homophobic rage were the ugliest this town could get, and I'd survived. Neither one of us was hurt; we were both laughing at the intensity the morons felt for people they didn't know. I really did think for a moment that if this was as bad as it got, I could survive.

Of course, no matter how far down you think you've fallen, there is always a place beneath that you can sink to with enough effort.

Turns out my father was out drinking at the Rodeo Club that night, and he had watched his son get verbally abused with the rest of the drunken patrons, all of them laughing at the punishment the freaks were getting for being out on the street. I suppose it was lucky for me that no one could connect me to my father, because the beating he gave me that night for almost embarrassing him was so painful that I spent the next week walking very slowly to avoid further injury. I can only imagine how much more he would have done if the people at the bar had laughed at him as they'd laughed at me. It was the first time he had actually whaled on me for being something other than what he had wanted me to be, and it wouldn't be the last.

That summer became the summer my dad tried to force me to be normal through corporal punishment.

He threw away all my movies and comic books. Posters of bands I liked were torn down and thrown away, along with any clothes he deemed "not normal," which meant almost anything. Jeans and plain T-shirts were forced on me as I went to work with him every morning and labored in the fields with a handful of undocumented workers who did the job for pennies an hour. I found it ironic the illegal aliens were getting paid more than me.

No one was allowed to come over. No one was allowed to talk to me on the phone. I would say I was a prisoner in my own home, but by that point I didn't consider the place a home anymore. In the end it was Sammy who saved me from a fate I was pretty sure included my dad and I killing each other in a drunken rage.

She called the sheriff, and he came by to check on me since there had been some reports that I hadn't been seen around town. My dad pulled me up from my room and shoved me at the policeman. "See? He's just fine. Now get the fuck out."

If there is one thing you shouldn't do to Sheriff Rogers, it is tell him what to do. He doesn't take kindly to it.

"You okay, son?" he asked me, ignoring my dad completely. I just stared at him, not trusting myself to even nod and not burst into tears. "You can tell me if anything is wrong."

"He's fine," my dad growled from behind us, the warning in his voice unmistakable. "Aren't you?"

I nodded mechanically to the sheriff, who gave me a sympathetic look.

"There," my dad bellowed. "You got your answer. Now get off my property."

Sheriff Rogers seemed so unimpressed with my father's order that it was like he couldn't even hear him. "Not your property anymore—it's the Mathisons'," he said as he did a casual lap around the living room. "Not even your house—it's theirs."

"So?"

The sheriff looked back at my father. "So when I get called out to investigate something, the person who I am investigating doesn't get to tell me to leave. Especially if he's just a renter."

"This was my family's property forever, and you know it." Spittle flew out of my dad's mouth as he became incensed about a whole new topic.

"And now it's not." The sheriff paused and moved some papers off the table. "Richie, you're going to tell me that you have a license for this gun, right?"

My dad and I looked over at the policeman, who now had a hand casually on his pistol. On the table was my father's .357. Its action was open, and from where I was standing, I could see a half-loaded clip on the table.

"I have a legal right to own that gun!" my dad insisted, moving toward the table, no doubt to retrieve his property.

Sheriff Rogers had a different plan.

He spun and placed himself between my dad and the table and now had his gun half drawn out of its holster. "Richie, you take one more step towards that gun, and I am going to take it as a hostile threat." My dad stopped walking. "You are drunk, you are belligerent, and you have a loaded gun on your kitchen table where anyone can get to it. You may have a license to own and operate a firearm, but I am damned sure you don't own one allowing you to be a fucking idiot." My dad's eyes locked with Rogers's, and they said nothing for a few seconds, communicating solely through forms of anger and disgust.

It was the sheriff who broke the silence. "Richie, I need you to turn around and put your hands behind your back." My dad gave him an unblinking look, and the sheriff added, "If you don't, I assure you I can make your arms go behind your back by myself."

With the speed of molasses, my dad's hands moved behind his back as the sheriff fastened the cuffs on his wrists. As soon as my dad was locked down, the sheriff got on his radio and asked for immediate backup to our location. He had an exposed firearm and an intoxicated citizen, and he wanted some witnesses. The dispatch lady rattled off something I couldn't understand but made the sheriff relax as he looked back over at me. "Do you know if he has a gun safe?" I nodded. "Do you know the combination for it?" Another nod. "And do you know how to handle a firearm with respect?" Last and smaller nod.

The sheriff went over and made sure the piece was completely empty. Once he was satisfied, he handed it back to me, grip first. "Find its bag, secure it, and lock it away in the vault. And Jeremy?" he asked as I started to move. "Hide the key somewhere only you know of it, okay? For right now, at least."

I nodded quickly and dashed up to the attic, where Mom had made my dad store the gun safe. I never told my dad where the key was. He never asked me.

They took my dad away to jail to sleep it off. The next day a social worker came to talk to me. She asked a lot of questions that might have scared someone a lot dumber than me. Her pity was dripping from every word, and though she might have thought she was helping me, all I could see was the cowlike dullness in her eyes as she tried to understand a problem bigger than she was. Though my father was an idiot, his general apathy about my life was a good thing, because it allowed me to do what I wanted. When she asked me about the bruises I was sporting, I told her I had fallen down the steps. It was as useless a lie as her question was, and we both knew it. After a while of this verbal sparring, she put her pen down and took off her glasses.

"Jeremy, you know I am here to help you, right?" The condescending tone in her voice as she looked at me like some abused creature was enough to make me want to puke. I wasn't some poor, mistreated child who had no out. This was my life, this was my world, and so what if my father got drunk and felt like hitting me? He was as useless as everyone else in this godforsaken town, and when my time came around, he would pay just like everyone else would. They would all look up at me and wonder why they'd treated me so badly and beg me to forgive them.

I would look down at them and say no.

"I tripped and fell down some stairs," I repeated, not bothering to make it sound convincing. I knew the rules here as well as she did. She needed proof, and without me, there wasn't any. This woman was not going to disrupt my life just because Brad Graymark and his merry band of assholes decided to use me as target practice. Brad and his jock friends would pay too, not me. Them.

The next day my dad came home, and things returned to as normal as they got for us. He never said anything about the social worker or the arrest, and I went out of my way to stay out of his life the best I could. For the next year or so, it was a perfect arrangement. He let me be the person I wanted to with my friends in the basement, and I didn't tell the world that he got off on punching his son.

Everything was okay until the summer before my senior year.

I was now undisputed lord of the drama club. Only Sammy and I possessed a set of keys to the place, meaning we could stay as late as we wanted and enter whenever we felt like it. I was practically faculty by the time I finished junior year, and it was only going to get better after summer. One of my friends got a used car for his graduation present, which meant for the first time in my life, I had a way out of Foster, even if it was only for a night.

We went to Dallas and saw *Rocky Horror* on a big screen. We got to see Scum Allegiance, H.R.A., and Daggerwound live, which was insane on so many levels because live shows are way better than just hearing the music. I got to be around other kids who were like me, who were considered lesser than others. Angry like me, fed up like me, tired of getting kicked like me. I slowly started thinking I might fit in somewhere once I left Foster.

It was on one of these trips to Dallas with my friends that I ran into Kelly Aimes.

We had gone to the Tin Room in Dallas to see the strip show. It was one of the few gay clubs that allowed teenagers in the door, even though we couldn't drink. Though all of my friends were straight, no one minded going to these places with me because they played great music, and who doesn't like to see naked guys?

Even the straight boys who were part of the group seemed to like the attention they got in gay clubs, so no one complained.

I had walked out of the club to get some fresh air and to have a smoke. Dallas was pretty Nazi about nonsmoking establishments, so there was a group of us outside grabbing our nicotine while we could when Kelly walked past us and into the bar. I almost choked and dropped my smoke as I pushed my way past the smokers to see if I had imagined him. When I looked in, there he was, paying the cover and getting his hand stamped as a minor by the doorman.

I looked around to see if there was anyone else following him in. A pack of straight guys from Foster invading a gay bar just to fuck with people didn't sound completely crazy. I knew that Tony Wright and his friends spent most of the weekend cruising by the gay club outside of Foster and calling out names of the guys who walked out. But Kelly was alone. I didn't see anyone else from Foster with him. Curious, I followed him inside, trying to find out what he could be doing there.

It was Saturday night, and the bar was packed, so it wasn't easy to find him again. I scouted around, trying to see if he was near the bar or the dance floor. I almost tripped over my jaw when I saw him over by the bathrooms, staring up at one of the male strippers. At first I thought maybe he knew the guy and was trying to talk to him.

And then I saw the dollar bill.

I could not believe my eyes as I watched the stripper kneel down and let Kelly put a dollar bill in his G-string. This had to be a joke or something. My first thought was to look around for Ashton Kutcher because this had to be *Punk'd*, and then I saw the guy lean down toward Kelly's face and give him a kiss. I swear I almost passed out in shock.

The stripper went back to dancing as Kelly went back to staring. I was about to walk up to him when one of my friends tapped me on the shoulder. "Hey!" she yelled over the music. "I was looking outside for you. We're thinking of hitting BuzzBrews. It's, like, five minutes away. You coming?"

Normally the answer to that question would have been "Of course I am— you're my ride, you idiot," but this was not normal. I shook my head and yelled back, "I'm not hungry. Call me when you guys are done and I'll meet you out front."

She paused, obviously not expecting that answer any more than I was. "You sure?"

I assured her I was. "Just don't forget me," I said with a smile.

I watched my friends leave, all of them looking over their shoulders at me in confusion since they all knew I didn't have a car. As soon as the last one was out the door, I turned and made my way to where Kelly was still staring up at the stripper. I had to give him credit; the dancer was gorgeous, but then again he got naked for money, so if he wasn't, it would have been weird. As I got closer, I noticed that the guy looked like an older version of Brad Graymark, almost. He had the same dark red hair and clean-cut look that Brad had, though this guy obviously took way more steroids than Brad did. Looking at the trancelike state Kelly was in staring at the guy, I wondered if he looked at his friend the same way.

I took a deep breath and moved next to Kelly. "Didn't anyone tell you if you keep making that face it will stick like that?"

The complete and abject horror on his face told me everything I needed to know in one expression. Kelly here was a closet case and was terrified that his straight little jock friends would find out. So he drove hours away just so he could sneak into a gay bar and stare at naked guys all night. He had thought that Dallas was far enough away that he would never get caught, but here I was, catching him and loving it.

"Cat got your tongue?" I asked him, relishing the power I had. "Oh wait, that would mean you like pussy, and we both know that's not true." I nodded up at the dancer. "He a good kisser? 'Cause you seemed to like it."

Kelly tried to say something but failed miserably as his brain began to melt out his ears. His face was bright red, and he looked like he might pass out. Instead, he pushed past me and made a beeline toward the exit. I was hot on his tail. When we hit outside, I reached out and grabbed his shoulder, which I realized instantly was a mistake.

"Get off me, queer!" he roared at me, grabbing the attention of everyone outside smoking. Once he realized they were all looking at him, Kelly mumbled something under his breath and took off down the street.

I chased after him, though I couldn't tell you why. It wasn't like I cared if he was gay or not—well, cared past the point of laughing my ass off about it. Kelly was a first-class asshole, and everyone knew it. If it wasn't for his skill on a football field, he would have been a moderately good-looking guy who couldn't put three words together to form a sentence. But I chased him because I wanted to know more.

Kelly was the guy who shoved freshmen into trash cans every year because he thought it was funny. He was the guy who would slap your books to the ground for no reason whatsoever. If there was a poster boy for being a complete and total tool and making other people miserable, Kelly was it. I swear to you that at the time, I didn't have a thought about rubbing in the fact he was a closeted gay. I wasn't chasing him so I could threaten to tell others I had seen him there; I really wasn't. I just wanted to know why he was there, even though I knew most likely I was going to get my teeth knocked out for my trouble.

He had parked his truck three blocks from the club, no doubt hoping that was far enough away in case someone saw it. He fumbled with his keys as I stood behind him. "You don't have to run away." He spun around and glared at me, and I really thought he was going to punch me. "Seriously! It's okay."

He looked like a bull standing there, nostrils flaring as he huffed and puffed at me. I knew that look from my dad; he was too mad to even speak. His rage had overridden all rational functions, and all that was left was a red haze.

"No one else saw you," I threw out there quickly. "I didn't see anyone else from Foster, so you're safe."

That seemed to calm him down some, which gave him back the ability to talk. "I'm not a fag."

It was such a stupid statement to make, I had to force myself not to laugh out loud at him. I mean, he was just in a gay bar getting a kiss from a stripper. I wanted to scream, "Dude, if you're not a fag, you have some issues." Instead I opted for nodding slowly. "Okay, cool. Never said you were."

He looked around the parking lot, no doubt trying to see if there was anyone else nearby waiting to ambush him. "You tell anyone about this, and I'll fucking end you."

He actually said that— "fucking end you." I swear, as a generation, people my age have been ruined by horrible dialogue in action movies. The things we think are intimidating and threatening sound so stupid coming out of anyone who isn't Arnold Schwarzenegger that I honestly don't think we will ever recover. Instead of reacting to his Terminator-like threat, I decided to move past that and ask, "So, you know that guy?" I motioned back toward the bar.

Even in the dark I could see his face flush, and I went back to thinking I was going to get slugged.

"I'm not going to tell anyone," I said, holding my hands up in surrender. "I was just wondering if he kissed everyone who tipped or if it was just you."

I waited patiently for the gears in his mind to make a complete cycle. It was obvious I had seen him kissing the guy, so there was no use in denying that, but it looked like he was struggling with saying it out loud to someone else. Finally he spit out, "I've seen him a couple of weeks in a row. I've never seen him kiss anyone else."

That made sense to me; with the abundance of ugly old guys who pawed on male strippers every night, getting tipped by a young jock like Kelly must be the closest thing to a vacation they get. I, of course, would never possess the body to strip nor the face to attract a stripper, so it was all theoretical to me. "He's hot," I said, when it was obvious Kelly wasn't going to continue talking.

He nodded and then leaned back against his truck. "Okay, so what do you want?"

It was so abrupt I just stood there in confusion.

"Not to say anything, what do you want?" he clarified.

"Nothing," I answered quickly and honestly. He gave me an unbelieving look, and I added, "I'm not going to blackmail you. I mean, if I did that, I'd have to admit I was gay too."

He came off the truck so fast that one second he was there, and the next he was in my face, gripping my shirt tight. "I. Am. Not. A. Fag," he enunciated slowly. "You say that again, and I will kill you."

See, that was a much better threat, all around more believable.

"I won't," I babbled, seriously scared of being beaten to death in a parking lot. "I swear!"

His fist hovered there above my head, my own private sword of Damocles for me to marvel at. I could see the wavering in Kelly's eyes, unsure if he could trust me or not. I suppose the fear on my face was enough because he let me go, and I fell to the ground. "If you say one word about this, no one will believe you." He opened the door to his truck. "And then I will crack your head open like a pumpkin."

And back to the lame threats again.

I didn't say anything as he started his truck and pulled off into the night. I watched his taillights fade away as I wondered what exactly I would do with the information that Kelly Aimes liked guys.

I didn't say anything to anyone the rest of summer. After all, what was there to gain from it? The people I ran with wouldn't care about Kelly's sexuality, and no one else would even believe me. So I filed it away as one of those things I knew and no one else did and went on with my life. When school rolled around again, I was pretty fired up, not only because it was my last year but because I was finally a senior, which meant it was my time to shine.

I held that thought for almost two full class periods before I was rudely informed by the universe that it was never going to happen.

Our school had a tradition—well, not so much a tradition as it was a reoccurring nightmare for those who endured it. The ones who did it called it trashing; the ones who suffered it called it the worst thing imaginable. Basically, two douchebags grab you from behind and carry you to the nearest trash can. Now, I guess if they had bothered to pick out a trash can beforehand that, say, wasn't already filled with trash, it might not be as bad, but they don't, so it is. Now, the joy of this little spectacle is that there is a crowd of people who already know what is about to occur to you and have gathered around the trash can in anticipation of seeing someone's whole day ruined.

I don't have to tell you that trashing doesn't happen to many jocks.

Normally this happens to freshmen the first week of school, as a kind of welcome-to-hell thing, but occasionally it's done with older students, especially if they can't defend themselves. So in other words, it happens to whoever the jock overlords deem are lacking in their undying faith to their popularity. It had been done to me three different times my freshman year until I learned how to get to my classes without going through the quad, so the thought of being trashed had faded from my mind, which of course was a huge mistake.

It was the first day back, and I was wearing the vintage Ramones tour shirt from when they played Mothers in 1975 because I thought it was safe to inject a little culture into Foster High. Instead, all I did was add to the mindless enjoyment of the masses when I was grabbed and thrown into a trash can. Now, it is easy to brush this off since it was the first day of school and barely third period. I mean, how much trash could be in there?

Well, it turns out it can be halfway filled with the nastiest spoiled food that had been tossed out when the cafeteria staff got back from their break. It seems the jocks had decided an empty can wasn't nearly as funny as a can filled with rotten fruit and meat. All I could think as I slowly sank into the gunk was that the shirt had cost me thirty bucks on eBay and was ruined.

Now, when one is thrown into a trash can, there are certain limitations placed on your movement that may not be obvious to the random observer. If you were thrown in ass first, which I was, your body is then squeezed to a V shape as you sink into the wretched mass of organic material beneath you, your arms pinned to your sides as you find your knees hanging on to the side of the can, keeping you from falling all the way in.

The long and short of it is that you are stuck like a turtle on its back, and the process of getting out is as humiliating as getting thrown in.

I could barely hear the roaring laughter over the deafening sound of blood rushing to my head in anger. The smell, which had been fleeting in my panic, was settling in, and the automatic revulsion caused by it made me try to get away from it violently, which then caused the laughter to get louder. It wasn't the humiliation—well, at least it wasn't at that very moment—it was the fact that this rotting concoction was seeping into my clothes, and that there was literally no way I was going to be able to continue to classes without going home first and changing. That thought brought more and more anger as I flailed about helplessly.

In the end I was so pathetic that I was saved by a girl.

Sammy's voice broke the almost thunderous laughter as she came running up to the trash can. "What the fuck is your malfunction?" She put her hand out to help me up, but she didn't have the strength to get me free, and I eventually fell back into the can, spilling even more trash on me.

The laughter exploded like we were a comedy team.

"Looks like Punky Smurf didn't eat her spinach today," a guy taunted her from the crowd. I couldn't see who it was because my head was pressed up against the side of the trash can, but I knew the voice all too well.

Kelly.

"Fuck you, Aimes," she said sadly. "Hold on."

I closed my eyes and held my breath as she kicked the side of the can with her Doc Martens. The world tilted to the right as the can fell over to its side. I came flying out onto the blacktop, propelled by a virtual river of muck that washed over me. I tried to wipe my face clean as well as I could before daring to try to breathe.

The moment I did, I threw up violently.

I'm not sure what kind of sadistic bastard came up with the evolutionary process of human vomit, but if I meet them in the afterlife, I plan on kicking them squarely in their higher-power balls. There is nothing that makes you aware that there are things about your body you cannot control like projectile vomiting uncontrollably in front of a crowd. Of course, this was easily as funny as me getting thrown in the can, which brought even louder peals of glee from the people watching me struggle to my knees.

Luckily my nose began to lose all function, no doubt from the overload from rotten food and vomit all over me. I looked up and saw Sammy kneeling next to me. The pity in her eyes was too much to bear. She reached out to help me to my feet, and I pushed her hand away angrily. "Get off me," I roared, causing even more approval from the studio audience. From across the quad I could hear Mr. Raymond's voice calling out, asking what was going on. People began to scatter, as was the protocol when being caught at the scene of the crime. Everyone ran in different directions, knowing they couldn't catch them all. All you could do was pray you were one of the lucky ones who escaped.

I took a deep breath and got ready to stand when Kelly's face appeared next to mine. His smile was everything a smile shouldn't be, and it struck a chord of terror in my chest. It was an evil smile, a smile that not only said he was enjoying seeing me so debased, but also that the fact it had turned out so badly for me was almost orgasmic to him. I froze as he said in a low voice, "Welcome back to school. We clear on where we stand?"

I looked at him, confused. "But I didn't say anything," I confessed uselessly.

"I know." His smile faded instantly. "And now you know what happens when you do, right?"

Neither one of us said a word as Mr. Raymond came rushing up to me. "What is going on here?" he demanded.

Kelly stood up and shrugged. "No idea, sir. Looks like someone was hungry and went dumpster diving."

I slowly stood up as Mr. Raymond glared at Kelly. "Get out of here, Aimes, before I kick you off the football team." Kelly held his hands up in surrender and backed away. His eyes locked with mine, and I saw the menace in them before he turned around and walked off with his friends.

It was at that moment, August 21, 10:44 a.m., that I made my choice. I decided right then and there, Kelly Aimes was on my list, number one with a bullet.

Sammy and I didn't talk to each other for almost a month after that. I am sure she was pissed I had snapped at her, and I was just mad. I planned and planned to find some way to get Kelly back for what he had done to me. There had to be a way, something I could do to get justice. I couldn't just walk up to him and beat him senseless. I wasn't strong enough, and he had too many friends. I was smarter than him, smarter than all of them. There had to be a way for me to get even.

That was when I heard about Brad and Kyle.

It was sickening how fast the word spread around school about how Kelly had tried to bully Kyle and how Brad had not only stuck up for him but actually kissed him in the middle of the quad. And in one fell swoop, Kyle Stilleno had unknowingly taken the only unique trait I possessed and made it his own. Thursday I was the only gay guy at Foster High. Friday, Kyle and Brad were the only people in the world who had ever kissed before. It was as infuriating as it was insulting, and I voiced my opinion loudly over lunch to the drama crew.

"I was gay way before those two ever thought about liking each other," I proclaimed as we ate lunch in the auditorium. "I don't even think Graymark is gay. He's just using this as a chance to be considered open-minded and cooler than he actually is."

Everyone but Sammy nodded as I went on. She just watched me talk with an odd look on her face. Finally I turned to her and asked, "What? You don't agree with me?"

She paused, obviously weighing whether she should say something. "I can't believe that anyone would pretend to be gay in this school, even if they thought it would make them cool." She locked eyes with me. "And we both know that it won't."

"You're on his side?" I was incensed she would even argue with me about this.

"I'm not on anyone's side. I'm just saying that if anyone in this school should know how hard those two are going to have it, you're the person."

Everyone looked back to me, and I literally bit my tongue not to explode at her. Taking a deep breath, I said, "The only reason anyone cares what they are doing is because it is Brad Graymark doing it. I've been gay forever, and has anyone ever said one thing about it?" She opened her mouth to respond, but I kept talking. "Also, it is a huge sign of how shallow Kyle is. I mean, come on. He's going to fall for the dumb jock? That is all about looks when he knew I was available."

Most everyone else nodded, but Sammy didn't. "How would he know? I've never seen you talk to him before."

"And you're with me all day every day? Trust me, I've talked to Kyle Stilleno before, and he is just another shallow, stuck-up queer, only caring about looks and nothing about what is inside."

More people nodded and agreed, since most of the drama crew were not the best-looking people in the world. It was a popular belief that anyone who didn't give us the time of day were shallow assholes who didn't know what they were missing. Of course, I didn't add that I wouldn't touch one of them with a ten-foot pole, because, I mean, the first thing a leader must know is not to piss off the little people.

The subject was dropped, and we went back to eating lunch, but I knew this wasn't over with Sammy.

I spent the weekend ignoring the whole town by locking myself in my room and working on mash-ups. With my headphones on, an atomic bomb could have gone off outside and I would have no idea. I tried to put Kyle and Brad out of my head, but it was that sore on the top of your mouth you can't stop messing with. There was no way Kyle couldn't have known about me. I mean, since junior high I have been teased and beaten on because I was gay. How clueless could he be not to know that I was gay and maybe liked him?

I liked him? Where did that come from?

It was like a lightning strike. I just sat there for a few seconds and realized I had liked him. He was cute, he was smart, he was socially awkward... the more I thought about it, the madder I got. We could have been perfect—well, if not perfect, certainly not as miserable as I had been most of my life. In seconds, the perfect, polished image I had of him crumbled to just another superficial asshole from Foster. He wasn't different. He was just like the rest of them, and I had been stupid enough to think otherwise.

By Monday I hated Kyle as much as I hated everyone else.

When I got to school, Sammy was waiting for me in the drama room. I ignored her, put my stuff down, and started to look over the schedule for the week.

Friday's rehearsal had been scratched out, and an emergency school board meeting had been written in. That didn't sound like a good thing.

"So you plan on ignoring me forever?" she asked from across the room.

I looked over at her with a raised eyebrow. "Didn't even see you there."

She rolled her eyes and grabbed her purse. "Fuck you, Jeremy. I came in here to talk it *out*, but if you're going to be shitty, I am *out*."

I stood there as I watched the closest thing I had to a real friend walk away.

"Wait," I called after her. She stopped and looked back at me. "You pissed me off."

She made a face. "Do you think you never piss me off? It is always about you, Jeremy, and it's getting boring."

I sighed and put the clipboard down. "You don't know what it's like to be gay in this town, Sam. It just gets to you."

She looked at me sympathetically. I knew I had her. We talked it out for a while, but she was back on my side, and that was the only thing that counted. She didn't know it, but by walking out on me, she had made the list too.

The next day we began to do the prep work for the school board meeting, and I came face-to-face with Brad and Kyle hiding in my theater. They were up in what used to be a balcony for the theater, but was now closed down and used for storage. I knew that sometimes people hid out up there to get away from it all, but that privilege did not extend to douchebags and their boyfriends. I did not plan on passing up the opportunity to make sure they knew whose house they were in.

"Oh," I said, clearing my throat to get their attention. They both looked back at us. "What are you guys doing up here?"

Kyle held a paper bag. "Lunch. More than enough room," he said, gesturing to the other seats.

Sammy put her hand on my shoulder and whispered, "Let them eat. We can come back."

I shook my head and said, "No, we don't have to leave. They're the ones who are lost." I ignored the look Sammy was giving me as Brad began to stand.

Kyle's hand moved to his arm, no doubt silently pleading with the Neanderthal not to beat me senseless, as his type is wont to do. "We're not lost. We're just looking for a place to eat lunch." It was obvious from his voice he was pissed to even be speaking to someone like me.

Todd said from behind me, "Jeremy, let it go." Todd went on the list too.

The sarcasm dripped off my tongue. "What's wrong with the Round Table? Couldn't get a reservation?"

Now Kyle's caveman stood up fully and began to browbeat me. "Look, Jeremy, we don't want any trouble. We just want to eat lunch. Why don't we just all calm down and think a second." He raised his hand, and I flinched, because people like him always hit first and ask questions later. "My name is Brad, and this is—"

When it was obvious he wasn't going to slug me, I cut him off. "I know who you are. You don't even know who I am, do you?" From the cowlike expression of ignorance on his face, he didn't. "You and your friends threw beer bottles at me last year outside the bowling alley. You guys screamed 'drama fag' and took off. Ring a bell?"

He shook his head, looking like he had just eaten dirt.

"You don't remember me? Or you don't recall because you jerks have done it more than once?" I demanded. Since he was going to try to act nice in front of Kyle, I planned on taking advantage of it.

"Both," he mumbled, not even looking me in the eyes.

Now it was Kyle's turn to make an ass of himself. He got between Brad and me and said, "Come on, guys."

I never stopped looking at Brad, since there was an even chance he was going to swing at me at any moment. "You can stay here, Kyle. You, I have no problem with, but he is going to have to go." It wasn't the entire truth, but I had to admit, if I could get Kyle to see what kind of asshole he was dating, maybe, just maybe there was a chance he could see me.

"You know me?" Kyle asked, the shock obvious in his voice.

I tried to play it off cool, but the fact that I didn't even register enough for him to remember me made something inside of me ache. "I've had a crush on you since the seventh grade. Pity you never noticed." I could see the blood drain out of Kyle's face as I went on. "Just because douchebag here is experimenting with his sexuality, it doesn't mean he's an outcast." I glared at Brad. "It just means karma works and that bad things do happen to bad people sometimes."

A weird look began to come over Kyle's face, and I wondered briefly if I had bitten off more than I could chew. I could recognize the cold fury in his eyes; I had seen it in the mirror looking back at me every day of my life. Was it possible that Kyle was making a list as well?

Brad saw it too, 'cause he looked at Kyle and said, "It's cool. I'll see you after school." He had to walk past us to get out of the room, and from the outright disgust on our faces, it was obvious he wasn't our favorite person.

He did stop and say to me, "For what it's worth, I'm sorry."

I like that he added "for what it was worth," because it was worth shit, and we both knew it.

I looked back to Kyle and was ready to lay into him, but he exploded at me. "What the fuck was that?"

I must have looked shocked, because I just stared at him for a second in silence. Finally my brain engaged. "You can't tell me you are attracted to that asshole?" Of course, I knew he was attracted to that guy. I mean, who wasn't? Brad Graymark had the face, the body, and the car that made everyone want to kneel down and kiss his feet. To clarify, I wouldn't, but I could see how looking like a model and having a six-pack could do that to people.

Kyle ignored my question and came screaming at me full force. "I get that he and his friends were dicks to you, and that sucks. But you know what it's like to walk around this town and have people hate you for no other reason than you're different, right?" I nodded. "Then why the hell would you treat anyone else like that?"

My stomach lurched as he went on.

"You may not like him, but he stood right next to me when no one else would. He came out to the entire school for no other reason than he liked me. He didn't have to do that. It would have been so much easier to deny everything and stay who he had been, but he didn't. So whatever problems you may have had with him, he is ten times the man of anyone else I have ever met. So back the fuck off."

His anger was so self-righteous, I hated it as much as it turned me on.

"You don't even know who I am, do you?" I asked defiantly, already knowing the answer.

"You're Jeremy Kimble. We went to the same junior high, and you're in two of my honor classes. You think you're smart, but you're too arrogant to learn anything you don't agree with. Oh yeah, and I guess you're an asshole too."

My mouth hung open in shock. He knew who I was? He really knew me?

I had no idea, but my mouth asked, "Would you have even gone out with me?"

He sighed, and I knew the answer instantly. People like him never went out with people like me. Life wasn't a fairy tale. It was a horror movie, and no one but the one pretty chick got out alive. The rest of us were just there to add to the body count.

He surprised me by asking a question. "You said you've known me since seventh grade?" I nodded. "And in those six years, did you ever talk to me? Just walk up and let me know how you felt?" I opened my mouth but then shook my head. "He did." He pointed to where Brad had walked out. "He came after me and told me that he liked me. You don't get to say that I wouldn't go out with you. You never even asked."

It felt like he had gut-punched me. Hard. My mouth was dry, and my eyes stung as I tried to get a grip on my emotions.

Luckily Sammy jumped in and saved me. "Jeremy, count the chairs and let's go."

At the moment I could give a shit. "The school board knows how many chairs we have. They can bite me."

Kyle popped up. "School board?"

She nodded at him. "They're having some emergency meeting Friday, and want to know if we have enough up here to cover the seating."

I wanted to tell her to shut up, but before I could, Kyle mumbled something and ran out the door.

"I hope they make your fucking boyfriend burn," I said as he ran out the door.

I stood there in silence for a couple of minutes, realizing no matter how much I hated everything, there was always more I could hate it.

"Jeremy," Sammy said carefully.

"Count the damn chairs," I said, shrugging her off and pushing past them.

My list continued to grow.

Of course, the school board didn't do anything to their golden child. In fact, I'm not sure they even bothered to have a meeting. Suddenly gay was okay, as long as you looked like an extra on *Teen Wolf*. Everyone was talking about how Brad had stood up for everyone, and it made me sick. Once again the masses followed along behind a pretty face like lemmings dying to go leap off a cliff. I found even more hate in my soul for Foster and its denizens.

Leave it to Sammy to not see the truth around her.

"It's a good thing," she tried to tell me during lunch. "If people can accept the two of them, then maybe they can accept everyone."

I said nothing as the bile in my heart simmered. There was nothing wrong with Sammy, nothing she didn't do to herself. She insisted on dying her hair a ridiculous color of blue and dressing like she had just come from a funeral, but all those things were superficial. She was as normal as everyone else in this fucking town, and just because she felt like rebelling, it didn't mean she understood one second of my life and my pain.

"You want to be accepted?" I snapped, tossing the rest of my lunch into the trash. "Wash your face off and dye your hair back, and like magic you'll be accepted. I'm gay, and there is nothing I can do about that. I will *always* be hated and always will be an outsider."

I guess I had expected her to just sit there and take it like she always had, but this time she jumped out of her seat and screamed back. "People hate you 'cause you're a dick, Jeremy! And you're an outsider because you hate everyone else. Brad and Kyle are just as gay, and trust me, they are going to change things in ways you could never do because it is always about you."

My hand clenched into a fist, and before I could stop myself, I took a step toward her to teach her to keep her mouth shut. The look of terror in her eyes stopped me cold as I realized it must be what I looked like when my dad came at me.

"Fuck you" was all I could spit out, and I rushed past her and out of the auditorium. This was why I hated people, because they always made me do things I didn't want to do. She couldn't just keep her mouth shut, could she? Screams of insatiable hatred bubbled just below the surface, but I held them in because I knew. I knew the day was coming when I would get even against all these people. I needed to bide my time and just keep it together.

And then make them all pay.

The next month all people could do was talk about the perfect couple and the water they walked on. I wasn't shocked to see Sammy start to hang out with them. I suppose when one is a fag hag, you take the jobs that are available. When a new popular fag comes along, you need to go where the hagging is needed. She wasn't the only one who changed sides.

Everywhere I saw people begin to suddenly care about homosexuality who literally had spit on me as they walked by. I muttered to myself as I walked through school. Now that a couple of perfect people had caught the gay, it was suddenly a thing to be okay with it. My loathing threatened to spill over as each day passed. More and more people made their way to my list as I waited. As we went into winter break, I was at the end of my rope. The only thing that gave me solace was slaving on my computer, making mash-ups. I don't know why, but throwing myself into the music was the only way I could escape my anger for even a second.

It was the week before school got out that Sammy came crawling back into my life.

My dad opened my door and screamed down, "That freaky raccoon girl is here for you."

It took almost everything in me not to scream back, "Tell her to go fucking die." Instead I closed down my computer and walked up my steps to the front door. She stood there looking like there were a million places she would rather be. I reveled in the fact she understood maybe a millionth of how I felt about being in Foster.

"What?" I said, standing in the doorframe, making it clear I did not want her to come any closer.

"Look, I get we're in a fight, and we both said horrible things, but I need to talk to you."

I stared at her like she was a lizard or something. "One, I didn't say horrible things, you did, and two, we aren't in a fight. We aren't an anything."

If this was a Stephen King book, her eyes would have glowed as her hair was blown back with a wind machine. The music would have gotten all dramatic as I burst into flames. She literally closed her eyes and took a mental deep breath before talking again. "Can you just think past your monumental ego for, like, three seconds and at least pretend to be a human?"

My right hand really, really wanted to slam the door shut in her face something fierce. "What?" I asked again.

"So Kelly is throwing his party this weekend."

I waited for her to continue. "Yeah, Douche-a-palooza is this time every year. What's your point?"

She looked down and took a deep breath. "Kyle thinks we all should go."

"And I assume when you say *we*, you're actually speaking French?" I replied.

Her look was scathing. "He thinks everyone who never gets invited to the party should crash it by showing up."

I rolled my eyes at her. "Crashing a party *is* showing up, and Kyle is an idiot." Before she could retort, I kept going. "He's not worried about his ass getting kicked since he is dating his own personal jock, so it sounds like a setup to me."

"You do know that Brad got his ass kicked in the locker room by those very same jocks?"

I didn't even hesitate. "Good. He deserved more."

The anger in her eyes was like burning coals deep inside of blacksmith's forge. "You know, I told him this was a waste of time. I tried to explain to him that you were a complete and total asshole who cared nothing about anyone save yourself, but he still begged me to come ask you. So I have, and I was right." The silence that followed said clearly that she hoped I died in a fire.

As she turned to walk away from me, I stopped her. "Wait, Kyle begged you to ask me?"

Her sigh was withering. "Yes, even after I told him you were a complete—"

"I'll get everyone else from the drama club organized. Just let me know when he wants us there."

It reminded me a lot of those cartoons where the bird just stopped, and the coyote went flying past him. That was the look on her face. "You're going?" I nodded. "Why?" she asked, completely shocked, but then I saw the suspicion in her eyes as she began to doubt my intent.

"Kyle wants a show of solidarity. He'll get one. Isn't that enough?" I asked casually.

"For anyone human? Yes."

"You have my answer. Let me know when and where." And I slammed the door in her face. It saved me from any more of her ridiculous chatter and prevented her from seeing the grin spread slowly across my face. This was as close to perfect as life got in Foster.

Kyle begged her to invite me. Begged. This was it—everything I had dreamt of was coming to fruition, and all I had to do was wait for it to happen. Obviously he had grown tired of his muscle-bound boy toy and was looking for someone who could at least give him intellectual stimulation. And it gave me a perfect chance to out Kelly in front of everyone, a twofer that no one could have predicted.

What could possibly go wrong?

Brad

As soon as I realized Kyle was out there alone, I jumped up and made a mad dash toward the door. Mr. Powers threw himself between me and the only exit. "Brad, sit down." He was whispering, but it was obvious it was what a yell would sound like if you had to whisper.

"Move," I said, ignoring him completely. I reached to push him out of the way, but he slapped my hand away. I had to give him mad props for thinking he could stop me, but we both knew I was, like, three times stronger than him, and he was going to be moved.

"Mr. Graymark, sit down," he hissed, bringing both hands up to force me away from the door.

I said nothing as I began to move him out of my way.

"You're putting us in danger," he added, the first sounds of desperation entering his voice. He stopped talking as if he felt himself begin to weaken.

"Graymark, sit down!" someone whispered at me from across the room.

I saw Mr. Powers's left leg start to shake.

Digging in, I pushed him to the ground with a shove. My hand reached out to grab the doorknob as something stung me in the middle of my back. Before I could even react, my entire body exploded into pain, and I fell to the ground instantly. I lay there in a fetal position, shaking, as Jennifer moved a step closer to me, still brandishing her Taser.

Tears were falling from her eyes as she looked down at me. "I-I'm sorry, Brad. I can't let you endanger everyone else."

I wanted to scream at her that I needed to get to Kyle, but all I could manage was some pathetic-sounding noises as I drooled onto the floor. My eyes closed as I tried to will myself to get up and get to Kyle.

Jeremy

SO THE night of the party, I found myself standing outside of Kelly's house, wondering if this had all been one huge joke Kyle was playing on us.

Sammy had said we were early, but I wanted to make sure Kyle and I walked in at the same time so everyone could see us together. I know it sounds petty, but Foster had been just as petty to me, so some payback seemed justified. The rest of the drama people kept looking around nervously, like we were breaking into a bank or something. They were so pathetic it made me laugh.

"Something funny?" Sammy asked me as I shook my head.

She was wearing this ridiculous dress that looked like someone got kicked off of *Project Runway* for it. It was black with these slashes through it that had blue under it, obviously stolen from the set of *Wolverine vs. the Prom Queen*. How she wore such idiocy out in public was beyond me. "All of this is funny," I said to her, looking around. "We're sitting across the street from jock central, and the guy who wanted us to come isn't even here. I'm sure the YouTube video of us getting our asses kicked will be all over the net by Monday."

She had an odd look on her face. "I'm not sure what you think is the punishment in that scenario, the ass kicking or the fact it's on YouTube."

Before I could answer, someone said they saw a car coming.

I wasn't sure if I understood what she had been talking about. Getting your ass kicked was a finite experience. Your dad goes out on a Friday, gets so drunk he can barely walk, comes home to find that the magical house cleaning fairies have not miraculously picked up his mess during his absence, so he whales on you until you beg him to stop or he runs out of breath. Either way, once he is done, it's done; once on YouTube, it is forever.

For example, ever see the video of the big girl dancing on the table, and she slips back and falls on her face? One moment of pain; a lifetime of infamy. What about the girl in the horse mask who nearly knocks herself out by hitting the corner of the TV? Ten minutes of being dizzy; years and years of laughter. I had honestly been shocked that images of me being tossed into the trash can hadn't ended up online. I suppose that was just poor planning on their part.

"It's them," Sammy called out as she walked toward the now parked car.

I knew instantly that Kyle Stilleno had fucked me over again.

He was there smiling next to Brad, ignoring me completely as the rest of the nerds crowded around him. No one said a word to me as we all walked toward Kelly's house. I wish I could say I was actually surprised, but I wasn't. This was just the way fate rolled, making sure every single time I had the smallest glimmer of hope, something I moved toward, she slapped my nose like the badly trained dog I was.

Kelly's house was everything mine wasn't: clean, expensive, and decorated with a ton of money. The glares we got from the jocks who had shown up early solidified my belief that this was an initiation stunt Kyle had to pull to get into the cool-kid club. Get a bunch of losers to show up to a party, thinking they were going to be welcome, and then do something horrible like spray them with Coke or throw paint at them. I nudged Sammy and whispered to her, "This doesn't look good at all."

From the expression on her face, she wanted to argue with me that everything was going to be all right, but as she saw the guys in the kitchen, staring at all of us intently, she knew I was right.

"We should leave before it gets ugly," I suggested.

She took a half step away from me. "Then leave. Kyle thinks this can work, so I'm staying."

The way she said his name, the admiration and gushing pride... it made me sick. What did that loser do to get that kind of respect? I'd been struggling in this town for years, and I get bottles thrown at me. He decides we should go to a party and he's fucking Martin Luther King Jr.? Instead I stood in the corner with the rest of the drama geeks, which was as physically far away from the jocks you could be and still say you were inside Kelly's house. The other idiots whispered nervously to themselves, but I ignored them and watched the drama unfolding in front of my eyes.

Kelly was pissed, about what I wasn't sure, but he was not happy to see Brad and Kyle show up. Normally I would have assumed he was mad we were there, but he honestly didn't even look past the two of them to see us. Instead he stormed off to the kitchen and huddled there with his other friends, looking like a tribe of short-haired Neanderthals who had stumbled upon an alien species. Kelly drank almost half a beer as he glared over at Brad, Kyle, and Jennifer on the couch. I still couldn't figure out the genesis of his anger until I saw Kyle give Brad a small peck on the cheek.

Kelly yelled, "Fuck!" and threw his beer bottle across the room. Everyone froze as he charged upstairs and away from the party. Slowly everyone went back to being simply uncomfortable and not looking at each other. Kyle watched Brad follow Kelly out of the room, and then asked Jennifer something. That was when it started to dawn on me.

Kelly had the hots for Brad.

I laughed to myself at the idiocy of the entire problem. I liked Kyle, Kyle liked Brad, Kelly liked Brad, and God knew what Brad liked besides being scratched behind the ears. My entire focus was drawn to the stairs and what conversation was taking place up there.

The music stopped, and the sound of one of the library nerds shouting "— but no way Hulk could take Loki if he was ready" practically echoed through the house. They couldn't even come to a party and not discuss the uselessness that was comics. This was why people hated nerds and geeks. It was why I hated us.

Kyle jumped up off the couch and asked, "Anyone have any good music? A Spotify playlist? Anything?" No one answered, of course, because no one acknowledged Kyle as anything more than a guy who was here because his boyfriend could hit a ball. "Seriously? No one has anything?"

Sammy looked over at me and mouthed, "Your mash-ups."

I scowled at her and shook my head, but she nodded and practically threw my hand up. Kyle looked over at me, and I stammered a weak, "I have some mash-ups on mine."

"Sweet," he said, grabbed my phone, and began pulling wires out of the CD player. I wish the skill with which he handled the equipment wasn't impressive, but within thirty seconds, he had my music coming out of the speakers.

He nodded and smiled at me as he walked toward the library nerds.

I could feel a tingle somewhere inside me from even that brief moment of acknowledgment, and in that second, my anger was gone. "Did you make this?" one of the drama people asked me.

"This is incredible," another chimed in.

Maybe I had been wrong. Maybe this night wasn't going to be as bad as I thought it would.

Tyler

I ALMOST hit two other cars while I was running red lights to get to the high school.

A lot of thoughts were racing through my mind, but the first and foremost was that I was never fucking having kids. If this panic and absolute terror could be brought on by two teenage boys I had barely known a year, I could not imagine the day-to-day ordeal it would be to wonder if they were okay. Sheriff Rogers had two patrol cars in front of the school as we pulled up. One of the deputies was already putting up barricades to prevent people from getting any closer.

Robbie said something to me as I jumped out of the car. My heart felt like it was going to explode, and I hadn't sweated like this since the first day of practice in Orlando. My ears were doing that weird ringing thing that meant my blood pressure must be a thousand points too high, and the edges of my vision were blurry. All were indications I was too old for my own good.

"*Stop*!" Robbie yelled, getting in front of me. I paused, wondering how long he had been yelling at me. "What do you think you're doing?"

I cocked my head in confusion. "I'm going to go help."

"Help?" he asked. "Help who? Kyle and Brad?" I nodded and began to move around him, but he stopped me. "Did you gain superpowers at some point and didn't tell me? Because last time I checked, there isn't a thing you can do in there except get shot."

"They're in danger!" I screamed, not sure why he wasn't getting this.

"And you are incapable of changing that right now!" he screamed back. Neither of us blinked as we tried to drill holes into each other with our eyes. "If you go in there, whoever has a gun will just shoot you. Is that what you want?"

"Of course it isn't, but I can't just stand here and do nothing."

"No, that is in fact all we can do right now. See the big men in the dark shirts with guns? This is their job. If the whackjob in there who has a gun wants sporting goods, then it becomes your job, but right now all you can do is get hurt or die."

"So?" I asked him, fed up with the whole conversation.

"So maybe this isn't the time to go charging in to be a hero."

Something inside my brain snapped. "*I can't watch someone die again*!"

I hadn't known I was going to say it—fuck, I didn't even know I had been thinking it. But there it was, big as life and twice as ugly.

"Well, maybe I don't want to lose anyone else," he said back quietly.

There were a few seconds before I said anything. "I thought you'd jump at the chance to see me die." He gave me such a look that I knew instantly it had been the wrong thing to say.

After a second he sat down on the sidewalk; his entire demeanor was one of surrender. I sat down next to him. "What do you want me to say, Tyler? I can never forgive you for what you did, but as much as I hate to admit it, you are the last thing of Riley's that is still here, and I can't imagine losing you too."

Hesitantly I asked, "So you don't hate me?"

He quickly looked over at me. "No, I hate you with the fiery heat of a thousand suns, but I don't want to see this town kill anyone else. I just can't do that again." Looking out across the street, he said, "I hate this town. I hate it more than anything in the world. What is it about Foster that just preys on people? It's like a big fucked-up shark, slowly swimming in circles until it can find someone to pull under. I fucking hate it." Angry tears fell from his eyes as he talked.

I sighed and looked down at my shoes. "I miss him too."

"Tell me about it."

Another squad car pulled up in front of the school, and one of the deputies got out and pulled a large box from the back seat. As soon as I saw it, I knew this was serious.

"This is bad," I told Robbie, nudging him and nodding toward the box, which was now being set up on the trunk of the sheriff's car.

He shrugged. "Not to sound all Brad Pitt, but what's in the box?"

Before I could answer, the sheriff pulled out a nasty-looking sniper rifle and began to attach a scope to it.

"Oh" was all Robbie could manage as we watched him assemble the weapon.

Jeremy

THE LIBRARY nerds went outside and came back with tablets to play Hearthstone on. I'd never played the game, but I had seen it all over school; it was the geek equivalent of crack cocaine. Why Kyle would have them bring that crap in here was beyond me. Kelly's pack of rabid jocks were still standing in the kitchen, trying to distance themselves from the rest of the unclean in case being a loser was contagious.

So far, though, it was better than I thought it would be. No one had screamed at anyone yet, and my music seemed to be well received, so there was a kind of balance in the air. It was something that couldn't last. Instead of being actual peace and acceptance, this was forced cohabitation, and it was just a matter of time before one of the monkeys went apeshit on one of the others.

Brad came back downstairs and began talking to Jennifer. It was easy from afar to see why they'd gone out with each other. There was a sameness that the eye was drawn to and said, "They should be together." It was the same program that made you think celebrities should only date other celebrities. Perfect people gravitated toward perfect people. Thinking about it, I realized everybody gravitated toward perfect people.

He was upset about something, and he was trying to explain it to Jennifer. When Kyle walked over, the three of them talked for a second, and then Kyle began to walk upstairs. Instantly I knew what was about to happen. Kyle was about to confront Kelly about his feelings. This was it—my chance to get them all back.

I began to follow him and then stopped, realizing I couldn't make the same mistake I'd made in Dallas. I needed proof this time. I needed something to get Kelly back with. My phone was still playing music, so there was no way for me to take it with me. Sammy was swaying to the music, drinking something next to me.

"Can I borrow your phone?" I asked, wanting to run upstairs before I missed the explosion.

"Sure, why?" she asked, handing her phone over to me.

"Need to check in with my dad before he goes all psycho on me for being out." It was a complete lie, but my dad was a big enough dick to make it believable. I took her phone and practically sprinted upstairs. I listened at two doors before I heard talking on the other side. With a skill that had been perfected over the years of not waking up a hungover father, I turned the bedroom doorknob and slowly cracked the door open.

Kyle's voice became clear. "—about; this is what's going to kill you. Even if you got what you wanted tonight, come tomorrow, how could you live with it?"

Kelly started crying, and I tried not to jump up and down in glee. This was exactly what I needed. I stuck the phone in the crack of the door and began recording it. I'd have time to go over it in detail once I got home, but from what I could catch on the other side of the door, this was pure gold. I would destroy Kelly with this video. I was going to bring him and all his douchebag friends to their knees.

As the conversation went on, I heard someone burst in downstairs, and it sounded like he was making trouble. Cursing under my breath, I pulled the phone away and dashed back downstairs before Kelly and Kyle came out and found me. I ducked into the kitchen and hid while Tony Wright made an ass of himself in the living room. I was about to join Sammy and the drama crew, but then I realized I had to give her phone back.

Fuck, how did I get this video off without her knowing? I supposed I could email it, but that would take time to upload, and I still wanted to get Sammy back for going against me. I looked over the icons and saw she had the YouTube app. Crossing my fingers, I opened it up, hoping she was still logged in. When I saw the account name BluehairedgirlinTx pop up along with her password, I knew I was going to kill two assholes with one bullet.

I began to upload the footage to her account and then hit the home screen. The network icon was still spinning, meaning even though the phone looked normal, it was still uploading Kelly's confession to the web. All I needed to do was get home, pull up Sammy's account, grab the video, and edit the boring parts out. Once I had done that, it was a simple matter of posting it to Facebook and watching the world fall down around Kelly. The best part was if anyone tried to find out where the video had come from, it would lead them to Sammy, who deserved whatever crap she got as well.

Kyle was right; this could be the most important party in all of Foster, Texas, history.

Linda Stilleno

I HAVE a problem.

It's a statement that has rolled around my brain more than once, and though it may seem like an incredibly obvious thing to you, for me it was just starting to seep in. Once again I had the closing shift at work and ended up going to the Rodeo Club with friends after, knowing that Kyle would already be asleep. As usual, I drank too much, took the party back to my house, drank some more, made a complete fool of myself, and then passed out just as the sun was coming up.

There is little chance of me ever winning mother of the year.

Growing up, I was never one of those girls who thought about being a mom. I didn't like dolls all that much, and playing house seemed about as much fun as watching paint dry. I ran with a pretty wild crowd, and for a time I behaved like I was Peter Pan and never going to get old. I met Brandon, the wrong guy in so many ways, ran off with him, and then did the best and worst thing in my life. I had Kyle.

There are some people who will tell you having a child changes your world instantly, that the moment you stare into that baby's eyes, the universe adjusts itself around you and the baby becomes the center of everything. There are also people who will tell you that Bigfoot is real and that aliens took them far away and probed them intimately. I'm not saying that having a child doesn't change you, nor am I saying there is absolutely no chance that something like Bigfoot exists out there. I'm just saying it sure in the fuck doesn't happen the way those people describe it.

Kyle was a gift, no doubt, but he was also a curse as I realized there was no one else to take care of him. I have spent the better portion of my life wondering if he would have been better off with someone else as his parent.

At first I tried to do the whole "responsible mom" thing, but since Brandon, who was partly responsible for Kyle, wanted nothing to do with him or me, I was forced to go it alone. My parents, who had moved to California once my father retired, offered to move back to help, but in what could have only been temporary insanity, I told them no, I could do it myself.

That's a mistake I don't think I ever recovered from.

Looking back on it now, I can see what I did to screw things up. I decided to be stupid and not ask for help, and the instant it got too hard, I used the excuse to climb back into a bottle or worse. Of course, the reason it was too hard was because I wouldn't ask for help, but I was too fucked-up to see the logic loop I had created. Instead, I would go through cycles, getting worse and worse, realize I was ruining Kyle's life, try to get clean and sober, and then give up because it was too hard.

That isn't an excuse; that's just how I got myself into this situation.

The specific situation I'm talking about was me passed out while someone pounded on my door. At first I thought it was just a headache or possibly my pulse, but as I became more and more awake, I realized the sound was someone almost breaking down my door. Slowly I stumbled toward the noise. You can tell how zoned I was because I didn't even check the living room to see if there was anything illegal left out, just in case it was a cop. My mind was nowhere near awake even as I opened the door.

Gayle from the diner was standing there, looking four kinds of pissed.

"Typical," she practically spat at me as she pushed past into the house. "You know, I honestly gave thought that you might just be at work instead of hungover, still asleep. Against all odds I really did want to believe that, but I should have known."

I had no earthly idea what she was talking about, so I closed the door and asked in a quiet voice, "What are you doing here?"

She had already walked away and into the kitchen. I heard the water from the sink turn on and tried to figure out what the hell was happening. Was she in there doing my dishes? I walked into the kitchen and was met head-on by a glass of water thrown in my face. Now, I'm not sure what the protocol is when a crazy lady walks into your house and throws water in your face. Miss Manners never covered that when I was younger. I do know that if I had been awake, my reaction would have been different.

"What the fuck did you do that for?" I screamed at her, wiping my face off.

"Because you need to be sober and awake, and since the first part is impossible right now, I'll settle for the second." She brushed past me as she started toward the living room.

My mind had finally woken up, and it was pretty pissed. I grabbed her hand as she walked past. She turned back to look at me, and the expression on her face made it pretty clear she did not like me at all. Since I had been awake all of about forty-five seconds before I was doused, the feeling was mutual.

"What makes you think you can walk into my house and treat me like this?" I asked her, as ready as I had ever been to hit an older woman.

Instead of answering, she turned the TV on with her other hand. Rather than game shows or soap operas, it was showing local news. I saw half a dozen cop cars in front of Foster High, the words "Shooting at Local School" scrolling beneath the images. I felt my hand drop to my side as I stood there in shock. This could not be happening, not here. This was Foster. This place was safe.... This wasn't real.

Gayle slapped my face, not hard, but enough to get my attention back.

"Your son is in trouble, and he needs you. Get dressed now." It was pretty clear from the tone in her voice she was going to wait for me.

I opened my mouth to argue with her, to fight with her, to do *something* to defend my life to this woman. Instead I saw the police push the news crew farther away from the school and knew this nightmare was real, and I was wasting time.

I turned and ran back into my room.

Jeremy

IT WAS like watching a car crash in slow motion.

Or better, it was like watching one of those YouTube clips where this hot jock douchebag thinks he's going to be all cool and grind down a stair rail but instead biffs it and nails himself in the balls. It was like that except the guy just kept falling and falling and falling. I grabbed the video from Sammy's account, edited it down to the golden moments, looped it, and then uploaded it back to her account again. It was a simple matter to make a dummy Facebook account, link the video to Kelly's wall, and wait.

I didn't have to wait long.

It's a well-known fact that sharks will consume their own in the middle of a feeding frenzy. The same is true for high school douchebags trying to be as popular as they can. I labeled the video "Who's the fag now?" my very own cryptic clue to who I was, in the same manner that Joker left clues for Batman. Of course Kelly and his ilk weren't detectives, so I was in no danger of being discovered.

By noon it had become a thing.

Kelly had removed it from his wall, but it made no difference. People just kept passing it around and linking it back. Each time, more and more people took the opportunity to remind Kelly of what a worthless human being he was. By the end of that weekend, it was pretty clear that Kelly's life as he knew it was over. His so-called friends had thrown him overboard, since all he was now was social chum to the bottom-feeders waiting in the deep water. Kelly eventually deactivated his Facebook account, but not before some guys spray-painted FAG across his truck and posted pics all over Instagram.

It would have been painful if it wasn't so fucking funny.

That afternoon, after my dad had gone to work, someone woke me up pounding on the small window that looked out onto the street. Not having a door or a real window was the only drawback to having a room in the basement, but I didn't mind since no one really came by anyways. I could see Sammy's face glaring in at me from the other side of the glass. When she saw me look at her, she pointed toward the front door and vanished.

I took my time getting dressed before walking up the steps to the door. I took a deep breath before opening it.

"What in the fuck did you do?" she roared, pushing past me.

"Please, come in," I said dryly as I closed the door.

She held up her phone. "What did you do?"

I looked at her blankly, making sure I kept any hint of a smile off my face. "I have no idea what you're talking about, Sammy."

"You posted that shit on my account," she raged. "Why would you do that?"

"I have no idea what you're talking about," I said, sounding bored as I sat down in my dad's chair. "But if I did, I'd hazard a guess that this is the day all family business is dealt with." She gave me a confused look, and I knew she had never seen *The Godfather*. "You turned on me, Sammy, and this is the price. Learn to deal with it."

Her face turned four shades of red as my words sank in. Her hand holding the phone trembled, and I assumed she was fighting the urge to throw it at me. "We're supposed to be friends," she more pleaded than said.

"Life isn't what's supposed to be." I was sneering at her, but only because of the openly weak stance she was taking. Someone always has to play the victim. "You think I'm supposed to be stuck in this nowhere town while Kyle Stilleno lives my life?"

"People will kill you when they find out," she said, turning around, ready to flee my living room.

"People will kill *us*," I clarified. That stopped her dead in her tracks. "I mean, who's going to believe you had nothing to do with it? It's been almost four days. You had to have found out before now. You think you aren't going down in the same ship I am if you tell? Trust me here, Rose, we're both hanging on to the same iceberg this time, and I will kick your fat ass off before I go down first."

She looked at me like I was holding a severed head in my hand. Some people have to make everything a thousand times more dramatic than it *really* is. It *really* makes me sick. Her mouth opened like she wanted to say something, but nothing came out.

"Let me help your brain figure it out. You tell people about what I did, I will tell them you helped me, and they will believe me. Period. So if you're feeling superior, then you march right on out there and tell them what I did. With all due respect to Benjamin Franklin, we are going to stand together, or we will hang together."

She gaped at me openmouthed like I was a supervillain petting a fluffy white cat or something. It was so ridiculous to see the naïveté on her face. How I ever thought she was a peer was beyond me. No one in this town was on my level, and it was obvious the only way I was going to make it out alive was to force events into motion.

"So you rush on over to your precious Kyle and tell him what *we* did and see how long he is your friend, because I assure you, he won't care either. You asked me once what it was like to be hated for just being me. Well, congratulations, because you're about to find out what it feels like. No matter what you say or how hard you deny it, no one will believe you, and that will be the end of you in this town." I gave her a patronizing smile. "So you show me what a morally superior person does and go slit your throat socially. I'll be waiting for that."

Her astonishment turned to cold fury as she seethed at me. "You know what, Jeremy? I know why your dad beats the shit out of you. It's not 'cause you're gay. It's because you don't have a fucking soul, and if I had given birth to something like you, I would have smothered it in the crib to save the world."

I sprang to my feet, but she didn't back up an inch. "You don't know what you're talking about," I warned her.

"Thank God your mother died when she did, because if she saw you like this, she'd kill herself."

"Get out." The words pushed their way out of my mouth before I could say anything rational in response. My heart was racing, and I took another step toward her. "Get out, and don't come back."

She took a half step back, more likely to keep space between us than in actual fear, judging from the look on her face. "Don't worry, I won't," she said, opening the door. "You're going to die alone, Jeremy, alone and miserable, and you will have no one to blame but you."

"If I'm dying, bitch, it won't be alone."

Again the words bullied their way out of my mouth, quietly shocking me as much as it did her. She stared at me like I was a complete stranger and then slammed the door as she left, leaving me shaking, furious at the world.

Susan Graymark

THERE IS very little in my life I have done right.

I dated the wrong boy in high school, I had unprotected sex, I got pregnant and was unable to walk across the stage to get my diploma because my parents didn't want me to embarrass myself, I listened to my father and married that same wrong boy when he got kicked out of college, and then I made my son suffer what it felt like to grow up in a house constantly at war. I hid behind a smorgasbord of prescription drugs that didn't so much make me happy as they made me unaware I was miserable, and I used my son as a bargaining chip against my husband in the cold war our marriage had become. I could go on, but there's no point, because no matter how long my list of sins got, they would never equal the way I warped my son into someone who was unable to see what an incredible young man he was.

Brad always blamed himself for Nathan's and my troubles, even though the two of us had fought just as bad in high school. I tried to shield him as much as I could, but it honestly became impossible after a point, because I was just as guilty as his father was in making him feel that way. I'm not asking for sympathy; I'm just outlining my thought process so when I say what I'm going to say next, you'll understand I am serious.

Brad is the only thing in this world I did that was truly good.

I tried to tell him that, but he's a boy, and boys both gay and straight seem to shy away from open affection from their mothers. I did my best, but I know it wasn't enough. All I wanted in life was for him to be happy, and when he met Kyle, I finally saw what that looked like. From that moment on, I swore to myself I would change my ways to make the rest of Brad's high school life be better than what came before.

Which is, of course, why I was racing to the school, not sure if my son had been shot or not.

It was just a matter of time before something like this happened in Foster. We had been bucking fate for years by thinking we were better than the rest of the country somehow. That intolerance, shame, and inbred hatred was a small price to pay for not having to watch our kids die in front of us. Of course, that's only true if your kid wasn't judged by the town and then quietly executed on the outskirts. Everyone my age knew about the Mathisons' boy and how he was run down years ago in the middle of nowhere. Everyone knew, but no one talked about it, because what was there to say? Riley was just a sacrificial lamb, and all of us silently gave thanks to God above that our child wasn't the one who'd had to pay.

But now there was a maniac at the high school with a gun, and all bets were off on who was going to pay this time. As I pulled up in front of the police barricade, I fancied just running through it completely and driving my car into the side of the school. As if a couple of tons of plastic and steel could save Brad and vanquish whatever demon had taken the town hostage.

Stephen Rogers was there in his sheriff's uniform, barking out orders to his people, who were in turn barking out orders to the onlookers. A crowd was gathering, and not everyone had kids who went here. Pushing through them, I got to the edge of the police barrier and locked eyes with Deputy Justin Mayer, age twenty-two. I had known Justin since he was old enough to pick his nose, and the years had not done anything to divorce me of my image that he was just a boy playing dress-up.

"Mrs. Graymark." He gulped, looking around for backup. "You can't come in here."

Note, I hadn't actually tried to come in yet. That was how afraid of me he was.

"Get out of my way, Justin," I said in the same voice that could make Brad clean his room and Nathan retreat into his den. "I need to talk to Sheriff Rogers. Now."

He looked over his shoulder toward Stephen, and I took the moment to duck under the tape barrier and move past him.

"Hey," he called out to me. "You can't be in here."

I ignored him as I walked to a foldup table they had set up in front of the school. Stephen saw me, and I saw the deputy next to him take a step toward me. This one didn't know who I was, but it was okay; I had made contact. "It's okay, Phil," Stephen assured him. "Get someone over there with Mayer before he starts giving guided tours of the crime scene."

Deputy Phil gave me a wary glance as he walked over to ream out poor Justin for my presence. I wish I could say I cared more. As soon as we were alone, I asked, barely above a whisper, "Are they okay?"

Stephen and I hadn't talked much since Jennifer and Brad broke up, since there wasn't much to say. One day our kids looked like they were going to get married someday, and the next they were of different sexualities. I'm pretty sure Hallmark doesn't make a card for that. But I knew Jennifer had become friends with Brad and Kyle over Christmas break, and I had been happy to hear their generation seemed to get past this crap better than ours did.

He nodded and looked around to see if anyone was close enough to hear us. "She sent me a text—three shots from the west side of campus. She and Brad are in the east portables."

I let out a breath I hadn't known I was holding in as I leaned against the table. "Oh God, I was so worried...."

He put a hand on my shoulder. "They are safe from the shooter, but Jennifer had to Tase Brad." I looked up at him to see if there had been an infinitesimal chance he had picked the worst time ever to make a joke. "He tried to force his way out of the classroom—he was worried for Kyle."

I put a hand to my mouth, not trusting myself to say anything.

"He's okay, just stunned, but we need to figure out where the shooter is before I can get anyone out of there. Now you know everything I know." He sounded as tired as I felt, and this was just starting.

"They're going to be okay, right?" I asked, fearful for the answer.

Before he could reply, the sound of a car coming to a screeching halt tore through the assembled crowd. People parted as the black Mustang came to a rest inches from the barricade. Nathan almost jumped out of the door and pushed past both Phil and Justin, the whole time screaming, "Where is my son? Get off of me. Where is my goddamned son?"

I saw Stephen's face harden as he gritted his teeth in anger. I put a hand on his chest. "I'll get him out of here. Just get the kids. Please." Before he could answer, I turned back and walked directly in front of Nathan's path. Each deputy had one of his arms in a grip and seemed to be wondering if they should take him down or not.

"Get out of my way, Susan," he bellowed, ignoring the fact that he had a police officer on either side of him. "Brad is in trouble. I'll help him."

"Nathan," I said as calmly as I could, "they are doing everything they can do."

He wasn't talking to me anymore. "He's my son. Let me go. My son is in danger."

I reached out and touched the side of his face. "Nate, he's going to be okay."

His eyes were wide with emotion as he looked down at me. He was still struggling against the two police officers, but he had stopped moving forward.

He reminded me of a spooked horse who was ready to rear back and attack at any second.

"Brad is okay right now. You need to let them do their job." I kept my voice as still as possible. I'm pretty sure it wasn't my words but my tone that was keeping his attention. "He's okay right now. Calm down."

He stopped moving, much to the deputies' surprise. They let his arms go and watched him warily. A kaleidoscope of emotions danced over my husband's face as he tried to talk. Rage, terror, manic paranoia. I waited to see where his roulette wheel of reaction was going to land.

Out of nowhere he sank to his knees, his hands covering his face as he began to sob. It was so un-Nathan-like that I just stared at him, not understanding for a few seconds. With tears falling down his face, he looked up at me and asked, "What if he dies and I never get to tell him how proud I am of him? What if I lose our little boy?"

And for the first time since I could remember, I saw the face of the man I fell in love with.

I fell to the pavement with him and cradled him in my arms, oblivious to how many people were watching us. "We aren't going to lose him, Nathan. It's not too late."

As I rocked him, I said a silent prayer to God not to make me a liar.

Jeremy

THE MONDAY after winter break, I was ready to enjoy the fruits of my labor.

I felt like a master chef who had painstakingly added each ingredient to the pot, stirring slowly to let everything get good and mixed up. The rest had been just watching my creation come to a boil under the heat. Now it was time to feast on his despair. I wore the same Ramones shirt I had been thrown into the trash with earlier in the year. I knew there was no way Kelly would remember it, but I would, and after all, this was all about me.

I wandered around the quad, my iPhone blaring "Karma Police" by Panic! at the Disco.

This is what you get, Kelly. This is what you get when you mess with me.

I was sitting by the library, waiting for the show to begin, when Kyle came charging across the quad, making a beeline right at the Round Table. I pulled my earbuds out as Kyle pushed Tony Wright back with both hands. He was screaming at Tony about Kelly. I moved closer to hear the specifics.

As soon as I got in earshot, Brad said to Tony, "I'm his boyfriend, and Kelly killed himself, you douche."

The blood in my veins turned to ice water as I knew he wasn't lying. My feet wouldn't work as I staggered away from the table as more people moved toward it. Of course no one noticed me as I turned around and ran toward the bathroom. I barely got into one of the stalls before I vomited violently. My shame and horror spilled out of my mouth as I tried not to think that Kelly was dead. I gripped the edges of the toilet, because I felt like I could fall into that whirlpool of water that led to nowhere and be lost forever. I sat there on the bathroom floor, wishing my guilt would come out of my mouth as easy as my bile.

There was an announcement over the loudspeakers telling everyone that school was canceled for the week, and that we should go home. I waited almost an hour before leaving the bathroom. I was certain Kyle was going to be standing there in the hallway, waiting for me with those accusing eyes. I ran home, half crying the entire time as it really began to sink in. He was dead. Kelly Aimes killed himself, and….

No, I will not say that.

I slammed the door behind me and slid down to the floor, blocking the door with my body as I began to shake uncontrollably. Kelly was dead because he'd killed himself. That was a fact. I wasn't in the room with him. I hadn't been whispering in his ear. It was his choice, and that was what I kept telling myself until I ended up passing out right there on the floor.

I didn't wake up until my dad got home and tried to push his way into the house. At first I had visions of the police crashing into the house, trying to grab me and lock me away for killing Kelly. In a blind panic, I pushed against the door, slamming it shut, which brought a series of cursing from my dad on the other side. He kicked the door open, which knocked me back into the living room.

"What the fuck are you doing?" he roared, tossing his lunch pail to the side. "Why can't you just be normal?" I kicked back away from him, but it was too late. I had messed up his daily ritual of coming home from work, changing, and drinking a beer in his chair while watching ESPN. And like an overgrown, muscle-bound baby, he was cranky and going to take it out on me.

The ironic part was that as he hit me, I thought this was as bad as my day was going to get.

After a while he got tired, and I retreated to my room, knowing that after a full day's work and beating me, my dad would be too tired to bug me anymore for the night. I had no idea if he had heard about Kelly or not, but I honestly didn't care. I put my headphones on and tried to focus on my music. For a few moments, it pushed the dark thoughts away….

And then a photo book was put on my computer.

I jumped up in shock and saw Kyle standing there. "Kyle? What are you doing here?"

He just stared at me.

"Kyle?"

His expression changed and he suddenly started talking. "I brought you a present," he said, gesturing to the book. "We're going to take a little trip."

"What the hell are you—" I began to say, but he grabbed my neck and forced me to look.

He opened the book and there were baby pictures.

Of Kelly.

"He was a big kid, his mother said fifteen hours of labor to get him out." He turned the page. "Look at him; that's his first birthday."

There was a toddler smiling at me, a toddler who was now dead.

I tried to get away, but he held me fast.

"That's his fifth." An adorable baby looked up at the camera, a tiny football in his hand. "That was his first football. See? These are pics of him that day playing with it. Doesn't he look happy?"

I tried to get away again. "I don't know what Sammy told you, but she—"

"Shut up!" he barked. "We aren't to the Q&A part yet. We're moving on to elementary." Another page turn. "This is his third-grade picture. He insisted on wearing that jersey. His fourth, see his missing tooth? Pop Warner, he made a touchdown that week. Oh, and look at sixth grade. He had just gotten his braces off; look at that smile."

"I don't know…," I began to deny again.

"You know all that work at straightening his teeth? Wasted now, the impact of the gun broke most of them when he fired."

My stomach soured and I broke his grasp. "What do you want me to say? I posted it? Fine! I did, but he deserved it!"

Ignoring my words, he grabbed the book and kept flipping pages, "This is junior high, Jeremy. This was his first boy-girl dance. He insisted on wearing sneakers with his khakis because he didn't want it to be too serious."

I couldn't help but look and then turned away quickly. "I didn't mean for him to do that! He was an asshole! He picked on both of us! You know that!"

"This is football camp," he said, turning the page. "You see this? You see that smile?"

I was backing away from the book like he was holding a gun on me.

"He had thought Brad and him were a thing, and were at the very least friends. Brad threw him under the bus for fooling around with him, and the other guys all snubbed him for the rest of the summer. Look at that smile!"

I had to look.

"That is a guy who is dying inside because he is in love with a guy who doesn't love him back. Sound familiar? You think somewhere in your life you can relate?"

And in that moment I didn't see Kelly, the big, bad asshole who had made my life hell. I didn't see the monster who had tortured me for the past four years. Instead I saw a guy who was dying inside and couldn't tell a soul about it.

"You have a picture like this, Jeremy? A picture where your heart is breaking but you have to smile anyways, because to tell people what was actually wrong would get you killed? Do you?"

I nodded, knowing all of my pictures were that.

"Cool, then I have an idea," he said, closing the book.

I slipped down the floor.

"Put a gun in your mouth and pull the trigger, because that's what Kelly did. He had all this pain and suffering and humiliation, he had his whole world fall down on him, and he couldn't handle it."

"I didn't want that!" I screamed.

"But that's what happened. You thought you'd be cute and get back at him by doing the thing that if it happened to you, would cause you to blow your brains out too."

My eyes burned as tears formed.

"He was like us!" he screamed at me. "He was gay too, and you fucking pushed him to this."

I finally broke down and sobbed. "You don't know the things he did to me."

"Bad things?"

I nodded.

"Cruel things?"

Another nod.

"Things that made you want to kill yourself?"

Slow nod.

"Well, then congratulations, Jeremy, you were just like him." With slow deliberateness Kyle took one of the photos out of the book and held it up to me. "Take a good look, Jeremy, because this is the human being you helped kill. You are directly responsible for his death, and that's a fact you will live with for the rest of your life."

He tossed the picture at me. It floated between us, Kelly's face staring at me the whole time. "Have fun living with that."

He turned to walk out and stopped at the bottom of the steps. "By the way, you asked if I would have ever gone out with you. The answer is no. I don't date bullies."

He left me alone with the ghost of the boy I had killed.

Sheriff Rogers

THERE ARE a lot of reasons to become a police officer.

Some guys do it for the power it gives them; others like the thought of protecting people in general. I've heard just about every reason under the sun since I graduated from the academy, but in all that time, not one person ever said they became a cop to kill teenagers.

And yet that was what I was about to do.

Jim Kelly's voice crackled in my ear. "I got eyes on the campus, boss."

He had served two tours in the Army and could shoot the wings off a mosquito at a thousand yards without blinking. He was the best shot within five hundred miles, so when we found the money in the budget for a Remington 700, he was the only person I allowed to take it home to practice with. I vividly remember watching him pack it up and giving a silent prayer we never had to use it.

Thanks again for that, God.

"Roger that. Stand by," I said back, trying to shake those feelings out of my head. I didn't have time for this kind of hesitation. I'd called this play; now I needed to run it before someone got hurt.

Mr. Raymond was talking to a couple of his teachers, looking like he was as close to falling over from a heart attack as the rest of us. It didn't help that I had no love for this man already. Walking over to him, I said as uncurtly as possible, "I need you to call for a position check."

From the look on his face, I could tell I was about as curt as I ever had been with him. "Very well. Do you have the remote set up?"

Foster High had a pretty expensive security system, about the only good thing that had come from a series of random shootings across the country. The teachers were trained to respond to a siren system to communicate. Two blasts meant they were in lockdown; three would mean all clear. One was the signal for them to say if their position was clear or not. We had set up a remote system so we could communicate outside the office. Again, another piece of hardware I had hoped never to use.

Raymond gave one siren call and waited.

There were buttons in each classroom. If the teachers were able, they would push their buttons to indicate they were in a safe zone. A diagram of the school was displayed on my laptop. One by one the rooms began lighting up. Each light meant another safe zone, another place I could evacuate right now.

Each light meant the odds of me losing my daughter dwindled.

Stop, do not go there. Stow that shit and focus.

After two minutes the diagram was full of lights. There was only one place still dark—the library.

I asked Raymond, "We have any idea what was going on in the library today?"

He began to shake his head and then paused.

"What? What's in there?" I prompted him.

"Fucking Stilleno and his club," he answered.

Goddammit.

Turning away, I said quietly into my mic, "Okay, Jim, our target is in the library, East campus."

About thirty seconds later, he answered. "Roger that. I have eyes on the library. Not a lot of access from where I am."

I glanced over at the digital school on my computer. "Move over by East Street. There is a bank of windows there."

"Eagle one is on the move."

I couldn't move anyone out of the school until I could see who we were dealing with. So I waited and counted down the last few minutes I had left to say I had never killed someone on duty.

Jeremy

IT'S PRETTY easy to see how I ended up here, right?

I spent a month or so watching my personal world crumble around me. Kelly's death became a rallying point in the town, and people actually started talking about him like he had been a freaking saint when he was alive. Kyle used it to get his precious gay-straight alliance pushed through, and once again he was the golden boy of Foster.

While I remained the horrible and unnamable villain.

It was a harsh downward spiral, which of course meant nothing to anyone. I became despondent, started skipping school here and there, stopped caring about anything. I just sat in my room and tried not to think about the images of Kelly's corpse. One particularly bad night, I ended up finishing a bottle of something my dad had left upstairs and found out two things at the same time. One, getting drunk numbed the pain slightly, and two, I was a cheap drunk. I ended up alone in my room, pondering how I had gotten there and testing for myself how much courage it took to put a gun in your mouth.

Turns out a bit more than I possessed.

It became a morbid game for me after a while, taking the gun and placing it in my mouth. At first it was like a snake, something to gingerly hold, hoping it wouldn't bite, moving to a more relaxed tone until it became just a bad taste on my tongue. I wanted to pull the trigger, wanted to so badly. The pain, the memories, the utter failure that was my life made any chance of ending it sound like a good thing.

Yet my finger refused to pull the trigger.

Turns out Kelly was a braver man than I was.

Weeks turned into months, and one day I woke up, and Sammy was there in my room. I hadn't been to school in over a week, and to be honest, it had been longer than that since I had taken a shower. How she got in my house, much less my room, was a mystery, yet there she was. At first I thought she might be some kind of delusional image brought on by my cracking mind, but I quickly dismissed that, because if I was going to imagine people in my room, she wasn't even on the list.

"Which ghost are you?" I croaked, looking over to my nightstand for my cigarettes.

"The ghost of 'Jesus Christ, take a fucking shower.'" She handed me a cup of coffee from Nancy's, which I cradled like a crack addict coveted their pipe. "Seriously, man, there is ripe and there is people complaining because there might be a dead body in here." She walked over and cracked open the small windows that looked out to the street. The sunlight was almost as unbearable as the fresh air while I sipped the coffee. I liked the dank, dreary style of my pit, and she was fucking it up.

"If I wanted the window opened, I would have opened it," I pointed out.

She glanced back at me with a pretty upset look. "Yeah, and if I cared, I would have asked." She began to wander around my room, looking at everything casually like it was a museum. "You look like shit, by the way."

"So I've been told," I said finally, finding the almost empty pack of Marlboros under my well-read copy of *Catcher in the Rye*. "You done?"

She moved the mouse on my computer and woke it up. "Make any new music lately?"

Obviously she wasn't.

"No, I haven't made any music; no, I haven't been to school; no, I have not showered in a while; and yes, I am thinking about killing myself. Did I cover the rest of your questions?"

She paused and just looked at me like I was an alien.

Ignoring her, I lit the smoke and took a long drag, the nicotine chasing off the last remnants of sleep. "Yeah, I said it. I'm a hot mess, and that isn't saying anything new, so anything else?"

"Your dad was right," she said, marveling at the train wreck that was me. "You do need help."

Ah, and the penny finally drops.

"So this is what it takes?" I asked her, flicking my ashes onto the floor. "Eighteen years and nothing, but have a nervous breakdown and suddenly he realizes he has a son. Of course, what does he do with that knowledge? Does he actually walk the fourteen stairs down to the basement to talk to him? Of course not. Instead he calls the person who rolled over on me and told Kyle everything I did." Her eyes narrowed in anger, so I flicked the butt at her. "Don't glare at me. You know you did."

She took a good ten seconds before responding. "Only you could try to frame me for outing Kelly and then claim to be the victim when I tell someone about it. You're...." She searched for the right word but never found it. "Fuck this. Enjoy your stink, Jeremy. It's the only thing that will stay with you as you get older."

She began to walk up the steps and out of my life for good.

I heard a voice call out to her. "Wait." She paused and looked back down the stairs at me. I looked back, confused, not sure who had said that. Again I heard the voice. "Please don't go. I don't... I don't know what I'm doing anymore."

She paused and walked back down the steps as I tried to figure out who was talking. "I just sit down here, and all I can see is Kelly, and I ask myself what did he really do to deserve that, and I don't have an answer. And then I ask, if he didn't deserve to die, do I?"

She looked shocked and shook her head. "Jeremy, stop."

I was about to ask her what she was talking about when I saw it.

There was a gun in my hand, and it was pointed at my head.

"Jeremy, put the gun down," she said carefully, like I was holding a bottle of nitroglycerin, and if she shouted, it would go off. It took me a second to realize it was me and not the gun she was afraid would go off.

"Why?" I asked her. "Who would care? My dad would be happy he didn't have another mouth to feed. I was horrible to you, so you wouldn't. Everyone in this town either hates me or wishes I was dead. I mean, be honest with me, Sammy. Who would care?"

"I would," she said, sounding like she was going to start crying.

"No, you'd feel guilty, but you wouldn't care. We haven't talked since the Party's aftermath, and even then I was a dick. You'd feel bad because another human being killed himself, but I mean, who would care if I was gone as a person? Who would miss me?"

She said nothing, which was an answer in itself.

"See, we're all told we are special, unique people, but that's crap. We are all the same stupid, self-centered pig of a person and only care about what we want. We wallow around pretending to be more than we are, but in the end, what's the difference between a pack of wild animals fighting for the last scrap of food and a bunch of fat people fighting over a waffle iron at Walmart during Christmas? In the end, we all only care about what we want and are willing to do anything to get it." I took a pause as my own words seeped in. "Even cause someone to kill himself."

Sammy took another step toward me and sat down slowly on the bed. "Jeremy, put the gun down. It's not that bad."

I gave her a hard look.

"Okay, it might be that bad, but we can fix it," she amended. Holding her hand out, she suggested, "Let me help you fix it."

I hadn't even realized I was crying as I handed the gun over to her. She put it down and pulled me into a hug. I broke down as I hugged her back. I had cried a lot since Kyle threw those pictures in my face, but this was the first time I really let it all go. I just held on to her and wailed.

"I would miss you," she said, whispering into my ear.

"Thank you," I said between sobs, grateful I had at least one person in the world.

So, yeah, after that you kinda know. Sammy said she had asked Kyle if it was okay for her to bring anyone to the meeting, and he had said he didn't care. I kept pushing her to ask about me specifically, but she said it was okay and that I should go. That I needed people to talk to, and that was what the alliance was all about.

It sounded more to me like she knew if she had asked, Kyle would have said no.

That Monday was the first time I'd been to school in almost two weeks. My father had talked to the school and seemed to convince them that I had been out on a perfectly normal medical problem and was coming back. In all my first days of class, I had never been as nervous as I was that day. I walked around campus expecting someone to see me and let out a scream as they ran away. Either that or just beat the shit out of me for good measure.

Instead, I was ignored.

It was like I was invisible, and I had to say, it was kind of cool. I gathered all the work I had missed in the past weeks, trying not to stress over walking into that meeting. Sammy met me outside the library as I paced up a storm, finishing my smoke down to the filter.

"Calm down," she said, giving me a warm smile. "It's going to be okay."

"You don't know that," I said, rubbing the butt out under my boot.

"I have faith." I looked over at her, and she burst out laughing. "Sue me, I don't do Pollyanna that well."

"Pollyanna if she was raised by the Addams Family," I muttered back.

She paused and gave me a huge smile. "That might be the nicest thing you've ever said to me."

"How sad is that?" I remarked, getting nervous all over again.

She must have noticed because she put one hand on the library door. "You ready?" I shook my head. "Too late now," she said, pulling the door open and walking in.

I took a deep breath and thought about just turning around and running back home. Instead, I followed her in and readied myself. As I walked in, I could hear Kyle's voice.

"No one is turned away."

He saw me and froze in place. I saw the same look in his eyes that he had when he'd thrown the photos at me. I knew in that instant this was a mistake. "Get the fuck out," he ordered. "Don't stop. Turn around and get out."

Something soured in my stomach as everyone turned to look at me.

"Kyle," Sammy tried to explain. "He's sorry and wants to—"

That was as far as she got.

He came rushing at us. I really thought he was going to swing at me. "Sorry? You're sorry? Oh well, then that makes it better, doesn't it? It doesn't matter what you did as long as you say sorry at the end. Is that how it works?"

He was talking to me, but my mouth refused to work. My heart was exploding in my chest, and I shivered in a cold sweat. "I-I just wanted...." Between you and me, I had no idea what I was going to say I was sorry for and will now never know.

"I don't care what you wanted, you dick. I mean, you didn't care what he thought, right? So why should anyone give a flying fuck what you want?"

We both knew he was talking about Kelly.

The teacher, the weird one who liked cats, came up behind Kyle. "Kyle." He ignored her, so she asked a little more forcefully. "Kyle, what's going on?"

He never stopped staring at me. "Jeremy was leaving."

Sammy's voice sounded really pissed. "I thought anyone could be here. Wasn't that what you were just saying?"

Kyle turned to gape at her. "Really? You want him to stay?" Before she could answer, he looked back to me. "Sure, he can stay. He can stay as long as he wants. As soon as he tells everyone what he did." People gasped all around me. "So go for it, Jeremy. Share with the rest of the class and you can have a seat anywhere you want."

I had never been so close to someone who hated me so much. I was unprepared for how unpleasant it was to see such raw emotion radiating off of someone like that and not flinch. Time began to slow, and I could see everyone looking at me with varying degrees of confusion on their face. I looked back at Kyle and pleaded under my breath, "Please don't do this."

If he heard me, he didn't show it. "Leave, or I will tell them what you did."

There was a time when I would have argued with him. A time when I possessed enough arrogance to stand and shout back at him. I had admired this guy from afar for so long, but standing here, inches from him threatening me, I couldn't honestly find a thing about him that I found appealing. Did I do this? Did I make this Kyle when I killed Kelly?

And there it was. The first time I thought it to myself.

I had killed Kelly.

Sure, I wasn't there loading the gun or putting it in his mouth, but as plain as day, I was the reason he was dead. Me. I had done that. And there was nothing I could do to take that back. So instead of arguing or trying to convince him of anything, I turned and scurried out of the library like any good monster does when confronted by the hero. I just turned and ran as fast as I could.

I can't tell you where I ran or for how long. All I knew was, the next thing I remember was being in my room with the gun in my lap. It was night, and I had no real memory of how I got there. I just knew it was where I had ended up. All paths led here eventually. There wasn't anything I could do about it. I could fight and kick and scream, but I was a horrible person, and I needed to die.

It really couldn't get any plainer than that.

I sat in the dark and began listing the reasons I should die in my head. Like water bursting from a dam, they came rushing to me, one after another after another. With the echoes of all my failures racking up in my brain, I tried to find a reason I should live.

The silence was overwhelming.

Days passed, and every time I came up for air, I found myself sitting on my bed looking at that gun. Sometimes I saw Kelly standing at the edge of my bed, his unblinking eyes telling me to do it. Sometimes it was Kyle and his burning hatred of me asking who would even care. After a while I couldn't tell the difference between them.

That weekend I ignored calls from Sammy as my sorrow darkened into something else. Where did Kyle get off treating me like that? When did he get elected king of the gays? Kelly was an asshole, and what I did was wrong, sure, but Kyle wasn't his friend, so why should he care? As Saturday turned to Sunday, the darkness warmed and became a rage as my emotions began to simmer. Kyle was just as guilty as I was. What did he do to make Kelly's life better? I had done what I did out of defense, and it may have been the wrong thing, but Kyle didn't have a right to punish me.

I was the only one who got to hate me.

None of this would have happened without Kyle's bullshit. If he and Brad had never gotten together, this whole thing wouldn't have happened. I'd still be on my way to college and out of here, and Kelly could still be alive, being the dick he was. My life was over just as much as Kelly's, if not worse. Kelly was gone. The pain was over.

Mine was just beginning.

What this town needed was a wake-up call. They needed to know that Kyle wasn't the golden child they all thought. He didn't have the answers, and his hands were as bloody as mine. Of course, no one would listen to me. Why should they? I was just a loser in a long line of losers in Foster, and they would just ignore me. What I needed was a spectacle, a show. I needed something spectacular to grab them by the balls and make them pay attention. And once they were looking my way, I could say my piece, and they'd know the truth.

And in the end, should someone die?

The only answer was yes.

That Monday I showered and got dressed with a vigor I hadn't possessed in forever. It was the first few minutes of my last day on Earth, and somehow that knowledge was liberating. This was my last shower, the last time I was going to brush my teeth. It made everything seem… I don't know. More important? Less stressful? Nostalgic? I didn't know what the word was, but it was different, and I liked it.

I put the gun in my messenger bag and walked out of my house for the last time.

Life is different when you walk with a gun on you. People cease to be people and are just potential targets. No one is a threat because you know you can just blow their head off if you want to. Maybe that was it. Maybe this was what being a god felt like. Every person I let walk by was a person I let live because I had death in my hand, and there was nothing they could have done about it. For the first time in my life, I walked down First Street not afraid for my life.

As I walked onto campus, I went over my plan in my head. I would go into Kyle's precious meeting, point my gun at him, and get him to admit that he was just as guilty as I was. Once he did that, I would put the gun in my mouth and pull the trigger.

My place in Foster High history would be sealed.

I smoked half a pack waiting for lunch and his meeting to start. What was the worst that could happen? I could die of lung cancer? That made me laugh, a little too loud since people walking by gave me a scowl. My hand twitched toward my bag before I stopped myself. I had a part to play. I couldn't waste it on random assholes. Though that did give me a thought.

Surely Kyle wasn't the only person who needed an attitude change in this school.

What if there was a way I could get him to admit what he had done, tie him up or something, and then go poke my head in some classrooms. Kelly's friends were just as bad as he was. Making them pay would be funny.

And then it came to me. What I should do became perfectly clear.

I needed to get Kyle to admit his shit, and then I needed him to see he had made the wrong choice. In one move I could get him to see the greatest mistake he had made was not picking me, and I could do it in one fell swoop.

I'd make him watch Brad beg me not to kill him right in front of Kyle's eyes.

A huge smile spread across my face as I settled on my course of action. The lunch bell rang, and I watched people begin to file into the library. I waited until they closed the door before I got up and took a deep breath. Looking around, I realized this was the last time I was going to see this school.

Good.

I put my hand in my bag and walked into the library.

The moment Kyle saw me, he got up and began walking toward me aggressively. He had that look again, like he was going to hit me. I tried to pull the gun from my bag, but it got stuck. Kyle kept coming, screaming something at me as I struggled to get the gun free. He kept getting closer, and I felt fear clamp down as I yanked the gun free and pointed it at him.

My heart stopped as it spit out three bullets.

Oh my God, what had I done?

Kyle

SO MOVIES are mostly crap.

I say that because they show you all this stuff, and in your mind, you think you've seen it and would be ready for it in real life. Like a car crash. You see them all the time, and you think, well, that guy just got the one cut they always get on their forehead. He stumbled out and chased the bad guy for, like, fifteen blocks. How bad could it hurt?

Car crashes fucking hurt.

Another lie? Guns.

You see guys shooting them all one-handed, jumping across the room, and the noise is all *pop-pop*. Fucking *pop-pop*. You know what they could do if they wanted to make it like real life? In the movie theater, they could come up behind you and light a firecracker and stick it in your ear so it goes off when the gun fires. That is the only way you can get the deafening roar that shakes you to your very bones when the gun goes off. Your whole body jerks away from the sound, because it is literally the loudest thing you've ever not heard.

As for one-handed shooting like it's nothing?

Jeremy was firing a Glock 33 semiautomatic pistol. The bullet leaves the barrel traveling roughly around 900 feet per second and can stop a grown man in his tracks. I didn't hear the bullet because I was instantly deaf in that ear, but there was a rush of hot air past my cheek, and I stumbled backward, falling to the ground. Another shot went off right on top of the first, and I could see out of the corner of my eye that shot was as random as the first one. We all froze as Jeremy stood there, his hand over his head, with a smoking gun in his hand. There was an endless second of silence followed by utter chaos.

People started screaming and running, and I saw Mrs. Axeworthy scramble toward the back wall. Everything sounded like it was underwater, and I realized it was because I was deaf in one ear. There was this very surreal moment where it felt like a dream. Everyone was moving in slow motion, and the sound kept coming in and out of focus.

Jeremy fired the gun again over his head.

"*Stop moving!*" he screamed at them. To me it sounded like a speech coming from a broken speaker, but I understood his meaning well enough.

People stopped moving, and I couldn't hear a thing for what, to me, felt like a long time.

And then I saw lights flashing by the library door and heard a low buzzing from above, and it hit me. Mrs. Axeworthy just pressed the school lockdown signal. Jeremy swung around toward her, and all I could see was his gun. It's like he was just a mass of nothing holding a gun in his hand, and it was now pointed at her. I huddled on the floor, everything in my mind telling me to stay down and away from him. *Don't move; don't speak; just lie here and hope he ignores me.*

He was going to shoot Mrs. Axeworthy. Who was here because of me. All these people were here because of me. In fact, Jeremy was here shooting because of me.

I slowly began to stand up.

"Don't," I said to him, trying to sound as not-pissing-my-pants as I could. He looked over at me, and I felt my legs wobble. "This isn't about them. This is about you and me."

I don't know if that was the right thing to say or not, but it certainly got a reaction from him. He grabbed my arm and looked over to Axeworthy. "Turn that damn thing off."

"I can't. It can only be cleared from the office." If she was lying, then I never wanted to play poker against her, because she seemed 1,000 percent truthful.

"Get out of here while you can," I said to him quietly. "Just run before the police show up."

He gave me a wild-eyed look, like he hadn't even thought about the cops. "Does that signal at the police station too?" Axeworthy nodded. I could hear him cussing under his breath as he tried to figure out what to do next.

"Just run," I whispered, watching the barrel of his gun the entire time. "You haven't done anything yet."

"You really think they're just going to let me go?" He looked manic as he shook me. "You aren't that stupid."

I wasn't. I was just afraid.

"Everyone, get in the reading room," he ordered. There were only six people total, counting the three people who showed up to the meeting. None of them moved until he pointed the gun at them, and then they flinched their way to the room. "Take out your cell phones." Before they could even comply, he screamed, "Don't lie and say you don't have one. Give me the fucking phones!"

People dropped their cell phones to the ground as they filed into the room.

He knew what he was doing. The reading room had no windows or phone. Once inside, the only way to communicate with the outside world would be through this door. Mrs. Axeworthy stopped and looked at Jeremy. "You don't need to do this."

His face contorted through about fifteen different looks from shock to sorrow before he raged at her, "Get your ass in the room."

She looked over at me, and I just gave her a small smile.

He slammed the door and took a few steps back. "Okay, grab that shelf and push it in front of the door." It took me a second to realize he was talking to me.

"What, me? No. I'm not locking them in there."

He walked toward me, the black circle of his gun staring at me like it was the Eye of Sauron. "Move the fucking shelf. *Now*."

Sighing, I put my shoulder against the bookshelf and began to push it in front of the reading room door. It took some doing, but I found that having a gun pointed at you gave you access to previously unheard-of reserves of strength. Once it was in place, I looked back at him, almost out of breath. "So now what? You shoot me?"

I saw his eyes move across the room, and I knew he had no idea what was next.

"I'm not going to shoot you," he informed me, pulling me over toward the front doors. "Grab those magazine racks and put them in front of the doors."

So now I was effectively locking myself in there too.

As I pushed, I kept talking. "So if you aren't going to shoot me, why did you shoot *at* me?"

He ran a hand through his hair, and it was obvious he was pretty close to the edge. "You came at me. What the hell did you expect me to do?"

"Not have a gun?" I answered, pushing the rack until it covered the main doorway in. It wasn't a great barricade, but there was no way in or out without pushing it out of the way, and I had a feeling I wasn't going to get that much time.

"The gun wasn't for you," he said, walking behind the desk, taking all the phones off the hook.

"Then who was it for?" I asked, trying not to sound sarcastic because I believe that guns don't react all that well to snark. You ever see anyone mouth off to a gun and come out better for it? I rest my case.

"It was for me," he answered, way too casually to be a lie. He saw my mouth open in surprise. "Oh, please. What do you care if I live or die? Weren't you the one screaming for me to get out of here a few minutes ago?"

He had a point. An ugly, hard-to-swallow point that had a hidden razor blade inside it, but a point nonetheless.

"Oh, nothing to say?" he asked, kicking some chairs in front of the back fire exit. Again, if someone was to charge in through there, they would have to take precious time to clear the chairs and tables away. "It's funny how holding a gun suddenly gets you newfound respect."

"It's called fear, Jeremy. Not respect. Don't mistake the two."

See? That was snarky, and the gun wasn't happy with me. I know because it came rushing at me, held by a furious Jeremy. "I don't fucking care what it's called. I have this in my hand and you pay attention to me. That's all I care about."

I said nothing and tried not to flinch away from him.

"See? Instant respect—just add gun." He jumped up on the counter, and we waited in silence.

After a few minutes, we could hear police in the distance. "I guess we're in it now," he said quietly.

This was insane. I mean, of course it was insane. I was sitting in a library with a guy with a gun pointed at me, but I mean, it was crazier than that. "What are you trying to do, Jeremy?" He looked over to me. "I mean, what's your endgame here? What stops this?"

In less than a second, he broke down, and his face grimaced in pain, and it looked like he was going to burst out crying. He put the gun to the side of his head and pushed it like he was trying to force it through the bone and flesh. "I just fucking want it to end."

I reached out to him, out of instinct.

He jerked back, almost falling off the desk, and pointed the gun at me. "Fuck off."

Needless to say, I did indeed fuck right the hell off.

"Don't pretend to like me now that I have your life in my hands," he warned me. "I can see through that shit."

I have no idea what happened next. I would blame it on some kind of aneurysm or possibly just plain old stupidity, but however it came to be, it happened.

I stopped being afraid.

Like a switch, it went away, and I was just tired. So he could shoot me. So I could die there. If it happened, it happened, but I didn't care anymore. At least not enough to be afraid of it.

"I was reaching out to comfort you because you looked like you were hurting, not because I like you. And if you're going to shoot me, then fucking do it. But stop waving that thing in my face to make a point." I went over and sat down in a chair. "So I ask again, what's the endgame here? What do you want?"

He jumped off the counter and came at me, gun first, of course.

"You think I won't shoot you?"

I shrugged. "I think I can't stop you from shooting me. So what's the point?"

He continued to wave that thing at me for several seconds. "I will do it."

I nodded. "I believe you."

"Don't think I won't."

"I won't."

"Good."

He lowered the gun and sat down across from me.

"Jeremy, what do you want?" I asked after a few seconds.

He put his head down on the table. "I don't know anymore."

I looked at the gun and wondered if I could take it away from him, but it seemed like a dumb idea. "Do you want to, I don't know, talk about it?"

He looked up at me, and we stared at each other for a few seconds, saying nothing.

And then we both burst out laughing.

Through tears I croaked out, "I'm sorry, that was a little too after-school special."

He was trying to catch his breath, he was laughing so much. It was weird because I couldn't recall ever seeing him laugh before. That thought alone depressed the shit out of me.

"What did Kelly do to you?" I asked out of the blue.

He wiped his eyes as his laughter evaporated suddenly. I saw his hand tighten on the gun and mentally berated myself for ruining the moment. "Lots of people have done lots of things to me," he said darkly. "It doesn't matter anymore."

"Did you come to kill them?"

He looked up at me, his face pale from the suggestion. "What? No. You think I came here to shoot up the school or something?"

I looked down at the gun and back to him and just nodded.

When he looked down at the gun, he seemed surprised, as if truly seeing it for the first time. "Oh God, what did I do?"

Seeing a crack in his armor, I dove in.

"Nothing yet," I assured him quickly. "You haven't done a thing yet, Jeremy. There's still time to make this right." He was crying now, and I felt like I was losing him. "No one is hurt, and no one needs to be. This can be fixed."

He looked up me, anguish etched across his face like a tribal tattoo. "Is that what you told Kelly?"

If he had pulled the trigger, it wouldn't have hurt as much as those words did.

"Is that what you told him? That everything would work out, and if we all just worked together we would overcome it? Did he believe it? Did it do anything to help him?"

There was a feeling like I was answering him from the bottom of a very deep and dark well. "No."

"*Then stop trying to sell it to me*," he screamed at the top of his lungs. "It's not going to be okay, Kyle. I am going to die. That's how this ends. There isn't another ending, so just shut the fuck up."

While I was struggling to find something to respond with, one loud blast sounded over the loudspeaker. Jeremy jumped at the sound like a startled cat. "What the fuck?"

I realized that Jeremy, that both of us, were running out of time.

"Let them go," I said, standing up. He turned to me, and I tried not to stare at the gun. "Let the other people go. If you let them go, it's a sign of good faith."

Things were moving too fast for him. I could see it by the way his eyes darted about like a trapped animal. "Good faith? To who?"

I didn't think he actually knew what he was doing.

"The police, Jeremy. The police are outside. That was a signal for teachers to check in. They're going to figure out where we are. If you let them go, then the police will calm down some."

"You just want me to let you all go?" he asked out loud, but I honestly didn't think he was talking to me. "If I let you all go, then what's stopping them from killing me?"

"I'll stay with you," I volunteered before the voices in my head could shout me down.

"You'd stay here? With me?" It was obvious he didn't believe what I was saying.

I nodded, wondering why I would offer that.

He didn't say a word for a couple of minutes. The entire time, I kept expecting Jennifer's dad to come bursting in with a SWAT team.

"Fine," he said, making his choice. "Help me get them out of here." We both moved toward the door. "This isn't a trick? You'll really stay?"

I nodded but was shocked to find that I meant it. I really was going to stand here next to him.

No matter what happened next.

Brad

SLOWLY BUT surely I got control of my body back. And with each passing second, I grew angrier and angrier. I sat there glaring at Jennifer, not believing what she had done to me. I didn't trust myself to talk, so I just sat there, fuming in my own thoughts.

"You think I wanted to do that?" she asked me after a while.

That was it.

"I think no one was holding a gun to your head making you. So I guess that makes you one up on Kyle, right?"

She tried to shake off my words, but I could tell they had landed. "You don't know Kyle is in trouble. We do know that there is someone out there with a gun. We need to stay put, and you know it."

I did know it, but at that particular moment, I didn't care.

"Your dad teach you that?" I asked her, my anger lacing every syllable.

She was starting to cry, but I knew her well enough to know it was from anger and not because she was breaking down. Jennifer didn't break down. In all the time I had known her, I had never seen her lose it completely.

"You want to hate me, Brad? Fine, hate me. If Kyle is in trouble, I will be just as worried as you are, but I am not going to let you endanger everyone else in this room because of it." She wiped her eyes. "I am not sorry for what I did, and if you move toward the door again, I'll do it again. So sit down and shut the fuck up, because we are scared shitless, and you aren't helping."

I was about to say something back when there was a pounding at the door.

We all jumped back in shock as Mr. Powers tried to figure out what to do.

Whoever it was pounded on the door again and yelled, "Let me in already."

It was Josh.

"It's Josh Walker," I said to Mr. Powers. "Let him in."

He shot me a look, and I could tell that even he was losing it a little. "And if he's the shooter?"

Jennifer tossed out, "If Josh Walker had a gun, he would have already shot himself in the foot. Let him in."

I expected Powers to argue with her, but damned if he didn't go over and unlock the door. Josh came barreling through the door like he was being chased. He glanced at me and then to Jennifer and asked, "Are you okay?"

Jennifer looked over to me, assuming he had been talking to me.

"Yeah, we're good, dude," I said, gesturing for him to come sit down. "Did you see Kyle out there?"

He shook his head. "No. I had a free period. All I heard were shots, and then all the doors locking."

"Why did you come back here, then?" Jennifer asked. "Why didn't you get off campus while you could?"

Josh opened his mouth to answer and then closed it again. Finally he admitted, "I panicked."

Jennifer rolled her eyes and let it go.

Josh looked back at me and could tell I knew what the hell was going on. He pleaded with me silently to keep my mouth shut.

"Did you see anything at all?" Mr. Powers asked.

Josh shook his head. "I just took off running."

"Yeah, ran across campus, down two hallways, and past half a dozen doors to end up here," I said quietly.

He nudged me with his elbow. "Be. Cool. Brad."

I had almost succeeded in not worrying about Kyle for five whole seconds when one blast came over the loudspeaker.

"Everyone stay down," Mr. Powers said as he crawled over to his desk. He picked up the phone and pushed a few buttons before hanging up. "This is almost done."

He didn't sound that reassuring.

"So, you guys are okay?" Josh asked, not meaning us guys at all.

"She Tased me," I said, jerking a thumb toward Jennifer.

Josh looked at her and then back to me. "Well, you must have done something to deserve it."

God, he had it bad.

About ten minutes later, the phone rang, and once again we all jumped at the sound. Mr. Powers picked it up and listened. "Got it," he answered to whoever it was.

"We're about to get out of here," Jennifer said quietly, watching him talk.

"How do you know that?" Josh asked.

Jennifer looked over at me. "Because my *dad* told me so."

Only I could make a school shooting worse than it was by just being me.

"Okay, listen up," Powers said, getting our attention. "When the phone rings again, we are going to head left out of here single file, toward the fields. Once we get to the backstops, we are going to move around them and go through the gym to the parking lot. There is no talking, no running, no leaving your place in line. We leave as a class, and we arrive as one. When I call your name, line up at the door." He had a clipboard in his hand.

He went down the list. One by one we lined up. When he called Jennifer's name, Josh raised his hand. "Since I'm not actually in this class, should I just line up now?"

Powers nodded, not caring. "Fine, Walker, you're behind her."

I shook my head. Leave it to Josh to find time during a school shooting to make a move on a girl.

We all crouched down, waiting for the phone to ring. Thirty pairs of eyes stared, all of us knowing when it sounded, the longest five minutes of our lives were about to begin.

"Graymark," Powers called out to me. "You know the field and gym better than anyone. Lead us down the hall."

I nodded and moved to get in front of the line.

Jennifer grabbed my arm. "We're following you. Don't take off to find Kyle."

The phone rang, and I waited for Powers to open the door. He gestured at all of us and then to me. "Take it slow, but not too slow, and don't stop."

I took a deep breath and began to move down the hall, away from the quad and toward the baseball field. No one else was in the hallway. As we passed by rooms, I could see people watching us in some; others were empty. They must have been emptying the rooms one at a time, which seemed like a good idea now that I thought about it. Every sound seemed a thousand times louder than it really was. Every movement was a person coming at me. I ignored it and kept going until I got to the back doors and opened them up. The girl behind me walked out after me as I headed to the backstops.

I held the door to the locker room open as everyone dashed in past me. Jennifer didn't even glance at me as she passed, but Josh patted me on the shoulder and gave me a small smile. Mr. Powers was the last person in. I closed the door behind us and moved toward the parking lot exit. There was an explosion of something metallic that echoed throughout the room. More than half the class screamed as they hit the ground.

My heart skipped a beat for a second, but then my mind identified the sound as one I had heard about a thousand times.

"It's okay," I called out, trying to calm people down. "It's just the bats. Someone must have bumped into them." I walked over to where we kept the bats stored, and sure enough, someone had caused them to spill out, bouncing everywhere across the cement floor. "It's nothing—just an accident."

I helped the guy up and then picked up a bat for good measure. Josh let out a sharp whistle, and I saw him behind me, holding a hand out for one as well. I picked up another and tossed it over to him. Rationally I knew there was nothing I could do against a gun with a baseball bat, but it made me feel a thousand times better having it in my hand. Maybe it was habit; maybe it was because baseball was one of the only things I knew I could do; all I knew was the bat calmed me down.

Once we hit the parking lot, any instructions not to run were forgotten as we saw the police cars and tents set up in front of the school. There were dozens of people just beyond that, watching. When they saw us, they cried out, waving us to hurry. I tried to keep it together as long as I could, but the moment I saw my parents in the crowd, I just took off, running as fast as I could toward them in the same way I did when I was little kid being chased by bad dreams. My dad actually broke through the barrier and held his hands out toward me. I practically knocked him over as I dove into his embrace.

I was crying, even though I couldn't tell you why. He hugged me tight as he patted my back. "Shhh, it's okay. I got you. I got you, bud." His voice was as comforting and as soothing as I could ever remember. I was six years old, and I had broken my leg falling from the tree in our backyard. I was nine, and a wild football had broken two of my fingers as I tried to catch it. I was fifteen, and I was on my back trying to see as the echoing sound of the line drive that had careened off my batter's helmet rang in my ears. I was eighteen, and I thought I was going to die. And as with each time before, my fears and pain faded away because my dad was there to hold me.

"Brad, are you okay?" I heard my mom ask from behind us.

"You okay?" my dad asked me in a whisper, somehow knowing I didn't want to take my head off his chest. I nodded, keeping my eyes closed. "He's fine, just shaken up." He maneuvered me back behind the barrier, and I felt my mom hug me from behind. I kept feeling like I was regressing in age. Mere seconds ago I was a brave young man trying to keep his class in check, and now I was a crying baby who just wanted his mommy and daddy to make everything better.

It was a nice place to be for the next few minutes.

"Brad?" I heard someone ask from the crowd. I looked over and saw Tyler standing next to Robbie. The thought that I might actually still be unconscious from Jennifer's Taser crossed my mind. Tyler looked at my dad. "Is he okay?"

My dad nodded. "He's a little in shock, but he's okay." Looking down at me, he asked, "Right?"

The years started to come back to me as I realized I was in public, clinging to my dad like a damn howler monkey. Pulling myself away, I nodded as I cleared my throat. "Yeah, I'm cool."

Tyler smiled and was about to say something, but then Robbie interrupted. "Where's Kyle?"

And just like that my panic was back.

Jennifer and her dad were hugging and talking by the main tent. If there were answers, he would have them. I took a few steps toward them, and my mom tried to stop me. "Brad," she pleaded. "You have to stay here."

"I need to find Kyle," I told her, but she wouldn't let me go. I looked up to my dad, hoping he would understand.

He put his hand over my mom's and said softly, "Susan, he's okay. You need to let him go. He needs to find Kyle." He looked me right in the eyes, and for a moment I knew he understood perfectly what I was feeling. "There's no way he is going to be able to relax until he knows the person he loves is out of danger."

She let my shirt go, one finger at a time. The second I was free, she turned and embraced my father; it was her time to cry hysterically.

My dad nodded at me and mouthed the word "Go."

I had never loved him as much as I did at that very moment.

One of the cops was too busy trying to keep the local news back, so it wasn't that hard to slip under the tape and head over to where Jennifer was. She saw me before her dad, and I could tell she was still pretty pissed at me. "You can't be back here," she said, just begging me to argue with her.

"Look I'm sorry, okay?" I said quickly. "I need to know where Kyle is."

Jennifer looked over at her dad, and he sighed and put down the radio he was holding. "Look, Brad, Kyle is…. Kyle is in there with the shooter."

This had to be what it felt like when you were in a car that started to roll over. The whole world begins to spin around you, but you are just there, perfectly still, unable to move.

"We think the person with the gun burst in to his alliance meeting. So far, the guy has let the other people go, but Kyle is still in there with him."

I suppose I stopped breathing at some point, because Jennifer was screaming in my face, but she wasn't making any noise. All I could hear was Kyle's laughter and how I was never going to hear it again.

Something stung the side of my face, and I started breathing again. I touched the side of my cheek and saw Jennifer's hand reared back to slap me again. "Brad. Snap out of it."

"Is he… is he…." I couldn't say it. I couldn't say anything at all.

Her dad shook his head. "He's fine right now."

"I have to get to him," I said, ready to fight my way into the school. "Me and Josh have bats, and we could—"

Sheriff Rogers put his hand up to stop me. The look on his face was as grim as I had ever seen before. "You don't need to do that, son. This is about to be over with."

I was about to ask him how the fuck he knew that—how did he know when this was going to end?—when the radio crackled, and I heard a voice call out. "Eagle one is in position. I have eyes on the target."

Oh my God.

He picked up the radio, and in a voice that sounded like he hadn't slept in days, he said, "Eagle one, if you have a shot without endangering the hostage, take it."

"Wing?" the voice called back.

Sheriff Rogers said nothing for a long time. The voice asked again, "Base, wing or not?"

He closed his eyes and pressed the button on the radio. "Jim, end this thing now. If you think you can wing and incapacitate him without endangering the hostage, do it. If you don't, end this. Now."

Small pause. "Roger that, base."

He put his radio down and looked back at me. "This is about to be over with." To Jennifer he said, "Honey, I need you guys to get behind the line." Before she could argue, he added, "Please, I can't have you here."

She seemed to consider arguing with him but then grabbed my arm. "Come on, Brad, we need to go."

I let her drag me away, not sure I'd heard that right.

Someone was about to die.

Kyle

THE LIBRARY was eerily quiet once everyone else was out.

We put the chairs back in front of the door and sat down by the front desk again. Neither one of us knew what was next, so we sat in silence for a while as we tried to figure it out. Finally he sighed and said, "This really isn't turning out like I thought it would." It was such an absurd comment that I started to giggle. Not a normal giggle but one of those nervous laughs you can't stifle even if your life is on the line.

Like now.

He looked up at the sound, and I could tell he wasn't thrilled by my reaction at first, but as my laughter doubled, he cracked a smile in return. "Yeah, it's been a day for me too," I spit out before letting the nervousness and panic spill out in the form of hysterical mania. Jeremy began to laugh too, but we weren't laughing at something funny; we were on the edge of losing our minds and had no other way of expressing it.

"I'm sorry," he said finally. "I shouldn't have dragged you into this."

I took a few deep breaths, holding my sides as my stomach ached from laughing. "It's okay. This is kind of inevitable, don't you think?" He cocked his head in confusion, and I elaborated. "I mean, since that day in the theater, it just seemed like we've been on a collision course. It's my fault."

His mouth dropped open. "Yours?"

I nodded. "When you told me you were gay, I should have tried to be friends with you. I mean, how many of us are there in Foster? I guess I was just put off by how matter-of-fact you were about it. I spent most of my life trying not to give it a name, and you were so 'whatever' about it."

"I didn't kiss a guy in front of the whole school," he said, still obviously shocked.

I grinned at that memory, wishing Brad was here. "To be honest, he kissed me. I just stood there trying not to pass out."

"People like Brad don't kiss people like me," he remarked darkly. "So it all worked out for the best."

"Not for everyone," I added, wishing I hadn't almost instantly.

"There we go," he said, the anger coming back into his eyes. "I had almost forgotten that I was the bad guy here because precious Saint Kelly killed himself."

Common sense told me to shut up. Common sense told me to just shut the fuck up and let the Wookiee win.

Of course, me and common sense had never been the best of friends.

"You outed him in the worst way possible. You came to school with a gun. Jeremy, no offense, but yeah, you're the bad guy."

There was half a second I thought he was going to argue with me on it. He stood up to make his point and then paused. I could see it right there in his eyes when he opened his mouth—this was going to be another fight. Then he looked down at the gun and sighed. "How incredibly expected."

He sounded as tired as I did as I sat there wondering how I got myself into these things.

There are a lot of things that movies get wrong, as I have stated. Turns out, red dots for snipers aren't one of them. In a second that began to telescope out in front of me, I saw the flash of light from across the street through the window and knew I was about to see someone die in front of me.

There are actions you have no idea why you take. I don't know why I attacked Kelly in the assistant principal's office. I don't know why I got in that preacher's face at Kelly's house. I don't know the real reason I broke up with Brad, and I am still clueless why I told Jeremy I'd stay there with him. In fact, my life seems to be random actions that are connected through long bouts of regret that I had done them. Everyone has had them before, blind impulses that move too fast for your brain to think about. I say all this because I have no problem admitting that there are a ton of things I've done that make no damn sense.

This wasn't one of them.

"Get down," I screamed, grabbing his knees and pulling. Part of my mind noted how incredibly surprised he was, which probably meant I could have made a grab for the gun at any time. The other part tried to stop me from screaming as the surface of the table behind us exploded from the force of the bullet screaming through it. Glass showered down on the other side of the room as I pulled him behind the reception desk. One shot. It was only one shot.

They were going to kill him.

Jeremy was panicked as he kicked away from me and huddled against the desk. He clutched the gun with both hands as he tried to steady himself. "What the fuck was that?"

The very last dregs of control I possessed flew away like a kaleidoscope of butterflies. Gone in a rush of panic and movement, never to return.

"Are you serious? What was that? That was the police trying to kill you because *you brought a gun to school*!" I was screaming, but I didn't care. "There's a sniper across the street, and he just tried to kill you." I paused. "Well, it might not be a he because I don't want to be sexist, but are there is a person across the street with a high-powered rifle waiting for you to poke your head up."

He was starting to hyperventilate.

"You need to end this, Jeremy. It's over."

He nodded and put the gun in his mouth.

"Don't," I called out, not sure if I should reach out to him or not. "Don't do it."

He slowly pulled it out of his mouth enough to talk. "Why? You just said it, Kyle. It's over."

"I didn't mean kill yourself. I meant give yourself up."

"Why? What's to live for? I fucked up even worse than last time. There is something wrong with me, Kyle. Everyone else seemed to know about it. I just happen to be the last guy who figured it out. It's why everyone stays away from me, why I can't make friends. I'm not right, I'm… I'm just…."

He didn't know the exact moment he broke, but this was the very second when he realized how bad it had gotten.

"You don't have to die," I pleaded with him.

"Don't I?" he asked bitterly. "That's exactly what I have to do, and you know it. The weird kid no one liked comes to school with a gun, threatens everyone, and he ends up either shot or killing himself. Only thing I'm missing is a black trench coat and an angry website listing the reasons I snapped. This is how it always ends, Kyle, and you know it." Tears were falling down his face. "And in the end, should someone die?"

He sounded like he was quoting something, but I had no idea what.

"Just take it back," I said, not even sure what I was saying anymore. He looked at me, confused, and I repeated it. "Just take it back. Put the gun down and walk out with me. We'll just go back. We just go back to the way it was, and no one has to die." Tears burned my eyes, but I wiped them away. "This isn't some stupid movie, Jeremy. You don't need to die because you made a mistake. Just put it down, and let's go back to the way it was. If you kill yourself, all that happens is that Foster claims another victim, and people will shake their heads, saying they had no idea. Screw that. Don't let them kill you, please. I already lost Kelly. I can't lose you too."

"Why do you care?" he asked, sobbing.

"Because I'm not going to be like them. I refuse to only care about certain people and let the other ones go. You want a friend, Jeremy, then let's try." I held my hand out to him. "I'm not saying that because I think you're going to kill me or because I'm scared. I'm saying that because that's what I should have said years ago. My name is Kyle, and I want to try to be your friend, Jeremy. Just put the gun down, and let's walk out of here. Together."

I took a sobbing breath, not even sure if my words meant anything to him.

"And if I wasn't going to kill myself? This is just pity."

A scream that came from deep inside me exploded out of my mouth. My eyes were closed, my fists clenched as I wailed at the world. There was nothing else but that scream as I railed against the entirety of the world and the idiocy of how unfair it was. It didn't need to be this hard. It shouldn't be this fucking hard.

"We aren't friends because that's what the rest of the world wanted us to think," I began to say with a hoarse voice. "We walk by hundreds of people every day in the halls, and we *never* say anything to them. We just flock to the same people over and over and ignore the people who aren't like us and think it's okay. It's just these packs of like-minded assholes thinking they're the only ones feeling this way. We're all lonely, we're all hurt, and we're all broken, Jeremy. *We are all broken*. I don't know why no one wants to say that out loud, but I don't care anymore. I'm broken, I'm fucking broken, and I need a friend, Jeremy. I need to know that it's okay to be like this and that I'm not alone. I can't lose you, not like Kelly. Please…."

I broke down and really began to cry, no longer able to even form words.

I felt his arms wrap around me and heard his voice whisper, "I'm here. You aren't alone. I'm sorry, Kyle. I'm sorry for all of this. I really am." He was crying too now. "I'm sorry for Kelly, and I'm sorry for hating you…."

Minutes later the front door of the library burst open, and Jennifer's dad and two other cops came storming in. They found us lying there, crying. The gun was kicked across the room away from both of us. No one died.

Nothing to see here, just two broken people who realized they were more alike than different.

Brad

I HELD my breath as I heard the sniper's shot ring out.

There was no sound as the entire crowd waited to see what happened. Sheriff Rogers's radio called out, "No shot. I repeat, no shot."

People made sounds of disappointment as the sheriff asked back, "What the hell happened?"

I moved forward through the crowd to hear the response.

"The hostage just pulled the gunman out of the way. They ducked behind the desk. I don't have a shot." The frustration in the man's voice was pretty clear even over the radio.

"Are you...." The sheriff seemed ready to throw a fit as he started cussing under his breath. Into the radio he said, "Hold your position," as he scanned the crowd. It didn't take long for him to find me.

He made a beeline toward me, the radio still in his hand.

"Anything you're not telling me about this?" he demanded. "Like why your boyfriend would be protecting the guy with the gun?"

I was about to answer "I don't know" but then stopped.

Everyone started talking at once.

"He's doing what?"

"Brad, do you know something about this?"

"Honey, tell him if you know something."

"My son did what?"

I heard Jennifer whisper next to me, "He's being Kyle again, isn't he?"

I nodded, trying to weigh which impulse was stronger—kiss him or strangle him.

Sheriff Rogers was going to ask me something else when a commotion started to move through the crowd. By the time it got to us, it was pretty clear something had happened.

"Someone says they can hear screaming coming from the library," someone exclaimed.

"Fuck this," the sheriff said to himself and then called out, "Sharon, you're with us." He keyed the radio. "We're about to bust it. Get ready for cover."

My heart hammered against my chest as I watched them get ready to go in.

Jennifer grabbed my hand. "My dad will get him out safe. He's good at this."

I squeezed back, wanting to believe her instead of asking her how she would know. This had never happened here before.

Matt had shown up and was standing next to Tyler and Robbie. Well, closer to Tyler than Robbie, who seemed to be actively keeping him at arm's length. My parents were holding each other, and I felt a thousand times more alone than I had before. I closed my eyes and asked God to give me a break, just once. Please let Kyle be okay. If he did that, I'd do anything he asked. And I meant it, I really did. I didn't care if the price was having to go bald or losing an arm or whatever. I just needed Kyle to be okay. Because if he wasn't... if he wasn't....

I started to cry as I realized I didn't know what followed that sentence. If something was to happen to Kyle, if I didn't have him, I had no idea how I would get along. I wanted him to be in my life now, and I just couldn't imagine one without him.

"Brad," Jennifer said, nudging me.

I looked up, and through blurry eyes I saw Kyle being led out with a blanket around his shoulders. At first I thought maybe I was hallucinating, but as he got closer, I saw him look up and see me.

I took off running toward him as fast as I could.

I jumped the police line and almost knocked down one of the deputies as I dashed to him. He threw off the blanket and ran toward me too. We met halfway, and I don't know who was holding on to the other one tighter. We were both crying again as I realized he was there. He was really there in my arms.

And I wasn't going to let him go.

"I'm sorry. I didn't mean to—" he began to babble.

I cut him off by saying, "I don't care," and kissing him.

He relaxed into my arms as he kissed me back.

Nothing else mattered.

Kyle

HE WAS there, waiting for me.

I shouldn't have doubted it, but for a second I thought maybe I had gone too far, done too much, and pushed him away. But as he held me, I knew I had been scared, just plain fucking scared of this and the future. I had mentally painted myself into a corner and done the worst thing possible; I just gave up.

Brad never had.

"Are you okay?" he asked after a while. "Are you hurt?"

I shook my head, not trusting myself to talk without breaking down into a huge crying baby.

"Oh God," he said, hugging me tight again. "I thought...." He squeezed me close, and I knew what he had thought.

The crowd erupted into boos and screaming, and I looked behind us.

They were bringing Jeremy out in handcuffs. His head was down, and the people behind the police line sounded like an angry mob aching to lynch him. I wanted to stay in Brad's arms and let them take him away, but I couldn't. Not anymore. This shit was over now.

"*Hey*," I screamed at the crowd. "What's wrong with you? I was the one in there, not you. If anyone gets to be mad at him, it's me. I'm the one with the reason." The cops had stopped, and Jeremy looked up at me. I gave him a small smile. "And I don't like people screaming at my friend, so shut up already." Everyone froze, not sure they had heard right.

"Thank you," Jeremy said quietly to me.

I gave him a quick grin. "What are friends for?"

Before he could respond, I was almost tackled by my mom, who was talking a million miles a minute. She was apologizing for everything she had done since I was three, which I think included skinned knees and possibly chicken pox. Normally I would have found that kind of physical affection off-putting, but at that moment, it felt nice to have my mom hug me and tell me it was okay.

So of course, it couldn't last very long.

The cops took Jeremy into the squad car, and the people started yelling again. Sheriff Rogers put his hand on my shoulder. "You need to get checked out, just in case," he said, gesturing toward the ambulance waiting. "Brad and your mom can ride along if you want."

I nodded, ready to pass out. "Sure. Don't be too hard on Jeremy. He's sick."

He paused and looked at me for a second, and I had the feeling he was really seeing me for the first time. "That kid held you at gunpoint, and you're trying to stick up for him?"

I nodded weakly. "He's not bad. He's just broken like the rest of us." I looked over at Brad and saw him smile, understanding what I was saying. Sheriff Rogers shook his head and motioned at the EMS guys. "Get out of here."

As I walked over, Robbie came under the police line and almost crushed me with hugs. He seemed really upset, as he almost shook me. "You are the worst, most aggravating, backwards-ass piece of…."

"I love you too, Robbie."

He pulled back and flipped his imaginary weave. "Bitch, please, everyone loves me."

That made me laugh as I saw Tyler still standing behind the line, looking like he was afraid to make eye contact. Robbie looked over at him and rolled his eyes. "Oh yeah, he was worried too." I shot a grin at Robbie, and he slapped my shoulder. "Whatever, I still hate him, but he was worried." When I just stood there, he whispered, "Go talk to the goon before he starts to cry."

We all walked over to the police line, and Tyler smiled. "I'm so glad you're okay."

"I was a little asshole," I said in response. "I'm sorry I said all that."

He was in the middle of saying, "No, it was okay. I deserve—" when Robbie interrupted him.

"No, you deserved it from me. He was just being a good sidekick. Stop beating yourself up already—that's my job."

Tyler closed his mouth and looked at me. "Apology accepted, I guess." He turned back to Matt and nodded toward me.

Matt sighed. "I'm sorry I threatened you and all that. I'm just a bit overprotective of Tyler."

I looked over at Brad. "I know the feeling. It's okay."

"Let's get you checked out," my mom suggested and started to lead me over to the ambulance when Mr. Raymond stopped us.

"Stilleno," he said, angrier than I had ever heard him. "Are you happy now? I told you that club was a mistake, and now look at it." I was too tired to fight and honestly didn't care anymore. "It's done," he went on. "The club, you starting problems, it's over. Do you understand me?"

I just nodded, wanting him to get out of my face.

Brad moved toward him, and Mr. Raymond held up a hand. "And Mr. Graymark, before you get any smart ideas, if you so much as look at me funny, you're expelled. I will not have you two boys running around thinking you're in charge. This is my school, and if you want to graduate, you'll step in line."

"Brad, stop," I said, pulling him back. "I just want to get out of here."

Both Robbie and Brad looked at me to make sure I meant it, and I did. "Whatever, Mr. Raymond, you win. I just want to get my diploma and leave."

My mom, on the other hand, was more than willing to fight for me. "My son just had his life threatened and you come over here to make threats? What in the hell is—"

Someone stepped between her and Mr. Raymond before she could finish.

"You're done here, Jeffrey." My jaw dropped open as Gayle from the diner stood there, glaring at Mr. Raymond. "Do you honestly think chastising a teenager who was being held hostage is the best use of your time?"

He looked as flustered as the rest of us felt. "Y-you're not involved in this."

All Gayle said was, "I am now."

And just like that he wilted. His eyes darted back and forth and then fell on me. "I'm sorry for that. Kyle, we can talk about this another time." You could have pushed me over with a feather when he turned around and walked away.

"What was that?" I asked her, dying to know how she did that.

She continued to watch him work his way through the crowd and away from us. For a moment it looked like she wasn't even close to being done with him yet. I called her name again, and she looked over to me and smiled. "Long story. Go get checked out. Don't worry about this."

I was about to ask, but after the day I'd had, I just nodded and allowed Brad to walk me to the ambulance.

MAY 18
THE GREAT ESCAPE
28 DAYS LEFT

Kyle

FOR THE next two weeks, the whole school seemed to hold its breath.

Everyone was in some stage of shock. We had whole days set aside to talk about our feelings if we wanted to. Jeremy was charged with about half a dozen crimes, but none of them were filed by me. Though Brad, my mom, Tyler, and just about everyone who talked to me tried to convince me otherwise, I refused to say one word against Jeremy and what he had done. I told Jennifer's dad he was sick and that he needed help, but I don't think he was in any mood to listen, since all of a sudden the real world had come to Foster.

Brad was never more than three feet from me the entire time. The only time he left was to go home and sleep and when I forced him to finish the baseball season. The team had made it to the playoffs, and there was no way they had a chance without him playing. At first he said he didn't care, he wanted to stay with me. It was sweet, but I wanted him to play. He had already given up on A&M, and though we hadn't said anything yet, it was pretty clear he wanted to come to California with me.

And yes, I know it's silly, but I felt like I was taking parts of his life away from him, and I wanted him to at least have one last winning season. He deserved it. And it only took about six hours of debating for him to see that as well. He hit a seventh-inning double that allowed the guy at third to score and won us the game. He was so freaking happy after that moment, he stopped fighting me and started playing again without argument.

He also made a big thing about giving the phone back.

"So this," he said, holding the box up, "is yours. And when I say yours I mean that in the same way as this," he took my hand, "is your hand. What that means is," he put the box in my hand, "the phone and the hand are the same. Try to give me this back again and I'm taking the hand."

I cocked my head. "That was supposed to be romantic, right?"

He nodded. "Yeah, it became a little Confession Tapes at the end. But I mean it, this is your phone, no matter what happens."

I leaned in and kissed him, "Nothing is going to happen again."

God, I hoped I could back that up.

So while he focused on baseball, I went off to mend a lot of burned bridges.

I started with Sammy, who hadn't been to school since the shooting. There had been a flurry of gossip flying around. Most of it revolved around Sammy, who people had assumed was still friends with him. It was one of those things I really hated about high school: you see two people, don't know them, so you write this little story in your head about who they are and then that becomes the reality. Sammy was just the blue-haired girl who hung out with that goth guy and nothing more. I had no illusions I wasn't referred to as the mouthy kid who'd made Brad gay.

The only good thing about getting held hostage was that when you wanted to cut school, they assumed it was because you were still traumatized from the experience and said nothing about it. I told Brad that I was going to talk to Sammy, and of course he wanted to go with me. Not to talk to her—to make sure I was okay. Overnight I had become Whitney Houston, because Brad thought he was Kevin Costner all of a sudden.

If you don't get that reference, seriously, go watch that movie. I can wait.

I assured him I needed to talk to her alone and that he needed to practice for the playoffs that weekend. It was a bit of misdirection, but dangling baseball in front of him was the only way I could get him to stay.

I picked up some doughnuts downtown and made my way to Sammy's house.

She answered the door in midknock. It was pretty clear she was still pissed off at me. She said nothing, just stood there staring at me.

"Um, hey," I said, not sure how to handle silence.

Nothing.

"I, I wanted to come talk and…."

"So talk."

Going to be one of those kinds of talks.

"I was an asshole and completely rude to you. You were right; Jeremy was the kind of person that club was made for, and I shouldn't have chased him off. You were my friend, and I should have listened to you, but I was too busy freaking out over college and Brad and everything. I forgot what all this was about."

It was a lot to say in one breath.

"And I brought doughnuts," I added.

She sighed and looked away for a second, trying to compose her thoughts. "Look, Kyle, I don't think I can do this anymore. You and Jeremy, you're, like, the exact same type of person in a lot of ways. One of them is how you treat your friends. I wasn't your sidekick, wasn't your little helper. I was supposed to be your friend and an equal, and when push came to shove, you treated me no better than Jeremy did. So fine, I accept your apology. But I don't think I can be friends with people who treat me like that anymore."

I wished I could argue with anything she said, but I couldn't.

"You're right, and I'm sorry," I admitted, feeling so guilty for doing that. "You shouldn't be treated like that, and if you ever give me the chance again, I never will." It was super-awkward as neither one of us commented. Finally I handed the doughnuts over to her and mumbled, "Sorry."

I practically ran away from her house. I didn't expect her to call after me and tell me to stop.

Turns out I was right—she didn't.

The next stop on my redemption tour of Foster was Tyler's store. I was hoping Matt would be there too so I could apologize to both of them at the same time. I'm pretty sure I didn't make the best of first impressions, so I needed to let him know I wasn't always a judgmental prick.

When I walked in, I saw the two of them behind the counter in a playful embrace, laughing. I paused as I wondered if it was too late to back out.

"Kyle?" Tyler asked as I began to backpedal.

"Oh, hey, Mr. Parker, you look busy…," I began to explain, but he shook his head.

"Come in. Matt just dropped by to have lunch."

Matt had moved away from Tyler, like he was embarrassed to have been caught in a public display like that. It was weird because everyone knew they were gay and dating now, so why hide? I shook it off because it was none of my business, and even if it was, I would have no clue of how to fix it.

"I wanted to come by and say sorry," I said, coming all the way into the shop. "I said some horrible things, and I wanted you to know I didn't mean them."

Tyler smiled. "Sure you did, but it's okay. We all say things we regret when angry. Apology accepted."

That was one.

I looked over at Matt and said, "And I wanted to say to you, I get it." He looked confused. "I understand why you said what you did. If someone came at Brad like that, I would have gone at him with a bat. You were just protecting what you love."

It was hard to judge his feelings by his face, but he didn't seem pissed. Tyler nudged him, and Matt rolled his eyes and said, "And I apologize for being a huge asshole. Foster has changed a lot since I left. Still not used to not making waves."

"Foster's changed?" I asked, surprised. "Seems like it's trapped in amber to me."

"That's 'cause you're a kid...." I gave him a look. "No, that's 'cause you're young. Nothing moves fast enough for you. When you get older, you realize that you'd pay cash money for the world to stop spinning. Even if it was for a day."

I understood what he was saying, but it didn't sound like anything I would ever feel. I felt like I was like a hundred years old and getting older every day I was forced to live in this town. If I had one of those silver cars from *Back to the Future* or a police box, I would have just jumped past this part of my life and got to the next one. But I was here to make amends, not debate Tyler's boyfriend on the concept of linear time.

"So again, I am a horrible little brat and very sorry," I said, giving them a half bow and a flourish with my hand. They both laughed, and I felt the tension leave the room.

"So, Brad nervous about the playoffs?" Matt asked while Tyler got us all Cokes from the back.

I sighed, glad to be able to talk to someone about this. "He's gone all protective den mother on me since the shooting. Like I'm made of glass or something."

"That's not it at all," Matt said with infuriating certainty. I arched an eyebrow at him, but the fact I was trying to be extra nice Kyle stopped me from commenting he didn't know a damn thing about Brad. Seeing my disbelief, he elaborated. "He's not afraid you're made out of glass. He's afraid he is, and if he loses you again, he will shatter into a million pieces and just die. I saw him the day of the shooting. You aren't his crush, and you aren't his love. You're the center of his universe, the sun he orbits around, and if you were gone, he'd just go flying out into the dark, never to be seen again."

My mouth dropped a little because it was the most romantic thing I had ever heard, and coming out of his mouth, it sounded so... matter-of-fact.

"Don't kid yourself, Kyle," he said in a softer tone. "There are guys out there who search their entire life to find the person who makes them whole. Rogue planets that no one can see because the sun doesn't shine on them anymore. Life, like space, is a big place, and the odds of you hitting something else is so remote, it isn't worth mentioning. So don't take what you guys have for granted. It's the most important thing in the universe."

Tyler walked out with the Cokes, and Matt's whole posture changed. I saw the serious mask slide down over his face. He sat up straighter. I didn't get it until Tyler handed him the Coke and gave him a smile. I could see their fingers touch as they passed the bottle and the way Matt smiled back at him.

Suddenly I got it. Tyler was his sun.

It wasn't obvious, but his eyes lingered when Tyler walked away, and his entire posture leaned toward Tyler. From the outside you'd think Matt was the one in charge, since he was so aggressive to defend Tyler, but that was the illusion. Where Tyler went, Matt would follow, and neither one would ever question it.

Tyler handed me the Coke, and I understood Brad a little bit more.

Matt took a drink and asked me, "So, not that I'm complaining, but what brought about this whole mea culpa?" Tyler gave him a questioning look, and Matt added, "It's a religious thing." Satisfied, Tyler went back to his Coke.

I explained to them my whole tour of apology and that they were one stop in many.

"So who's your next victim?" Tyler asked.

"Robbie."

No one talked for a while.

"Be careful," Tyler warned. "He's been in a bad place for a long time. I don't think this whole shooting thing went down well with him."

Matt gave him a quizzical look. "Did it go down well with anyone?"

"You know what I mean. Robbie has… he's lost a lot, and when faced with losing more, he just shuts down. So if he's snippy, it isn't you."

I finished my Coke and handed the empty bottle over. "Well, no time like the present. Wish me luck."

I had a feeling I was going to need it.

WHEN I got to Twice Upon a Time, I wondered if it was even open. The blinds were still closed, and the sign hadn't been turned over. But Robbie's car was in the parking lot, so he had to be there at one point. I rapped on the window a few times before the door cracked open.

"Why aren't you in school?" he asked like a bouncer at a speakeasy.

"Because a guy pointed a gun to me," I quipped back. "I have a feeling if I'd been winged, I wouldn't have to show up for the rest of the year."

Robbie's voice sounded darker than normal. "Don't joke about that." He opened the door a little more. "Come in before someone sees you and thinks I'm open."

"Why aren't you open? I mean, it's…." And I froze.

Half the clothes were missing from the racks, and there were giant cardboard boxes scattered throughout. I looked around in amazement, and then I got a good look at him. His hair wasn't styled, and he hadn't shaved in a few days. He was dressed… well, not like he *normally* dressed. He was wearing *normal* jeans and a T-shirt that didn't have any rainbows or anything glittery.

"What's this?" I asked, worried.

"What's it look like?" he almost snarled at me. "If there's anything you want, better grab it before I pack it up, because once these boxes are sealed, not even Tyler Hoechlin could get me to open them." I gave him a look, and he half smiled. "Okay, maybe him, but you don't have a chance. So take now or forever hold your tongue."

"I don't understand…," I began to say, but he just kept talking.

"Think of it like an episode of *Supermarket Sweep* but without the shopping carts. The good stuff is over on the right, but you know the store well enough. Also—I think in the back—there might—"

"Robbie!" I shouted, trying to get him to stop. He glanced over at me and sighed. He looked exhausted, to be honest. "What's going on?"

He sighed and then sat down on the stool behind the counter. "I'm done, that's what's going on. Game over, exit stage left, th-th-that's all, folks." I was confused, and he asked dryly, "Which pop culture reference did you miss? *Aliens*, Snagglepuss, or Porky Pig? I swear, I don't even know what they're teaching you kids in school these days. In my day the classics were—"

"Robbie, seriously, what is—"

He slammed both fists down on the counter, and the glass cracked under his blow. "I'm not going to watch anyone else fucking die, okay?" I froze, not sure what to do. "I'm done with caring about people so I can just watch them die. I'm not burying anyone else in this town again. I've hit my corpse quota for this lifetime. Foster wins. It always does. I just wish I'd known that before I let Riley move back here."

He sounded so defeated, so unlike himself. I was terrified. There was no sarcasm, no biting jokes. He was just done. I had honestly never heard him talk like this.

"When I was growing up, me and my sister played a lot of board games, mainly 'cause we were poor, and it was the cheapest way to spend an afternoon while my mom worked. I always liked Monopoly because I liked the different-colored money, but Nicole loved Clue. She would want to play that damned game over and over, each time someone new dying in a new room a new way. And I remember one day we were shuffling the cards and I said, 'You'd think after a while these fucking idiots would just not come to the house where all these murders happen. They're just asking for it.'"

I saw a tear fall down his cheek.

"We were just asking for it," he muttered, looking at his broken reflection in the glass.

My mind seized up for a moment, the mental equivalent of grinding gears, as I tried to figure out what to do.

"Well then, this is for the best," I said as nonchalantly as I could. "Some kids have to wait a lifetime to figure out what lies they were told growing up. I'm glad I got this out of the way now." He barely raised his head and looked at me. "I mean, if this didn't happen, then I would have graduated, moved to California, and thought this whole time everything I tried to do was worth something. Kelly, the school board, everything was worth something if someone got better from it. I mean, that is what you were trying to tell me at the Bear's Den, right? That if this town was going to be fixed, it had to be fixed from the inside, so you gave me this song and dance about how I needed to step up and do something."

He didn't say anything, but I could tell he was listening.

"Now I can leave and know that none of it matters. If it gets too hard, give up and run away. There is no fighting the good fight. There's just surrender."

"You don't know what you're talking about," he proclaimed darkly.

"Of course I don't, because I'm, what? Five and a half years old and know nothing? Also I've only known you fifteen seconds, so I couldn't know a thing about you, right? Did I miss anything? Well, you're wrong, Robbie, because I know everything I need to know about you. I know everyone thinks you stayed here because you wanted to wallow in your misery of losing Riley, that you were just a bitter old queen who hated the world. That's what they think, but they're wrong. You stayed here to make sure it didn't happen again. You gave up the rest of your life to make sure that what happened to Riley would never happen again."

I'm not even sure he was blinking.

"You want to play that whole diva card, but that's the same reason that Bruce Wayne dresses up as a bat every night. Because it conceals who you really are from everyone else. You hide away the real Robbie so they can't get to him, but the whole time, you're just looking for the next innocent to save from this town. You want to give up? Fine. You want to just walk away, good, but you don't get to walk away thinking it was for nothing. You were the one who put these thoughts about fixing Foster in my head, and that counts for something. No matter how hard you try to deny it."

I was panting like I had just run a marathon. I had no idea if anything I said got through to him. At this point I wasn't even sure if my words made sense to me.

Finally he croaked out a gruff, "You're wrong."

And I knew I hadn't gotten through.

"I am nothing like that. I'm not a superhero, Kyle. I'm just a man. A tired man who has gambled away too much and can't afford to lose more. You can look at it like I'm giving up, but all I'm doing is stepping away from the table before I lose everything."

"So is that what I should learn? That when it gets bad, to just walk away?"

He sighed and pulled at his hair in frustration. "Kyle, you can take anything you want from this. You're a big boy and can find your own messages in life. I'm not fucking Yoda."

I wanted to argue with him, wanted to debate his whole mindset with him, but something told me that it was a losing battle. He wasn't going to listen to me. My words were going to be wasted on him.

Luckily, I knew who he would listen to.

Once I took care of that, I had two more names on my list. The first was Jennifer, which I was going to have to do tomorrow since she was at school. The second happened to have the same address as me, so I knew where she lived.

I had no idea what I was going to say to her, but I did know that we needed to talk. Only someone who had lost their sense of smell would have missed the fact my mom was trashed during the shooting. Luckily for… well, I have no idea who it was lucky for, to be honest, so scratch that. In a twist of fate that had no real effect, good or bad, on someone's life, my mom was a pretty functional drunk. She could go from completely trashed to acting completely normal in no time flat. I suppose in some college-party type of movie that ability would be seen as wicked cool, but in real life it was scary as shit.

I guess if I was a guy who had sex with a pie or a Van-something-or-other, going from stupid drunk to sober would be awesome, 'cause then I could outwit the hapless dean who was out to close down our frat or whatever and get the upper hand. But as just a person, having someone around when it was almost impossible to know if she was under the effects of a mind-altering substance was terrifying. You walked around in a constant state of concern that the person who was supposed to provide food and shelter for you might actually be in the middle of a three-day drunk and had no real idea how long the milk had been bad or that we've been out of bread.

Also, if a guy comes to school and holds your son hostage in the library, being drunk is no state to be making choices.

It'd be easier to deal with if she was always a horrible person, because then I could hate her with impunity and move on. And don't give me that look of "But Kyle, you could never hate your mom. She gave birth to you." Don't kid yourself—that whole "they are family" argument doesn't fly with everyone. Sometimes the people in your family are just that, people. They aren't warm balls of love who you wish would stop being so mean to you. They are people you are legally required to live with until you can find a way out, and you can hate them as easily as you can hate a stranger.

In fact, it's easier to hate family than strangers, 'cause odds are the strangers haven't done nearly as much to you as so-called family has.

But see, my mom wasn't all bad, and that was the crux of my problem. It was like she was being held hostage by a much darker version of herself that came from drinking and drugs and all that crap. And there would be days, weeks, she would get free from her captors, and things around our house would change for the better, and all would be well. Except I had become used to the fact that it wouldn't last. Sooner or later she would be taken again, replaced by the drunk and uncaring woman who resisted the urge of being a mother so much that when I was younger, she had her boyfriends discipline me instead of her.

I'm sorry. I got off topic.

There needed to be a talk, but I had no idea what to say. Mom, don't be a drunk? Mom, stop killing yourself? Mom, go to hell? Yeah, it was a multiple-choice question that didn't have a right answer. I felt the familiar pain of my stomach souring as I approached the house, wondering if I should just drop it and let it go as I always did. I was almost out of this town, and with it, her drama.

But from past experience, it was pretty clear I never really did what I should do.

When I opened the door, I had that weird disorienting moment where you recognize everything around you, yet it all looks completely wrong. I knew I had walked into the right house because my key worked, but it couldn't be my house because Gayle was standing in my living room. I was so confused I looked back at the number on the apartment door and then back at her. I opened my mouth to ask a question, but it just kinda hung open as I gave her a quizzical look.

"Oh, you're home early," she commented, like her being in my house when I got home from school was normal, and me coming home early was the only abnormal thing about this situation.

My mom walked out of the bathroom. She was wearing clothes that, compared to her normal wardrobe, would be considered fancy. "Did you say something...?" she began to ask Gayle and then saw me. "Kyle? What are you doing home?"

"I live here," I finally blurted out. "Least I thought I did when I left this morning, but now I'm not sure."

Gayle chuckled. "The place doesn't look that different, does it?"

I had no idea what she was talking about until I looked around again. I had never seen our apartment this clean, ever. Everything was polished and sorted and just... not normal. Also, the ashtrays were gone, along with the bong that sat on the bookshelf like it was supposed to be a work of art or something. "What's happening?" I asked, sitting down before I passed out.

The two of them looked at each other, and Gayle nodded to my mom and said, "I think I'll make a cup of coffee while you guys talk."

My mom sat down on the couch, and I just stared at her as Gayle walked out.

"So… I've made a choice," my mom said hesitantly.

I held my hand up. "I swear to God, if you say you and her are dating or something, my head might explode."

She made a curious look like she had no idea where I had gotten that from and then laughed at my observation. "No, this is not me coming out. This is something else."

I edged forward as I waited for her to say something.

"You know how I've always had this…." And she hesitated. "Well, you know how…." She paused again.

"Your mom is an alcoholic," Gayle said, standing in the kitchen. I looked at her, and she added, "You do know you're going to have to stand up and say that in front of a lot more people, right?"

My mom closed her eyes as Gayle's words hit home.

Gayle came in and sat down as well. "Your mom is sick," she began to explain as she pulled her keys out of her pocket. "And she wants to get well. I'm helping her with that."

She handed me the keys, and I took them, not sure what I was supposed to do with them. Then I noticed what looked like a bronze poker chip hanging on the ring. There was a triangle on one side and some writing on the other. I looked back at Gayle, not understanding.

"That's a ten-year chip of sobriety. I'm a recovering alcoholic as well."

Gayle? Like my mom? Not a chance.

"She's going to be my sponsor," my mom tossed in. "I know I've let you down, but I need to change. I need things to…." She trailed off, and I could see the pain in her face. "I'm just tired of letting you down."

"I was going to take her to a meeting this afternoon before you got home from school," Gayle said, taking her keys back.

"Then go," I almost shouted. "I mean, yes. I want you to go and get better."

I could see my mom's eyes tearing up, and mine started to in sympathy. "I never meant to…," she began to say, but I stopped her because I didn't want to hear all that.

I'd heard everything she was going to say before, several times, in fact. She never meant to hurt me; she was trying her hardest; she was upset I was the one to suffer. I was done with her telling me stuff. I wanted to see her do something about it.

"Just go to your meeting," I said as firmly as possible. "We can settle the rest later."

I don't know if she got the hint or if she bought it, but either way, she looked at Gayle. "You ready?"

Gayle nodded and got up. When my mom walked into her room to grab her purse, she said quietly, "You don't have to forgive her." I looked at her, and she added, "Just because she is getting help doesn't mean everything she did wrong is ignored. You have a right to be mad. This doesn't take that away."

"But if I don't, I'm a dick, right?" I asked her, not even realizing how mad I really I was.

"No," she answered. "You're a human being who has been hurt. You have the right to feel any way you want."

Words would not form in my head, which was good because my mom walked out and asked Gayle if she was ready. "I'll be back at three thirty," she said as they walked to the door. "You going to be okay?"

I nodded as they walked out.

What the hell just happened?

From the window I watched them drive away, wondering if this actually meant something or was just the latest in a long line of disappointments. Either way, it was out of my hands for right now.

WHEN SCHOOL got out, Brad came by, and we stayed in my room and pretended to do homework, but mostly made out on my bed and then lay there just enjoying being together again. It was weird because all the sexual energy I had before we broke up was still there, but there was a calmness now. Like just lying on him and feeling him run his fingers through my hair was as, if not more, important as before. Don't get me wrong, if my mom wasn't in the kitchen, making dinner, I would have jumped his bones something bad, but lying on his chest listening to his heartbeat was just as satisfying.

"I missed this," he said after a long stretch of comfortable silence.

"Me too," I said, clinging to him as only howler monkeys are capable of.

"So you're going to school tomorrow, right?" he asked, trying to be as nonchalant as he could be. Luckily I spoke fluent Brad.

"What's up?" I asked, knowing he was up to something.

"What?" he asked, trying to be, like, fifty times more innocent than he was. "It's just a question."

This is why I will never worry about him cheating on me. If he did, it would be so obvious that I'd know before he even opened his mouth. "You don't just ask questions," I said, sitting up.

"Sure I do, all the time. How are you? What's up? How you been? Do you know where the bathroom is? See? I am Question Guy."

I stifled my laughing as best as I could. "You're up to something. I don't trust you."

The smile went away from his face, and he looked at me dead serious. "Yes, you do."

He was right. I did.

"You're right. I do."

His smile came back, and he kissed me, and I felt the world move beneath me. I don't know how he did that. I just hoped he'd never stop doing it.

THE NEXT morning I sought out Jennifer before class started. I needed to clear things up with her before the guilt caught up with me and hacked me up into little pieces like the horror-movie monster it was. I found her by her locker, changing out her books from the ones she brought home to the ones she needed first period. She smiled at me when I walked up, which was a good sign.

"So I'm a dick," I said outright.

"I don't completely disagree," she said, still smiling.

"And I treated you horribly and should have never done that."

"Go on."

"And… um, I'm sorry?" I added, not sure what she wanted.

"And?" she prompted me.

"And I should eat a bug?" I tried.

"And?" she repeated.

"I don't know what you want to hear," I finally admitted.

"And I was being a tight-ass overreacting about one of my best friends hearing about my sex life, and that I should try to remember that Jennifer is always right, and Kyle is mostly wrong."

"I am not saying that," I said, grinning myself.

"Oh yes you are," she said, closing her locker door. "Or I will go into messy detail about your sex life to anyone and everyone who can hear me."

"You wouldn't," I said, not sure if she was joking.

"Oh, I would," she answered, loving this. "Messy and graphic detail."

"You don't have that kind of detail. I know Brad didn't tell you all that."

She shrugged and began to walk away. "Who cares? I'll make it up. You just know they'll believe me."

"Jennifer, please don't."

She paused and looked back, bursting into laughter. "Oh God, Kyle, you are so wound up. I am not going to do that. Apology accepted. A wise person once told me we all get one free crazy, and you used yours. All is forgiven."

And just like that, a little of the guilt was gone.

"Sammy isn't talking to me," I told her as we walked across the quad.

"She's in a bad place, Kyle. She trusted Jeremy, and Kelly happened. She trusted you, and you ended up snapping at her. She trusted Jeremy again, and he almost killed people. I'm willing to bet she isn't talking to anyone."

It made sense but didn't go far in making me feel any better.

Brad met us on the music hall steps, a Cheshire cat grin on his face. "Morning, guys," he said, leaning over and kissing me.

I looked at Jennifer. "Do you have any idea what he is up to? Because it's starting to worry me." Jennifer looked at him, and he mouthed a word at her. Her eyes got wide, and then she looked to me and then to him.

"Seriously? You're going to do that?" He nodded. "Today?" He nodded again, his smile getting even wider.

"Okay, now this is just mean," I protested, but neither one seemed to care.

"Make sure he's in place?" Brad asked her. "If it's not, like… a thing…."

What the hell was going on?

"No, it isn't a thing, dumbass. I'll make sure he is there," she said, grinning at me like a hungry cat would grin at a delicious-looking bird.

"Awesome," he said, almost jumping up in excitement. "This is going to be wicked." He pecked my cheek again. "I have to get shit ready. See you guys later." Before I could stop him, he waved and took off across the quad.

I looked at her. "You're really not going to tell me anything?"

She let out a laugh the Joker would be proud of. "Oh hell no. This is too good to spoil."

I hated everyone.

I SAT through three periods, wondering if I should just go home before whatever this was could explode. I trusted Brad. What I didn't trust was the rest of the school. Whatever Brad was planning could be made horribly wrong by just one asshole, and we all knew that.

Yet I stayed because if I left, Brad would never forgive me.

As I walked out, Jennifer was there, waiting.

"Any chance you're going to give me a heads-up?" She shook her head. "Oh, come on." I was whining now, literally three-year-old baby not wanting to go to bed whining. "I'd tell you."

She laughed evilly. "Then you're an idiot, because if you knew what was about to happen and didn't let me get blindsided by it, then you have no idea how friendship works."

None of that made sense at all.

She began to walk us toward the student union. I stopped walking. "We aren't going in there," I said firmly.

She reached back and grabbed my arm. "Oh yes we are."

I swear that girl is surprisingly strong, because she pulled me into the building like I was a rag doll. The noise of the place was thunderous, and I was instantly reminded of why I didn't eat in there. No one even gave us a second look, but I still couldn't help but feel like I was in enemy territory. She began to drag me through the crowd, heading right to a table filled with the most popular girls in school. I really expected one of them to scream "No, you can't sit with us," even though I wasn't wearing sweatpants.

"Nononono," I pleaded as she pulled us over to the table and sat down. She looked at the seat next to me like she was daring me to run. I slowly sat down as all the girls stopped talking and looked at us.

I looked around the lunchroom in confusion. This had to be a mistake.

Of course they weren't going to talk to me, and what in the world would I say to them? "Hey, so you guys make anyone feel inferior or fat lately?"

So I just sat there, fumbled with my tie, and waited for Brad to come and save me.

"You know, I've seen that look before," Jennifer said casually. I gave her a confused look, and she went on. "That look on your face is the same one I've seen in history books of people waiting to get their head cut off."

"Really?" I asked her, raising an eyebrow. "You've read a lot of guillotine fan fiction in your time?"

She laughed and actually snorted before she covered her mouth.

One of the other girls looked over at her and then to me and gave us a stink look. Jennifer noticed and got in her face. "Hey, Amanda, you ever get that prescription for your cream filled? I know how red it gets if you let it slide."

Amanda looked away in disgust. The way her face got red pretty much confirmed that whatever dirt Jennifer had on her was pretty dead-on. "Any more of you bitches want to look over here?" she said louder. "Because trust me, I have no shame."

They rustled in their seats, and all I could picture were cartoon chickens sitting on their eggs. I bit my bottom lip to stop myself from laughing like a loon.

"See?" she said to me quietly. "It's not all that bad."

"What am I even doing here?" I asked her, sounding way too much like a drama queen.

I was about to lunge at her to make her talk when the lights in the lunchroom dimmed. There were nervous giggles all over the room, and the girls sitting next to us felt like they were vibrating in their chairs. I looked over to Jennifer in panic as Josh Walker half strutted over to our table. "Can you guys bring your chairs over here, please?" he asked, gesturing to the center of the room. I didn't move as the other girls got up and dragged their chairs with them.

"Come on," she said, nudging me. "Get over there."

I refused to move and literally grabbed the sides of my chair with a dead man's grip. Josh looked over at Jennifer and added, "You too."

She froze, one hand paused over her chest as she pointed to herself. "Me?"

He nodded and walked behind me. "Yeah, both of you," he said, pushing my chair across the floor like I weighed nothing. I put my feet down and tried to stop him, but it was useless. He pushed my chair right next to the other girls.

Finally the other brain cells in my head got some oxygen and reminded me I could always stand up and walk away. I was about to when Jennifer put her chair down next to mine and grabbed my hand.

Hard.

"Do not leave me," she said in a voice that would have made Darth Vader pause.

I slowly sat back down and forced myself not to whimper as she crushed my hand.

Seeing we were in place, Josh nodded and walked away. I looked over at Jennifer. "What the hell is going on?"

She shook her head slowly as she talked to herself. "Who would even be asking me?"

"Ask? Ask you what? Who is asking who?" I was babbling now.

I could hear the PA system turn on, and a guitar strummed a few notes. I instantly knew the song. It was that One Direction song. Though not a fan, it was impossible not to find it catchy as hell. The crowd began to talk among themselves as the words started.

Tony came out from behind the curtain, wearing his letterman jacket and a pressed pair of khakis. His hair was styled, and I had to admit, he looked good. He started lip-synching the song as he walked out. The second line brought Josh out singing. The third was Brad. They were also wearing jackets and nice slacks. The crowd held its breath as Cory walked out with Adrian right behind him.

They lined up next to each other as they got to the chorus.

As they sang that we lit up their world like nobody else, they began to dance. It was a boy-band routine that they had obviously practiced more than once as they began to grind and move to the music. I went pale as I realized what was going on.

I was having a *Glee* stroke.

I knew it would happen someday; it was inevitable, I suppose. My brain was probably dying, and of course it compensated by making people sing and dance in public. I looked around, and no one seemed bothered by the fact that the five most popular guys in school were suddenly dancing and singing in the lunchroom. In fact, they were clapping and singing along. I was the only one who seemed shocked.

No, scratch that, Jennifer was looking forward with her mouth half-open like she was not believing what she was seeing either.

"You can see them, right?" I asked her. "They're singing and dancing?"

She didn't look away but nodded slowly.

"Oh, thank God," I sighed as I realized I wasn't brain-dead and stuck in a musical.

The second chorus started, and one by one, the guys peeled off from their line dance and moved toward us. Tony moved toward the first girl, and I dimly realized she was his girlfriend. Adrian moved toward Amanda, and Cory moved toward a redheaded girl sitting next to me. Brad gave me a huge smile and began to move toward me, and I felt like I was going to throw up.

"Oh, come on," Jennifer said under her breath as Josh moved toward her.

I wished I could do something for her, but I was in a blind panic as I watched my boyfriend dance in front of me like he was Justin Timberlake's stand-in.

"What are you doing?" I asked in a squeak that was barely above a whisper.

He just looked at me and said, "You don't know you're beautiful. That's what makes you freaking hot to me."

They took three steps back and went into their dance for the second chorus, giving Jennifer and me time to freak. "What is going on?" I asked, grabbing her arm.

She looked over to me. "You really have no idea?"

I shook my head and forced myself not to scream. *Do I look like I have an idea?*

"This is how they ask their dates to prom. It's a tradition that really sucks," she said, glancing back at Josh, who was singing to her.

They got to the middle of the song, which consisted of a lot of na-na-nas, and they walked toward us again. The song got to the point where it slowed down, and they all got to one knee. Brad grabbed my hand and gave me that "no worries" grin. "Go to the prom with me?" he asked, breathing hard.

Time slowed as I looked down at him, my heart bursting with love and my brain screaming in shock. I felt my face burn from embarrassment as I saw he had his ring out. I knew he was asking me to prom, but he looked like he was asking me to marry him, and in that moment I froze.

"Kyle?" he asked. I looked up. "Go with me?"

I nodded mutely, my eyes tearing up. I gave him a small smile as he slid the ring on my finger.

I swore I would never again take it off.

His face exploded into a smile as he leaned in and kissed me. I barely noticed that the other guys were kissing their girls too.

Including Jennifer and Josh.

I pulled away from the kiss and looked over at them. Brad followed, and we watched them kiss. And kiss. And kiss.

Everyone in the lunchroom cheered and clapped as the other guys stood up, pumping one fist up in victory. Brad was still kneeling, looking over at Jennifer and Josh still kissing. Slowly the rest of the crowd noticed too, and the room got quiet as the kiss extended into something epic. The song went on and on, but no one was singing. They were all looking at the two of them. The song ended, and they continued to lock lips.

"Wow," Brad said as the kiss went on and on.

Finally they stopped. Josh pulled his face back. "So that's a yes?"

Jennifer, who looked like she had just been mugged, nodded with wide eyes. He jumped to his feet and screamed a rowdy "*Yahoo!*" and the room went wild.

Brad pulled me to my feet and wrapped his arms around me as everyone celebrated around us. "I hate you," I said to him before he could kiss me.

"Prove it," he said, leaning in to call my bluff.

How could I not kiss him back?

"How long have you been planning this?" I asked him after catching my breath.

"Since I was a freshman," he said with a goofy grin on his face.

"You've been waiting since you were a freshman to sing and dance for me?" I asked him, shaking my head.

"Oh that, no, that has been since I gave you my ring before break." He leaned in, and his voice dropped to an almost whisper. "But I've been waiting for you all my life, so does that answer your question?"

I nodded and just enjoyed the moment as best I could.

"Did you know about this?" Jennifer asked, shattering the moment.

We looked over and saw Josh with his arms around her waist, a look of complete love in *his face*. She was pointing at *his face*.

"I had an idea," Brad admitted. "But some things are best done as a surprise."

Josh kissed her neck, and she her closed her eyes for a moment and then shook the feeling off. She moved out of his embrace. "Look, pal, I said yes to the prom, not to be your piece of ass. You wanna be my boyfriend, you have to earn that."

Josh nodded so earnestly I almost lost it right there.

"You will wine, dine, and court me to the best of your ability. If you don't make a complete ass of yourself, then I might go out with you. If you do, then we are prom dates and nothing more. Got it?" She sounded like a drill sergeant, which seemed to be exactly what Josh needed, since he nodded again and looked more than ready to follow her orders. "So… just keep that in mind."

"Can I kiss you again?" he asked, and I covered my mouth to stop from laughing out loud.

"Maybe," she answered, a small smile crossing her face. "That's on a case-by-case basis, so don't push it." He nodded again, but the look of devotion in his eyes never wavered.

He had it bad for her.

"So we should go together," Jennifer said, looking at us. "Safety in numbers and all that."

"We can get a limo," Brad suggested.

"The town is, like, five blocks wide," she said in disbelief. "Even if we could get a limo all the way out here, where would we go with it?"

"Limos are cool," Josh added.

She looked at him. "No, they aren't. They're big cars that are nothing but eyesores unless you're driving in one."

Almost immediately his face changed, and he looked at us. "Yeah, limos are lame, Brad. Bad idea."

"Oh God," Brad said, covering his eyes with his hand. "This is going to be fun."

We spent the rest of lunch making plans for the prom. Jennifer said we should all have matching colors, which confused me since she was the only one who was going to be in a dress. I got worried for a moment. "Wait, how am I going to rent a tux?"

"I got it," Brad said casually.

"You're going to pay for both of ours? That's not fair."

He shrugged. "I already own one, so it's just a matter of getting you one."

"What kind of teenager owns a tux?" I asked incredulously.

He looked a little embarrassed. "My dad bought it for me freshman year for parties."

"I don't need you to rent my tux," I declared, even though I badly needed him to rent my tux. "I'll get one on my own."

How, I had no idea.

We spent the last of that lunch and the next few days making plans and generally enjoying ourselves. I was going to head to fifth period when Jennifer pulled me aside. "Nice speech, but we both know a tux is out of your price range. You thinking Robbie?"

I froze, not sure what to tell her. Robbie always seemed so damn private. I'm not sure he would appreciate me passing it around he was in a funk. But on the other hand, Jennifer had known him longer than I had, so maybe she could help. I decided to split the difference and tell half the truth. "I was, but I hate asking him for so much stuff." I tried to sound as pathetic as possible.

"Screw that. Come on, let's go ask him," she declared as she headed toward the parking lot.

"What about prom committee?" I asked her, following behind.

She rolled her eyes. "Ugh, please. We've had everything planned for months. All we do is sit in there and bitch. It's a waste of time."

It did sound like a waste of time, but I wasn't going to say that. Instead I pulled out my phone and sent a quick text before getting into her car.

Robbie's car was there, even though the place looked like it was completely closed. I let her go up and knock on the door as I stood behind a little bit. I wasn't sure he wanted to see me all that much. After the fifth knock the blinds pulled back, and his face peered out from the other side of the glass. He looked even worse than before. He still hadn't shaved, his clothes looked slept in, and his hair didn't look anything like the old him since there was no product in it. The worst part was the dark rings under his eyes that made it look like he hadn't slept in weeks.

He looked at Jennifer like he didn't even know who she was, and then I saw his eyes flicker past her to look at me. I could almost hear him sigh through the glass as his head vanished and the door unlocked. Jennifer looked at me, wondering if that was an invitation in. I nodded, knowing it wasn't going to get any nicer than that. When we walked in, the entire shop was packed up. There were empty fixtures on the wall and racks in a corner, but minus a couple of things on the ground, it was all gone.

"What's going on?" she asked.

"Okay, please," he answered, retreating behind the counter. "Like Encyclopedia Brown over there didn't tell you what was going on?"

Jennifer looked back at me and I shrugged, feigning innocence.

"Are you moving?" she asked him.

"I don't know," Robbie replied, putting his head down on his arms. "I have no answers for you, Jennifer."

I tapped her on the shoulder and gestured we should leave. She shook her head.

"Brad asked Kyle to the prom," she announced like it was actual news.

"Of course he did," Robbie muttered, still facedown on the counter.

"And Kyle doesn't have anything to wear," she added.

Robbie slowly looked up, and I knew this was a bad idea.

"Oh, Kyle needs something," he said, sarcasm dripping from his tongue. "I didn't know it was an emergency. Kyle needs something, so let me put my midlife…." He paused and reflected on it. "My early midlife crisis on hold so I can help him. What are you, a twenty-eight waist? Thirty-two inseam? By all means, let me gather some mice up and get them to working. Any color you have in mind? Particular style? Please, allow me to be your own personal sweatshop." I said nothing as he came from around the counter. "Or wait, I have a better idea. Why don't I just find something of Riley's, and you can…."

"Robbie!" a voice bellowed from behind me, and I might have pissed myself a little.

Tyler was standing there, looking six different types of angry.

Told you I knew who Robbie would listen to.

"He goes five years without even acknowledging my existence and now twice in the same month," Robbie bitched, turning away from us. "I think I liked being ignored."

"You kids get on out of here," Tyler warned more than said to us. "This is personal."

"Take it easy on him," I whispered to Tyler.

From the way he glared at me, it was pretty obvious that he was not going to be easy on him.

"Come on, Jennifer," I said, grabbing her hand. "Let's go." We fled out the door like they were going to have a shoot-out.

I had a feeling it wasn't going to be that different from one.

"What was all that about?" she asked me once we were in the car.

I considered telling her but then thought better of it. If Robbie hadn't told her the story of Riley by now, he didn't want her to know. It wasn't my place to spread it around. Instead I gave her a shrug and said, "Looks like typical Foster drama to me."

I don't think she bought it completely, but she knew I wasn't going to share any more.

THAT NIGHT as Brad and I pretended to do homework at my place, he paused our kissing and asked, "So am I allowed to buy our tickets to the prom?"

"Depends," I said, leaning into him and gnawing on his neck.

"O-on?" he asked, his voice quivering from my mouth.

"If you're going to expect me to put out." I pushed him back onto his bed.

"I wouldn't expect you to…," he began to say and then saw me shaking my head.

"Wrong answer," I said, giving him an evil smile.

It took him a few seconds, but his face brightened, and he grinned back at me. "I would totally expect you to put out, then."

"Good," I said, glancing over at the door to make sure it was locked.

"What time is your mom going to be home?" he asked.

"Shut up and get naked," I said breathlessly.

He did exactly that.

THAT MONDAY, tickets to the prom went on sale. There was a line around the student union as everyone gathered up to grab tickets. I stood with Brad and Josh, the latter of whom had spent the entire weekend with Jennifer, and if anything, seemed more entranced by her than before. He kept going on and on and on about how she smelled and her laugh, and I saw Brad nod in agreement and then roll his eyes to me when Josh looked away. I wondered if I looked that goofy when I talked to someone about Brad. Most likely.

"And she does this squeak…," Josh began to say, and Brad's head snapped toward his friend like it was a martial arts movie.

"Say what?" he asked gruffly.

"I mean…." Josh was getting red now. "Oh damn, I completely forgot you used to be with her," he stammered.

"You got her to squeak?" Brad asked, not seeming angry but more confused.

Josh nodded.

Brad glanced down at Josh's jeans and then back to his face. "Did you… you know?"

Josh looked down in curiosity to what Brad was looking at. It took him a couple of seconds to realize what Brad was saying. "Oh. Oh no, we didn't do that," Josh answered, half laughing.

"Then how… I mean, why did she squeak?" Brad asked.

Josh put his hand up to his mouth and stuck his tongue between his fingers.

"Oh God," I cried, looking away but knowing I was never going to get that image out of my head. "Why did you tell us that?"

Josh laughed at my squeamishness. "Your boyfriend asked, dude. Trust me, you can be crazy in bed and all, but if you don't have any cunnilingus skills, you are a one-trick pony." I saw Brad's face turn a little pale, and I didn't feel so bad. "Oh, come on, you guys have to know this," he joked. "I mean, you guys have to at least have rimmed each other, right?"

"I withdraw the question," Brad said sternly. "Just please stop talking."

"Seriously? Oh, you guys have to try that. There is nothing like it in the world. Trust me," he said, slapping me on the chest, laughing.

"When were you rimmed?" I asked, not even sure how we got on this topic.

Josh held a finger up in front of my face and waggled it back and forth. "A gentleman does not kiss and tell."

"You just told us you went down on Jennifer," I shot back. "That is almost the very definition of kissing and telling."

Josh paused and thought about it. "Damn, you're right." He looked back to Brad. "Forget all that. We watched movies all weekend."

I rolled my eyes at Brad, who turned back to the line.

"Man, for gay guys, y'all are prudes," Josh complained to no one in particular.

When we got to the front of the line, Josh saw Jennifer sitting at the table collecting money with the other girls from the prom committee. He froze as he realized how close she had been to him bragging.

"So you think she'll mind if I ask what made her squeak?" I whispered to Josh.

"Dude," he said, looking back at me with wild eyes. "Be cool, Kyle, come on."

I laughed and shook my head. "I couldn't do that, 'cause if I did, she would just kill you. Not Tase you, just straight out kill you." I saw the look on his face when he realized I was telling the truth. "So maybe you should learn not to brag about what you did last weekend, huh?"

He nodded mutely as we got up to the front of the line.

Josh handed his money over to Jennifer. "Two, please," he said with a huge smile on his face.

She gave him a sly grin and took his money. "You coming over to watch a movie tonight?"

I slapped my hand over my mouth to stop from laughing.

Josh slammed his foot down on my foot as he nodded to her. "Oh yeah, anything you want to see."

She handed the tickets over and gave me a weird look. "What's so funny?"

I shook my head violently as I tried my best to stop laughing.

As luck would have it, fate was about to help me out on that real fast.

"What the fuck?" I heard Brad exclaim loudly. He was standing in front of one of the other girls at the table, who had a pretty ugly smile on her face. "Since when?"

She crossed her arms over her chest. "Doesn't matter," she said. "It's the rules."

"What is?" Jennifer asked her.

"She says I can't buy tickets for two guys," Brad explained.

"And if he buys two tickets and shows up with him," she said, looking at me, "then they will be turned away with no refund."

Jennifer's face got serious fast. "What the fuck are you talking about, Stacy?"

"It's school rules," she said smugly.

"Since when?" Jennifer growled at her.

Stacy looked over at one of the other girls. "Since last week, right, Patty?" Patty nodded at her and smiled. Stacy looked back at Jennifer. "Since last week, you know. When you decided not to show up."

"This is bullshit," Brad complained, getting loud.

Of course, that was when Mr. Raymond appeared. Speak of the devil and he shall appear with cloven hoofs.

"We have a problem here?" he asked out loud, but he was looking right at me.

"Since when can't I bring my date to prom?" Brad asked.

Raymond looked back at him. "You are more than welcome to take your date, Mr. Graymark, as long as that date is of the opposite sex. This is out of my hands. The prom committee voted on it themselves. I have no power over it."

Such bullshit.

"You are really going to do this?" I asked him, ignoring everything else around me.

He looked back at me, and I could see the gloating in his eyes. "I am not doing a thing, Mr. Stilleno, but if I was, I would say you were warned. Every action has a consequence. Try to remember that in the future."

I felt the familiar fire in my chest as the indignity of this shit rained down on me.

And then I just felt tired.

"Just fuck it, Brad," I said, looking away from the petty man. "It's not worth it."

Brad looked at me, shocked. "What? You're going to just take that?"

I sighed and shook my head. "I'm tired of fighting."

And I was. Raymond had won.

Brad

JOSH TURNED off the music and looked at me harshly. "Dude, do you want to be the Joey of the group?"

We were alone in my garage as he tried to teach me how to dance, and I had no idea what that meant.

Before I could tell him that, he shook his head and tossed me a towel. "Joey Fatone? Of *NSYNC?" Still clueless. "Jesus, every boy band has a member who can't do the dances as well as the others. Joey Fatone of *NSYNC, Brian Littrell of Backstreet Boys, Donnie Wahlberg for New Kids on the Block. Do you want to be that guy?"

I wiped the sweat off my brow. "I'm more concerned about your encyclopedic knowledge of all things boy band."

He gave me a look. "What's wrong with that?"

"You're straight?"

He flipped me off and cued the One Direction CD up again. "You ready for this?"

I tossed the towel onto my garage floor. "No, but let's do it."

We had been practicing this stupid dance for almost a week now, and I wasn't getting any better at it. The Foster High tradition of the sports guys doing a song and dance to ask their dates out to prom was legendary, and honestly, I never gave it a second thought. If I knew it was going to be this bad, I would have started practicing when I was a freshman. On the other hand, Josh seemed to be the world's youngest male stripper by the way he bucked and gyrated effortlessly to the music. If I hadn't met Kyle, I would have found the sight of him dancing around my garage shirtless and sweaty more than a distraction.

Now he was just another guy who wasn't as hot as Kyle to me.

There were five of us who were going to sing this year, and we decided on "You Don't Know You're Beautiful" because it seemed to be the easiest to dance to, and everyone knew it. It took Josh about an hour to teach the other guys the steps we were going to do in front of what promised to be the whole school. A week later, I was no closer to getting it than I had the day he showed me.

I went to try to spin and my feet got tangled up and I almost fell over. The only thing that stopped me was Josh grabbing me before I hit the ground. "Wow, you must suck in bed."

I pushed off him. "Hey, what the fuck does that mean?"

He chuckled and paused the music again. "You know the saying, if you want to know how a guy is in bed, watch him dance. I've seen you naked, so I can't imagine it can be all that pleasant."

I sat down to catch my breath. "Dude, do you even hear the words that come out of your mouth, or is it a straight shot from your brain to the outside world?"

He laughed at my criticism and grabbed a couple of waters out of the fridge. "Dude, no one cares what I say. I'm an idiot, remember? Besides, why can't I mention the fact I've seen your dick? We shower together, and I'm secure enough in my sexuality to say it's an impressive sight."

"Oh God, please stop talking," I pleaded, taking the water. "My boyfriend and me don't talk about our junk as much as you do."

"That's 'cause you two are insecure about your sexuality. You're both good-looking guys who should be proud of what you got."

"There is 'secure in his sexuality' and then there is 'confused.' You're skating that line, Josh."

He laughed and finished his water. "Nah, I already had my experimental phase, and it wasn't for me." He stood up and held out his hand. "You ready to do this?"

I took it and stood up. "You're really okay with just telling me you fooled around with a guy before?"

He took my empty bottle and shrugged. "Why not? Everyone does it, and you're gay. If I can't tell you, who can I tell?"

I could not believe he was so cool with it. "How did you even deal being Tony's friend for so long?"

He actually paused and thought about that for a second. "You don't know the *real* Tony. He has *real* problems at home, so he picks these stupid things to focus on. Like that whole thing with you and Kyle at the diner? That was all his dad. Tony could give a shit, but what was he supposed to do? Let his old man just stand there and look like a dick? You could tell his heart wasn't in it. He was ready to drop it until...."

And he stopped talking.

"Until Kelly attacked him at school," I finished for him.

Josh nodded. "That was why Tony went after Kelly after the video. Spray painting his truck and the dildos, that really didn't have anything to do with the gay thing—that was Tony trying to get him back for making him look the fool at school." His voice got really sad. "Can't help but wonder how it would have gone down if Kelly hadn't done that."

The mood was depressing as shit, so I decided to change it.

"So, we going to dance or what?"

He gave me a grin and moved toward the CD player. "Well, I'm going to dance. You're going to make a fool of yourself."

And he was right—I did.

So I asked Kyle to the prom, didn't fall on my face and crack my nose in front of everyone, and even managed to get him to wear my ring again. And Josh grew the balls to ask Jennifer out. All in all a good day. Which was canceled out by how horrible it was the day I tried to buy our tickets.

"Are you fucking kidding me?" I raged as the bitch behind the table told me I couldn't bring Kyle to the prom.

She gave me a sour look like she had never heard that word before. "I'm sorry, but those are the rules."

"What the fuck?" I made sure to use the word again just to piss her off. "Since when?"

She crossed her arms over her chest. "Doesn't matter. It's the rules."

Jennifer had been selling Josh his tickets and looked over. "What is?"

"She says I can't buy tickets for two guys," I explained.

"And if he buys two tickets and shows up with him," she said, looking at Kyle, "then they will be turned away with no refund."

I took a step back as I saw a bad look cross Jennifer's face. Every other time I had seen that look, someone was getting Tased. "What the fuck are you talking about, Stacy?"

They started to argue, but I watched Kyle's face. I kept waiting for him to jump in and say something, kept waiting for him to stand up for himself.

Instead he said nothing.

"This is bullshit," I complained, not just talking about the ticket thing. I looked over and saw Tony standing there off to the side. I expected to see a shit-eating grin on his face, but instead he was just watching everything. Scowling.

I had known these two broads for nearly forever, and I knew they didn't have the brains to pull something like this off, not over Jennifer. It wasn't until Mr. Raymond walked out that I understood what was really going on.

"We have a problem here?" he asked, but he was looking right at Kyle, who still hadn't said a word.

I moved a little in front of Kyle. "Since when can't I bring my date to prom?"

Raymond looked back at me, and I felt the urge to punch him pass through my body. "You are more than welcome to take your date, Mr. Graymark, as long as that date is of the opposite sex. This is out of my hands. The prom committee voted on it themselves. I have no power over it."

Lying piece of….

"You're really going to do this?" Kyle asked him, like they had been in the middle of a whole other conversation.

The urge to hit him grew as he said to Kyle, "I am not doing a thing, Mr. Stilleno, but if I was, I would say you were warned. Every action has a consequence. Try to remember that in the future."

This was it. This was when Kyle let him have it. I almost smiled as I felt it coming.

And then, out of nowhere, Kyle looked at me and said, "Just fuck it, Brad. It's not worth it."

I almost choked, I was so shocked. "What? You're going to just take that?"

He sounded so sad when he answered. "I'm tired of fighting."

And just like that, Mr. Raymond won.

He walked away as people behind us started to talk among themselves. No doubt laughing that the fags got what was coming to them once again. I caught up to Kyle. "Hey, we don't have to take that," I assured him. "That asshole can't just…."

He spun on me, and I could see he was on the verge of tears. "I don't want to go, Brad. Seriously, if every single thing in life is going to be a fucking fight, then

I'm done. It's a fucking dance with a bunch of assholes. I'd rather just stay home instead of forcing my way into my own prom." He wiped away an angry tear, and my brain erupted in fiery anger. "We're gone in a month. I just want to leave."

He walked away, but there was no way I was going to let this one go.

After practice, I headed over to Tyler's since Kyle said he needed some alone time after school. When I walked in, Tyler was in the middle of helping someone, so I went in the back and grabbed a Coke and tried to calm down some. Once I heard the customer walk out, I came back in and instantly started to complain.

"Do you know what they're doing to us now?"

He closed the cash register and sat down on the stool. "By 'us' you mean you and Kyle and not you and me, right? Because I'm sure no one is doing anything against you and me."

I went over everything he just said and shook my head in frustration. "I mean Kyle and me. Do you know what they're doing now?"

"'They' being?" Tyler asked.

"The school," I almost yelled. "They won't let us go to prom together."

His face got serious, and I could tell now he was paying attention. "They're what?"

"They said a guy and a guy can't go, and that if I buy tickets and take Kyle, they'll kick us out. Can they do that?"

I saw him open his mouth to answer no, but he paused. "I don't know," he finally admitted and pulled out his cell phone.

Twenty minutes later Matt was there, and he wasn't sure either. "I think they can," he answered after some thought. "I mean, I've heard them do it at other schools."

"That's crap," I spat, trying to find some way around this. "What did they do at the other schools?"

Matt was looking over something on his laptop. "Well, a couple got lawsuits brought against them. Others just had a gay prom for themselves at another location." He paused and then added, "But it's important to note that none of those kids actually got to go to their prom. These articles are more about what happened after."

"Why don't we do that?" Tyler suggested. "Have a gay prom the same night?"

I tried to keep the anger out of my voice. "So what, the entire school goes to their prom and, like, five people stand around and wish they were at the real thing? I don't want to force people to choose between going to their prom and making a statement." And I was suddenly starting to get why Kyle was tired of fighting all the time. "I really thought this shit was done with."

Matt closed his laptop. "I don't think you have many choices here, Brad. The only possible way this could get changed is if all the parents were to protest it, but we all know that for every family who would stand up against this, there are two ready to defend the school's choice. That's just how it is."

"Well, it fucking sucks," I said, not trusting myself to look at them.

"I took Kyle's mom to the prom," Tyler admitted. "Maybe you guys take friends and go as two couples? It's not perfect, but you aren't missing the prom, at least."

I understood what Tyler was saying, but I already knew Kyle's answer, as I asked that night.

"Do you know what would be worse than not being able to go to prom with you?" Kyle asked over the phone. "It would be going to the prom and not being able to dance with you. It's just a dance, Brad. I don't care anymore. I just want to graduate and leave, okay?"

It wasn't okay, but I let it go because it was obviously making him miserable, and I needed to focus on the last games of the year.

It was a four-day series of games at Round Rock that went from playoff to championship—if you got that far. We had been here before as a team, but this was my first time as a captain. I had seen a little game tape on the other teams, and we were in for a pretty serious fight. There's no such thing as lucky when you get this far. It all came down to blood, sweat, and determination. The entire game could simply come down to the team who wanted it more, since they were evenly matched in skills.

And I wanted it very bad.

We checked into our hotel and got our stuff stowed away for practice. Games started the next afternoon, which meant we had a couple of hours in the morning and then nothing but playing for our lives the next few days. I knew we could win this. I had no doubt that as a team we were the best there was this year. The key was keeping the team from turning confidence into cockiness.

That meant spending that night going over what we were still coming up short on and making the guys aware that the only way we were in this was if we all worked together. I'm pretty sure they just wanted to order room service and watch pay-per-view, but I kept them focused for most of the night, which made me feel a little better.

I was sharing a room with Josh, which meant I spent most of the night listening to him talk to Jennifer in a baby voice that made me want to claw my ears out. Luckily I had Kyle and FaceTime, which meant I could ignore that train wreck altogether.

"Is he talking like a baby?" Kyle asked me as I lay in the hotel bed with my headphones on.

I nodded and rolled my eyes. "Yeah. Lovely, isn't it?"

"We don't do that, do we?" he asked.

I had to pause and think about it. "Well, if we do, it's not in front of other people."

He nodded and smiled. "That works for me."

"When do you get here?" I asked him, knowing he was driving up with Tyler and his mom to watch the games.

"Tomorrow morning. We went and got food for tailgating before the first game. Are we really going to cook stuff and eat it in a parking lot?"

The look on his face was priceless. "Dude, tailgate food is the best," I tried to convince him. "Nothing else like it."

"Yes, there is. A ton of food is like it, except it's made inside, with washed hands and stuff."

That made me smile. "Trust me, when you take a bite of a tailgate hot dog, your life will change."

"Food poisoning?" he asked.

I burst out laughing.

"Hey, man," Josh said from the next bed. "Can you keep it down? People are trying to talk."

I glanced at Kyle, and he gave me that small grin of his back. Looking over at Josh, I said, "Oh, is wittle Joshy upset he can't hear his wuvey-dovey?"

I could hear Jennifer's voice scream from his phone. "You didn't say he was in the room with you!"

Josh immediately forgot me and tried to calm Jennifer down.

"You're bad," Kyle commented.

"So... lots of things we can do with a video phone," I said, arching an eyebrow at him.

He got red and looked around like there was someone in his room. "Brad, we can't... not over the phone."

"Wanna bet?" I said suggestively.

Which was when someone knocked on our door.

"Damn," I said, sitting up. "I'll call you back?"

"I'll see you tomorrow. I need to get some sleep so I can be awake when Tyler gets here."

"But what about the video phone?"

He winked at me. "Use your imagination." And he hung up.

Son of a bitch.

I adjusted myself as I opened the door.

Shayne Fuller was standing there.

There is no easy way to explain Shayne Fuller to you without sounding like I'm a stuck-up asshole, so let's just pretend you know me better and know I don't believe everything I'm about to tell you but am using it as reference so you can understand, okay?

Shayne Fuller was Granada's version of me.

We were the same age, grew up playing baseball against each other just about everywhere we went, and we were both playing our hearts out for our senior year. He was taller than me with darker hair, but we had that same build most baseball players had—part muscle, part lean runner, all of it necessary for what we need to do. Where my arms were big from batting, his looked like carved cables from continuous pitching. The only difference was that he wasn't gay, least as far as I knew. I mean, he had a girlfriend, but so did I for a few years, so what does that mean in the long run? Either way, he was what Kyle would call the Bizarro version of me, and he was knocking on my door.

"Hey, Shayne," I said as if we always talked instead of the three times we'd ever actually exchanged words.

"Hey, dude, have a second?"

He had that tone of voice that made you want to do what he said no matter what. It was the voice of a leader, of an alpha dog, and it was damn annoying because I didn't have it. People usually went along with what I said because they either liked me or liked what they thought I was, but it was rarely because of a commanding presence or anything. Shayne was the opposite. He was Granada's Captain America and would grow up to be a cop or a firefighter, and people would automatically do what he said even if he was wearing a T-shirt and jeans.

"Let me grab my coat," I said, realizing I had done exactly what he wanted without even asking why.

Josh looked at him in the door and then back to me. "You want some backup?" he asked quietly.

"Do you think he knocked at the door to invite me to get jumped?"

Josh had no answer for that. Instead he called out, "Take your phone just in case."

I shook my head and closed the door behind me. "Where we going?" I asked Shayne.

He looked both ways down the hall and said, "DQ is across the street?"

"Sure," I said, slipping my jacket on. I was expecting some version of trash-talking since Granada was in the playoffs as well. After all, the rivalry between our schools was pretty intense. There was no basis for it; it was just the way it had always been and most likely will always be in Foster.

We got in the elevator and headed down to the lobby. "Congratulations for getting here, by the way," he said absently.

"Um, thanks, you too, man." This didn't feel like trash-talking.

"You know it's going to come down to us, right? I've seen the same game tapes as you have. You're the main competition we have this year."

I nodded. "It'll be a good game."

He smiled as we got off in the lobby. "You can count on that."

We walked out of the hotel and crossed the street to Dairy Queen. We each ordered a sundae and sat on the benches out front. Neither one of us talked for a while as we consumed the ice cream. Finally he said, "I heard what happened."

I looked up at him, having no idea what he meant.

"About the prom thing. I heard what they did. That sucks, man."

"Yeah," I said bitterly, trying to have some form of a poker face. "Just more shit on top of a shitty year."

"Did you turn down A&M?" he asked, paying acute attention to my answer. "I heard rumors, but I want to hear you say it."

I finished my sundae and nodded. "Yeah, they wanted me to lie about being gay and all that. Was a whole set of things I could and couldn't do. So I told them to fuck off."

"Wow" was all he could say as he took another bite. "I don't know if I could have done that."

"Yeah, but you're not gay," I reminded him.

"No, but still, I can't think of anything I wouldn't give up to be an Aggie. Had to be hard."

I nodded but didn't say anything, 'cause what was there to say?

"Anyways, I asked about our prom, and they said you had to actually go to the school to be able to get in and all that, which sounds like bullshit since no one ever cared who went to what prom before. So I'd say you guys can come to ours, but I have a feeling they're going to do the same thing."

I stared at him for a long time, not even sure how to compute what he'd said.

"But what they're doing, it's crap. I just thought you should hear that from someone else, and I'm not the only one who thinks that."

"I don't get it," I said slowly. "We're not friends. Why do you care?"

"I can only care about friends when they're being fucked over?" he asked rhetorically. "I knew Kelly too. He went to football camp with my brother, and he was cool enough. I just think after everything is said and done, what you do in your bedroom doesn't matter to me. And it shouldn't change if you can go to your fucking prom or not."

He grabbed the empty sundae container and tossed it into the trash. "I just wanted to let you know, no one who counts cares if you're gay, man."

I was kind of blown away. "Thanks, man."

He gave me a grin and said, "You want to thank me? Kick the shit out of those losers so I can play you in the championship. I've been dying to take you down since I was twelve."

I laughed. "You can try, Fuller, but I got your number."

He held his fist out for me to bump. "Then we're cool?"

I bumped it back. "More than cool, dude. Consider yourself a friend."

He nodded as we got up and walked back to the hotel. It was going to be an interesting few days.

THE BASEBALL nut in me wants to explain every single moment of the next two games, but I have a feeling you'd doze off somewhere around the third inning. So let me tell you, we won both games and ended up in the finals against Granada, just like Shayne had predicted. We were tired, but there was no way any of us were sleeping the night before the game. Tyler, Matt, Kyle, and his mom went to dinner with me and my parents that night. It was the first time all my families sat at one table, and I was more than a little nervous about how they would get along.

"So, UC Berkeley?" my dad asked Kyle after we had ordered. "That's not an easy school to get into."

Kyle's mom beamed with pride as Kyle blushed slightly from the praise. "Neither is A&M," Kyle remarked after taking a drink of water. "A lot harder to get in on a baseball scholarship than an academic one."

My dad paused for a moment. This was his first exposure to Kyle's underhanded snark, and as always it took a moment for a first-timer to recognize it. "I agree, and I was very proud of Brad for both achieving it and for turning it down."

"It's hard to read emotion on some people sometimes," Kyle replied, sounding apologetic, even though I knew he wasn't. "Was just making sure."

My dad studied Kyle for a long few seconds and then said, "I think maybe you were just busting my balls because you're not my biggest fan."

Kyle nodded, putting his glass down. "That too."

It took everyone half a second to realize what Kyle had said.

And then my dad started laughing boisterously. Everyone else followed hesitantly. "You really are my son's defender, aren't you?"

Kyle gave him a small smile, which indicated he was publicly acknowledging the mirth of the situation but wasn't sharing in it. "Your son can defend himself just fine. What I refuse to do is let someone belittle him ever again. That isn't going to happen on my watch."

Kyle's mom nudged him and whispered something to him, but he refused to acknowledge it. Instead he locked eyes with my dad and waited.

Slowly my dad nodded. "Agreed." He looked over at me and added, "I am as proud as I can be with the way you've been playing the last two games, and it doesn't matter what the score is for the next game. In my book you already won everything that counts." He looked back at Kyle. "Better?"

Kyle smiled for real. "Completely."

My mom looked over to Kyle's mom. "You mind if I borrow him sometime? I need to know how he does that."

Linda looked at Kyle, and the expression on her face looked like she was seeing him for the first time. "I'd like to know that too."

After that, the tension at the table went away, and we began to talk randomly about the game, graduation, and everything else. Under the table, I grabbed Kyle's hand and squeezed it in thanks. He squeezed it back, and I knew it meant "I love you too."

You couldn't have pried that smile off my face with explosives.

"So what are we going to do about prom?" Tyler asked after dinner but before dessert.

"I put a complaint in to the school," my mom said. "But they said the rule came from the prom committee, which is voted on by the students, so there was nothing the school could do."

"That's bull," I said, stopping myself from finishing that word. "Raymond put them up to it. He's had it out for us from the start."

"We're just not going to go," Kyle said out of nowhere, ignoring the way everyone looked at him in shock. "What? Why would anyone think we would want to spend our prom at a dance that the people don't want us attending? What is there to get out of it besides pissing people off? I'd rather stay at home and be with people who actually like us than sit in a dance in some form of protest." He shook his head and refused to look anyone in the eyes. "I've charged at all the windmills I can in this town. I really just want to spend the rest of my time here drama-free."

No one said a word. The sounds of the restaurant were deafening in the silence. Finally my dad cleared his throat and said, "Well, that just sounds like you're chickenshit." Of course, everyone looked at him, but he was staring at Kyle. "It's hard to read emotion on some people, so just wanted to make sure we were clear. That is a chickenshit reason."

Kyle gave him a half smile. "I think maybe you were just busting my balls because you're not my biggest fan."

My dad gave him the same smile back. "Then you'd be wrong, because right up to you saying that, I was becoming a huge fan. Now, not so much."

My mom hit him on the arm, but he ignored her as nicely as Kyle had ignored his mom.

"Sorry to disappoint you," Kyle answered diplomatically.

My dad finished his drink before responding. "That's the problem with the world, young man. No matter what or who you believe in, you're going to disappoint someone. What separates the boys from the men is how much you care about it."

Kyle said nothing, and Tyler chimed in, "He has a right not to go," even though he had made it pretty clear a couple of minutes ago he thought we should go under protest as well.

My dad looked at Tyler. "Yes, he has a right not to go. But I think the point of the conversation is that he also has a right to go. The decision should be his, and instead, he has let someone make it for him."

"I'm still in the room," Kyle said, sounding a little annoyed.

My dad didn't miss a beat. "Are you? I couldn't tell by the way you weren't saying anything."

"Nathan," my mom exclaimed. "That's enough."

"Is it?" my dad asked Kyle. "Is it enough?"

Kyle tossed his napkin down. "I'm not hungry anymore." He pulled his chair away from the table. "I'll meet you guys outside," he said to his mom and Tyler.

I got up as he walked out. I shot my dad an evil look before chasing after Kyle. He got to the parking lot before I could get him to slow down. "Come on, please," I said, panting. "I've played, like, three games in a row. I do not need extra running."

He spun around and looked at me. "How did you live with that man?" he demanded. "He is so… arrrrghhh," he screamed.

"My dad is a dick. I thought you knew that," I said, trying to calm him down.

"'Dick' doesn't even come close to… I mean, where does he get off…." His words tumbled out of his mouth carelessly, like each one was fighting with the other to get said first. "Do you agree with him?"

This would be the moment, if I was in one of Kyle's comic books, that there would be squiggly lines all around my head telling me danger was close.

"If you don't want to go, then we shouldn't," I answered as neutrally as possible.

"I didn't ask that. I asked if you agreed with him," Kyle reiterated.

"Yeah, I do," I said bluntly. "I think what they're doing is bullshit, and I can't believe I'm not going to get to dance with you in front of the entire school and show them how stupid they are, but I'm in love with you, which means if you don't want to fight, then I don't want to fight. But if you ask me if what we're doing is chickenshit, then I'd have to say yes, it is."

He stared at me for a long time. It was pretty much the same look I'd expect from him if I had grown a second head or a third arm.

"Why didn't you say something?" he asked after a while.

"Because I'm in love with you." I tried not to make that sound like duh, but I'm pretty sure I screwed that up. "If you don't want to fight, Kyle, that's your choice, and I will respect it, completely. But you asked if I agreed with my dad, and I do."

"If you want to fight it—"

"No," I said, cutting him off and walking over to put my arms around him. "We don't fight because I want to. That's not how it works."

He pressed his face onto my chest. "But we don't fight if I say so? How is that fair?"

"It isn't." He looked up at me. "It's not, but trying to fight Raymond again isn't something we do because the other wants to. It has to be both of us or nothing. That's the only way it works."

He leaned into me again, and he sounded like he was going to cry. "I'm so fucking tired. I just want to close my eyes and wake up and have this whole thing over with."

I kissed the top of his head. "Then close your eyes. Before you know it, we'll be gone."

A couple of minutes later, Tyler, Matt, and Linda walked out into the parking lot. "Honey, you okay?" Kyle's mom asked. "That man is...." She looked at me and smiled. "Sorry, I know it's your dad, but he is a real gem."

"It's okay, I've called him worse," I assured her. "You okay?" I asked Kyle quietly.

"I feel like an asshole. This is supposed to be about your game, and now it's—"

I kissed him, which was the nicest way to tell him to shut up I knew.

When I was done, he smiled at me, and I knew it was going to be okay. "Kick their ass tomorrow?" he asked.

"For you, anything."

It wasn't a perfect night but close enough for my life.

The next morning the locker room was quiet as a library, which, let me assure you, was not normal at all. Usually there was laughing and wrestling as we tried to burn up a little energy before we went out onto the field. But now, no one said a word as we got dressed. You could swear we were going to a funeral. Shaking my own worries out of my head, I decided to change that.

"Okay, listen up," I said, walking to the center of the unfamiliar locker room. "I have something to say." Everyone looked over at me. I didn't see a calm face in the bunch. "This is just another game, same nine innings as every other one. It is no different than any other one we've played this year. We are going to walk out onto that field, and we are going to play the best game we know how to. And you know what? We're going to win. And you want to know why? Because we don't go to the newest school, and we don't have the shiniest equipment or the most expensive gear, but you know what we have that they don't?" I pointed to the black armband on my sleeve. "We have something we're playing for. I don't want to go out there to beat them, and I don't want to win because it would make us cool. I want us to go out there and play one more game for Kelly, and I want to show him how much we miss him. Not by crying, not by being sad, but in a way he would understand. By kicking Granada's ass off the field."

Everyone started to cheer *with me*.

"We are not players, we are warriors, and we are fighting for those who cannot fight anymore. Who's *with me*?"

The sound was thunderous in the small room. One by one they began to chant "Kelly," again and again. I looked around at my team, and I had never been so damn proud of a group of guys, ever. We charged out of the locker room as a team, ready to take blood if we had to.

So it turns out that Shayne wasn't lying. His team was every bit as good as he implied.

He was a wicked good pitcher, and he had taken me out swinging twice. Each time I wasn't even close to the ball. It was just dumb luck that we were only behind by two runs. It was top of the seventh, and I was beginning to have a bad feeling about this. I looked out to the stands and saw my parents sitting with Kyle and the rest of our patchwork family. They didn't look like they were feeling any more positive than I was. I looked a couple of seats down and saw that Frank guy from A&M sitting there looking at his iPad.

There were two guys on base, and I watched Shayne pitch to Kenny. The ball dropped low as it got to the plate, an obvious ball. I ignored everything else and watched Shayne wait for his catcher to toss him back the ball. I could see the sweat soaking through his cap and the way his eyes looked at the batter with a sense of dread.

He was out of gas.

He was at his breaking point, and his arm was about to give out. He could still pitch, but he was about to lose his heat, which meant he had maybe a couple of pitches left before he was going to have to tag out and be replaced. Kenny took another ball, and I saw Shayne cuss quietly to himself, no doubt telling himself to keep it together until the end of the inning.

I was up next, and I knew I finally had a chance to catch us up or pull ahead if Kenny got on base.

Looking over to Frank, I saw him watching intently, no doubt looking for someone to take the hole I opened up when I walked away. Shayne threw a weak strike that Kenny fouled off. Yeah, he was about to lose it.

"We got this," Josh said from behind me. "Now's your time to hero it up."

I looked back at him and heard the umpire call the third ball. Every particle of my being told me to shut up and just agree with Josh. Go out, slam the fuck out of that ball, and be the guy who turned the championship around once and for all. Shove the fact that just because I was gay didn't make a damn bit of difference on how I played ball. I thought about the cheering and the celebration, and then asked myself what would Kyle do.

"I can't," I said, grabbing my shoulder.

"What?" Josh asked, sounding like I had just said I had shot his mom. "What do you mean?"

I looked past him to Coach Gunn. "I got a problem," I said, wincing as I tried to raise my arm.

He walked over as Kenny took his base from the fourth ball. Gunn called a time-out real fast. "What are you doing?" he asked, pulling me away from Josh. "Not a damn thing wrong with your shoulder."

I looked over at Josh and then back to Coach. "Let him bat for me," I pleaded. "A&M is out there watching. Let Josh take the shot."

"You're our best hitter," he said, not exactly arguing with me. "If he flies out, the inning is over and we left three men on base, along with our only chance to catch up. You really want to risk the entire championship on getting your friend seen by a scout?"

"You think that guy is here to see Josh play? We both know he isn't, and that's not fair 'cause he is a damn good player. All he needs is something to get the man's attention. He won't miss."

"And if he does?" Gunn asked me.

"If he does, I'll tell everyone it was my fault," I answered instantly. "It won't be a thing on you." He seemed unconvinced, so I added, "I thought you already won championships. Wasn't this for us to win or lose?"

He didn't say anything for what seemed like forever. The umpire called his name, asking if he was going to play or not.

Finally he shouted, "Walker, you're in. Graymark, have a seat."

Gunn told the umpire, and I heard the announcer call out, "In for Bradley Graymark, Josh Walker."

Josh looked at me with panicked eyes. "Dude, what's wrong? We have bases loaded."

As calmly as I could, I put a hand on his shoulder and looked him right in the eyes. "Listen to me, you can do this. He is going to throw a hard left. Ignore it. He's going to try a hummer over the plate. Ignore it. When he leans in real low, that means he's had enough. He is going to throw it down the middle to the left. Take a step back, stop crowding the plate. When he throws that third pitch, swing low and then push forward. Got it?"

He *looked* at me with a terrified expression.

"Fine, just remember this. Jennifer is out there. How sexy do you think you'll look winning this game right now?"

He opened his mouth to say something and then just grabbed his batting helmet and walked out to the plate. I watched him tap the dirt off his cleats as he looked out across the crowd. "I hope you know what you're doing," Gunn growled from behind me.

So did I.

I saw Josh search the stands, and I did the same. Once I saw him look at Jennifer, a smile came over his face, and he brought the bat up to his shoulder.

For the record, we won 5-3. They never got close to catching up to us.

The stands were on fire as people rushed the field, all of them in some zealous state of joy for our victory. Jennifer jumped into Josh's arms and gave him a kiss that looked like it could bring back the dead. I smiled as I watched confetti fall all around the stands. It was a truly perfect moment. I looked over and saw my dad screaming his head off in celebration. Tyler and Matt looked like they were doing their own celebrating as well.

"Well done, Mr. Graymark," a voice said from behind me. I turned around and saw Frank from A&M standing there. "Your shoulder okay?" he asked with a small smile.

I rotated my arm a little and pretended to wince. "It will be, I'm sure."

"Think it will get better if you introduce me to your friend?" he asked, nodding to Josh.

I gave him a huge smile back. "I think it will, in fact."

I led him over to where Josh and Jennifer were still kissing. "Ahem," I said, trying to get their attention. "Josh," I said when he ignored me. "Josh," I yelled when he ignored that too. He waved an arm at me to go away without ever breaking from that kiss. I looked over to Frank. "Sorry, they're a couple."

He chuckled. "I'd hope so, 'cause that's a hell of a kiss from a stranger."

I finally kicked his leg. "Josh."

He pulled back. "What the fuck?" he whined. "What is so damn important that…?"

"This is Frank. He's from A&M."

Josh almost let Jennifer fall to the ground, and he went to shake Frank's hand. "Sir, pleasure to meet you," he said, pumping the man's hand like he was trying to get water from a well. Jennifer looked around, confused as to where he had gone.

"He's going to be busy," I told her, leading her away a couple of steps.

She shook her head. "He can really kiss," she said distantly.

"Better than me?" I asked, trying to sound hurt.

She just nodded. "Oh yeah, way better."

I suddenly wondered if I'd made the right decision.

Not really, but I'm a better kisser than she's letting on.

THAT MONDAY back to school was insane. Everyone was cheering. There was an assembly for us in front of the whole school, where Mr. Raymond once again looked like he was taking credit for the win instead of Coach Gunn. Josh was the hero of the moment, and he loved the attention he was getting. I remembered liking it at the time as well. He got his letter of intention from A&M during the celebration, and the lunchroom went nuts for him. His dad walked up and gave him a maroon-and-white letterman jacket to wear, which he did proudly.

I felt really good for him.

"Wait, wait, wait," he said, settling the crowd down. "Hold on. I need to say something." Everyone stopped talking and waited for him to speak. "I need to thank God and Coach Gunn and everyone for getting me here." He turned around and looked at me. "But there is someone else I need to thank." He smiled at me and then said to the crowd, "Let's hear it for our team captain, Brad Graymark."

The room went crazy again as he pulled me up to the podium. "Nothing would have happened this year without him." He raised my hand, and I started to laugh with him. "Come on, scream," Josh ordered them.

And they did. It was pretty cool.

Not a bad way to end a season, if you ask me.

Tyler

"YOU HAVE to talk to Robbie," Kyle said, walking back into the shop.

I looked up, confused. "I thought you were going over there to say you were sorry and stuff."

He nodded and closed the door. "I did, and there is something seriously wrong. He's packing his shop up."

That made me pause. "Like in boxes?"

"Like in moving," he assured me. "I'm worried."

I thought about it as I folded uniform shirts, wishing Matt hadn't taken off. Life had shown I have a pretty bad track record making decisions when it came to Robbie. After a few minutes, I said to Kyle, "I'm not doubting your read on him. I just don't know if I'm the best person to talk to him about... well, anything."

He countered with "You guys seemed okay at the shooting."

I unconsciously chuckled at the absurdity of that statement. "It was a panic situation, Kyle. I don't think anything was actually resolved except neither one of us wanted to see someone else die."

"But you're the closest thing he has to a friend. He may not think so, but you might be the only person in Foster who really knows him."

A statement that was as terrifying as it was true.

I assured Kyle I would do something and then brought it up at home with Matt. We were tag-teaming making dinner, and he stopped at the fridge. "What does Kyle want you to do?"

My kitchen was not large enough for both of us to actually stand and do stuff in it at the same time, hence the tag-team dance we had worked out in the past few months since he'd moved back. So when he stopped, I ended up bumping into him and almost spilling the bowl of green beans I was carrying. "Um, I think talk to him," I said, taking a few steps back and putting the bowl down.

Matt closed the fridge door and thought about it for a moment. I really wished he could think and cook at the same time, because I was starving. After a minute or so, he said, "I can't imagine Robbie even listening to you. Do you want to talk to him?"

That was the question, wasn't it?

On one hand, of course I wanted to talk to Robbie about everything that had happened, but on the other hand, there was no way he was going to actually listen to me. After what I had done, why would he? But it didn't really matter if I wanted to talk to him or not; I needed to talk to him. What mattered was if he would actually listen to me for once.

And I had to agree with Matt. I didn't see that happening anytime soon.

Like everything else in my mind, I spaced it out and went about my business, waiting for life to tell me when the time was right to make a move.

A couple of days later, I got a text from Kyle saying he was heading to Robbie's, and asking if I had talked to him yet. I knew I couldn't keep putting this off. I closed the shop and headed over there, ready to ignore Robbie's protests until he talked to me once and for all. When I got in, I heard the tail end of one of Robbie's rants.

"—color you have in mind? Particular style? By all means, allow me to be your own personal sweatshop." I said nothing as he came from around the counter. "Or wait, I have a better idea. Why don't I just find something of Riley's, and you can—"

That was enough.

"Robbie!" I shouted at him. Both Kyle and Jennifer jumped out of their skin, but he looked almost bored.

"He goes five years without even acknowledging my existence, and now twice in the same month." He leveled a look at me. "I think I liked being ignored."

Normally that look would make something inside me wither, but I was done with feeling bad about this. "You kids get on out of here. This is personal."

Kyle whispered to me, "Take it easy on him."

But easy was not how this was going to go down.

"Are you insane? Since when do you throw Riley's name around to make Kyle feel like shit?"

"Am I insane?" he asked, mimicking my voice. "Am I insane? Of course I'm fucking insane, you asshole. This town has taken everything I ever wanted away from me. What am I supposed to do?"

"Get over it," I said with no humor in my voice whatsoever.

"Get? Get over…," he sputtered, too pissed to complete a sentence. "You think something like that, you just get over? You think it's that fucking easy?"

He was trying to bait me, but I wasn't going to nibble this time. I had done the wrong thing too many times. It was time to stand and fight for once. "I didn't say it was easy. I said you should try to get over it, which you haven't. You haven't made one effort to get over his death, and we both know it. Instead you'd rather walk around town hating everything and everybody as if they were accomplices."

"They were!" he screeched at me. "They did everything but drive the getaway car. Did they try to find out who did it? Did they even acknowledge me as his partner? What were they, if not in on it?"

"People who had no idea what happened," I explained as patiently as possible. "You can blame the guys driving the car. You can blame his parents for locking you out. You can even blame me for being a complete asshole and bailing on you. But you have to stop blaming the town like it's a living, breathing entity out to get you."

"What if it is?" he asked, sounding crazier than normal.

"Then I have to assume you want to die too, since you chose to open a store here."

He froze, my words striking far deeper than I expected.

"Riley died, and that is a horrible thing. You know how I feel about it, but Robbie, what are you doing to yourself? The only reason to stay here is to punish yourself. What are you expecting to happen?"

He visibly got smaller as he slowly sank to the floor. He wasn't fainting. His body just seemed to give up, and he knelt on the ground. "I just want it all to stop. Why doesn't it all fucking stop?"

I knelt down next to him. "Robbie, do you want to die?"

He looked up at me, tears streaming down his face. "I just want to see Riley again."

I hesitantly reached out to hug him, and he didn't scream at me. I held him and said quietly as I began to cry, "I want that too."

After a while, I dropped him off at his house, telling him to get some rest and that I would be over in the morning to talk.

"Who said I wanted to talk to you?" he asked, none of the normal acid in his voice.

"Who said I cared what you wanted?" I shot back, smiling.

He turned back to the house and unlocked the door. "If you're waking me up, you better well bring fucking food." He went in and slammed the door on me.

The next morning I brought doughnuts and coffee for good measure.

He looked like death warmed over, but he let me in after taking one of the cups from me. "So what is this, an intervention?" he asked, sitting on the couch and lighting a cigarette.

"No, it is a long overdue talk," I assured him.

"You were a coward and fled. You're sorry, and if you had to do it all over again, you would change it all. Anything I missed?"

"You have to get better," I said, ignoring the bait. "Are you moving?" Nothing there was packed, but the shop was completely shut down.

"I'm closing down the shop," he said, opening the box of donuts. "Does this look like I'm moving?" He gestured around the house.

It was nothing like when Riley was alive. There were dishes in the sink, clutter all over the place. When Riley was alive, you could have eaten off the floor in this place. Now I wasn't sure I should eat the donuts I brought. "It looks like you've started using crack, to be honest." He glared at me, but I waved it off. "Seriously, Robbie, if not the shop, what are you going to do?"

"Why do you care?" he asked me. "Is this about guilt? Because if it is, then just go. I forgive you, and all is right in the world."

"It's not guilt," I assured him.

"Then what? Going for sainthood?"

"I just care," I said.

"Well then, why, Tyler?" he asked, growing increasingly upset. "If you insist on staying and bugging me, I deserve to know why."

"Because it's what Riley would have wanted me to do," I said quickly.

His hand began to shake. "What Riley would have wanted? How do you know what Riley would have wanted or not wanted? Since when are you an expert in all things Riley? You played sports with him, for fuck's sake. You weren't really friends. You didn't even know he liked guys until he walked up to you and told you, so how would you know what he wanted?"

I didn't say a word, knowing there was no right answer to those questions.

"You want to know what Riley wanted?" he asked, getting up. "You want to hear what he expected from life?" He grabbed an envelope off the desk and stomped back over to me. "You want to know the truth? Here." He handed it to me. "Read it for yourself."

I took the letter out and began to read, and I suddenly knew what had been bothering Robbie so much. My heart sank, not sure how to take what Riley had written years ago. Robbie was right. Riley wasn't my best friend. We knew each other well enough in high school, but we were never that close. It was only when he tried to reach out and get me to admit I was gay that we became close, and look what that got him. But reading this, I had to come to terms with the fact I might not have known him at all.

"So tell me, Tyler," Robbie said, waiting a respectable time for me to absorb the letter. "Tell me how to live with that, and I'll do it. Show me how to get over it, and I will get right on that. You tell me what I am supposed to do with the check that came with that letter." He leaned toward me. "But if you can't, then shut the fuck up and leave me alone."

I handed the letter back to him, my mind struggling to find something to say. Some germ of an idea that could make this even a little better for him. But as Matt joked with me once, I am a bear of very little brains, and long words bother me. It was why I loved Matt and why Brad loved Kyle, because in a very large world, it helps to have someone smarter than you standing by your side.

And then I had the answer.

"So then do what the letter says," I suggested. He paused in putting the letter away, and gazed at me with bloodshot eyes that looked like they hadn't closed for days. "You won't cash the check because you know what he meant it to be spent on, so spend it like he wanted."

Robbie sighed and put out his cigarette. "It's impossible. We didn't do anything, in case… I mean, we never got around to even talking about it." He fell back onto the couch. "Well, we had barely started talking about it when…."

He didn't need to say anything else.

"I have an idea," I said, sitting up in the chair. "One that will make you feel better and honor what Riley wanted. But you have to want to feel better, Robbie. You have to want to stop feeling this way." He looked over at me with a desperate stare. "You have to stop waiting to die and start living."

The silence in the room was like nails on a chalkboard to me as I waited for him to say something. I could feel the ghost of Riley there, leaning over my shoulder, waiting to see if Robbie would nibble on my bait. If he didn't, I had no idea what to do next.

He closed his eyes and asked in a very small voice, "What do you have in mind?"

I could feel Riley slap me on the back in congratulations as I outlined my plan with Robbie.

The next step was making sure what we were planning was legal and didn't get the two of us arrested or, worse, shot. While I was waiting for the right opportunity to take that step, Brad came in and told me he wasn't going to be allowed to take Kyle to the prom, which was about fifteen different kinds of fucked-up. This time I was smart and called Matt to come over and go over the options, but in the end, it really did look like the school was going to get to fuck over the boys one last time on their way out.

After Brad left, I was still pissed and nursed a Coke, bitching to Matt about it.

"It's not fair." Which was the most obvious thing in the world.

"It's Foster. I know you love those kids and all, but were you expecting something different? Because it seems pretty SOP to me." I gave him a look, and he explained, "Standard operating procedure. I dated a military guy—sue me."

Matt was right, but I didn't have to like it.

So a couple of days before the playoffs, when I knew Brad was at practice, I headed over to his dad's dealership to have a talk.

It had been a long time since I had talked to Nathan Graymark—almost four years, to be honest. We had both been sitting on folding chairs in the middle of the Foster High gym, each holding a cup of coffee in both hands so it wouldn't look like we were going through DTs as bad as we were. It was a couple of years after Riley had died, and I decided to climb back into the bottle to forget that one moment when he tumbled over the hood of the car and hit the pavement like a bag of discarded meat. Sheriff Rogers had arrested me for my third DUI and gave me a choice: either go to AA or take my chances in a courtroom.

Needless to say, I chose AA.

Nathan had played football for Foster when I was playing for Granada. The only times we ever went up against each other were those rare preseason games where the whole town picked sides and then become the most obnoxious, rabid fans you can imagine. You'd swear it was the Blue and the Gray instead of two high schools in the same town, the way people got worked up. So the two of us were never friends, but we knew of each other, and we both knew that in a sea of faceless players, only the two of us were good enough to get out of town based on it.

And we also knew how crippling having to come back was.

He never said why he was there, but it was pretty obvious that he didn't think he needed to be there, which meant, like me, he was being forced. We talked some, shared very little, and after a few months decided that if we were going to drink, we'd best do it responsibly. I hadn't said a word to him since that last meeting, but the few times we saw each other around town, we made eye contact long enough to acknowledge that we knew each other and where we knew each other from.

So me walking onto the lot was probably as much a surprise as him walking into my shop would have been.

He was in his office on the phone, and once he saw me walk in, he hung up and headed out to the lobby. One of his salesmen came up to me with the same demeanor a golden retriever would have if you were holding a ball—too eager and way too slobbery. "Can I help you?" he asked, which sounded way too much like "Throw the ball?" to me.

Nathan came up behind him and patted him on the shoulder. "I got him, Keith."

Keith walked away like he had been kicked repeatedly.

"Tyler," he said, once the salesman was out of earshot. "Here for a car?"

I shook my head. "Nope, I needed to talk to you."

I had to give him credit; he was a very good salesman because his smile didn't waver an iota. "No, you're here to see a car," he said forcefully. "If we talk while you look, then that happens as well."

I suddenly understood.

"Yeah, show me the red one," I said, pointing to a midlife-crisis special, complete with shiny rims and all.

"Pete," he called out behind him. "Toss me the keys to the coupe, will you?"

Pete took a set of keys off a pegboard and tossed them across the salesroom. We walked outside, and he asked, "Mind if I drive?"

"Be my guest," I said, getting into the passenger side.

He turned the engine over, and the car purred like it was alive. He gave me a grin as the automatic seat belts locked us in. "Hold on." The second the car was tossed into Drive, we took off like a bullet. I wasn't in the market to buy a new vehicle, but it was hard not to want this car just a little by the way the dealership faded into the rearview mirror like a distant memory. "So talk," he said as we pulled out onto the interstate, leaving town.

I explained to him what Robbie and I wanted to do and the reasons why. Nathan said nothing as I went over the key points of our plan and then the thoughts behind it. This went on for about ten minutes, until he pulled over in the middle of nowhere. He turned the car off and got out. From the look on his face, he was no longer trying to sell me the car. I got out too, not sure what was going on but pretty sure I had fucked it up once again.

"I'm just curious; do you really think I'm that bad a father?" I opened my mouth to answer but honestly had no idea what to say to that. "Do you think my son needs your help?"

I shook my head. "I'm not saying Brad needs anything. I'm just saying we want to help him."

"And I can't do that?" Nathan demanded.

"I didn't say that."

"Didn't you? Aren't you saying I can't take care of my son, and you and your friend are more than willing to help him?"

"It's not like that, Nate," I assured him. "Brad is a good kid, and him and Kyle deserve every chance to make it work."

"And I will give him that chance," he raged back at me. "I don't need someone else coming along trying to be his dad. He has one."

"I am not trying to be his dad, and neither is Robbie. What Brad did was… well, shit, it was braver than anything you or I could have done back in the day, and you know it. Could you imagine telling a college to go fuck themselves after they offered you a full ride? He shouldn't get punished for that. He should be rewarded. He should be fucking celebrated, and that's all we are trying to do. You're his father, Nathan. I'm just trying to be a supportive friend."

"Why do you care so much about my son?" he asked, his eyes narrow with suspicion.

And that was when I lost it. "Oh, of course, I forgot. I'm a faggot, so I can't have friendships with anyone unless there's an ulterior motive, right? Doesn't matter if I'm in a relationship or even that you're talking about a teenager. I have to want to get into your son's pants because I'm a pervert, right? Is that what you're asking, Nathan?"

He didn't say a word, but we both knew that was exactly what he was saying.

"You can't be that stupid, Nate," I went on. "You have to know what an incredible kid Brad is. He has a thousand times the guts I ever had at that age. I'm not sexually attracted to him, you asshole. I'm blown away by the decisions he has made, and I want to celebrate that. And by the way, if I was some dirty fucking creep, I wouldn't have told you a thing about this. I would have just done it, and you would have never known. This isn't about you or me, Nathan. This is about him and Kyle and showing them that the entire world is not against them. Can you look past your own shit and see what we're trying to do here?"

He looked away, out across the endless horizon that made up the Texas landscape, and sighed. "You know, I thought he really made a mistake turning A&M down. I just thought, why not shut up and do what they say? How hard can that be?" He shook his head. "I swear, I could have never walked away from that like he did."

I stood there as the wind howled around us.

"I know I didn't teach him that," he said finally. "That was all his mother, and I had never been so proud of him." He leaned against the hood of the car and shook his head. "I've been a shitty father, and your offer just made it sound like you were trying to rub that in."

"I swear to you, we weren't."

He laughed. "Yeah, I get that now." He looked out across the nothingness. "He is going to graduate and leave town with that boy, and he is never going to talk to me again. I did it with my father, and he did it to his. I really thought I was going to be different."

"Nate," I said, putting a hand on his shoulder. "He loves you, trust me. You aren't losing him at all. He's just growing up."

He looked at me and then back to my hand. "I'm really not one for touching."

I took my hand off, and he thanked me.

"Okay, sure, you and your friend want to do that, be my guest. Just wait until it's closer to graduation, can you?" I gave him a questioning look. "I just want to be his favorite dad for a little while longer. Once his gay dads get in on it, I don't have a chance."

He gave me a smile, and I knew it was going to be okay.

"So about this car…," he said as we got back in.

By the time we got back to the dealership, I was almost ready to trade in my Jeep.

So I saw Brad and his team win state, all the while drawing up the papers with Robbie to get it done. I had been at the school dropping off some gear the day the Walker kid got his A&M papers, and Jennifer pulled me aside in the lunchroom. "I need your help," she said as the crowd went wild.

I took a couple of glances to the stage as Josh pulled Brad to the podium. "What's up?" I asked her, already feeling weird for being a grown man on campus.

She began to talk, and I began to smile. It seemed I was not the only one with plans.

I couldn't wait to tell Robbie.

"You're joking," he said when I told him.

"I am not," I said, not commenting that he looked 1,000 percent better since we last talked. "So what do you say now?"

He took a sip of his coffee and finally admitted, "I'm shocked. Which makes my decision even easier."

"And that is?"

"I'm moving," he said simply. I stared at him, openmouthed. "Back home. To Long Island." I just gaped. "Oh, for Gaga's sake, close your mouth. You look like the world's gayest trout."

I closed my mouth. "You're really leaving?"

He nodded. "After they graduate, I'm out."

I wasn't sure what to say, so I just sat there and stared into my coffee.

"Oh, please. I thought you'd be doing backflips," he teased.

"But we were just… I thought…." I was babbling. "I just thought we were getting back to being friends."

He sighed and put his coffee down. "One, we were never friends. You were Riley's friend, and I liked you for that. Two, what did we ever have in common except him? You and I would never have even talked if it wasn't for him." With every word, I felt my stomach souring. "And three, we are friends, you idiot." I looked up, and he was smiling. "What, you never heard of the internet and this new invention called an airplane?" I smiled back. "God, you really are lucky you have that face, because seriously, you're as dense as a rock."

"Can we hug?" I asked, standing up.

"Don't push it," he warned, and I sat back down. "And stop looking like a dog that just got caught peeing on the carpet. I said we were friends. Don't push it."

I didn't.

THE NIGHT of the prom, Matt was gone getting stuff done when I knocked on Brad's door. Nathan answered and gave me a warm smile and a handshake. "If it isn't the other dad."

I shook his hand back. "Part-time. You can have the holidays and every other weekend."

He laughed and let me in. "Brad, you have a visitor."

A couple of *seconds* later, Brad came down a few steps from upstairs. "Tyler?" he asked, confused as to why I was there.

I began to walk up the stairs. "Hey, got a few *seconds*?"

"Um, I was about to head over to Kyle's," he warned. "We're going to spend the night watching movies, pretending the prom isn't going on somewhere else."

"Yeah, Kyle isn't there," I said, following him into his room. He paused and turned around to look at me. "Get dressed—something nicer than jeans and a shirt."

"Where is Kyle?" he asked, not moving.

"Somewhere other than his house," I said, smiling. "Clothes, nicer than that. Now," I ordered, picking up a pretty cool-looking baseball-shaped clock from his nightstand. "We're on the clock."

He grabbed some clothes from the closet and walked into his bathroom. From the other side of the door, he called out, "What clock?"

"Dress faster," I said, tossing the ball up into the air.

Five minutes later he walked out in khaki slacks and a button-up shirt. He held his arms out. "Better?"

I looked at him and shook my head. "Need a tie and some kind of jacket."

He growled as he stomped to his closet. "Would be easier if you just told me what I was dressing for."

"Hey, you know, you're right," I said, sounding surprised. He looked at me expectantly. "But I'm not, so jacket and tie, and something other than sneakers."

He growled under his breath, pulled a blazer on, and began to knot his tie. "Anything else I need? Cologne? Condom? Shot of whiskey?"

"Maybe less talk and more changing?" I offered.

He flipped me off as he slipped on a pair of loafers. He stood up and turned toward me. "Better?"

I assure you, Brad did absolutely nothing for me sexually, but I had to admit, he was a good-looking young man. I wondered how far I would have gotten at his age with a guy like him by my side. "You look perfect," I said, getting up. "Come on, let's move."

He followed me out of his room. "Move to where?"

I didn't say a word as I walked toward the front door. "See you later, Nathan."

From another room I heard him call back, "You guys have fun."

Brad's eyes looked like they were going to pop as we walked out. "How did you do that? My dad would have grilled me on where I was going."

"Didn't you know?" I said, getting into my Jeep. "I got mad skills."

He rolled his eyes as he climbed in. "So, a hint?"

I zipped my lips shut as we backed out of the driveway.

He sighed and looked out the window in silence.

Robbie

SO I lost it, and then I got better.

Happy?

Maybe Tyler was right. Maybe I was just sitting here waiting to die. Maybe for once in his Neanderthal life, he had one decent thought in that pretty, pretty head, and maybe, just maybe, his words got through. It's not like he invented fire or something, so let's not dwell on it, shall we? Instead let's look at his idea on how to get me to alleviate the guilt of having all this money Riley left me.

And before you start to think how stupid I was to not just keep it and be done with it, let me explain how guilt works, my dear. You see, anything I bought with that money, anything at all, would remind me how it was purchased, which would be with money that came from Riley's death. Now you might be able to somehow get around that kind of soul-crushing experience, but I assure you, I couldn't. Bad enough I lived in a tomb of everything that once belonged to the man I loved, because I refused to throw anything of his away in case I forgot even the smallest part of him. But to add new things that would be associated with his absence was just too much to ask of my brain and my heart.

So Tyler came up with a way to enact *Brewster's Millions* without the comic genius of Richard Pryor.

I have to admit, his solution was a little ingenious, especially coming from Tyler. I would expect that kind of problem solving from Matt, he has that annoyingly smart look about him, but coming out of Tyler's mouth, it was obviously a message from Madeline Kahn. Hey, you're allowed to call God by whatever name you want. I'll refer to her as I want to, okay?

What I wasn't expecting was the universe to open up and show me that I might have had the wrong idea about Foster.

This was how I found myself knocking on Kyle's door the night of the prom, knowing I was about to change the poor boy's life forever. He answered in a pair of sweats and a T-shirt that looked like it was about three thousand miles past its expiration date. "You're early. Did you pick up the…"

He saw me standing there with a suit bag over one arm and a pair of shoes in the other.

"…movie?" he finished, shocked.

"Yeah, change of plans," I said, walking past him into the house. "I'm gonna need you to take a shower, burn what you're wearing, and then put these on." I handed him the suit bag. "And we're on the clock, so you need to hustle before you go turn into a pumpkin." He just stood there, not sure what was going on. "Though I will admit I do enjoy it, right now I'm not talking for my own amusement. So shower, burn those, wear that. Simple enough?"

"What's going on?" he said, kicking the door closed and setting the suit bag on the back of a chair. "Because if this is some lame 'fake prom' at Nancy's with, like, three people, I don't want to go."

I put the shoes down and put a hand on each of his shoulders. "Kyle. Look in my eyes. We need to be one in this instant, okay? Feel what I am feeling." He nodded slowly. "I don't give a fuck what you do or don't want to do. Go get dressed before I set fire to the sweats with you still in them."

He blinked a couple of times, checking to see if I was joking.

Finally he grabbed the suit bag and headed toward the bathroom. "Fine, but I don't have to have fun."

Madeline save me from teenagers.

Twenty minutes later, he walked out wearing the slacks and shirt, holding the jacket in one hand. "Am I going to a funeral or something?"

I looked over at him. "Do you want to? Because I swear to all that is unholy, if you come out here without all that on, I will…."

He turned tail and slammed the door behind him.

After another ten minutes, he came out, fully adorned in his new dark blue suit. He was in socks, so the outfit was not quite complete, but it was close. "Why do I feel like I'm auditioning for *Doctor Who*?" he asked.

I held up a pair of red Converses and a bow tie. His face exploded into a smile. "Oh, you rock on so many levels." He grabbed them from me and slipped them on in a flash. The key to getting any teenage nerd into a suit is one part fear, two parts peer pressure, and one part Time Lord. If you don't know what I mean, look it up. It will serve you well in the future, trust me.

He jumped up, and I could see him wiggling his toes in the new shoes. "Are we going to a convention or something?"

"Better," I said, smiling at the unbridled joy on his face. "Come on, we need to leave."

"I need to leave a note for my mom," he said, dashing to the kitchen. "She's working late, and I don't want her to worry."

I grabbed his arm and turned to lead him out of the kitchen toward the door. "No, she's not. She's waiting for us." He looked at me, once more confused. "You do need to lock the front door, though," I said, pointing.

He shook himself out of his stupor and locked the door behind us.

As we pulled out onto East Avenue, he asked me where I was taking him. I ignored his questions as we took First Street past Nancy's so I could show him it was closed, so there was no way it was our destination. All that did was cause him to question me even more.

"We need to talk," I said in a rare moment of him not talking. "And it has nothing to do with where we are going."

"Are you dying? Is my mom dying? Is Brad? Okay, answer me this—is someone dying?"

I gave him a sideways glance. "God, I thought I was morbid. No one is dying—well, not that I know of. I mean, we're all dying in a Sylvia Plath kind of way, but... oh God, why would you even ask that?"

He gestured to the road. "'Cause you're driving me somewhere out of town in the middle of the night. Either someone is dying or I'm going to die, and I can't imagine you would dress me up just to kill me."

"We need to talk," I repeated, opting to ignore the last few seconds. "Before you start to ramble about serial killers or something equally quaint, I want you to tell me why you decided to just not go to prom." He gave me a silent look, and I prodded him. "Don't glare. Answer the question."

"Why?" he said, starting to sulk. "You already know the answer."

I tried not to sigh. "Well, if I did, then I wouldn't be asking you, but let's pretend I did know and still wanted you to tell me. Why?"

He said nothing for a while, just watching the road unfold in front of us from the darkness. Finally he muttered, "Because why fight to be somewhere they don't want you to be?" I didn't say anything because I knew he was just starting. "I get the whole 'treat us equal' thing and 'let us have the same rights,' but when it comes to something like a prom or a celebration, if straight people don't want us there that fucking bad, why go? All we would be are the assholes who insisted on being able to go, ruining the party for everyone else, and who wants to be that guy? I just don't see why everything about our life has to be a fight. Please let us get married, please let us serve in the military, please stop killing us. I mean, seriously, after a while I'd just rather stay around gay people and tell everyone else to go fuck off."

I wish I could say I was surprised, but I wasn't, since everything he'd said had run through my mind at least a dozen times. I pulled over to the side of the road, because I didn't trust myself to be able to drive, talk, and not burst out crying like I was menopausal. He looked over at me as I put the car in Park.

"Okay, look," I said, not looking him in the eyes because I needed to get through this without breaking down. "I understand why you think that, trust me, I do. But I need to say something that you aren't going to believe, and I'm not going to waste time arguing. You just need to hear it." He nodded. "You're wrong this time. You are dead wrong." He opened his mouth to argue, but I wouldn't let him talk. "You can't do what I do and just lump people into one huge group like that. It may seem like it's easy and right, but you can't do it. Every single time you think you have people figured out, they do something to surprise you. You're not even twenty yet, and you can't be this jaded, and I think I'm partly to blame." I took a deep breath and steadied myself. "The reasons I hate Foster are my own, and I should have never tried to make them yours."

"But you weren't," he blurted out. "You weren't wrong at all. They locked us out of going to the prom, and look what happened. Nothing."

He sounded so bitter for his age, so set in his hatred. It made me feel older than I already did, and trust me, I felt like I was as old as Cher, circa *Believe*.

I shook my head and wiped my eyes. "You're wrong, Kyle, and I can prove it." Before he could argue, I started the car and pulled back onto the road.

"Where are we going?" he asked. "What's going on?"

A little ways up, I pulled off the main road and onto a dirt lane. I prayed I didn't get lost like I did the first two times Tyler tried to show me where it was.

We parked in the middle of a field next to Tyler's Jeep, where Brad and he were standing.

"Is that Brad?" Kyle asked, almost jumping out of the car.

"And just like that, our conversation is forgotten," I said to myself as I turned off the car. "Mom, I owe you a serious apology."

By the time I got out of the car, the two boys were drilling Tyler for answers.

"—middle of nowhere?" Brad asked.

"And what's with the clothes? Tyler, seriously. Is someone dying?" Kyle asked.

"Oy, again with the dying," I said, slapping the back of Kyle's head. "What did I say?"

He rubbed his head. "So then why are we here?"

I pointed into the dark woods. "To prove you're wrong," I said as cryptically as possible.

"Is this where we run?" Brad asked Kyle quietly.

"Shall we go?" Tyler asked me, smiling with pure mischief on his face.

I smiled back. "I like seeing them squirm, to be honest."

Tyler rolled his eyes. "Come on, kids, this way."

"This is how every person ever dies in a horror movie," Brad said as they followed Tyler.

"I knew having sex would get me killed," Kyle muttered. "Before I met you, I was the virgin nerd. I would have made it at least until the last part of the movie."

Brad nudged him. "Yeah, but that would have meant no sex."

I saw the look on Kyle's face as he smiled at Brad, and I remembered smiling like that at Riley. And part of me knew I would smile like that again someday.

We walked into the dark copse of woods. I had no idea how Tyler was navigating, but I'm sure it had something to do with outdoors and manly crap, which made tromping through the darkness even more annoying. Finally I saw them stop, and Tyler looked over to the boys. "We're here," he said solemnly.

"We're where?" Kyle asked.

There was the sound of a switch being pulled, and floodlights lit up the area like it was an outdoor field. Across the branches of the trees were strung Christmas lights, making the whole grove look like it was a magical place instead of just a campsite by Lake Foster. There must have been over a hundred kids standing there, all of them dressed up and waiting for the shock to settle in before they screamed "Surprise" at Brad and Kyle. Music started playing, and people came up to them, every one with a huge smile on their face at the boys' shock.

Kyle turned around and looked at me. "Did you do this?"

I scoffed at him and shook my head. "Did I plan a party in the middle of some old woods, outside, with bugs? Bitch, you don't know me at all."

Brad looked at Tyler, who laughed. "Nope, I was just the getaway driver. He's the brains."

Both of them looked back, and there was a kid standing there, looking three kinds of uncomfortable.

"Tony?" Brad almost spat. "Tony Wright?"

Tony nodded and looked around. "Guilty. You like it?"

"Why?" Kyle asked, obviously not believing any of it.

Tony took a deep breath. "Look, I didn't do this 'cause I was guilty about Kelly or I felt sorry for you, if that's what's you're thinking. I'm still not a fan of what you guys do behind closed doors, but that doesn't mean you shouldn't get a prom. I mean, that's just not fair. You went to school, you won us state, and you had a gun pointed at you. If you guys didn't deserve a prom, then none of us did. I may not like what you guys are, but I can also understand that some things are just taking it too far. It wasn't hard to set up, turns out a lot of people were pissed about it. So to repeat, this is just me being nice and nothing about Kelly." He got quiet, and I could see his eyes tear up. "Okay, maybe it's a little about Kelly too," he said, wiping his eyes. "But anyways, welcome to prom."

He held his hands up, and a couple of people around them cheered and held up their red plastic cups in celebration.

"Enjoy," he said, taking a few steps back.

Brad took a step toward him and gave him a hug. I saw the boy freeze for a moment and then hug him back. "Kelly would have loved this," Brad whispered, and Tony hugged him tighter.

I nudged Kyle. "See? You were wrong."

Kyle turned around and looked at me, and I could see the absolute wonder in his eyes at how incredible the world could be if you just gave it a chance. I saw that because I'd just learned that lesson myself.

"Third wish granted." I smiled at him.

He dove at me and gave me a hug. I thought of something sarcastic to say in response, but instead I hugged him back.

Then the two of them went running into the prom, holding hands, while Tyler stood next to me and smiled. "They did a good thing here."

I watched them grab drinks and start talking to people. "I still can't believe it."

Brad's parents and Kyle's mom joined us, with Matt tagging along behind them. This was only part one of our devious plan; part two came later.

"I'm still worried for them," Matt said as we walked over to a bench.

The DJ stopped the music and announced, "This one is for all of those who aren't here." "Some Nights" by Fun. began to play, and the kids sang along, their voices raised in tribute. I looked over at Matt and smiled. "I'm not. I think they are going to be fine."

It was incredibly saccharine coming out of my mouth, but it was how I felt.

"But what if they think the rest of the world is like this? What if they go out there and are met by the assholes we know are real? What if they aren't ready for it?"

I walked over and put a hand on his shoulder. It was the first time I had actually touched him. "Listen to them, Matt. I mean, really listen to them." We paused, and they were practically screaming as one.

"That isn't a song, it's a war cry. They aren't just kids anymore; they are warriors. Those kids have it more figured out than we ever did. And they're just graduating high school. Can you imagine when they have kids? Can you imagine what their kids will be like?" I shook my head, marveling. "No, my dear moose, they are going to be just fine."

And for the first time in a long time, I meant it.

Jennifer

IF THERE is anything sadder than an empty gym made up for a prom, I don't know what it is.

I sat at the front door, my hands on the lockbox for the money, and waited. The rest of the bitches who made up the prom committee were inside, no doubt ready to peck themselves to death over blaming why no one was there. Mr. Raymond looked like he was about to throw up.

My phone chirped, and I looked down and saw a text message from Tony. *they r here.*

I smiled and gathered up my stuff.

"I don't understand," Mr. Raymond said with a cup of punch in his hand. "Where is everyone?"

I smiled again as I walked up to him. "Oh. No one is coming," I said as cheerfully as possible. Stacy and Patty swiveled their heads toward me like two dogs smelling fear. Once I was sure I had everyone's attention, I said, "Everyone canceled their tickets a few days ago. Didn't you just hear me? No one is coming."

Raymond put his drink down. "What are you talking about, Ms. Rogers?"

The girls moved in closer too, dying to know what was up. "Well, most of the school have been coming to me this past week, saying they couldn't make it to the prom." I tried to look as innocent as possible. "What, no one told you guys?"

"This is not funny." Mr. Raymond tried to sound threatening, but honestly, my dad has caught Brad sneaking out of my room before. This guy had nothing on him. "What is going on?"

Someone whistled behind me, and I turned to see Josh standing at the door. He smiled and tapped his watch. I felt a glow in my chest, and I realized I really liked that boy.

I looked back at Raymond and his bitch squad and gave him a curt smile.

"What's going on is this," I said, handing him the lockbox. "School isn't for you, it's for us. You and everyone who work here, I think you've forgotten that, so we, as a school, have decided to remind you. You see, the school is here for us, to teach us, to guide us, and to make us better people, not only for you to come and get a paycheck. It doesn't matter what you like and don't like. What matters is if it helps us grow as people. So we have taken prom away from you." I looked around. "As you can see. Now, if you're lucky, and I mean really lucky, the class next year will let you give them a prom, but I would suggest not excluding people, because that's just going to piss them off."

I took a step closer to him. "And, Mr. Raymond, do not piss them off."

He looked upset for a moment and then gave me a predatory smile. "Well, you and your friends can laugh all you want, but at the end of the day, they still paid for their tickets," he said, shaking the box. He froze when there was no sound. He scrambled to open it and saw the huge nothing inside. "Where is the money, Ms. Rogers?"

"Oh, that," I said, sounding like I just remembered. "Well, like I said, I had people coming to me all week, asking for refunds because they weren't going to make it."

He looked like he was going to spit. "You can't give refunds."

I cocked my head. "Really? You sure of that? Because according to the guidelines, it says the prom committee can refund money for tickets if the circumstances are unique. So I held a meeting and decided to define what 'unique' meant."

"When?" Patty demanded.

I thought about it for a second. "Since last week, right, Josh?" I answered simply, looking over to him. He nodded. "Since last week when I held a meeting and no one showed up." I pulled out another stack of papers and handed them to Raymond. "There is a list of every penny we got and every cent we gave back. Feel free to ask them if they got refunds or not."

I grabbed Josh's arm. "You'll excuse me. I have a prom to get to." As we walked out, I waved behind me. "Have fun here, guys."

"You liked that too much," Josh whispered to me as we walked out.

"Damn right I did."

We both laughed as we headed into the night.

I was officially done with Foster drama.

Brad

I KNOW it's silly to hear someone who's eighteen years old say this, but I have to be honest. I had never seen anything like this. Gayle had set up a table of food, and Coach Gunn was helping her pass plates out to people. Two generators on the backs of pickup trucks were running the lights and music, and there was a tub full of ice and sodas.

I knew they were sodas because Sheriff Rogers was sitting over there talking to Kelly's mom.

There were people from all grades here, freshmen to seniors, all of them having a great time. There were a ton of guys I didn't recognize, and then Shayne came walking up to me with his girlfriend. It was only then that I realized Granada was here as well. He saw the look on my face and laughed. "I told you people were pissed about how prom went down."

"No hard feelings?" I asked him, hoping there wasn't going to be bad blood because of taking state from them.

He shook his head. "Hell no. I should have gotten off that mound before the sixth. That was just dumb pride. You took it fair and square."

He held his fist out, and I bumped it.

"This is my boyfriend, Kyle," I said proudly, nudging Kyle forward since he had been half hiding behind me.

"I've heard of you," Shayne said, extending his hand.

Kyle took it. "Anything good?"

"Depends," Shayne said wryly. "Is it supposed to be a secret you're a masked vigilante who protects the town from ass hats?"

I saw Kyle's face redden slightly, and I pulled him close.

"Don't mind him," I said, gripping Kyle tight. "He's not used to being a superhero yet."

"You should be," Shayne said seriously. "I mean, take a look around. You did this." Kyle looked at him for a second, not sure what Shayne was talking about. And then it started to dawn on him. He had changed Foster, just like he had promised. "We all did it," Kyle said, trying to deflect like he always did.

"Sure," Shayne agreed quickly. "But it took one person to stand up and say it was fucked-up for anyone to do that." He pointed a finger at Kyle's chest. "Trust me, that's all you."

Kyle said nothing, still struggling to accept what Shayne was saying.

"Anyways, just wanted to say hey and good game."

I nodded as he walked off.

"Do you think he's right?" Kyle asked.

I moved and faced him. "I think this town sucked, and no one had the balls to do anything until you said it needed to stop. Look around you. You didn't need to fight for this. Everyone did it on their own, not because you're the most popular or they were trying to score cool points. They did it because it was the right thing to do, and you showed them that."

"You were the one who told the school board you'd walk off the team unless everyone was protected from bullying."

"Yeah, and what did I tell you that day after I said that? All I was thinking was 'What would Kyle do?'" He was still resisting it, but the proof all around us was pretty hard to deny. "Face it, Kyle Stilleno—you changed Foster."

"We changed it," he amended.

"Hey, you know me, I'll take any credit I can," I said, giving him a smile. "Give me a week, and I'll say I set this whole thing up."

He laughed and pulled me into a kiss. There was literally nothing in the world that could have stopped me from kissing him back.

"So the music sucks," someone said from behind us. We turned around and saw Sammy standing there, looking fourteen different kinds of uncomfortable. "Everything else is pretty cool, but that DJ sucks balls because no one here wants to hear 'Call Me Maybe' anymore."

Kyle smiled at her. "You came."

She shrugged. "I heard this was going down, and I thought...." She sighed and shook her head. "I thought not showing up would just make me a bitch."

"I'm glad you came," I tossed out.

But this was really between the two of them.

"I am sorry," Kyle said, sounding sincere.

"I know, and so is Jeremy, who says hi, by the way."

"How is he?" Kyle asked.

"Well, they aren't going to throw him in jail, they're sending him to a facility instead. I hear that was because you argued with Sheriff Rogers about it."

Kyle nodded. I didn't even know that.

"He's not well. That doesn't deserve jail time."

She looked around at everyone, and the silence became unbearable for a few seconds. "Anyways, I just wanted to stop by here and say good job on all this."

Kyle looked confused. "But I didn't set this up."

She gave him a smile, a ghost of her normal smile, but a smile nonetheless. "Yeah, you did, Kyle, in every way that counts." She looked over at me. "Treat him well, or I will hire a hit on you."

I saluted her, and she laughed.

"You're not all bad, Graymark."

It was the nicest thing she had ever said to me.

"You can stay," Kyle urged her.

She shook her head quickly. "Nah, I never wanted to go to the real prom. I mean, it's just...." She sighed and then looked away. "Actually, Jeremy and me said we would go, way back when, and just make fun of people. It doesn't feel right being here and him being locked up."

"You're a good friend, Sammy."

She looked at him and smiled. "Yeah, I really am."

She walked away and out of the prom without another word.

"I screwed that up," Kyle said, hugging me.

I had nothing that could make him feel better, so I just hugged him back. "She'll be okay."

He seemed so depressed that I had to do something to cheer him up, so I leaned in and kissed him softly. He was hesitant at first, and then responded. I think he was realizing no matter what, we still had each other.

"So before you guys start humping each other's legs, we need to talk to you."

I opened one eye and saw Tyler and Robbie standing there. I didn't stop kissing Kyle, just opened one eye to look.

"I will grab a bucket of water," Robbie warned.

Kyle pulled away and looked at him. "You lie—your kind is petrified of water."

He gave Kyle a sarcastic grin and nodded. "Keep that sass up. It will really make you popular once you get old."

"Speaking from experience?" Kyle shot back.

Robbie put a hand over his chest. "You, sir, are a twat."

"Come on," Tyler said, gesturing toward some picnic benches, and I saw my parents sitting there with Kyle's mom.

I looked over to Kyle, who shrugged. He was as oblivious to what was going on as I was.

We sat down, and my mom reached over and gave me a hug. "You look so handsome," she said.

"Mom," I protested, being mom-handled in front of strangers.

"So who's first?" my dad asked, obviously wanting to get whatever this was started.

Tyler looked at Robbie, who shrugged and said, "You go ahead."

My dad nodded. "Okay, so this has been a trying year for everyone, and it hasn't been easy for the two of you, but you came through it not only stronger but together. So that's saying something." Kyle grabbed my hand under the table. I grabbed his, not sure where this was going. "I'm not going to pretend to understand how everything works when it comes to two guys, but I do know true love when I see it, and when my son was the first person you ran to after being held hostage, it told me everything I needed to know."

I could not believe my dad was saying this stuff out loud.

"You're going to California, and I can't imagine a scenario in which Brad doesn't go with you. So in that case, I wanted to give this to Brad before graduation so you guys can make plans now."

He handed me a graduation card. It had a cap and gown on the cover and something corny written inside, but that wasn't what I was looking at. Inside was the pink slip for my car. It was made out in my name.

"You're going to need something to drive once you're out there, and now you have something."

I handed the card to Kyle and threw myself into my father's arms.

"I love you," I said, meaning it like I had never meant it before.

He hugged me back and whispered, "You grew up better than I could have ever asked, son. I love you too."

I didn't want to let go of him for a very long time.

Sitting back down, I could not believe I owned my car. It was just too much for words.

"So let me ask you something," Tyler asked once I had settled down. "What do you want to do after graduation?"

My mouth got dry as I realized I didn't know how to answer that question.

"I mean, what are your plans? Long-term ideas? You have anything in?"

I just shook my head, feeling like I hadn't studied for this test at all.

Robbie rolled his eyes and asked me, "Let me put it this way. If you could have just one wish, one thing to come true after graduation, no matter how silly it may sound, what would it be?"

Without a moment's hesitation, I said, "Be with Kyle."

Which sounded really lame as a long-term goal but was true.

"There are a lot of things that can mess up a relationship out of high school. You guys are going to be growing up and becoming new people. You're going to have a lot to get through. The very least of all is how to afford to eat."

I looked at Kyle and felt really dumb because I hadn't thought of any of that. I just wanted to be with him.

"So that's why you two are the first and only recipients of the Riley Mathison Scholarship for True Love." He handed Kyle a brown leather checkbook. Kyle took it, and Robbie motioned for him to open it up.

Kyle gasped at whatever he read.

"What?" I asked, looking over at what was inside. It was a joint account in Kyle's and my names. It said there was over a hundred thousand dollars in it. I felt myself go pale at the thought that this might be real.

"I can't take this," Kyle said, putting the book down and sliding it back to Robbie. "He left that to you."

Robbie reached into his jacket and pulled out an envelope. "No, he didn't, and here is my proof."

He handed it to Kyle, who pulled the letter out and began to read it.

I read along over his shoulder.

Robbie.

If you're reading this, then something terrible has happened.

My lawyer has instructions to give this to you only if I pass away unexpectedly, which is never a good thing. There are a ton of things I want to say to you, but I hope by this time we have said it to each other a million times over, but in case I am an idiot, let me say it again.

My life didn't start until I met you.

Sure, I may have grown up and went to school and all that crap, but the only thing that counted was the day you said yes. Everything else was prelude. You may find me silly, but this letter and this check is my proof I am not. It was our third date, and you asked me if I liked kids and I said I loved them and you seemed to think it was just a line I was saying to get you to like me. The first thing I did when you said you'd marry me was set this account up, just in case something we couldn't plan for happened.

Because by the time you open this, I expect us to have at least two kids, if not more.

Take this money and use it for them to be happy. I know it is just money, and I wish I could be there instead, but take this money and remind our kids how much I loved you and them and that even though at the moment of me writing this they don't exist, they are the most important people in my life.

Next to their father.

Or we may find this letter after they are all grown and moved out, in which case....

Smile, baby, we're going to Disney World.

Always Yours,
Riley

Kyle looked up at Robbie, who was openly sobbing. "If we had kids, I would hope they would have been as brave as you two have been. So you see, he didn't leave it for me." He slid the checkbook back toward Kyle. "He left it for you two."

Kyle broke down, and I was pretty sure we were all crying by then.

JUNE 4
BYE BYE BYE
11 DAYS LEFT

Kyle

I'M NOT even sure why they bother having school for the senior class after prom.

It's, like, a hundred times worse than normal summer vacation jitters, knowing these were the last days you were going to be sitting in this classroom. There was a ton of other things that needed to get done, but in the class itself, we might as well have played hangman for the next week for all we were paying attention.

And that we were kind of rich was distracting me.

If it seems incredible to you to hear about someone giving someone else that much money, try to think how it feels to get it. Tyler said it was what Robbie needed to make a clean break. It just seemed like an incredible, generous act that I was never going to be able to repay.

That and I think I was kind of related to Robbie now.

He said he was going to stay long enough to see us graduate, and then he was leaving Foster for good. I asked him if I was ever going to see him again, and he just gave me that snarky smile and said, "Don't ask me. I'm not the one with money to burn."

So yeah, sooner or later I was going to take a trip to New York.

But right now, Brad and I were looking online at places around Berkeley to rent while I was in school. Thankfully, Coach Gunn didn't care what we were doing on Brad's laptop as long as it was quiet.

That was when one of the office aids came into the class and handed Gunn a note.

"Stilleno," he said, holding the piece of paper up. "Principal's office, now."

"Jeez, what did I do now?" I asked Brad under my breath.

Brad flashed me a "no worries" smile and said, "Hey, if he's going to charge you for the prom, tell him you'll write him a check."

He had a point.

I walked into the administrative area, and there seemed to be a flurry of activity all over the place, more so than usual. There were boxes being moved and people on the phone, none of them sounding that pleased. I showed one of the secretaries the note, and she pointed to Raymond's office.

I took a deep breath and knocked on the open door.

There was a strange man on the phone pacing behind the desk. He motioned me to come in as he kept talking. "No, I don't think so, and frankly don't care if it is. Look, John, it's two weeks. All I need to do is keep the trains running on time." He pointed to one of the chairs as John spoke to him. "I agree, if I have any problems, I'll call, but we should be good." He nodded and rolled his eyes as John kept talking. "Great, call you later."

He hung up the phone and shook his head. "Let me tell you something—people in Texas can talk your ear off. You're Kyle?"

I nodded, confused. "Yes, sir, but I was supposed to see Mr. Raymond."

He shook his head as he sorted through the papers on his desk. "No, you were supposed to see the principal. That's me now." He pulled a file out of the mess. "Here we go, UC Berkeley? Nice school, fantastic GPA, and whoa... your SAT score is insane. Wow, can't say I've seen a record like this before."

"I'm sorry, you're who?"

"Mr. Fisher," he said, putting the file down. "So, looks like you've had a pretty shitty year."

I just stared at him, not even ready for an adult, much less a principal, to say that out loud.

"Coming out, your friend's suicide, and then the shooting." He shook his head. "And through all that, you got a full ride to Berkeley. I would have just fell apart."

My mind finally found some traction. "Wait, you're what now?"

He laughed and sat down. "Mr. Raymond doesn't work here anymore. He has decided to spend some more time with his family, which is a polite way of saying he was asked to leave or we would fire him. Mostly because of the way he handled the situation with you. So on behalf of Foster High, the school board, and, to be honest, the entire Texas education system, I apologize for everything and want to make it right."

Raymond was really gone?

"Now, I can't do much about everything that has gone on, but I can give you something that most people don't ever get." He paused for a moment to make sure he had my attention. "The last word."

I cocked my head, more confused than ever.

"If there is another student better suited to being your class's valedictorian, I haven't seen them." I began to shake my head, but he leaned forward. "Kyle, look, as a principal I'm supposed to tell you that you should give an uplifting speech about where you guys are heading and what you hope for the future, and I am, but I'm also saying something else. Tell the truth. Tell how it is and what you were never allowed to say before. Stand up for your class and speak for them, talk about this Kelly guy, about being gay, about whatever you want. I'm literally giving you the last word on this whole year. If you don't take it, you'll regret it."

I just nodded, not trusting my mouth to say anything that made sense.

"Anyway," he said, standing up, signaling the meeting was over. "Let the graduation committee know how much time you'll need and they will work you into the program. Any questions?"

"Was I the reason he lost his job?"

Mr. Fisher's face grew serious, and he shook his head. "No, Kyle. He lost his job all on his own. You just happened to be the person he was doing it to. The fault is all his."

"But I don't understand," I said slowly. "He's been here forever. Why do something about it now?"

Fisher was already back to deciphering his desk. "Austin got a complaint about him. Actually, turns out one of the commissioners' moms lives here, and she told him what was going on."

"Who?"

He looked up and thought about it. "He is Chad Cunningham." Um… Gayle. Her name is Gayle."

I walked out of the office without another word.

During lunch, Brad and I went to Nancy's to talk to her. She was in the middle of her normal rush when we walked in. She saw us enter, and a smile crossed her face. She said something to one of the waitresses and pointed to the kitchen. We walked out to the back of the diner. "So how was school today?"

"You got him fired?" I asked, completely seeing her in another light all of a sudden.

She gave me that all-knowing smile. "Honey, he got himself fired. I just got tired of seeing him bully innocent students."

"Why didn't you do something earlier?" Brad asked. I nudged him to be nice, but the question had already been asked.

"Because the Jeffrey Raymond I used to know didn't used to be filled with hate and intolerance. I thought he was just on the wrong side of an argument and needed some time to come around to the right side. Once I saw him the day of the shooting, I knew it wasn't something he was going to come back from. So I did something."

"You really run this town, don't you?" I asked her, slowly grasping how Foster worked for once.

She laughed. "I just serve food, silly. Foster isn't a thing that needs to be run. It's a collection of people, lots of people, who all feel and think different things. But at its heart, at the center of it all, it's a good place. It just needed someone to give them a kick in the ass."

"So you kicked them?" Brad asked.

She shook her head as she began to lead us back into the diner. "No, that was you two who did that. And by the way, good job."

Brad

THE DAY of graduation was like a series of sprints that made up a long-ass race.

We were waiting in line for our seats, and the line was pretty long. All our families were sitting together: my parents, Kyle's mom with Tyler and Matt, Robbie, Gayle, Jennifer's dad. I saw them all in the same place, and my eyes misted up as I realized how many people we had on our side. How could we ever think we were alone?

Kyle was already gone, getting ready to give his speech, as Jennifer, with Josh hanging on her, was arguing with her dad.

"But why not a real college?" he asked.

She shrugged. "Because I want to do this more. Maybe I can go to community college to get my degree in criminology, but this is what I want to do now."

"You want to do what?" I asked her, realizing I had spaced out at the beginning of the discussion.

She turned to me, looking like a model for a second as the setting sun hit her blonde hair. I know I was gay, and that girls didn't do anything for me, but not even a blind man could miss how beautiful she was. "I want to join the police academy."

Josh looked back at me with a huge grin. "Dude, she's going to wear a uniform and everything."

God, those two were bad.

"Brad, help me out here," her dad pleaded with me. "Tell her to go to school for something else."

She raised one eyebrow, and I was reminded of how ridiculously brave she was during the shooting. "Sorry, sir, but I think in five years she'll have your job."

He scowled at me, but she mouthed "Thank you" at me and gave me a huge hug.

Which was when they asked us all to take our seats.

There was a prayer, and the new principal gave a nice speech about the school, and then he moved aside and introduced Kyle.

The crowd grew silent as he walked up to the podium.

I had never been so proud nor so in love with a single person in my life. He reached into his gown and pulled out some index cards and looked at them for a moment. After a second he put them down and took a deep breath. When he looked up, I knew this was not going to be the speech they expected.

"They want me to talk about us," he said, sounding tired. "They want me to talk about the future and where we're going." He looked down at his cards and then back to the crowd. His eyes caught mine, and I smiled at him. He gave me a ghost of a smile back and then said to the crowd, "So here is my speech: I have no idea."

The crowd went *wild* as everyone under the age of thirty burst into *wild* cheering.

"I have no earthly clue to what we are going to do with the rest of our lives. All I know is where we've been and what we are." He waited for the crowd to calm down. "We are the ones who made it. We are the survivors." There were a few chuckles from parents, who thought he was telling a joke. "I know that may seem crazy to those who have already graduated. It used to be getting good grades and scoring a good college was all you needed to do. That's not true now. We don't care about that. We just care about living. We just don't want to die."

No one said a word. It was as if the whole crowd held its breath.

"There are those not with us. There are people who literally didn't make it through high school alive. We are the ones who made it, so we have an obligation now. We have an obligation to ourselves and to the world. We have to love and fight and to do stupid things and just live. We have to live for those who can't. That's our job now, and it's not fair. Life just isn't fair."

He took a second to gather his thoughts. "The world sucks, and everyone knows it. Kids kill kids, people are spit on because of things as stupid as skin color or who they love, the people who have everything refuse to share with those who have nothing, and no one does a thing. I see people much older than me just shake their heads and say 'Oh well, that's life. Not much we can do about it.' That is not life!" he said, slamming his hand down on the podium. "You want to make the world a better place? Do it. You want to be a better person? Be it. Those of us here, those of us who have survived Foster High, we know. We know the truth about the world, and we aren't going to be lied to anymore. We aren't going to be told that the problem is too big or there is only so much one person can do. We aren't going to accept there is a time and place for things, and that someday they will get better. The place is here, and the time is now."

A few kids cheered. The adults looked like they were in shock.

"We are tired of your world. We are sick of your hatred and your bigotry and of your bullshit. We are not going to stand for it anymore—we won't. We are going to go out into the world, and we are going to change it, one person at a time. We are going to meet people, and we are going to tell them these stories from where we grew up, and we are going to share them. And one by one we will change the way people think about the world and the people in it. One by one we will find hatred and intolerance, and we will destroy it."

More kids started cheering.

"We are going to go out into the world, and we are going to find those people who are filled with hatred, and we are going to tell them their time is done here. That we will not tolerate that crap anymore. You want to know who we are and where we are going?"

The kids were going crazy now, myself included.

"We are coming for you, and we are coming for your world, and we are pissed. If you stand for hate and for discrimination and you can't see that all people are worth something, then know this. We are the graduating class of Foster High, and your days are numbered."

He grabbed the microphone and screamed, "We are the ones who survived!"

Nothing much was said after that because we all rushed the stage and ran toward Kyle.

We had just been given our marching orders. We all had a life to live.

Kyle

THEY TELL me I stood up and gave a speech at graduation. I don't remember a word of it.

I remember walking out there on stage and seeing everyone looking back at me and being incredibly grateful I had a gown on so they couldn't see my legs shaking. I saw Brad smiling at me, and for a moment the fear and the trepidation passed because I knew, no matter how bad I was going to be up here, he was always there waiting.

I saw my mom sitting with Tyler and Matt, who was sitting next to Robbie, who was crying as hard as my mom was.

When I was done with my speech, the whole crowd went crazy. Well, the kids did. The parents looked a little scared, which was okay with me. Once everything got settled down and Mr. Fisher said I could have a seat, I saw one seat empty.

Robbie was gone.

Without a word, I ducked off the platform and dashed to the parking lot. In the back of my mind I knew he was going to do this. I hadn't even been sure he was going to make it to graduation, but now I understood his plan. He was going to run out while we were getting our diplomas, thinking I was going to be trapped onstage until it was done.

I caught him at his car, driver's side door half-open as he was about to get in. "J'accuse!" I called out at him. "J'accuse! Mon petit citron."

He shook his head and closed the door. "Inches from a clean getaway."

"You were just going to run out without saying goodbye?"

He sighed and leaned against his car. "I said goodbye. I even said goodbye with fabulous parting gifts. What more do you want?"

I had something snarky to reply when I noticed his clothes for the first time.

He was dressed normal. As in completely normal. Normal jeans, button-up shirt, hair combed without gel, nothing. Just normal Robbie. He looked like... well, he looked like just another person.

"Did you lose a bet?" I asked, gesturing at his getup.

He sighed and pulled a cigarette out. "No, just stopped doing drag." I didn't say a word and just stared at him, confused, until he explained. "Look, Kyle, I spent a lot of time being someone I wasn't as a defense mechanism. Foster hated me for being gay, so I shoved being gay in its face. They wanted me to be the token fag, so I made sure to play the part. I mean, don't get me wrong, everything I said about *Into the Woods* and the movie *Clue* is still gospel, but that wasn't really me. I haven't been me for a long time, and I think maybe I need to try to find him again."

"I feel like I'm seeing behind the curtain for the first time."

He nodded. "It's a lot like that. I was a great, flaming fake, and you're a small and annoying little dog that should have been left behind." I flipped him off, and he laughed. "Here is the last lesson I am going to give, so pay attention. There will be times in your life where people are going to make you want to act straight, through intimidation or peer pressure or whatever. Don't let them do it. But on the other hand, if you are ever in a place where you feel like you have to act gay, where you feel like you have to shove it in their face... then leave. Because the second is as bad as the first, trust me." In that moment I had a feeling of how the last few years must have been for him. "Come give me a hug before I go. I need to get out of here before I change my mind."

I moved over and embraced him. I really was going to miss him.

"Oh Jesus, you're as bad as Tyler," he said, wiping his eyes. "There is a fucking phone, FaceTime, and an airplane. I'm not dying. I'm going to Long Island. You'd know if I was dying because I'd say I was going to Jersey." When I didn't laugh, he rolled his eyes. "God, good humor is lost on you hicks."

"Call me when you get home?" I asked him.

He stopped getting into the car for a moment and looked at me thoughtfully. "I am going home." He said it like he was realizing it for the first time. "I really am going home."

I smiled at him. "This is where you're supposed to say, 'I'll miss you most of all, Scarecrow.'"

He leveled a look at me and shook his head. "Kid, you were the only one here with any brains. Don't ever forget it."

And with that, he closed the door, backed out of the parking lot, and drove out of Foster forever.

Between you and me, the town was lesser for it, but no one would believe me.

JUNE 15
HOME
THE LAST DAY IN FOSTER

Kyle

WHEN I walked out, Brad was waiting for me, making room in the trunk.

"So you have everything?" my mom asked for the hundredth time. "Your wallet? Phone? Charger?" I nodded each time, as I had each time she had asked me before. You would think it would seem annoying, but here, standing outside our crappy apartment, holding a suitcase, we both realized this was the last time I was going to be her teenage son living under her roof. As soon as I got in that car, I would drive off and take the first steps in a long line of steps toward being an adult, and everything would be different.

I was surprised to find that I didn't want it to end.

I dropped my suitcase and hugged her tight. Everything I was scared of was in that one gesture. All my childhood fears, all the things under my bed, the demons in my closet, everything in one life-changing hug. She hugged me back, and as with every skinned knee, black eye, and upset stomach, it went away for the brief moment I was in her arms. My mind knew logically I wasn't going to miss her, exactly, as much as I was going to miss the safety she provided me growing up, but I told my mind to shove off for a couple of minutes and give me some space.

"You can always come home," she whispered. "Always."

Even as she said it, she had to know I never would. Sure, I would come back for holidays and the odd school break, but I would never take that step backward into her life again. Sober or not, this was not the life I wanted, and she knew that. This was the moment I had been waiting eighteen years for, and I was never going to look back.

"Thanks, Mom" was all I could choke out as I held on to her.

And then slowly, deliberately, I pulled away and took a step back.

"We're losing daylight," Brad said behind me as he took my bags and shoved them into the trunk.

"Call me when you guys stop for the night," she called out as I turned toward the car. "It doesn't matter how late."

"I will," I promised her, closing the door behind me. Brad got into the driver's side and slammed his door.

"We good?" he asked me as I continued to look out the window at her.

I looked back at him and nodded. "I'm ready."

He started the car, and I waved to her as we pulled out of the driveway. He headed out East Avenue and then turned on First Street, heading *out of town*. We passed Nancy's, and I saw Gayle serving the lunch crowd, her smile beaming as she shared a story with a customer. Across the street I saw Tyler's shop. I couldn't see inside, but the front door was open, and I could imagine him behind the counter, giving someone one of his thousand-watt smiles as he offered them a Coke. Ms. Garner was in front of the Vine, sweeping the front sidewalk as she readied herself to open for the afternoon matinee.

We turned off First and hit the long road *out of town*. I saw Robbie's shop already closed down. The sign in the window read: Make Your Own Happy Ending. I laughed and wondered if it was a message to me. We passed the cemetery where Kelly was buried, and I pressed my hand against the glass as I said goodbye to him one last time. Slowly, building by building, the town went away, leaving the bleak countryside that surrounded Foster all around us. We drove past the Bear's Den, and I smiled as I wondered how many guys would walk in there and wonder who was the handsome green-eyed boy whose picture was on the wall, looking like a deer in the headlights as the flash went off.

We drove another twenty minutes, and I saw something in the distance.

"Slow down," I asked Brad, who had already begun to drum along with the radio. He saw what I was looking at and pulled over to the side.

I got out of the car and stood there for a second. The acrid afternoon air whooshed past me as Brad joined me on the side of the road. The only sound was the wind and our own heartbeats.

"Afraid?" he asked as he came up behind me and moved his arms around me.

I shook my head as I continued to look at what had caught my eye.

"Really? Not even a little?" he teased.

"No," I said, leaning against him. "Not even a little."

"Why?" He nuzzled my cheek with his nose, and I closed my eyes for a moment, relishing the sensation.

I turned around and hugged him back. "Because I am taking everything I loved about Foster with me." I smiled, and he leaned in for a kiss. As with the first time he kissed me in his room, the world stopped moving for a second, and there was nothing else but Brad.

It was that good of a kiss.

"You have a marker?" I asked him, pulling away.

"Are you planning on labeling me?" he asked with a grin.

I rolled my eyes. "No, when I do that, I'll make sure it's a tattoo and never coming off." I paused as I thought about it. "Also, might give you one of those chips they put in dogs in case you wander off."

He shook his head and turned back to the trunk. He popped it open and dug through our stuff before coming up with a Sharpie. "One marker, sir," he announced, giving me a half bow.

"I like the 'sir,'" I said, taking it before slapping his ass.

"We're still burning daylight," he said, heading back to his side of the car.

"I know," I said, moving toward it. "I just need to do one thing."

It took me a couple of seconds, and then I was done.

I got back into the car and tossed the marker in the back. "I'm ready to leave," I told him.

He leaned over and kissed me again. "Then let's go," he said, shifting into Drive.

As we pulled away, I turned around in my seat and watched the "You Are Leaving Foster, Texas" sign get smaller in the distance. I knew the first rain would wash it clean, but for now, it had one small message under that.

"Brad and Kyle were here."

I don't know when I was broken, but I know the moment that it didn't matter anymore. It was the moment I started my life with the green-eyed boy.

August 21
Where the Story Ends
633 days left

Jared

I DON'T know what I did in the sixteen years I've been alive to deserve this fate, but whatever it is, I am fucking sorry. I am not just saying that, either. I mean it. Whatever angry god up there I pissed off or stepped off to, I take it back. I take it all back.

Just get me out of this fucking town.

My dad turned down the radio and asked me, "So, what do you think?"

What do I think? What do I think? Oh, Dad, please don't ask me questions that you won't enjoy the answer to. Instead I looked over at the one movie theater in town and commented, "Well, I'm pretty sure both of those movies are on Netflix, so paying to go see them in a crappy, run-down building sounds like a hoot."

I usually don't use the word "hoot," by the way. I'm just trying it out since I'm now officially a citizen of Foster, Texas.

"Jared," my dad said, which was his way of prepping for one of his "buck up, kiddo, life is what you make of it" speeches. I can tell because he used my full name instead of the normal Jay. Like "Jay, take out the garbage. Jay, did you do your homework? Jay, that music is too loud." Jared was reserved for heart-to-heart talks, bad news, and the rare times he was going to discipline me. But then, Jared was usually followed by a lilting "Brandon" and then finished with a sharp "Fisher" to round it out. Jared by itself was more reserved for lemon-to-lemonade kind of talks.

"I know you didn't want to move here, and I'm sorry for that, but you know how much of an opportunity this is for me."

Yeah, some opportunity, to be a principal for a school that most likely has a hitching post in front of it for the kids who ride a horse to school every day.

"You'll make friends here," he said with the same validity in his voice that he might have said, "One day KJ Apa will be on Instagram, see your profile, and come to take you away from all this."

Yeah, when fucking pigs fly. And I mean literal pigs with superpowers that fly around and fight pig crime. Not a pig launched from a catapult and filmed on YouTube.

"I hear they have a great football team."

That was it. I slipped my earbuds in and began to thumb through my music. "I'm not playing football again, and you know why."

I was not going through what had happened to me last year. Never again.

If he said anything after that, it was drowned out by Jack Antonoff asking me what did I stand for? Most nights, I didn't know.

The school was every bit as underwhelming as I thought it would be. The main building looked like it was ancient, with a bunch of newer portables on the edge of the parking lot. It was too early for anyone cool to be there, only those few pathetic kids who actually liked school or had no other choice but to wait an hour for class to start. And kids whose dads might be the principal.

"You going to be okay?" he asked, pulling the earbuds out. "You have money for lunch?"

I nodded as I grabbed my backpack and opened the door. "I'm sure I have enough for a spot on the trough."

He grabbed my pack and stopped me from getting out. "This is your first day. Try to enjoy it."

I put my music back on as I got out of the car. He was right; this was the first day of the end of my life. Welcome to Foster High!

I wandered around and found a place on some steps to sit. I pulled out my Kindle and opened up *American Gods* to where I left off. As I sat there, my face in a book, my music blaring, the school began to come to life around me. It was as bad as I thought it would be. Most of the guys who showed up looked disgustingly jockish and seemed to know each other since birth, and the girls seemed to huddle together and talk whatever girls talk about to each other when boys aren't around.

If I wasn't trying to be an antisocial asshole, I would have felt like an outsider.

No one came over to me and asked who I was. No one inquired what I was reading or who I was listening to. Of course, I had never asked a new kid at my old school any of those questions in the past, but for some reason I half wanted someone to at least notice. I didn't even hear the bell ring and only noticed the time when the quad was almost devoid of people.

"Shit," I muttered, tossing my Kindle into my bag, and began looking for my class schedule. Precious seconds passed as I dug for the piece of paper in desperation. Even if I found it right *now*, I still had no idea where anything was. Fuck, I was so busy trying to be all brooding when I should have been figuring out where these buildings were so I wouldn't be the new kid who walked into class late.

"Fuck, fuck, fuck," I exclaimed, not finding the schedule.

Sighing, I closed up my pack and walked to the office. Perfect start, Jared. Sit there pouting about how stupid everyone in this town was going to be, and you're the idiot who has to get his schedule printed again because you're too stupid to live.

If that angry god is still listening, I get it. Really. I am so, so sorry, and if you want me to do some Hail Marys or whatever they do in confession to get rid of sin, just text me, dude. You so don't need to keep kicking me in the balls.

So, ten minutes and several hundred levels of embarrassment later, I walked into my first-period history class. And as *every* person who ever walked into a class late knows, I, of course, interrupted the teacher in the middle of something and got everyone's attention instantly.

"Awesome," I said to myself as thirty strangers looked at me blankly.

"New?" the teacher asked, grabbing his roll book off his desk.

"Um, yes, sir," I said in a voice that would have made Justin Bieber sound butch. I cleared my throat and tried again. "Yes, sir. Jared Fisher."

He nodded and checked something off. "Take a seat, Fisher. I'm Coach Gunn, and welcome to history."

I looked around for a seat in the back, but those had long been taken. The only one left was right up front, next to a cute-ass boy with dirty-blond hair. I moved into the seat, trying my best not to look at him since I so did not want people to start talking about how the new kid was perving on Johnny whatever-his-name-was five minutes into class.

"You have a good build," the coach said as I sat down. "You play football in your old school?"

I looked at him for a moment, wondering if somehow my dad had set him up to ask that. It was pretty obvious from the look on the guy's face he was deathly serious and was waiting for an answer. Of course everyone else was too, which made me feel like dying.

I nodded as I pulled out my notebook.

"A couple of players just graduated," he said, putting a history book on my desk. "You should try out today after school."

I don't know where it came from or why I did it, but something in me just snapped, and my mouth began talking before I could stop it. "Yeah, you should know before you ask that I'm gay."

I had told myself I wasn't going to take a step back into the closet, not after what I had gone through in Chicago. I didn't care if these backward fucks hated me or wanted to kill me. I wasn't going to spend the last couple of years of high school hiding who I was anymore, and they could just shove it. I looked at him defiantly and waited for his response.

He blinked a few times in confusion and then said, "So does that mean you don't want to try out?"

My mind came to a grinding halt as I tried to figure out if I had just heard what I thought I just heard.

"Huh?" I finally asked.

He chuckled and shook his head. "Son, I don't much care who you date. I'm looking for football players. If you want to try out, it's the boys' gym after school." He picked up some papers and flipped through them for a moment. "Okay, we were going over how much each test is going to be worth."

His words faded away as I looked around to see if anyone was watching and laughing at me.

They weren't.

"What the fuck?" I mumbled in complete confusion.

I felt someone tap my hand, and I looked over to see the cute boy trying to get my attention. "Hey, I'm Joel. We already did the gay jock thing last year." He smiled and winked at me. "Welcome to Foster High." He handed me a folded-up piece of paper before going back to his notes.

I slowly unfolded it and gaped. *You're cute, call me!* and then his number.

I looked at the note and then back to him and then back to the note.

I folded it back up and slipped it in my pocket, resting my hand on it lest it vanish in a puff of whatever things vanish into.

"Okay, let's open our books and jump into it," Coach Gunn said, grabbing his own book off his desk. "We have a lot to cover this year."

As we began to read, I had to smile. I thought I was going to like this town after all.

JOHN GOODE is fifty years old and was found in his floating crib by a strange man… wait, no that's Baby Yoda. I am a cat that gets constantly screamed at by a blond woman while I'm trying to eat… wait, no, not me. I am inevitable, nope. I am Iron Man? More no. I'm not bad, I'm just drawn that way? I can't pull that dress off. Okay, I am and shall always be your friend. Sigh, I think I stole that from somewhere. Let me try again. WHEN I WAS A YOUNG WARTHOG! Too much? I agree. Okay, how about a little Fosse, Fosse, Fossee, a little Martha Graham, Martha Graham, Twyla, Twyla, Twyla and then some Michael Kidd, Michael… I lost you, huh? Well whoever he is, I can assure you he isn't a black cat that wears glasses. Okay, how about this?

He is this guy who lives in this place and writes stuff he hopes you read.

Twitter: @fosterhigh
Facebook: www.facebook.com/TalesFromFosterHigh

JOHN GOODE

Tales from

FOSTER

HIGH

Tales from Foster High: Book One

Kyle Stilleno is the invisible student even in his nothing high school in the middle of Nowhere, Texas. Brad Graymark is the baseball star of Foster High. When they bond over their mutual damage during a night of history tutoring, Kyle thinks maybe his life has changed for good. But when you're gay and falling for the most popular boy in school, the promise of love is a fairy tale, not a reality. Isn't it?

A coming-of-age story, *Tales from Foster High* shows an unflinching vision of the ups and downs of teenage love and what it is like to grow up gay.

www.dreamspinnerpress.com

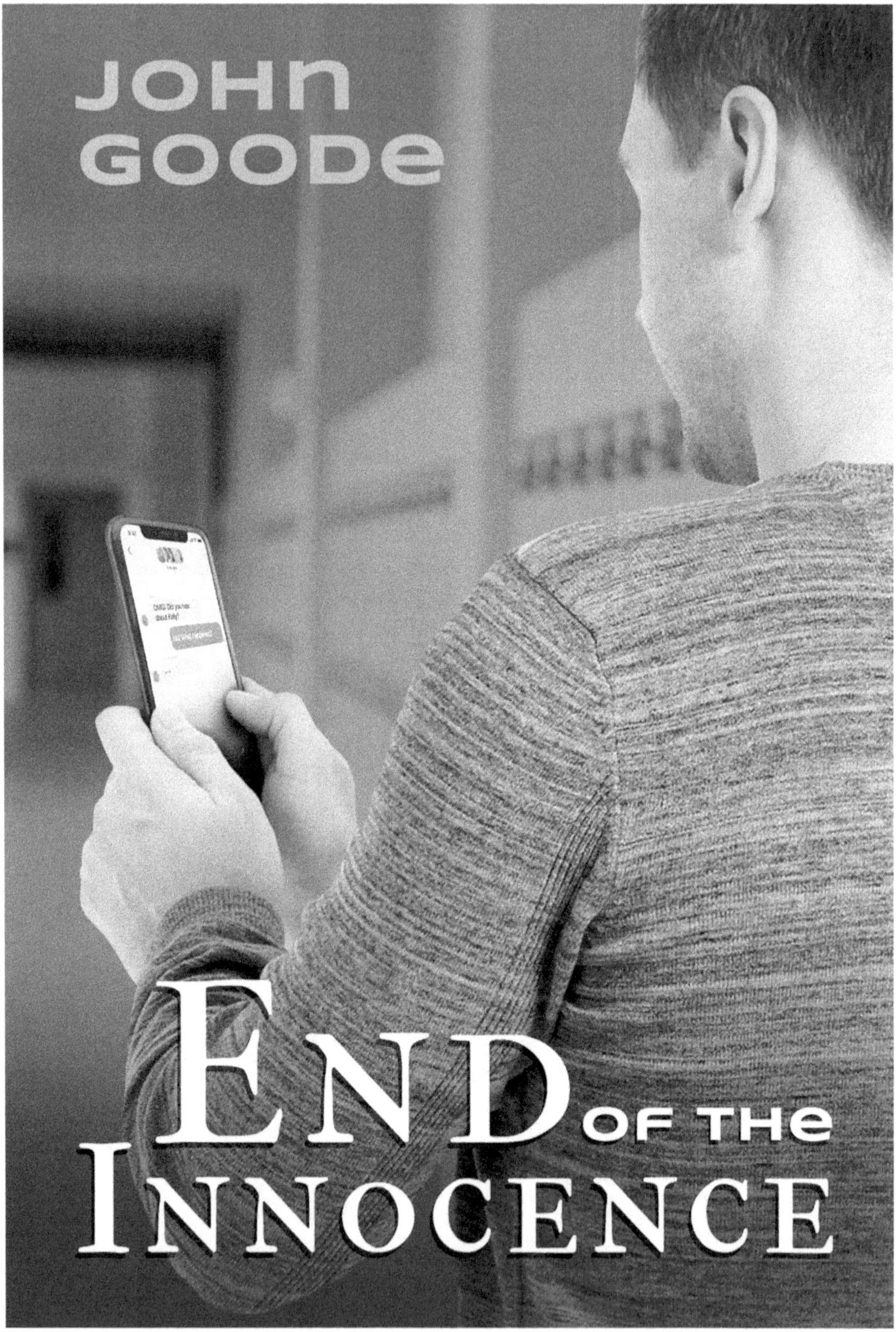
JOHN
GOODE
END OF THE
INNOCENCE

Tales from Foster High: Book Two

Kyle Stilleno is no longer the invisible boy, and he doesn't know how he feels about it. On one hand, he now has a great boyfriend, Brad Graymark, a handful of new friends, and even a new job. On the other hand, no one screamed obscenities at him in public when he was invisible.

No one expected him to become a poster boy for gay rights either—at least not until he stepped out of the closet and into the limelight. But with only a few months of high school left, Kyle doubts he can make a difference.

With Christmas break drawing closer and their trials far from over, Kyle and Brad have each other to lean on. Others are not so lucky. One of their classmates needs their help—but Kyle and Brad's relationship may be too new to survive the strain.

www.dreamspinnerpress.com

www.ingramcontent.com/pod-product-compliance
Lightning Source LLC
Chambersburg PA
CBHW050027030726
47506CB00001B/147